ADAPT OR BE CRUSHED

ADAPT OR BE CRUSHED

EXCEPTIONAL S. BEAUFONT™ BOOK 9

SARAH NOFFKE

MICHAEL ANDERLE

DISRUPTIVE IMAGINATION

LMBPN Publishing
PMB 196, 2540 South Maryland Pkwy
Las Vegas, NV 89109

First US Edition, October 2020
Version 1.02, November 2020
eBook ISBN: 978-1-64971-196-0
Print ISBN: 978-1-64971-197-7

THE ADAPT OR BE CRUSHED TEAM

Thanks to the JIT Readers

Peter Manis
Veronica Stephan-Miller
Dorothy Lloyd
Diane L. Smith
Deb Mader
Jackey Hankard-Brodie
Jeff Goode
Kerry Mortimer
Paul Westman

If we've missed anyone, please let us know!

Editor
The Skyhunter Editing Team

For Veronica, a good mother and an awesome friend.

— Sarah

To Family, Friends and
Those Who Love
to Read.
May We All Enjoy Grace
to Live the Life We Are
Called.

— Michael

CHAPTER ONE

The beast lunged, trying to break free of its restraints. Once the tarrasque was large enough, it would escape and the result would be complete destruction. The horned monster would easily smash through the sports dome where Nevin Gooseman was hatching his plans. Then the tarrasque would demolish the city of Dallas with nothing that could possibly stop it.

Nevin Gooseman smiled sadistically to himself.

He had never wanted it to come to this. All his life as a magician, he'd worked to help mortals, building his career as a public servant in their governments. But they'd turned their backs on him—all because of the Dragon Elite.

Now both mortals and dragonriders would pay.

The magic-reinforced chains clanged like giant bells as the tarrasque swung its head from side to side, its anger growing as it came to terms with its confinement. The creature was hideous with a thick orange hide and long curved spikes down its back and tail. On its head and chin were rows of more horns. When it opened its wide mouth to roar, the many rows of knife-shaped teeth were prominent.

Although the monster was considered only half-grown, taking up half the football field of the abandoned sports arena, it would mature quite fast. After securing it, Nevin Gooseman had hired a handler who specialized in rapid maturation of magical creatures.

The ex-politician turned his attention to Clyde Jackson. The man had a rough look and too many narrow escapes from dangerous animals based on the many scars marking his face, arms, and hands. He wore an eyepatch over his left eye and a sniveling grin on his crooked mouth.

"When will it be full grown?" Nevin Gooseman indicated the tarrasque that thrashed in the distance.

Clyde pulled back his arm and snapped the whip in his hand forward. It assaulted the beast and made its head stretch into the air as it arched its back. Bright blue sparks radiated from the magical whip and rained down on the creature, instantly paralyzing it. It fell on its stomach, its head lying to the side as it passed out from the spell.

Apparently the handler would mostly keep the monster asleep. It was safer that way. It was fed once every few days and put back into submission. When it was full grown and filled the entire sports dome, then it would be allowed to stay awake. The creature wouldn't be fed and therefore, would break free of its prison and thunder through the streets of Dallas where it would undoubtedly feast on the people.

Having decided that the tarrasque no longer demanded his full attention, Clyde turned his focus on Nevin Gooseman. "It's hard to say. Maybe a few weeks. Maybe a few months. There's no exact science to this since it relies on magic."

Nevin nodded and slipped his hands into his jean pockets. He missed the feel of his Italian suits. He missed his old life. That was all yanked away when the Dragon Elite stole everything from him— they'd pinned the outbreak and spread of the distortion disease on him.

He was officially on the run and hoping he could elude the House of Fourteen and mortal law enforcement, which were both looking for him. Nevin fled as soon as the world learned the truth, and went into hiding after draining his bank accounts. He left most of his possessions behind, but what he didn't, he sold. The resulting sum meant he could buy the broken-down old sports arena in Dallas, Texas.

There hadn't been much money left over after such a costly investment, but there'd been enough to purchase the last tarrasque in existence. Thanks to Bermuda Laurens, the world-renowned expert on magical creatures, Nevin had known where to look for the beast. Of course, the giantess didn't know she'd helped him find the animal that would destroy the entire city of Dallas, and hopefully go on to do a lot more than that. She thought she was answering questions for a college student researching magical creatures. People were so thick and talked if they thought it didn't have any consequences.

That interview with Bermuda Laurens had been more than fruitful. She not only told him where to find the creature, but that it would be too big to stop once it was full-sized. The giantess also gave Nevin information on where to find two other magical and dangerous creatures that would be almost as deadly, and ready sooner than the tarrasque.

"The leviathan and the simurgh?" Nevin questioned Clyde while keeping his focus on the comatose dinosaur-like creature.

"I'm working on tracking them both down based on the information you gave me. It shouldn't take much longer."

Nevin nodded, enjoying the feeling of triumph once more. "And when you do, you know where to lead them?"

"They'll make quite the scene if seen together in the Mediterranean Sea," Clyde stated.

"That's exactly the point." Nevin's nostrils flared. He knew that the Dragon Elite didn't stand a chance against the tarrasque when it ventured into Dallas. But maybe, just maybe he had a way of taking them down before then—or at least diminishing their numbers.

His time in isolation, hiding away from the world he once loved, gave him time to strategize. That's when it occurred to him how to take down dragons. Fight teeth and claws with teeth and claws. He'd been going about it all wrong by using politics. There was always a rebuttal to that. But giant sea creatures and birds and reptiles? Well, the Dragon Elite couldn't talk their way out of that, and they'd have to come to the rescue since they thought that was their mission—to save the world.

Nevin Gooseman had once wanted to help this planet to be a better place, but it didn't want to do things his way—and now it was going down. Mother Nature be damned.

"Oh, and I got that thing you wanted." Clyde reached into his pocket and dug like there were a lot of things in the small compartment. He withdrew a small vial of clear liquid. "This should do the trick."

"That?" Nevin questioned. "That's for the entire water supply of Scotland?"

The guy laughed. "If you can believe it."

"And it will only work on sheep?" Nevin asked.

"Yes, sir," Clyde Jackson answered. "It's about genetics and a combination of factors. Cost me pretty heavily since it's so specialized, which means it's going to cost you."

Nevin reached out and yanked the vial to himself. "Put it on my tab."

The man with the eyepatch nodded, but gave him an uncertain expression.

Nevin wasn't leaving anything to chance this time. He had multiple ways to bring down the Dragon Elite, and one would work. Then the world could go to hell for all he cared. He was tired of trying to help those who weren't grateful for it.

CHAPTER TWO

"I think I'm going to wither away and die," Evan complained with his head lying on the dining hall table and his voice muffled as he spoke.

"If only your predictions were accurate and came true," Wilder replied, a longing in his voice as he looked off dreamily toward the ceiling, like glancing at the heavens and making a wish on a star.

Evan pulled his head up, one of his dreads falling into his face. "Some of us don't have stores of fat to live off."

Wilder scoffed. "I can't believe you're calling me fat."

"I can't believe that you all are bickering like children," Hiker thundered from in front of the large fireplace behind his seat at the table, irritation heavy in his every movement.

"He started it." Evan pointed across the table at Wilder.

His mouth fell open. He held up his hands in surprise. "How? I've been here, thoughtfully listening to your incessant complaints like a good friend. I haven't interrupted once while you whined like a little baby and went on and on about your hunger pangs."

"You mock me," Evan fired back.

Hiker halted his pacing. "Enough. We're all hungry." He pointed at

Sophia. "Go and find out what's taking Trin so long to bring breakfast."

"Me?" she asked, offended. "Why me?"

"Because you're a girl and know where the kitchen is," Evan replied at once.

"Because Trin likes you," Wilder added.

"Because I want the job done right," Hiker argued and narrowed his eyes at the two riders before looking at Sophia.

She didn't budge. If the leader of the Dragon Elite wanted information from his new housekeeper about the status of breakfast, he could find out for himself. She crossed her arms over her chest and glared at him.

He threw his hands and chin into the air while sighing dramatically. "I swear, if I want anything done around here, I have to do it myself."

Sophia's stubbornness paid off though, because Hiker stomped toward the kitchen. She knew that he wasn't having an easy time since Ainsley left. He had to deal with more than the loss of his housekeeper for the last few hundred years.

However, she didn't think that coddling him with Trin would do him any favors. Whereas Hiker and Ainsley had been nothing but confrontations, the Viking was almost avoiding Trin, as if he hadn't come to terms with the fact that she'd formally replaced the elf as housekeeper.

"Oh, good," Mama Jamba sang as she strode into the dining hall. "I'm not late."

"Late?" Evan laughed. "You have time to do your hair and makeup and press your track suit and you still won't be late for breakfast."

Mama Jamba glared at the dragonrider. "I'll have you know that I've already done all those things."

Wilder glanced up at Mama Jamba and batted his eyelashes. "And may I say that you look lovely and all your efforts weren't lost on me? Although I don't think you need anything to enhance your elegance."

Evan coughed, and it sounded very much like, "Suck up."

Mama Jamba didn't seem to notice as she slipped into her seat and bounced her hand under grayish-blue curls. "You know, I did a lot of things right on the day I decided you'd be born, Wilder."

"You're the only one who understands me, NO10JO." Evan groaned and patted the cyborg dog's head who was stationed beside him.

"Ainsley didn't want the dog in the dining room." Sophia gave him a pointed glare.

"I don't see Ainsley anywhere around here, do you?" Evan looked around the dining hall.

"I think," Mama Jamba began, good naturedly, "That just because Ainsley is gone, doesn't mean her rules are."

Evan shook his head and continued to pet the dog under the table. "Of course they are. It's a new era. One where I can finally have a little freedom. Which is good because I'm going to stock up on food for the next time that Trin falls asleep on the job."

Hiker strode out of the kitchen, his face uncertain.

"And?" Mama Jamba looked at the placemat before her, as if wondering where the food was and hoping it would magically appear.

"It's going to be a little longer," he answered, little confidence in his voice.

"The Castle and her..." Sophia's voice trailed away.

He nodded and sat. "They're working things out. It seems that the more I tried to help, the worse it made things."

Wilder laughed. "By help, you mean you yelled?"

Hiker's face blossomed to a fine shade of red. "No, not at first...I didn't understand what the problem was. The food was sitting there on the main counter, appearing to get cold while we all waited."

Sophia lowered her chin and sighed. "You do know that even if the Castle has created the food, it doesn't mean it's ready until the timer goes off, right?"

He narrowed his eyes at Sophia. "That's why I told you to go and check on the kitchen. I didn't know that, but apparently you did."

She shrugged. "It's in the Complete History of Dragonriders."

"I wouldn't know since I'm not allowed to read the book," he grumbled.

"That's bizarre." Wilder looked sideways at Sophia. "So the food will appear but can't leave the kitchen until the timer dings?"

She nodded. "Sometimes. The preparation is different every day, depending on multiple factors." Sophia had taken it upon herself to brush up on this part of the history of the Castle, interested in some of the challenges that Trin would face. The factors that dictated food preparation or cleaning or maintenance were dependent on who was in the Gullington, the climate around the Expanse, the morale world-wide, and how many crickets were hiding in the Caves. It was quite the strange equation.

Quiet and Mahkah entered the dining hall. The gnome halted as his eyes narrowed on the cyborg dog, then Evan. He muttered under his breath, and Sophia felt his hostility.

"Speak up, little guy. I can't hear you," Evan sang and continued to stroke the dog. However, he disappeared a moment later—simply vanished from his spot. NO10JO also disappeared from the floor.

Sophia stood and looked around. Wilder did the same, then pointed.

"Looks like the dogs will be taking breakfast al fresco." Wilder motioned to the Castle window where Evan and NO10JO could be seen sitting outside on the Expanse, surprise on both their faces.

Mama Jamba shrugged. "I told him that just because Ainsley was gone, it didn't mean her rules were."

Quiet nodded and sat next to Mother Nature.

"Can we not talk about that?" Hiker seethed.

He said "that" but he meant "her," and Sophia knew it.

They all missed Ainsley, but each of them showed it differently. Many of them tried to be respectful to Trin, knowing that she was filling a big void in the Castle—or at least trying to.

The cyborg strode through the kitchen door with her face covered in sweat and her many electronic parts hissing. She carried a tray of buttermilk pancakes, which she set down in front of Mama Jamba with great relief, as if they weighed a ton.

"Very good," the old woman said proudly.

"About time," Hiker muttered.

Trin spun around to face him. "That's all I could manage after you stormed in and spooked me. The rest of you will have to settle for a store of protein bars that I have."

"I love protein bars." Wilder smiled.

"That's fine," Sophia stated.

"Absolutely," Mahkah echoed.

Quiet didn't at all look pleased, but simply kept his chin down.

"Fine, but you'll need to work on this," Hiker scolded.

"I have done nothing else," Trin assured him, hurrying back for the kitchen.

Evan stomped back into the dining hall, appearing madder than hell. However, NO10JO didn't follow him past the threshold. The cyborg dog stopped at the door and cowered as Quiet looked over his shoulder at him.

"That's a rotten trick." Evan glared in Quiet's direction.

Sophia was going to defend the gnome, but before she could, a strange purple glow took over her vision. It was happening more and more, and blanketed her ability to see properly. She blinked and tried to recover.

"It's happening again," Wilder said at her shoulder, more of a statement than a question. He'd been watching her and knew what was going on. When the purple glow overcame her, she appeared disoriented.

She shook her head and tried to dispel the effect, which was a result of being cursed by the evil spirit that put a mark on her soul. "It's fine."

"It's not," Hiker argued. "You need to get Papa Creola to help you."

"He's working on it." She was grateful that the strangeness was receding, making it easy for her to see again. The hallucinations were always different, but not bad when at the Gullington. She could sleep if she had the piece of hair from Mama Jamba. Still, things weren't ideal after being cursed.

"In the meantime, I don't want you on a case," Hiker stated. Before

SARAH NOFFKE & MICHAEL ANDERLE

Sophia could argue, he held up his hand. "That's final. You get cured first. But the rest of you..." He motioned around the table at the men. "Now that the Dragon Elite's name has been cleared once more, the adjudication missions are coming in fast."

"Woot!" Wilder exclaimed, either because he was excited to be on a mission again or because Trin had entered, carrying an armful of protein bars.

She dropped them on the table and strode back to the kitchen.

Evan eyed them, not at all impressed. "You outdid yourself," he called over his shoulder to the housekeeper.

"She's trying," Sophia argued as she grabbed a chocolate chip cookie dough protein bar and tore it open. She took a bite and chewed mechanically, hardly tasting it.

"Where are we with finding the demon dragons?" Hiker looked straight at Mama Jamba who was delightedly digging into the only hot food on the table.

"I started an hour ago." She licked off the maple syrup covering her lips.

"I can't believe you lied to me and said you were working on that tracking spell when you were creating that time ball," he seethed.

She calmly looked up. "Can't you, though?"

"You're not supposed to lie to us," he argued, sounding almost hurt. Maybe this was because Mother Nature had deceived him. Or maybe it was because what she had been working on was for Ainsley, to help her see how her life would have been different if she made different decisions.

"A mother's job is to make decisions that benefit their children," Mama Jamba stated. "You don't have to understand them, now or later. But if lying is what I have to do, well, so be it."

He shook his head, grabbed a protein bar, and looked it over like it was a piece of trash.

Everyone reluctantly took bites of their protein bars. No one appeared happy about the breakfast option.

It was Evan who threw his down, unsatisfied. "I'll go ahead and say it. I miss Ainsley."

Wilder nodded. "Yeah, me too."

Mahkah released a small commiserating sigh. "Every day."

It was Quiet's expression that made Sophia speechless though. She could have sworn that a tear slipped from his eye before he turned his head away and nodded.

CHAPTER THREE

The sunlight glistened across the glossy green grass of the Expanse, making it seem unreal. Sophia pulled in a breath of fresh air and enjoyed the coolness in her lungs. The herd of sheep baaed as they grazed. Quiet could be seen in their midst, but he seemed perplexed by something.

Sophia was about to investigate further. She didn't have a mission demanding her attention since she was cursed and Papa Creola hadn't yet alerted her to a cure. However, Lunis poked his head out of the Nest at that moment and immediately swooped down in her direction.

She smiled up at her dragon, feeling especially sentimental that morning with Ainsley gone and the realization that she wasn't coming back finally settling in. It had been a week since she departed and things felt like they'd never be normal again, but then, maybe that was because Sophia didn't feel normal.

However, to her surprise, Lunis didn't smile back as usual when greeting her in the morning. He had the same worried expression as Wilder plastered across his face.

"You've had another episode," he stated rather than asked.

Sophia sighed. "It was quick. Over before it started."

"That's impossible," he said smugly. "Something can't be over before it starts."

"Sure it can," she argued. "Time is a strange and beautiful thing. Just ask Papa Creola. It doesn't have to make sense."

"That's not the point. Don't try to derail the conversation." The blue dragon shook out his wings before folding them tight to his large body.

"Am I in trouble for having hallucinations caused by an evil spirit who I was forced to face to save Baba Yaga's grimoire from their greedy and dangerous hands?"

"No." He lowered his head, seeming suddenly guilty. "It's just that I'm concerned about you. You're not the same since then. There's something in your eyes."

Sophia's lips tightened and a sudden raw ache rose in her throat. "I'm not evil now."

"I know that, Sophia. It's just that a mark on your soul is evident in your eyes and it pains me to see you this way. We have to find a way to fix you."

She nodded. "Yes, I worry about leaving the Gullington where the hallucinations would be worse, but that will be the only way to find the cure."

"I think I can offer you some help in the meantime," Lunis began slowly. "If I divert my energy to you when you're away, maybe that will keep the hallucinations from happening."

"Won't that be costly for you?" she asked, concerned about the sacrifice her dragon would have to make.

He shook his head. "It's only a forced nap. A deep meditation of sorts. Not the worst thing in the world. And if I do it in Falconer Cave, then I'll probably have good results."

Sophia considered this for a moment. "Okay, thank you. I guess that will work so that I can run a few errands. I need to check on the healing elixir, which I wish could work on me."

"Souls can't be healed." He slipped into his "wise" voice. "The mark must be removed, is my guess."

"And only Papa Creola will know how to do that."

He nodded. "So pay him a visit. Prod him until he gives you some information. I don't like seeing you like this.

Sophia leaned against her dragon and hugged him. "I know. I don't like being like this."

She could sometimes forget about the mark on her soul when in the heat of battle or asleep at night, but she knew Lunis was right. When she looked in the mirror, she wasn't herself.

Sophia squeezed Lunis tightly, enjoying his warmth. Then a sudden blast exploded in the distance and made the blue dragon protectively swing his wing around her—holding her close.

CHAPTER FOUR

"What was that?" Sophia pushed out of Lunis' wing. She had trouble making out the scene before them on the Expanse that was peaceful and pristine moments before. The herd of sheep all scattered while baaing loudly in fright. In the center of where the sheep had been grazing was a small black spot where the ground had been scorched. Around it were bits of sheep... Or what had once been one.

Quiet ran in their direction with panic written on his usually calm face.

"What happened?" Sophia asked, noticing that he was running the opposite direction as the herd.

She couldn't make out his voice but she saw the shape his mouth was making as he seemed to repeat the same word over and over again: Sheep.

Looking between the scattered herd and the scorch mark, Sophia's brow scrunched up in confusion. "There's something wrong with the sheep?"

He nodded, adamantly. Turning around, Quiet pointed at the herd of fluffy white sheep, then at Lunis. Then he wagged his finger, his intention clear. He didn't want the dragon eating any of the sheep—a

SARAH NOFFKE & MICHAEL ANDERLE

dragon's main food source. It was what the dragons at the Gullington feasted on, but it was also a dragon's preferred food worldwide and harkened back to their Scottish ancestry, according to the Complete History of Dragonriders.

Lunis gulped as his eyes grew large. "Too late…"

Sophia gawked at him, suddenly worried. "You ate a sheep?"

He burped. "A little one. This morning."

"Are you okay?" she asked, looking him over.

Lunis nodded, but didn't appear totally right. "I've had indigestion all morning. Thought it was from the cheese puffs I had last night."

"Go back to eating cheese puffs." Sophia turned to face Quiet. "Will he be okay?"

He studied the dragon before nodding. And again, he pointed at the herd and shook his finger.

"So the sheep," Sophia began. "They're exploding. How is that possible?"

Quiet replied by simply shaking his head again.

"It's almost like someone is trying to harm the dragons," Sophia seethed while looking at the hills where the other dragons lounged in the morning sunshine.

"I think that's an accurate conclusion," Lunis stated.

"If it is Nevin Gooseman, then how could he accomplish this?" Sophia looked between the dragon and the groundskeeper.

Neither seemed to have an answer. "Okay," Sophia began, "well, I'll look into this. But in the meantime, we have to alert the dragons not to eat the sheep. We'll have to find a new food source for them."

"We'll be fine. I'll communicate with the clan so they know too. We will eat fish from the Pond," Lunis stated with authority. "In the meantime, you need to go to Roya Lane and find out how to remove the mark on your soul."

"Fine," Sophia acquiesced. She knew Lunis was right, but felt torn between helping her dragons and herself. There was always something pulling her in different directions. She'd remove the mark from her soul first though. Then she'd find Nevin Gooseman and make him pay.

16

CHAPTER FIVE

For maybe the first time ever, Sophia was grateful to run into King Rudolf Sweetwater upon stepping through the portal onto Roya Lane.

He didn't look any different after his imprisonment at Nevin Gooseman's compound, which was deserted when Rudolf took the Dragon Elite back there. The politician had unsurprisingly fled after the truth about him being behind distortion was exposed.

Sophia had hoped that Nevin went down with his magitech army, but it appeared that he had gotten away. And now, she suspected he was behind the exploding sheep. That man wasn't going to stop until he had ruined the dragons and the Elite.

Sophia was more worried about what the evil magician would do now. Before he had an agenda to take down the Dragon Elite, believing they had too much power that threatened his abilities to control mortals. He was against the demon dragons and made mortals believe they'd be the death of the world. However, now he had lost everything, and no one was more dangerous than someone with nothing left to lose.

If Nevin created and spread a deadly disease like distortion,

Sophia didn't want to think what he'd do now. She'd figure it out, right after she removed the mark on her soul.

Priorities, she told herself. First, remove curse. Second, figure out why the sheep were exploding and stop it. Third, take Nevin Gooseman down for good.

"You look different," Rudolf remarked upon seeing her on Roya Lane. "Did you get a haircut?"

She shook her head, disappointed that he could see the mark on her soul too. She expected that from Lunis and Wilder who she was close to, but not someone like Rudolf.

"Did you get glasses?" he asked.

Sophia tilted her head and gave the handsome but ridiculously dumb fae a confused expression. "I'm not wearing glasses."

"Which would be why you look different without them," he reasoned, and ran his hands through his shiny blond hair. His eyes widened. "Oh, I got it. You got a mark on your soul."

Not sure whether to be impressed or worried, Sophia glared at him. "How did you know that?"

He shrugged. "I know things. Met my fair share of evil spirits who have tried to curse me."

"You have?" Hope rebounded in Sophia's chest. "Do you know how to remove the curse?"

Rudolf gave her a sympathetic expression as he shook his head. "Sure don't. Sorry. For some reason, the evil spirits I've met always tired of me and ran away. Who knows why?"

"I think I've got an idea of why," she muttered, and wondered if she should ask Rudolf to teach her his ways so that she annoyed her villains into submission. It wasn't a common approach, but it sure seemed to work for the fae. He was like a cat and had multiple lives, having escaped things that he shouldn't have.

"Well, if I'm honest, I like the mark on your soul." He flashed her a toothy grin. "It makes you look dangerous."

"I thought the sword and dragon did that," she stated blankly.

He pursed his lips and shook his head. "No, those make you look unapproachable. That blue lizard probably makes it impossible for guys to work up the nerve to ask you out."

"It didn't seem to deter the one who stole my heart. And the dangerous appearance would be acceptable if it weren't for the fact that the mark on my soul makes it hard to sleep and gives me hallucinations."

Rudolf looked off dreamily. "Oh, that sounds like the sixties for me. Good times."

Sophia pointed toward the Rose Apothecary down the lane. "I was headed to see Bep about the healing elixir. Now that you're back, can you get her the dragon egg shells for the next batch of the potion?"

"Yeppers!" he chirped. "And sorry about that whole getting abducted thing and not being able to help with the healing elixir business. I've got a plan worked up now though, and want to review it with you after we visit Bep."

Sophia couldn't help but laugh. "You wouldn't have been abducted in the first place if it weren't for Nevin Gooseman's vendetta against the Dragon Elite. And thank you for getting us the information that helped bring him down. That saved us."

He bowed. "You are very welcome. I expect now that you all will owe me your lives, be indebted to me for eternity, name all of your no doubt destined to be gorgeous children after me, and always be available to get drunk with me and go bowling every Saturday night."

"You expect wrong," she said flatly. "And remember, we're not doing that binding agreement thing anymore that you fae always tie people to you with."

King Rudolf nodded. "It was worth a shot. And no, we're not. I do things for you because you're my friend. I'm always at your beck and call, Sophia Beaufont."

She couldn't help but smile at him fondly. "Same to you, Ru. Same to you."

CHAPTER SIX

W hen the pair entered the Rose Apothecary, Bep was holding a bundle of smoking sage and waving it at a corner.

"Just a regular day in the insane asylum, I see," Sophia muttered, mostly to herself.

"Oh, it's Tuesday." Rudolf slapped his forehead. "I forgot and totally didn't sage the penthouse."

Sophia wasn't sure why, but this surprised her. "You sage your Las Vegas penthouse?"

"And the yurt in Pismo, if you can believe it," he answered at once.

"I can," she said dully.

"Would you two be quiet? I need to concentrate to clear out the energies from that evil spirit, Tatiana." Bep swooped by them while wagging the smoking sage in the air. The smoke made Sophia cough right away.

The potions expert gave Sophia a sideways look as she passed and continued to wave the sage at the other corner of the shop. "Oh, I know why the sage affects you like that."

Sophia coughed a few more times as her eyes watered from the smoke. "Because I have lungs."

"Because of Tatiana's curse," Bep countered and strode elegantly to the next corner. Her long black gown billowed as she moved.

"Yeah, that's why," Sophia retorted sarcastically. "Any remedy for that?"

"I told her the mark on her soul made her look cool." Rudolf waved his hand to clear the smoke from in front of her face. "A real bad girl appearance."

"You would say something like that." Bep's disappointment showed as she regarded the fae. She then directed her eyes at Sophia, and they softened. "And no, dear. I can't help you. Neither can the healing elixir. But for every problem there is a solution."

"And for every season there is a scarf," Rudolf added.

Sophia blinked at him. "Are you drunk?"

He nodded. "Since 1981. Steadily. It's a gift."

"Impressive." She returned her attention to Bep. "About the healing elixir—"

"I did ask you two to be quiet while I cleared the negative energy from my shop, didn't I?" Bep scolded.

Sophia considered going on holiday right then and letting the entire world go to shit since everyone she had to work with made her doubt the whole mission of preserving the planet, but she decided that it would probably backfire on her. She'd pick a resort that was the first one affected by some apocalypse that she was meant to stop, and it would put a damper on the whole "escaping her problems" thing. The only option was to stick around and manage a business that healed magical creatures, remove the mark on her soul, and go on to save the world through various means. Very day-to-day stuff.

Having decided that the saging had worked, Bep blotted out the smoking herb and glanced up at the pair. "Now, what are you here for?"

"The healing elixir," Sophia answered without inflection. *It wasn't too late to turn evil and murder the whole world,* she thought. The curse on her soul must be responsible for making her think so darkly...or her patience had waned to that point...

"Yes, King Sweetwater, do you have the dragon egg shells that I require?" Bep strode forward, and scratched her arms as she did.

He snapped his fingers, and a large box materialized on the table in the center of the room. "They've been ground down to fine dust as you requested."

"Very good." Bep continued to scratch.

"Nice work," Sophia told the fae, glad that she could rely on him in this way. He had proven himself quite reliable lately, but then again, he was drunk, so it wasn't like she would count on him for too much.

"Oh, did you roll around in the grass and get chigger bites too?" Rudolf scratched his arms as well.

"No. I just finished washing the salt crystals from my skin and my body is already reforming them," Bep replied, irritation heavy in her voice.

Sophia blinked at the potions expert. "Why am I getting this information?"

"Because," she answered simply. "It's a result of living by the sea."

"Or of being a dirty hippie," Sophia remarked under breath.

"The waters affect everything," Bep went on, and swept her hand through the air in a broad motion. "They affect the way we feel, how our bodies function, and our minds."

Something about that phrase struck Sophia oddly. She gulped. Closed her eyes to think. Then realized something profound.

"The sheep!" Sophia exclaimed as her eyes popped open with excitement.

CHAPTER SEVEN

"Goat!" Rudolf exclaimed, his eyes dancing with excitement. "Donkey," Bep stated, not at all as enthusiastic.

Sophia shot them both confused stares.

"Your turn again," Rudolf encouraged. "Name another animal."

She shook her head. "No, it's about the sheep. Now I think I know why they're exploding. At least, I have an idea."

Rudolf nodded like exploding sheep were perfectly normal. "I remember in the summer of 1745 when crows kept exploding."

"Oh, really?" Sophia wondered if he had a clue for her on the subject. "Why?"

"I fed them explosives," he replied.

She sighed with defeat. "Anyway, Bep gave me an idea."

"I'm prone to that," the potions expert said at once. "It's because of my esoteric nature. It provides inspiration."

"Okay." Sophia drew the word out. "Anyway, I think the water at the Gullington might be contaminated. I can at least look into it and cross it off the list."

"Speaking of things to cross off lists, let's go get a cookie." Rudolf grabbed Sophia's arm and hauled her toward the door with surprising strength.

"Do you work out?" she asked, impressed and allowing herself to be led off.

"No, fae don't have to. We're naturally ripped. I have a six pack and everything."

"Of course you do," she muttered. "And why is getting a cookie on your list?"

"Because that's how I think best, and we need to discuss the business plan for the healing elixir. I've got ideas."

Sophia nodded. She could use something to eat since her protein bar breakfast left her wanting. Then hopefully she'd be ready to take on whatever challenge removing the mark from her soul would entail. It would no doubt be dangerous and convoluted and probably leave her with a new scar. But as long as she didn't have the curse anymore, she'd endure whatever she had to.

CHAPTER EIGHT

"Do you gals make cakes?" Rudolf asked Lee and Cat quite seriously as he stood on the other side of the case of pastries, cakes, and cookies at the Crying Cat Bakery.

Lee glanced at her wife with an exasperated expression. "Seriously, you say I can't kill the king of the fae? Are you still standing by that statement?"

Cat laughed and toddled off toward the back. "Just you wait. He'll kill himself off eventually."

Lee groaned as she watched the other baker retreat into the kitchen. "I'm waiting for a certain someone to die, and it's killing me."

"You ladies are cute." Rudolf slapped the counter impatiently. "But seriously. Cakes. Do you make them?"

"It's a bakery," Sophia pointed out.

"Yeah, but it doesn't mean they make cakes," he countered.

She pointed at the turquoise and pink cake with a unicorn decorated on it. "What about that?"

"It's a unicorn," he remarked. "What I need is a birthday cake for the Captains' one year mark. Something with chocolate and not too much rum."

"Are you sure about that?" Sophia asked.

He thought for a moment. "Yeah, you're right. Lots and lots of rum. They have pirate's blood in them after all, being captains and all."

"You realize that they don't, right, and giving them a name... Never mind." Sophia abandoned her argument since it would only give her a headache.

"Yeah, we can make your triplets a cake for their birthday," Lee stated.

"They aren't triplets," Rudolf corrected. "There are only three of them."

Sophia smiled sweetly at the assassin baker. "Isn't it great that he's so attractive?"

"So great that it makes my trigger finger jumpy," Lee replied. "But if you want to do something cool for your girls, who probably have everything already, I might have a suggestion."

Rudolf looked relieved. "That would be amazing. They really do have everything. I was going to buy their pony a pony, but I'm up for suggestions."

"Well, I need to check into it and see if it's still around," Lee stated. "It's invite-only and very exclusive, but I might be able to get you in. I offed the guy's wife a few years ago, and he owes me a favor."

Sophia closed her eyes for a beat. "Again, best if you don't share information about your assassin business with me."

"I mean offed as in... Yeah, never mind." Lee shrugged in surrender. "I can't figure out how to spin that one."

Sophia pointed at a chocolate chip cookie. "Is there anything magical in that?"

"By magical, what do you mean?" Lee asked.

"I mean something that will make me hallucinate—well, hallucinate more," Sophia answered.

Lee tilted her head. "What answer are you looking for here? Is hallucinating more a bad thing? Or is that what you're going for?"

Sophia sighed. "I'd prefer fewer hallucinations."

Whatever Lunis was doing to help against the curse's effects was working. She only hoped that it continued.

"There's a touch of Tormenium nutmeg in there, since that's my secret ingredient—" Lee's eyes widened as her mouth slammed shut.

"What?" Sophia wondered why the baker had a sudden look of horror on her face.

"Well, now that I let that slip, I have to kill you." Lee hung her head and looked disappointed.

"That totally sucks." Rudolf nodded like he understood. "Can I call my wife first? She'll be excited but pissed that I won't be bringing home dinner, so I need to let her know to fend for herself...forever..."

"She's not going to kill us," Sophia said dryly and crossed her arms over her chest.

"I'm sorry, I have to," Lee argued. "I'll make it fast." She pulled a knife from behind her back with a menacing look on her face.

"If the cookie isn't poisoned, can I have one please?" Sophia asked, not at all flustered. "Ru and I have a meeting, so we'll take the table in the corner since apparently no one wants to come in here, and we can have some privacy to discuss our business strategy."

"Fine." Lee put the knife down and trotted over to the counter. "I won't kill you, but you must forget that I said the secret ingredient in all our food is Tormenium nutmeg."

"Repeating it helps with the forgetting process," Sophia imparted, then took the cookie Lee offered her before giving one to Rudolf.

"And there are no customers here because I shooed them all away," Lee stated. "They kept buying stuff. That's going to require me to go in the back and make more stuff, and that's exhausting."

Sophia glanced at Rudolf as they sat at the corner table. "Remember that we don't take business advice from Lee."

He snapped his fingers, and a pad and pen appeared. The ball point scribbled across the pad hovering in the air—taking notes. "Don't take business advice from the assassin baker. Great stuff. What's next for our business plan?"

Sophia sighed. "Get a new business partner."

CHAPTER NINE

King Rudolf wasn't a bad business partner. As usual, he surprised Sophia with his competence. The king of the fae had a very savvy business mind. In less time than she would have expected, they knocked out a business plan for their new company that they were calling Heals Pills. One of the next steps was to put the elixir in gel caps so they were easier to pop on the go.

Of course, for everything remarkably intelligent that Rudolf said, he'd follow it up with something about how magicians wouldn't die out now since they'd find each other attractive enough after taking Heals Pills to breed.

Sophia was aware that one of the potential benefits was increased beauty, but her motive was to offer an option for ailments that couldn't be easily healed through other means. Heals Pills would be huge, and help tons of magical creatures.

The pair probably would have knocked out a lot more, but Sophia got a message from Papa Creola. It read, "If you don't want a mark on your soul anymore, then stop by the Fantastical Armory."

She couldn't help but laugh at his phrasing. Like she was going to say, "Well, I like not being able to sleep and having this brooding sense of doom in my spirit. Think I'll keep it."

After getting the message, she bolted out of the Crying Cat Bakery as fast as she could and sprinted all the way to the Fantastical Armory. When she entered the weapons shop, she found Subner unsurprisingly blowing smoke rings from a hookah sitting on the floor next to him.

"So you're getting high too." Sophia looked at the stringy-haired elf. "Same thing is happening at the Crying Cat Bakery down the way."

"Like a true Nature's child, we were born, born to be wild." Subner repeated the words of Steppenwolf.

"Not me," Sophia argued. "I was born to deal with weirdos, apparently."

"You're either on the bus or off the bus," he replied, this time in Ken Kesey's words.

"Anyway," Sophia drew out the word. "Papa Creola messaged me. Where is he?"

Subner took another hit off the hookah. "Always trust those searching for The Truth, never those who have found it."

"Cool, so you're going to be zero help. I've got a club you can join. It's getting very full."

"As Carl Jung said, 'Masses are always breeding grounds of psychic epidemics,'" Subner imparted.

Thankfully, Papa Creola entered from the back door a moment later, carrying a small metal box that appeared very heavy based on the strained expression on his face. He set it down with a loud thud.

He didn't appear to notice Sophia standing there with an irritated expression on her face.

"I'm here," she said when he bent down to eye the box from a different angle.

"Ram Dass said, 'Be here now,'" Subner advised in an airy voice.

Sophia tapped her foot. "Papa Creola, you messaged me."

"I did," he replied absentmindedly.

She pointed at the small metal box. "Is that the way to remove the mark on my soul?"

"War is over, if you want it," Subner stated in the words of John Lennon.

She ignored him. "Papa?"

He glanced up as if realizing she was there, or maybe had forgotten. "This? Oh, no. This is… Well, I can't tell you."

"That's typical. Secrets."

"Not a secret," he countered. "I simply haven't figured it out yet."

Subner began to sway. "Your mind is like a parachute, it doesn't work unless it's open."

"Is there a way to turn him off?" Sophia pointed at the owner of the Fantastical Armory.

Papa Creola shook his head. "No, but this pains him. He's worse than usual today. Probably all the drugs."

"He could try not doing them," she offered.

"He can't," Papa Creola amended. "It's part of who he is in this form."

"If I'm free, it's because I'm always running," Subner stated.

"I think you should run," Sophia quipped. "So you have a solution for me for this curse?"

Papa Creola shook his head. "No, unfortunately, I don't."

Sophia sighed. "That's cute, because your message implied that you did."

"I know where you can look to find a solution though." Papa Creola continued to regard the metal box with speculation.

"It all depends on how we look at things, and not how they are in themselves," Subner told them, his eyes closed.

Sophia ignored him. "Oh great. So not even a direct answer. Instead, a place to look for the answer. I love a good scavenger hunt."

Papa Creola nodded as if she was serious. "Then you'll love this."

"Love is a friend set to music," Subner quoted.

"How has Liv not murdered him yet?" Sophia pointed at the hippie sitting with the hookah.

Papa Creola blew out a breath. "I don't know. It's only a matter of time for us both. But then we're hopeful we'll be back as magicians or gnomes or something more tolerable."

"Or fae," she teased.

He shot her a repulsed expression. "Don't joke like that. I'd throw myself in front of a bus. I have…"

"Not weird at all," she stated.

Father Time shrugged. "Some things are worse than death. Fae, for one."

Sophia nodded. "So where's this place I get to look for my next clue?"

"Well, I do know that you need to find the original Door of Reflection to lift the mark from your soul," Papa Creola advised.

"You mean the entrance to the Chamber of the Tree in the House of Fourteen?" she asked.

"Yes. It was created from a source, but I can't tell you where."

She lowered her chin. "Can't?"

"Life is a journey, not a destination," Subner sang, still swaying.

Papa Creola nodded in his assistant's direction. "What he said."

"Okay, so where's the source?" Sophia asked.

Papa Creola simply gave her a look that said, "What do you think?"

"So you're not going to tell me, are you?"

"I will tell you that while you currently can't go to the Great Library, since it's under construction—"

Sophia's laughter cut him off. "You mean moved."

"Whatever." Papa Creola waved his hand dismissively at her. "There's another place to find the source location of the Door of Reflection, and it's one that you're acquainted with."

Sophia's eyes widened with a sudden realization. "Of course! Another source for the Door of Reflection's location would be the library in the House of Fourteen."

She didn't wait for confirmation from the elf known as Father Time before bounding for the door.

Of course, Subner had to have the last word and called at her back, "May every sunrise hold more promise and every sunset hold more peace."

CHAPTER TEN

When she stepped through the portal into the House of Fourteen, Sophia felt the familiar sentiment of nostalgia wash over her as she entered her childhood home.

Most didn't grow up in a hidden magical house disguised as a rundown palm reading shop off the Santa Monica pier, so most probably didn't have the same ambivalent feelings as Sophia. It wasn't that she didn't value the place that she'd called home for the first part of her life, but rather that it was constantly changing, so how could she miss it?

The House of Fourteen wasn't like a little cottage that one could return to and skip through memories as they strolled through the familiar rooms. The House was constantly changing depending on who was there and many other conditions, similar to the Gullington. It was a massive seven-story building with rooms that disappeared and reappeared and a magical chamber where only councilors and warriors could enter through the Door of Reflection. And the Dragon Elite, of course.

But in truth, Sophia mostly didn't have too many sad feelings when returning to her home because it hadn't ever felt like that to her.

She'd lived in one place with her parents until they died. Then she, Ian, Reese, and Clark moved to another apartment inside the House of Fourteen.

Then her older sister and brother died, and she and Clark lived alone in a smaller place. If anything, it had been nice to move to Liv's where there was no association with death and loss. When Sophia finally moved to the Gullington, it had been about growth and rebirth and starting a new life. So returning to the House of Fourteen was like stepping into an old life—one she outgrew long ago.

"What's with the weird look in your eyes?" Liv asked as soon as Sophia crossed the hallway from the portal connected to the Castle.

Her sister was propped up against the wall, next to a painting of a warrior standing in a dark landscape with their hair blowing in the wind and a murderous expression on their face. Liv appeared like she had been casually waiting for Sophia to enter from the portal all along.

"I love that I keep getting that question," Sophia muttered with no real joy in her voice.

"I love that you speak the language of sarcasm," Liv replied. "But seriously. The look. Looks like your soul has been scarred."

"Marked," Sophia corrected. "And ten points for the guess. Yes. That's why I'm here. Your boss is sending me on a scavenger hunt."

Apparently used to the people she loved getting their souls marked or bit by demons, Liv didn't act too shocked or concerned. Sophia loved that about her—and much, much more.

Instead, Liv rubbed her hands together and looked excited as she pushed off the wall. "Oh, a good scavenger hunt. That's so Papa's way."

"Yes, he and Mama Jamba refuse to give direct answers when they've got all the time in the world for us to figure things out on our own."

Liv cleared her throat and slipped into her Papa Creola voice. "Why tell you when you can risk your life to find the answers for yourself?"

"We should murder that man," Sophia said, earning a look of

surprise from Liv. She quickly added, "Sorry, it's the mark on my soul. It's making me extra irritable lately."

Liv nodded and understood at once. "Same thing happened to me when a talking toad cursed me. Worst two weeks ever. Clark nearly didn't survive."

Sophia laughed. "How is House business?" She nodded in the direction of the downstairs where the Chamber of the Tree was located and the Royals met.

"Boring. They love to hear themselves talk, especially Bianca. Lorenzo seems humbled since you punched him in the face. However, I'm still keeping an eye on the guy."

"Good," Sophia stated with relief.

"Plato wants our help with something soon," Liv began. "You might have noticed that he moved the Great Library."

"How could I have missed that?" Sophia joked.

"Yeah, it created a huge chasm in the folds of time and space according to Grumpy Pants, also known as Papa Creola," Liv related. "However, it had to be done and we're patching things up. Anyway, once the renovation is complete, Plato wants us to fetch the new librarian. You game?"

"Fetch?" Sophia asked dryly.

"Well, it will involve getting our hands dirty," Liv confessed. "We'll probably get a little sweaty."

Sophia groaned. "I don't like to sweat."

"Me either."

Still, Sophia grinned. "Yeah, as soon as I remove this mark on my soul, I'll have time. When do you think?"

Liv shrugged. "When the paint dries. I'll let you know. Sounds like you've got more pressing issues."

"I have to find the source that the Door of Reflection was created from. Any ideas on that one?"

"Unlike Papa, I'd tell you if I knew," Liv answered. "Alas, I do not and can't help."

Sophia nodded. "Well, I figure the information is in the library so I'm off to research."

"Don't get lost." Liv strode in the opposite direction after offering her sister a smile.

It was good advice, since the potential of getting lost in the House of Fourteen's library was an actual concern and had happened to many a wise magician—never to be seen again.

CHAPTER ELEVEN

The library in the House of Fourteen, although not nearly as big as the Great Library, was still magnificent. It was several stories tall and never the same on any given day. That was because it contained almost exclusively magical books that in many ways were alive. There was no librarian that Sophia was aware of. Instead, the reader was supposed to stay focused on what they were looking for and be "led" to the right section and book.

If one didn't focus properly, then they would be lost. And if the browser didn't know the right clues to look for, then they might never find the right book. That was because magic was inherently tricky in both a complex and mischievous way.

Reese, Sophia's oldest sister, used to say that magic had a personality all its own. "You have to be clever to understand magic. And you have to have a sense of humor to appreciate it."

The books in the House of Fourteen's library reflected this personality.

Sophia let out a deep breath and enjoyed the familiar smell of the many volumes sitting on shelves when she entered the large library. This was her favorite place in the House of Fourteen. She'd spent many an occasion playing hide-and-seek with Liv, hiding in strange places that only Liv could find. For instance, Sophia once hid as a book on a shelf and another time she was inside a painting. Her magic when she was young was very creative. Now she had to reserve it for more practical things—like staying alive.

Knowing that the library picked up on her thoughts the moment she entered, Sophia directed them intently, thinking of the book she needed.

I need to find the source of the Door of Reflection, she thought.

When nothing happened, Sophia deflated. It wasn't that she expected the library to rearrange itself right in front of her or illuminate a path to the book she needed. Well, that happened on occasion, but she thought *something* would happen. Usually a sign was presented. It was always different.

However, for nothing to happen at all was troubling. Sophia suddenly worried if the curse interfered with her ability to focus or work with the library in the House of Fourteen.

Sophia wondered what her options were as she glanced around, starting to feel desperate. That's when she noticed a familiar figure who she shouldn't have been surprised to find with his nose in a book. And he was exactly the right person to help her with her current dilemma. But first she was going to sneak up on her unsuspecting brother and scare him half to death—because that's how she rolled.

CHAPTER TWELVE

Sneaking up on Clark wasn't difficult since he was completely engrossed in the book he was reading. He had it pressed up close to his face and scanned the words intently as he mouthed them.

Sophia reached out from behind him and grabbed his shoulders. "Boo."

He jumped forward, then whipped around and held the book like it was a makeshift weapon.

Unable to control herself, she doubled over laughing at the frightened expression on Clark's red face.

He relaxed at the sight of her, and his eyes went from scared to annoyed. "Soph, that was a trick that Liv would have pulled on me. I didn't expect something like that from you."

She continued to giggle. "I know. I just saw Liv, so I guess she inspired me."

His chest rose and fell as he sought to catch his breath. Then he tilted his head with a sudden worried expression. "What's wrong? Are you okay?"

She nodded at once, wanting to put his fears at ease. Those who knew her best could obviously see the mark on her soul. "I'm fine, but that's why I'm here. I'm looking for something that could help me. Maybe you can assist."

His brow wrinkled more. "What is it?"

Sophia didn't want to tell Clark that she'd been cursed. He was a worrier and wouldn't take it as easily as Liv. "I'm looking for a book that tells me where to find the source that the Door of Reflection was taken from. You don't happen to know the answer offhand, do you?"

Clark was probably the most well-read person she knew. For a moment, hope filled her chest that she could bypass the research aspect and get the answer from him.

However, his frown deepened as he shook his head. "I don't, but why do you need to find the source of the Door of Reflections? You don't look like yourself. What is it?"

"It's something I can fix," she said with conviction. "I just need your help. Can you help me find the book that has the information?"

He blinked at her in confusion. "I don't understand. Why can't you search? I taught you how the library works a long time ago."

She shrugged. "I don't know. For some reason it's not working for me. Maybe it's because I'm a dragonrider now or something." What Sophia didn't say was what she thought was the actual cause. The mark on her soul made it so that the library wouldn't respond to her. Maybe it didn't trust her, or that was part of the curse.

"Why do I get the impression you're intentionally avoiding telling me what's wrong with you?"

Sophia sighed. "It's not worth going into. What's important is finding that book with the information on the Door of Reflection. Will you please help me, Clark?" She batted her eyes at her brother, giving him the look that she knew would always work on him.

Instantly, he softened, nodded and let out a breath. "Yes, you know I'll help you, Soph. Let me put this away so it doesn't interfere." He slid the book he was holding onto the nearest shelf. It didn't matter where he put it because the library would reshelf it to wherever it belonged.

"Now, it could be possible that the book isn't here and that's why you can't find it," Clark offered and turned to look down the row.

"I considered that. But Papa Creola sent me here."

Her brother nodded in understanding. "So then it's here."

"I think so."

He closed his eyes, obviously focusing on what they wanted to find. He walked forward without opening them, seemingly pulled by an invisible string. Blind but walking perfectly straight, Clark made a sudden turn at the end of the row and continued forward. Sophia followed him at a distance, not wanting to distract him as he navigated his way through the library.

After Clark had walked a great distance, he stopped abruptly and swung around to face a row of books. With his eyes still closed, he reached out and pulled a book of maps from the shelf. His eyes popped open and surprise hit his face. When he held up the book, Sophia knew why.

The book was entitled, *Hidden Places*.

CHAPTER THIRTEEN

"Have you ever seen this before?" Sophia took the book from Clark. It was thick, and full of dusty maps with faded colors.

He shook his head. "I'm certain that no one has in a long time judging by its appearance."

She knew what he meant when she opened it to find the pages stuck together. There were maps of the Earth full of blue waters and green lands, but it didn't look like the globe she was acquainted with.

Clark gasped as he looked over her shoulder. "This map..."

"It has lands that are hidden," Sophia finished his sentence. The map was full of places she'd never heard of like Ramycans and Fatima Islands and Bateman Peninsula.

"I wonder if the only way you can find these hidden places is if you have this book," Clark mused and scratched his forehead.

"That makes sense. Because otherwise they would have been discovered by now."

She suspected that Mama Jamba could shine some light on the subject, but doubted that she would offer much help. That woman was about as forthcoming with information as Papa Creola.

While flipping through the book, she found map after map with places she'd recognize, but with bodies of lands next to them that she didn't. "Since when is there a small continent next to Mexico?"

"Probably since forever ago," Clark answered.

Although the discovery of all these mysterious places was incredibly cool, it didn't help Sophia to narrow down where the source of the Door of Reflection was located.

Similar to how Bermuda Laurens had taught Sophia how to use the books *Magical Creatures* and a *Complete History of Dragonriders* to find things, she randomly flipped through the pages, not scanning them, but rather feeling directed. Suddenly, her hand stopped on a page. The map was full of tiny islands and looked to be in the South Pacific.

At first, Sophia wasn't sure why her instinct had made her stop on this particular page. Then Clark reached over her shoulder and pointed. "Look. That's got to be it."

Her mouth popped open, and she knew he was right. Nestled between the cluster of islands was a body of water labeled, The Reflective Sea.

CHAPTER FOURTEEN

Standing outside the Barrier at the Gullington, Sophia frowned. She'd continuously failed to create a portal to one of the islands around the Reflective Sea. And stepping through a portal close to the islands would have her swimming in the South Pacific.

"I think you have to go with me," she said to Lunis, who stood beside her with uncertainty written on his face. "We must need the map to find the hidden locations and that's why I can't portal there."

"But if I go, then there's no way to protect you," he argued. "The hallucinations..."

"The only way to remove the mark from my soul is to go to the Reflective Sea," she stated with confidence. "I don't know what I'm supposed to do there, but this is what Papa Creola told me I needed to do—find the source of the Door of Reflection."

He hung his head, obviously not liking this new plan. "It's just that leaving the Gullington is one thing and puts you at risk, but me not protecting you is another."

"I left the Gullington with you before, while I had the curse," she countered.

"It's getting worse."

They both knew he was right. Early on, the curse hadn't been so bad, but it was progressively worsening and Sophia knew that there were many risks if she left with Lunis. "Then that's why we have to do it now, rather than waiting any longer."

Although she knew that he was reluctant, her dragon obediently knelt and extended his wing so she could climb onto his back and slip into the saddle.

When she was in place, he took off at once, probably wanting to get this over with as soon as possible.

Sophia didn't look forward to being unprotected from the hallucinations, but she was intrigued by the idea of seeing a hidden land. With the book of maps tucked inside her cloak, she enjoyed the wind whipping through her hair as she opened a portal to the South Pacific.

It shimmered bright and colorful in front of her and Lunis as they flew. Soon they'd step foot on an island that most had never seen or knew existed.

CHAPTER FIFTEEN

When they slipped through the portal and flew over the sparkling waters of the South Pacific, Sophia expected to find little islands sprinkled throughout the area, like she'd seen on the map she'd studied all night. However, the blue ocean simply went on for what seemed like eternity.

Are you sure we're in the right place? Lunis asked in her head.

Not at all. It happens to be my first time using a magical map of hidden locations.

She pulled the book from her cloak and flipped it open to the map of the tiny islands in the South Pacific. There was no other landmark to give her reference.

I think whatever you did, worked, Lunis said, excitement in his tone.

Sophia jerked her head up and saw little islands covered in lush trees materialize, springing up one by one in front of them.

Oh. I guess I have to use the map or I can't find them.

That makes sense, Lunis imparted. *You can't simply know about the hidden places. The maps are the key to finding them.*

Sophia studied the map and located the islands around the Reflective Sea, looking for discernable traits. There was one that was shaped like a cat's paw and another like a crescent moon. The sea was right in between them, and one of those places seemed like the best spot to land.

She glanced up and searched the islands littering the South Pacific in front of them. There were so many that it was hard to believe no one knew they existed. Suddenly, she wondered what other strange things could be hidden in these places besides the source for the Door of Reflection. Then that begged the question of why the lands in the book, *Hidden Places*, were concealed in the first place. Maybe they had dark magic that if in the wrong hands would be dangerous. Or maybe there were secrets buried there. Sophia suspected that each hidden land had a different reason for being secret. She looked forward to exploring them more—when time allowed.

There, Sophia exclaimed to Lunis. She pointed to a small island that sat next to a bright blue sea that sparkled so much it nearly blinded her. The crescent-shaped island was directly across from the paw-shaped one. However, that one was covered in thick trees with little beach. The crescent one was mostly sand, and would hopefully offer them the best opportunity to investigate the Reflective Sea all around it.

Sophia didn't know what they were supposed to do at the sea, but it worried her. The Door of Reflection was the entrance to the Chamber of the Tree. Although it didn't work on her as a dragonrider, when Councilors and Warriors passed through it, the door served up their worst fears in an effort to cleanse them of it. If the door was sourced from the Reflective Sea, Sophia worried about what she'd encounter.

She knew without a doubt that it would have to be major to clear the mark from her soul. Although she was more than a little intimidated by the unknown challenge that lay before her, she would do anything to lift the curse. Sophia swallowed as Lunis dove in for a landing, realizing she would probably have to do what she feared most...

CHAPTER SIXTEEN

L unis' claws slid deep into the white sand of the crescent-shaped island when they landed. The smell of salt and the ocean breeze rippling the pristine waters of the Reflective Sea made Sophia long for a vacation.

According to the map, the island was called Buddha's Temple and had a long stretch of beach, which was why Sophia chose it for the landing. There was also a tropical forest that filled the center of the island. And lapping up on it was the Reflective Sea, which was what Sophia figured she'd come for.

However, as she slid off Lunis and made her way closer to the waters, she felt like something was pulling her back. Sophia picked up her boots one by one, wondering if she was sinking into quicksand.

The white sand of the beach wasn't easy to trudge through but it wasn't pulling her down like she thought. Sophia glanced over her shoulder, seriously feeling like something was tethered around her waist, tugging her back from the Reflective Sea.

Lunis was scowling at her with an undeniably angry expression on his face.

She wasn't sure why, but Sophia's words came out of her mouth before she could stop herself. "What's your problem?"

It was such an uncharacteristic way for her to talk to Lunis, or anyone. And the tone of her voice didn't sound like her.

"You, for starters." Lunis' scowl deepened. "You kicked up sand on me when you dismounted. And I don't know what you're waiting for, standing there staring at the Reflective Sea. We don't have all day. I'm ready to get back to the Gullington."

And now it was war. Sophia's head filled with heat. "Kicked up sand? Really! It's a freaking beach, Lunis. We're going to get sandy. But I guess that's too much for you to understand." She didn't know why she suddenly felt so hostile or how to make it stop. As she spoke, more angry thoughts came to her. Ones that she'd felt like she'd always had.

"And really, you don't have all day?" she continued. "What, do you need to go back and watch Santa Clarita Diet and veg on cheese puffs?"

His eyes narrowed with anger. "I have lots of important things to do at the Gullington. Most recently, I kept you from having hallucinations."

"You took a long nap," she spat. "Real freaking hard."

"I take care of the dragonettes while you gallivant, hang out with Liv, and eat nachos," he bellowed, his voice rising.

She stuck her hands on her hips. "I go on missions to save the world."

"Oh, I go on missions to save the world," he said in a high-pitched voice, impersonating Sophia.

Before, she was mad. Now she was livid. "To answer your question, I can't get next to the Reflective Sea or otherwise I would have already because being here with you is further marking my soul."

The dragon's face shifted suddenly. "Here…this place. It's causing us to be like this."

"Like what?" Sophia insisted, still fuming.

"Soph, this isn't us. Well, it is and this is how we're acting, and right now I despise you, but that's not us. It must be some weird magic of the island or the sea or this whole area."

That made sense. Sophia couldn't understand why she didn't see that from the beginning, but the argument exploded so fast and all she could see was red. Lunis was right. For some odd reason, she couldn't stand looking at him right then. She disliked him more than anyone on the planet...and dislike wasn't the word rebounding in her head, but that word, well, it made her soul ache more.

How could she hate her dragon? She had never loved someone that much before him. And now, for seemingly no reason at all, they were close to being at each other's throats.

"You're right," she said slowly as she processed it.

"Of course I am," he barked.

She cut her eyes at him with a look on her face that said, "That's not helping."

He nodded at once. "Yeah, I'm sorry. As much as it pains me to say it."

"So what are we supposed to do? And why are we so angry with each other?" Sophia asked.

"I think you need to stay away from the Reflective Sea," he offered.

A rude laugh popped out of her mouth. "We're on an island. How exactly do you expect me to do that?"

Lunis lowered his head and regarded her with a murderous expression. "I realize that it won't be easy, which is why this is supposed to be a challenge."

They were doing it again. Sophia wanted to yell, to battle the magical beast before her. But if they did, they would destroy each other. And that would be the worst possible way to die, by the teeth of her dragon. His heart punctured by her sword. She instinctively knew that if they started to fight it would be impossible to end, so powerful was the urge drumming through her body.

She let out a breath and tried to clear her head. "You're right. It's the water. So what do we do?"

"Well, I think you're repelled from it for a reason," Lunis stated. "Maybe it's your soul helping you, communicating to stay away. What else do you feel?"

That made sense, Sophia realized as she felt something ancient and wise flowing in her now that she was tuned into it. She closed her eyes and tried to focus on that internal flow. The voice of her soul.

For a moment, she heard multiple voices. Male. Female. Young. Old. It was like a compilation of everyone she'd ever been or known or loved across many lives. It was a chorus of voices, all with different messages that spoke the wisdom of the ages.

Sophia wasn't sure how she knew that, but she did, with all her being. Then the voices all wove together and didn't sound like they were speaking words anymore. It was a sound. It was music. It was the sound of water flowing.

Her eyes popped open. "We have to go to the center of the island."

CHAPTER SEVENTEEN

Buddha's Temple was thick with vegetation and appeared to be an unforgiving land full of dangerous animals and thorny plants and sinking mud.

After the first step under the canopy, Sophia and Lunis were cast in darkness. The cacophony of birds squawking in the trees overhead was nearly deafening, and made Sophia have to adjust her hearing. Through the darkness, she spied many yellow eyes blinking at her up ahead.

"We have company." Sophia felt a little better as they moved away from the Reflective Sea, although she was still irritated at Lunis for no apparent reason.

"Whatever they are, they smell delicious," Lunis stated in a low voice.

Whatever they were, they moved fast and made little squeaky noises as they darted between large leaves and the undergrowth.

Sophia halted after a few steps and gave Lunis a sideways expression.

"What?" he asked, his tone still not the one she was accustomed to.

She tentatively glanced up at the many colorful tropical birds in the trees that glared down at them. "Do you get the impression that we're not welcome here?"

"Impression?" Lunis questioned. "The welcome mat has pretty much been ripped out from underneath us. Are you certain we're supposed to go to the center of this island? Maybe it's a different one, like the one shaped like a paw or any of the others."

Sophia closed her eyes and listened again to the chorus of voices deep within her soul. She felt a pulse. Watched in her mind as the voices took shape and wove together like DNA. Heard them sing a song that again was unmistakably the sound of rushing water.

Her eyes snapped open. "We have to go to the center of this island or one of the others, but what we're looking for is the same on each and our experiences to get there will be the same as well."

"So there's no avoiding facing the little beast ahead or getting away from the birds that appear ready to bomb us with poop then," he groused.

Sophia shook her head. "Or any of the other obstacles that lay after that."

It was weird how she knew this information and yet, it was something she was absolutely certain of. The islands were all different, like souls, yet they were all the same. They were one. What happened on one affected the other. What lay at the center of one, lay at the center of the others. More poetic than that was the Reflective Sea connected them all—in essence making them one.

CHAPTER EIGHTEEN

"So do we deal with the birds first or venture toward the yellow-eyed beasts that I don't think are cuddly little creatures ready to assist us on our journey?" Lunis asked.

"They might be," she argued. "But I don't think there's anything to be done about the birds. They just seem to be throwing us death stares."

"I could torch them," Lunis offered.

She shook her head. "I don't think going on the offensive will do us any favors with the natives. Let's wait until they make the first move."

"I'm certain that's going to involve trying to murder us, but you can hold out for a fruit basket if you so desire."

She grinned. "I'm an optimist."

Sophia was grateful that the negative feelings towards Lunis evaporated as they moved farther into the jungle. They'd come on so fast and receded as quickly. Who knew why, but it seemed to have been a test of some sort. Or maybe it was a way to push her farther away from the Reflective Sea.

If Lunis and she hadn't had that argument, then there wouldn't have been any need for reflection and she might not have gone within and listened to the voice of her soul. The irony of the sea's name and this experience wasn't lost on her.

On Sophia's next step, a twig cracked under her boot. Suddenly, the loud calls of the bright-colored birds in the tree ceased. The sounds from the yellow-eyed creatures halted. The entire jungle fell silent, but not in a peaceful, "all is well on the prairies" way. More like a, "you're not welcome and about to pay" way.

CHAPTER NINETEEN

Sophia pulled Inexorabilis from its sheath. She had stalled doing that, not wanting to put the jungle creatures on the defensive. Now this was about self-preservation rather than avoiding offending the natives. And that's exactly the effect it had.

The birds overhead dove like kamikaze fighter pilots with no regard for their lives, it seemed. This left Sophia no choice but to swing her sword at them and knock them away like fly balls. Lunis opened his mouth and blanketed the canopy with fire.

This did little to deter the suicidal birds. They streaked through the flames, caught on fire, and dive-bombed the dragon. This made Lunis abandon his strategy and use his claws and head to bat the balls of fire to the ground.

Thankfully, the forest was wet enough that the trees didn't burn for long before the fire extinguished. Being on a burning island would make things much more difficult when Sophia didn't think she could handle any more complications.

Sharp beaks tore at Sophia's armor and face. A few times, she felt close to losing an eye. The birds were out for blood and not willing to negotiate. Since there was no reasoning with the murderous avians,

Sophia had no choice but to slice through bird after bird until it seemed they'd slaughtered every single one.

Lunis' claws and tail made quick work of the little feathered monsters. But still, the dragon took quite a bit of damage since he was unable to protect himself from being assaulted from every angle.

There had to have been over a hundred birds, but as Sophia and Lunis stood in the once again quiet jungle, it was hard to count all the bodies that littered the jungle floor. Feathers and beaks and broken birds lay all around them, but for some reason there was no blood, which perplexed both Sophia and Lunis.

A chill ran down the dragonrider's spine as she looked up at the forest canopy to see it lined with more birds. But then when she brought her chin down, all the ones they'd slain were gone—simply vanished. *So not new ones. The same birds.*

Well, that's annoying, Lunis said in her head.

Annoying wasn't the word I was going to use. Her hands gripped her sword as she backed up to her dragon.

Irritating, bothersome, frustrating. Take your pick, the dragon replied with laughter in his tone.

Troublesome is the one I choose, Sophia stated while eyeing the birds. This new set didn't appear any more endeared to the dragon and rider.

The jungle was once again quiet and in the distance, the yellowed-eyed creatures still blinked through the dark leaves.

The waters of the Reflective Sea still stood at Sophia's back, promising to bring other dangers—like fights with her dragon.

So what does your soul say to do now? Lunis asked in her head.

Sophia didn't have to go within to ask as the birds dove from over-head in attempt number two to take them out.

"Run!" Sophia yelled and sprinted for the unknown dangers that no doubt lay ahead.

CHAPTER TWENTY

The blades of the thick leaves sliced at Sophia's face and neck as she sprinted, trying to escape the homicidal birds. Lunis held out his wings as they ran, which created a wall and protected Sophia from attacks. However, as they progressed deeper into the jungle, the vegetation was denser and made it so he had to pull his wings down to slide through the branches. He could have used a compartment spell if he weren't focused on not being torpedoed.

When Sophia was moderately certain that they had a lead on the tropical birds, she pointed over her shoulder and threw up a shield barrier. It would cause a huge drain on her magic, but so would death.

Sophia knew the shield had worked when she heard a pelting sound at her back. She dared to look over her shoulder and briefly saw an image of the dumb birds colliding with the invisible barrier, hitting it like bugs on a windshield.

The pair came to a halt, but not only because the tropical birds were no longer chasing them. Mostly it was because they'd discovered what the source of the yellow eyes was.

CHAPTER TWENTY-ONE

Sophia assumed that the little tiny yellow eyes belonged to creatures, probably with sharp teeth and a motivation to murder them. She was wrong.

Sophia wasn't sure what she would have preferred. Fighting angry gremlins or the creatures they'd run up on.

Hundreds of fireflies hovering in front of them, their bodies aglow in the dark forest. However, these weren't like the enchanting little bugs that fill up the night. A quick study of them told Sophia that they were also murder bugs, much like their bird friends.

Their wings fluttered and kept them in place like a helicopter. The back of their bodies glowed with a large bulb. And on the front of their body where their heads should have been was a large stinger that buzzed like a bee.

I've got bad news, Lunis said in her head.

If it's about the swarm of most likely poisonous bugs, I'm already aware, she replied.

Oh, well never mind then, he joked.

The pair stood frozen in the middle of the dark jungle as the mutated fireflies simply hovered, seemingly deciding when to make their collective move.

Why do I get the impression that when we move the chase will be afoot? Sophia asked.

I think your impression is accurate, Lunis answered.

I was afraid of that. Sophia watched the giant stingers buzz in the air, all of them directed at them. *What do you think the odds are that we can stay like this for a while?*

I'm willing to stick it out forever on this island, Lunis teased. *It's now my forever home.*

Sophia had to stop herself from laughing.

Other impressions I have at the moment, Lunis began. *I think that much like the tropical jerk birds, if we wipe out these guys, they'll return.*

Safe assumption, I'd say.

So I'd blast them with fire but...

For some reason, I don't think magical fireflies will be harmed that much by fire, she stated.

I think this has to be about strategy. Lunis dared to look over his shoulder where the shield still kept the birds at bay. *What are the chances you can create another of those shields?*

Low, Sophia answered. *And even if I have the magical reserves for such a big spell, then I'm pretty much boxing us in.*

But we will be safe and can make our home here, he joked.

Something tells me that all the plants are poisonous and the water supply will make us hate each other, Sophia replied.

So no to living here then.

I think we have to plan an exit strategy, she imparted.

Does it involve running like hell like the last time? he questioned.

Pretty much, unless you have any other ideas.

Well, we could fly or portal—

But we need to be on this island, Sophia interrupted. *I know it. And taking off under this canopy of trees would be pretty dangerous. I don't want you to risk it.*

Then we run like hell, he stated with confidence. *Which way?*

She tuned into her intuition and listened to the voices of her soul. *You're not going to like this...*

It's straight ahead, isn't it?

Yep, Sophia answered.

Lunis groaned in her head. *All right, we'll go around them. Let the race begin.*

CHAPTER TWENTY-TWO

As Sophia had suspected, as soon as they took off, it triggered the fireflies and made them dart after them. The killing birds were fast, but they had nothing on these guys who sped through the air and made up the distance quicker than Sophia would have thought possible.

That's why she had to employ a spell to increase her speed. Lunis sped up too, taking down branches and foliage as they tore through the jungle. It was hard to come up with a strategy while they were running for their lives, but Sophia knew for a fact that there was no way they could outrun the deranged fireflies.

But facing them wasn't an option either. That would exhaust their magic, and the creatures would probably reappear once defeated.

What they needed was a way to escape the swarm.

As Sophia thought that, they approached a clearing where the rush of water falling was so loud, it could be heard over the buzzing and their thrashing through the jungle.

The feel of cool mist told Sophia that they were close to a waterfall. She knew they were near the sound she'd heard in her soul. They were approaching the source—the center of the island. Their destination.

Lunis, I know what we have to do, Sophia said in a rush in her dragon's head.

What, he asked urgently as they ran out into the clearing. A large body of water stretched out in front of them with a cliff reaching high above it.

"Jump!" Sophia yelled.

CHAPTER TWENTY-THREE

Sophia launched herself forward off the shore around the lagoon and bicycled her legs to propel herself harder—faster. Her hands clawed through the air as she screamed with a guttural force that seemed to pull her into the pristine, shimmering waters.

Sophia sank into the cool depths, her eyes wide open as she submerged. She hoped that this wasn't like the Reflective Sea and wouldn't make her insane with rage. It made sense that it was the same water since all the islands were connected by the Reflective Sea. But her instinct, the voice of her soul had told her to jump. As she looked up at the rippling surface, she saw the angry fireflies pass over.

Lunis had done as Sophia had ordered and jumped next to her. His size created a huge splash. The current his weight created quickly pushed Sophia to the bottom. She would have been pushed to the far side of the pool as well, but he wrapped his tail around her waist and anchored her to the bottom with him.

Sophia was relieved to find that the lagoon was big enough for them. She'd had a brief moment where she worried that it was too shallow for Lunis. But it appeared to be deep enough—barely, as if it was all planned this way.

For a moment, the fireflies hovered above the surface of the water.

Their yellow bulbs shone brightly above the two and their angry stinger faces buzzed.

Sophia held her breath, knowing they couldn't last long after running through the jungle and nearly exhausting themselves. She'd hardly had a chance to pull in a full breath before she leaped into the water.

When she looked at Lunis, she saw that the struggle was real for him too. His cheeks were puffed out and little bubbles trailed from the side of his mouth, then rose to the surface.

The psycho fireflies seemed to know that this was a waiting game as they hung out above the water's surface. Sophia's eyes bulged with frustration.

GO, she yelled at them in her mind.

However, as she saw the same panic in Lunis' eyes, she was grateful that she didn't want to murder him. That was at least something. Apparently, this water was somehow different than the Reflective Sea, but she didn't know why. Hopefully they would get a chance to figure it out.

Sophia was grateful that Lunis held her down. Otherwise, the urge to kick to the surface might be too strong to resist. Her chest convulsed and she opened her mouth, swallowing a sip of water. It burned her lungs and made her insides ache. This was it. She was going to drown. With her dragon.

Or she would risk getting stung. Those seemed like the only options.

Then the most remarkable thing happened. The fireflies didn't leave. That would have been a miracle too. Instead they faded as their bulbs dimmed.

Sophia blinked at them and wondered if that meant they were more reasonable, not on fire. Before she could check, they buzzed off and zipped back the way they came, leaving Sophia and Lunis at the bottom of the lagoon.

CHAPTER TWENTY-FOUR

L unis held Sophia under the surface of the water a few seconds
longer to be safe before he propelled her up, faster than she
could have gotten there on her own. She choked on the water she'd
swallowed once in the freedom of the fresh air, trying to breathe in as
she coughed.

Lunis did the same thing beside her. The dragon sputtered water
as he thrashed in the lagoon and turned it into a bubbling mess of
currents. Sophia struggled to swim through the rapids to the lagoon's
edge. The waves kept pulling her down and lapping over her head.

Lunis once again wrapped his tail around Sophia and launched her
into the air, making her fly over the water and tumble onto the sandy
bank. She landed less than gracefully, but thankfully the ground was
soft enough to cushion the fall.

The dragon soon joined her and slumped on the ground as he
continued to choke up water. Sophia took a cursory glance around to
ensure the mad fireflies were gone before lying back down with her
cheek against the cold sand.

"This place sucks," Lunis griped when he'd finally caught his
breath.

"No arguments there." Sophia was grateful to find that the lagoon was fresh water and didn't have the angry effects like the Reflective Sea. She didn't know how that worked since the islands all seemed to be connected by the water.

Figuring that they'd spent enough time resting, Sophia pushed up and studied the area. It was shaded and the water was settling down after their swim. Overhead was a large cliff, and palm trees and other vegetation surrounded the lagoon. The strange part of the otherwise pristine oasis was the rush of water. It was loud, like they were sitting under a waterfall. But there didn't appear to be anything like that.

"Lunis, where is that noise coming from?"

The blue dragon shared her confused expression. He nodded in the direction of the cliff. "It's right there. Unmistakably. I'm certain of it."

She nodded. "That's what I thought too, but why don't we see anything?"

"It's like it's invisible," he reasoned.

"But there would still be water displacement if it was," she countered.

He glanced down at her. "When did you become a physicist?"

She shrugged. "I know science. But I apparently don't understand the weird science of this place."

"I don't think anyone understands Buddha's Temple," he imparted, then nodded toward a strange set of stones, definitely arranged. "However, I think someone left us a puzzle to help us figure it out."

CHAPTER TWENTY-FIVE

The smooth stones were arranged in towers with the largest rocks on the bottom and the tops a tiny pebble. There were three towers, and they were all about two feet high. Sophia had seen them marking hiking trails in the Highlands in Scotland and other outdoor areas. They were definitely manmade.

"Those are cairns," Lunis offered.

"What are they for?"

"They have a few different purposes," he began. "Sometimes they're competitive."

"Oh, like I built a tower and the next traveler tries to build a bigger one?"

Lunis nodded. "Exactly. In modern times, I think they're used for navigational purposes. Back in the day in Scotland, it was tradition to carry a stone up to the top of a hill and place it on top of the stack. They also have history with marking burial grounds."

"So what do you think their significance is here? You said you thought this was a puzzle of sorts, right?" Sophia asked.

"That's what my instinct says," Lunis answered. "We're by the Reflective Sea on an island named Buddha's Temple. It stands to reason that these aren't here by accident or for decorative purposes."

"And they aren't marking a trail," Sophia added.

"No, and I don't think they're marking a burial ground." Lunis' eyes narrowed as he studied the space.

"They might be," Sophia joked. "Like, I don't know many who could survive this place."

"Although true," he began tentatively, "I think their purpose is more related to symbolism rather than anything of a practical nature."

"And that would be?"

"Well, one of the most common reasons to make a cairn is to leave your mark," Lunis explained. "And thinking about where we are and the reason for our visit—"

"To remove a mark from my soul," Sophia offered.

He nodded. "Yes, so therefore, I would suggest that they symbolize something to do with consciousness, which is what makes creatures with a soul unique from those who don't have one."

Sophia nodded and took it all in. "We have awareness."

"Yes," he affirmed. "And in my mind, cairns are connected to the idea of, 'I exist and therefore I matter.' Why else build them on your journey unless you want to leave your mark?"

"So," Sophia drew the word out. "I need to build one, don't I?"

Lunis' eyes brightened. "I think so. You need to tell Buddha's Temple, 'I was here. I have significance.'"

"Well, that can't be too hard, right?"

Lunis groaned. "You have to tempt fate, don't you?"

She laughed. "It's a rock tower. How hard will that be? But what do you think happens when I'm done?"

He shrugged. "Only one way to find out, but I don't think I can help you since this is your soul and your quest."

Sophia waved him off. "I think I'm good. You take a nap, I'll make a cairn."

CHAPTER TWENTY-SIX

B uilding the tower wasn't difficult. Well not in the physical sense. However, as Sophia stacked large rocks followed by progressively smaller ones, the mental strength became more demanding. A seemingly straightforward task was suddenly complex and required all her concentration.

Her surroundings suddenly blurred around her, but for some reason this didn't alarm Sophia. She kept her eyes searching for the perfect stone, which needed to be a specific size.

Not too big and not too small. She looked without seeing, spurred by her instinct rather than her vision.

Sophia felt like she was working out a complicated math equation. At the same time, it was also like she was working through a complex emotional problem. She felt heavy as a catharsis unfolded in her chest.

Sweat poured from her forehead and her fingers were pinched under the weight of the flat stone she carried. When she slid it onto the top, her heart thumped like it was about to give out and made her clap her hands to her chest.

"Sophia!" Lunis exclaimed in the distance. He was close, but she couldn't see him. Only the stones. The ones on the tower and the ones around for her to fetch. They were like all the memories of her life. The good ones and the bad ones, and they all stacked onto each other, creating….

"Creating me," Sophia said aloud.

"What creates you?" Lunis asked.

"Memories," she answered, then mechanically turned and searched for the next stone. It needed to be smaller. Round. It needed to fit into place, while also offering a place for the next stone.

"That's how experiences work," she said mostly to herself.

"I don't understand." There was undeniable worry in her dragon's voice.

"We are an accumulation of our experiences…our memories," she explained. "And they're all linked, like stones on a cairn. They stack on top of one another. Nothing about us is separate. It's all connected to another part of us."

"Are you okay?" Lunis was still out of her sight, no matter where she looked.

"We're never okay," she answered at once, not knowing where the response came from. "We're evolutions. If we're okay, by definition we're satisfied. We're finished. We're complete. But there is always room for another stone, it just has to fit."

"And a particle could fit on the top of a grain of sand," Lunis offered.

Sophia nodded as her eyes found the perfect last stone. It was crescent-shaped like Buddha's Temple.

Nimbly she picked it up and held her breath. Putting it in place could be tricky. The tower shook like one false move would bring it tumbling down.

"We are always at risk of crumbling," she mused. "One experience can put us over the edge."

"But they can also make us stronger," Lunis offered.

"They inevitably will, even if we crumble," Sophia stated, then dropped the stone on the top and watched as the cairn wobbled before standing firm.

Sophia smiled at her work, strangely proud of her accomplishment. She had previously thought it would be easy, but it was quite complicated and enriching. She got a lot more out of the experience than she could have ever imagined.

Then something else happened that Sophia hadn't expected, and sent droplets of water all over them.

CHAPTER TWENTY-SEVEN

At first, the waterfall was a trickle that ran over the side of the high cliff towering above them. Then the rush of water turned into a raging force that joined the already present noise.

Sophia and Lunis edged away from the splash zone while taking the gentle mist in the face.

"So that's where the waterfall was." Lunis looked up at the torrent that had materialized in a few seconds.

"It's quite the force," Sophia observed.

"It is. You know waterfalls represent chaos in feng shui?"

"How do you know that?"

"I watch a lot of Home and Garden Network when you're not around." He giggled.

"So, I made my mark." She indicated her cairn. "The waterfall appeared. Did I do it? Is the mark on my soul gone?"

Lunis looked her over and the expression on his face told her the answer before he did. "No, I'm sorry, but it's still there."

"So what am I supposed to do?" Sophia wondered suddenly if they'd made a mistake and maybe they were completely off base. Maybe this wasn't the place they were supposed to go to lift the curse. Maybe getting away from the killer birds and murderous fireflies and making the waterfall appear were other obstacles, unrelated to cleansing her soul.

"Wait, that's it," Lunis said suddenly.

Since she hadn't said anything, only stood there and worried, she flashed him a confused expression. "What is it?"

"What you were thinking," he answered.

Sophia brow scrunched up more. She had to trail back to remember what she'd thought. Sometimes she forgot that Lunis was often in her head although he didn't often do it when they were together and could communicate. The link was also stronger at different times depending on multiple factors.

"What specifically?" she asked.

"About cleansing your soul," he answered. "You made your mark to start the process of removing the mark." Lunis slung his head to the side and indicated the cairn she'd made. "Remember why the Warriors and Councilors pass through the Door of Reflection when entering the Chamber of the Tree?"

"It's to cleanse them of their fears so they can be objective in meetings."

"And the source of the Door of Reflection comes from here." He glanced at the waterfall. "What if that's it?"

Her mouth popped open. "I'm supposed to walk through there? That water will crush me."

The flow was at full force now and crashed into the shallow basin below it. There was little doubt that walking through this particular waterfall would be potentially deadly for Sophia.

"It's about facing your fears," Lunis offered. "If there's no risk, then where's the gain? Cleansing your soul can't be easy."

Sophia gulped. "Although this all makes sense, what if we're wrong about this being the way?"

"I think finding 'the way' is always about faith rather than logic. Do you feel like this could work? What does your soul tell you?"

Sophia closed her eyes and focused on the inner voices that she'd become acquainted with since coming to Buddha's Temple. Again, they sounded like a rush of water. They sounded like the waterfall in front of her. But she knew that their voices were inside her and the noise of the falls was outside her. Just like her fears weren't a part of her, but they did affect her soul. And that was all the information she needed to make the next decisions.

Her eyes sprang open and she looked at Lunis. "I'm walking through the waterfall. That must be the way."

CHAPTER TWENTY-EIGHT

The raging waters poured over the tall cliff and smashed down on the lagoon water, sending droplets all over the pool and banks. As Sophia edged closer, she felt the spray and it was sharp like little dull needles. But even a dull object can do damage.

The flat rock where the waterfall hit was slick with moss. Sophia took each step carefully, her head to the side as she prepared to step through the waterfall. She wasn't sure if she should dart through, in an effort to minimize damage, or if she needed to step, like the Warriors and Councilors did when passing through the Door of Reflection into the Chamber of the Tree.

Her heart pounded in her throat as she tilted her head to the side away from the spray. It intensified as she neared, and took over her vision. The water was cool but it burned her face when it hit.

You can do this, Lunis encouraged in her head.

She smiled, grateful for the dragon's words at that eleventh hour moment.

I'm doing this, she thought.

I'm here for you, he stated, again trying to be supportive.

Her smile faded. There was support, and there was lip service. She loved Lunis, but he was wrong. She was in this alone. There were times that he could be there for her. That he could save her. They'd experienced so many of those times already. But in this, Sophia was alone. She had to step through the waterfall alone. What she'd experience would be hers alone. And whatever came after that, she'd have to deal with by herself. All Lunis could do now was watch, and they both knew that.

Sophia held her breath and moved as close as she could to the waterfall before stepping through it. It fell in a thin sheet that created a mirrored surface. Now that she was this close, she admired the way the water sparkled with tiny little lights. Prisms radiated off its surface in various places. It was beautiful.

What wasn't as attractive was the explosion the sheet of water made when it hit the stone, violently sprayed up, and created a rush of noise.

Sophia allowed herself a moment to appreciate the sentiment of the water being both beautiful and chaotic. An elegant force and also one to be respected. It had the power to quench her thirst and also break her neck.

She hoped that it simply cleansed her soul, but there was no more time for stalling. Sophia had to take the plunge and step through the waterfall.

CHAPTER TWENTY-NINE

The spray was so strong that it forced Sophia to close her eyes as she stepped forward. The slick rock under her soaked boots nearly sent her off her feet. She clenched her hands by her side and strode forward, entering the waterfall.

Sophia expected the crashing water to hit her like an avalanche and knock her down as it assaulted her head. Burying her in the water of the lagoon. Drowning her instantly.

What she experienced was exactly the opposite.

When Sophia stepped through the waterfall, it was much like how Liv had explained going through the Door of Reflection. It felt like she was walking through soft water. It covered her instantly, and gently wrapped around her face and hands as if giving her a hug.

She smiled, relieved by the experience and grateful she wasn't dead.

But then she realized that she didn't know where she was anymore. Instead of stepping through the waterfall to the other side of the lagoon, she had entered total blackness. She didn't know where Lunis was. She didn't know where anything was. Suddenly, she felt blind and deaf. Even the sensation of the water on her skin disappeared.

Sophia felt nothing at all, and it was absolutely terrifying.

CHAPTER THIRTY

Sophia opened her mouth to scream, but nothing came out. She tried to pull in a breath, but her lungs didn't work.

Am I dead? she wondered.

Was this what nothingness felt like?

It wasn't uncomfortable, but to not see, hear, or feel anything...

But I have my consciousness, she told herself. That was meaningful to her. Because it meant she was still her.

A flash assaulted her vision and nearly blinded her.

Sophia was simultaneously grateful for the blinding light and repulsed by it.

She was grateful to see something. To have eyes that could be blinded. But the white was so bright it burned.

Then colors wove into place, like brush strokes on a canvas.

A rustling sound replaced the silence. The absence of feeling halted, and a warm breeze filled the air around her. The scent was chemical and burned Sophia's nose. Images took shape and showed Sophia what had to be her very worst nightmare.

CHAPTER THIRTY-ONE

L unis stood beside Sophia on top of a building in the middle of a city she once knew very differently. The pair looked out at Los Angeles and gazed at the burning buildings, the devastation, and the absence of life.

Smoke filled the air, but Sophia didn't cough. She also didn't cry. Even when she saw the dead bodies littering the ground, she didn't shed a tear. She recognized the bodies of dragons and various other magical races. They were all dead.

Instinctively, Sophia knew everyone in the city was gone. There were no sirens in the distance. No planes in the sky. No one coming to rescue them. There was no one left.

A war had wiped everyone out. The only ones who remained were Sophia and Lunis.

She realized then that her greatest fear wasn't what she thought it was.

Like the Door of Reflection, the waterfall served up Sophia's worst fear. She'd expected it to be death. At first, that's what she thought she was experiencing. Although she hadn't wanted to think about it, she thought she'd see Lunis dead in this vision.

However, his death would mean hers since they were linked

together through the chi of the dragon. But there were worse things than death, she knew now.

Surviving when everyone you loved was gone—that was worse.

Being the one left to tell the story, that was a curse.

But Sophia wasn't going to be cursed. Not now. Not ever.

She looked directly at her dragon and shook her head. "How did this happen?"

He continued to glare out at the war scene. "We stopped seeing the world the way we envisioned it and started seeing it the way it was."

Tears ached in her throat. "We lost faith in the planet becoming a better place."

He nodded.

"I have to fix this," she stated with total conviction.

He gave her an expression that spoke of ancient wisdom. "Then see the world the way you want it to be. Remember, you must see it to believe it."

Sophia pulled in a breath and closed her eyes. In her mind, she replaced the images of burning buildings and overturned cars and scorched roads with the city she loved. She saw Los Angeles with bright blue skies and diverse architecture. Sophia envisioned the beach and the people, laughing as they strode down the boardwalk in Santa Monica. She saw the House of Fourteen, protected by Warriors and Councilors. And beside them, she could clearly see the Dragon Elite, standing strong and brave.

The images of the world buzzing with life and love was so strong in Sophia's mind that sudden tears overcame her. They ran down her cheeks, warm and graceful, and fell on her collarbones.

Sophia saw the world not the way it was, but rather the way she wanted it to be—at peace.

And she knew that was the way to remove the mark on her soul. Sophia had lifted the curse.

CHAPTER THIRTY-TWO

"You look like you again." Wilder gazed deeply into Sophia's eyes, a quiet appreciation in them.

"I feel like myself," she admitted with relief, feeling like she was able to finally breathe after a long spell of holding her breath.

After stepping through the waterfall and having the vision of her worst nightmare, Sophia awoke to find herself lying on the sand next to Lunis. He said that she'd disappeared after entering the waterfall, then magically appeared there on the beach.

Apparently she didn't breathe for a solid minute, which no doubt terrified him. But then, like before when they almost drowned, she'd sucked in a sudden breath and bolted upright, coming back to life in a burst.

The whole experience had been cloaked in so much symbolism and strangeness that Sophia had a new respect for her soul. She'd never thought much about it, merely thinking she was her—Sophia Beaufont. But now she knew that like the dragons, she was so much more. A timeless being.

The experience had also been emotionally, mentally and physically exhausting. So when Wilder messaged Sophia and asked where she was and if she wanted company, she replied instantly with a very loud, "YES!"

Unable to have Wilder meet them at the Reflective Sea because first, she didn't want to hate him and second, because he wouldn't be able to find the hidden place without the map, Sophia met up with him and Simi in Bora Bora. It was close, and offered all the beauty she'd seen at the Reflective Sea without all the dangers.

The only danger Sophia was currently worried about was getting too tipsy on lemon drops. Her lips puckered as she laid down the mixed drink and looked out at the crystal clear aqua-colored waters of the French Polynesian Sea.

"This doesn't suck." Wilder let out a giant breath and also stared up at the mountain in front of them, directly across from their bungalow over the water.

"No, I could get used to this," Sophia replied. "Do you think in our next life we can vacation regularly and not have deadly professions?"

"Yes, but why would we want the latter?" he joked.

She nodded. "Good point."

A splash of water hit Sophia in the face. Not hard like the waterfall, but enough to make her bolt upright. "Hey, this is a no splash zone," she fired at Lunis, who was rolling around in the water next to their hut and splashing them.

He flicked his tail like a rebellious child and sent a wave of water at Sophia that instantly soaked her. She narrowed her eyes at her dragon but smiled.

"You're going to get yourself voted off the island," she threatened.

"I'd like to see you try," he fired back.

"I'll vote for him to leave," Simi said lazily, lying in the water on the other side of Wilder.

"That makes two of us," Wilder joked while drying off the water on his bare chest. He'd been in the splash zone.

Lunis rolled over in the clear waters and sent more of the sea up over the bungalow's side. "I'm off to fulfill a lifelong dream."

"Scare the tourists?" Sophia asked.

"Climb Mount Otemanu?" Wilder nodded at the mountain in the distance.

"No, swim with the dolphins," Lunis answered before he shot through the water, dived low and disappeared as he created ripples.

Wilder laughed. "Your dragon is so weird."

"I know. Isn't it grand?"

"What's grand is being here and having this view." Wilder wasn't looking at the mountain any longer, but rather Sophia in her bikini.

She blushed, then reached out and took his hand. "My view is quite nice too."

His dimples surfaced when he smiled.

The two stayed locked on each other until they were rudely interrupted by the loud buzzing of Sophia's phone. She would have ignored it, but it only rang like that when it was of great importance.

With a sigh, she pulled her gaze off Wilder and grabbed her phone.

"The message is from Evan," Sophia explained, seeing the worried expression in Wilder's eyes. He knew that if the phone buzzed, then it was someone like Papa Creola or Mama Jamba or Liv.

"Evan…" Wilder groaned. "How did he figure out how to take your phone off silent to get your attention?"

"I've found that he shouldn't be underestimated." Sophia read his text. There was only one, but he was currently typing out a second. "He says, 'Hi.'"

"Tell him I say that he should go jump in the Pond," Wilder replied.

Sophia giggled as another message from Evan came through. "He says, 'Hope y'all are getting sunburned on your much undeserved vacation.'"

"What a nice lad." Wilder grinned. "Send him a pic of our view and tell him 'Glad you're not here.'"

Before Sophia could do that, another message came through. She read it aloud, "How's everything here? Thanks for asking. I'm good. Tired, but probably because of all the work I've been doing while you slackers lounge around in your swim suits. Coral is grumpy, but that's because the sheep are exploding at an alarming rate and making things dangerous here."

"Wow, the sheep problem is still going on?" Wilder questioned.

Sophia sat up in her lounge chair. "Yeah, I need to address that now that I'm not cursed."

Another message came through, and Sophia's eyes widened. She tensed all over as she read it aloud for Wilder. "Oh, and random strangers keep turning up inside the Castle and no one knows why. But don't you worry. We'll manage while you losers waste time."

CHAPTER THIRTY-THREE

"What does he say his name is?" Wilder leaned against a wall and eyed one of the many strangers who had been found strolling confused through the Castle of the Gullington.

The man was an older mortal of around sixty-five, and wore a smart navy blue suit and a confused expression as he sat at the dining room table in the Castle. He didn't touch any of the food that Trin had tried to serve to him, but rather kept tapping on his phone and scowling—no doubt frustrated that it didn't work there on the grounds of the Gullington.

"He says his name is Christopher Dickenson." Evan slouched in the doorway of the dining hall. "Says he went into his walk-in closet to fetch a tie and when he came out he found himself here."

"Where exactly?" Sophia studied the man, who didn't seem to have any nefarious agendas, but rather appeared peeved that he was going to be late for work since he kept yanking up his wrist to glance at his gold watch.

"He was in the hallway on the second floor," Evan answered.

Sophia sighed. "You do know what the term exactly means, right?"

Wilder laughed. "We're talking about Evan. You have such confidence in this lad, but one day you'll learn."

Evan rolled his eyes at his friend but smiled. "Exactly. It means, accurately, precisely, just, closely, and specific." He stuck out his tongue like a child before turning his attention to Sophia. "And to answer your question, Pink Princess, all the others and Chris here, were found around the second door from the stairs on the eastern wing."

Wilder's eyes flashed wide. "And here I thought you were a lost cause, mate."

"Don't count me out yet." Evan winked. "Oh, and it looks like you got too much sun on vacation. That's going to make for a nasty burn."

Wilder stuck out his arms and appraised the golden tan he now sported from their time in Bora Bora. "Nah, I think I'll be all right."

"Well, it will no doubt give you wrinkles and freckles later," Evan replied.

Sophia shook her head at the antics of the two. "So it sounds like they're coming through the portal from the Great Library."

Evan shrugged. "One would think, but we can't get the door to open so who knows."

Sophia glanced up at the staircase and watched as Mahkah led an equally confused group of mortals toward the dining hall. All wore similar expressions as Mr. Dickenson and seemed completely disoriented as they studied the Castle while marching in a single line like reporting for basic training in the army.

The mortals had all been given rooms and allowed to rest since they seemed weary after entering the Castle.

"Where is Quiet?" Sophia asked, although she knew that it was probably a lost cause to rely on the groundskeeper to answer questions on the subject.

"He's been mad busy with the sheep situation," Evan replied. "You know they're exploding, right?"

Sophia nodded with a concerned expression on her face. "Yes, we were gone for a few days, not a fortnight."

"A few days, huh?" Evan questioned. "Must be nice. I've been managing things in your absence, which wasn't at all missed."

It was clear from the way Evan said it that he missed them, Wilder especially. As much as the younger dragonrider tried to act otherwise, it was clear he was a social being and adored his comrades. He seemed happy to have Sophia and Wilder back, and told them a series of jokes that he must have stored up, just for them.

The group of unintended trespassers paraded by the three and into the dining hall, not paying them as much attention because of the obviously overwhelming details of the Castle all around them. One lady with short brown hair and wearing a nightgown gave Sophia a strange expression, apparently thinking that she looked weirder than her in her armored top with her sword on her side.

When they'd all filed past, Sophia said in a low voice, "So, they all came through the portal from the Great Library from..." Her question trailed away, knowing that Evan would infer the rest.

His gaze studied the group of oddballs. Most were half-dressed, like they'd been interrupted during their normal routine. "They went into their closets to get clothes or whatever and when they came out, they strode out into the Castle." Evan laughed loudly, making many of the strangers in the group jump. "Imagine going to get ready for your boring job and winding up in a magical Castle in Scotland. Talk about a great story for dinnertime."

Wilder blew out a breath. "Let's hope we can get them home by dinner."

Sophia nodded and watched as Mahkah dutifully led them to where Christopher Dickerson was still trying to make his phone work, with no luck. They reluctantly took seats, their expressions flat as the overwhelming factors increased when they stared around at the large hall. Most seemed speechless, like the questions of "why" and "how" hadn't quite formed in their mouths yet.

"They're in shock," Sophia observed.

"I would be too," Wilder agreed. "I mean, look at what Evan is wearing. It's simply atrocious."

The other dragonrider huffed. "I was the first friendly face most of the blokes saw. I rescued them."

"From what?" Wilder asked. "Getting lost? Real jokes? Discovering a place no mortal has ever seen?"

Evan rolled his eyes. "Whatever, man. I hope that no more come through. Trin is having a hard enough time feeding us. Imagine having to feed a bunch of mortals all of a sudden."

Wilder nodded. "So the Castle sealed the door. I wonder why the portal door malfunctioned."

Sophia considered this for a moment. "It has to be because Plato is moving the Great Library. I bet it's going to several places in the process, and the portal is being shoved around until it finds its final location."

Evan laughed loudly again, making more of the half-dressed mortals whip around to face them, startled. "So when the portal malfunctions, it brings blokes into the Castle."

"Well, it probably creates a schism. Makes sense," Sophia offered.

"When is the Great Library supposed to be in place?" Wilder asked, suddenly serious.

"When the paint dries, apparently," she answered with a laugh, then added, "I'm not sure. But we need to get these people home."

"Oh shucks! I was hoping they'd become our merry bunch of court jesters," Evan said in mock disappointment. "Can't we keep them?"

Sophia shook her head. "No, they need to go back since they've been questioned."

Mahkah joined them with a thoughtful expression on his face. "I'm not sure the Castle is the best place for these people. It seems to disorient them more than they should be."

Sophia nodded. She'd noticed that many seemed to be having a hard time staying awake, and were falling asleep in their seats. The rest were almost paralyzed when Trin materialized from the kitchen carrying a platter of plates. The sight of the cyborg housekeeper must have been well over the threshold of what they could take.

"Yeah, it's time to get these people home," Sophia agreed. "And since the portal appears to be closed, hopefully this problem won't keep happening, but we still need to keep an eye on things."

Evan saluted dramatically. "Yes, Captain. We're ready for our orders, Captain."

Sophia ignored him. "Where is Hiker?"

Mahkah leaned in, his voice quiet. "I think he's been preoccupied by something in his office lately. He's aware of this situation, but not as concerned as one might have suspected. He told us to handle it."

Sophia nodded and chewed on her lip. She thought she knew why. *It had to do with Ainsley's absence,* she thought, but didn't dare say anything to the group. None knew what she'd seen that night when Ainsley left the Castle, and Hiker and she said their goodbyes. "And we will handle it. Can you guys get these people back to their homes and check their closets to ensure they won't end up back here or in some black hole?"

Wilder nodded, but Evan pursed his lips.

"How much does this job pay?" Evan asked.

She rolled her eyes. "It pays your room and board, and is why you work for the Dragon Elite."

"I'm listening," Evan said. "Keep talking."

Sophia shook her head. "I need you all to get these mortals out of here before they lose their minds from the Castle's magic. It can't be good for them."

"I agree," Mahkah said, always the voice of reason. "We need to get them out of here. It's clear they don't know anything about how they ended up here and don't have any reason for their presence. It seems to be a fluke."

"Which I can research," Sophia offered, but noticed Quiet materialize in the doorway. The gnome's sudden presence almost startled her for some reason. It was the solemn look on his usually expression-less face. "After I see what he needs."

Everyone turned their heads as she automatically strode in Quiet's direction.

"Yeah, fine," Evan called. "Just go gallivanting off with that trouble-maker while the rest of us clean up the messes. Sounds good, pigtails."

Sophia ignored him as she headed for the door where Quiet strode out to the Expanse, seeming to know that she was following him. At her back, she heard Evan say, "Man, Wilder, that short guy is gonna steal your gal. How you feel about that?"

CHAPTER THIRTY-FOUR

O nce on the grounds of the Expanse, Sophia had to pull her attention away from the angel dragonettes streaking through the air in the distance, their various colors like kites in the wind. She was always mesmerized by how the tiny dragons moved, so graceful from the beginning.

But like Lunis, they were playful and enjoyed gliding on the breeze and diving toward the grass. Their landings were less practiced than the elder dragons and more like that of football players victoriously rolling over the touchdown line.

Sophia pulled her gaze to the groundskeeper and tried to focus. "What is it, Quiet?"

He didn't look at her right on, but instead, pointed his stubby finger toward the little white specks that lined the hills. It didn't take Sophia's discerning eyes long to zoom in and determine that the spots on the grassy slopes were the herd of sheep.

A moment later, a small explosion scattered the herd in the opposite direction from the commotion. The sheep that was the epicenter of the ignition was only a scorch mark on the earth, which made Sophia grimace with regret and disgust.

"What's happening?" she asked Quiet.

He had his attention on the glossy lawn too, and looked back at her with somber eyes that very distinctly said, "I don't know."

She lowered her chin. "I have to figure this out, don't I?"

He nodded gravely.

Sophia sighed and wondered where she could go to figure out this complexity. It was true that someone had to figure out what was going on with the sheep. It was so ill-timed with the strange appearance of the mortals in the Castle. She wanted to ask why one thing couldn't happen at a time or what was Quiet doing about the invader problem in the Castle, but she realized that he was overwhelmed. As usual, they were all overwhelmed. The Gullington was overwhelmed. That was status quo at this point.

Finally, she nodded. "Okay, so find out why the sheep are exploding and stop it, right?"

Quiet simply gave her a nod that said so much more than yes.

"Okay." Sophia drew out the word. "I will devote my attention to the sheep problem. There must be a reason for why they're exploding."

Quiet nodded again. His eyes said, "Are you ready to set off yet?" Impatience hung heavy in his every movement. His Castle was being invaded and his sheep exploding. It must have been annoying. More than annoying. He was used to being in charge of this territory and suddenly so much was outside his control.

Sophia turned to him. "Don't worry, Quiet. I'll devote my attention to this. Keep the portal door to the Great Library sealed until I check with Plato."

He agreed simply.

"I'll find someone to help with the sheep," she went on, and jerked her chin back in the direction of the Castle. "But first, I need to check on someone."

Quiet mumbled, and Sophia could have sworn it sounded like, "It won't help."

However, she still set off for Hiker Wallace's office.

CHAPTER THIRTY-FIVE

"Son, I've told you a hundred times—"

"I don't need to hear it again," Hiker interrupted. His voice boomed into the hallway and made Sophia halt before she came to the crack between the door and Hiker's office.

She gasped, feeling very much like a voyeur similar to when she watched Ainsley and Hiker's goodbye that final night. She still felt guilty for witnessing their intimate moment. But, she couldn't help what she saw or that she saw it. The Castle woke her and led her to it, and showed her what was now imprinted on her soul...the goodbye of two souls who had spent five hundred years together and were now separated by circumstances—and choice.

"What does the message say?" Mama Jamba asked after a moment, sounding like her usual calm self.

Hiker blew out a breath. "It says... It says..." He seemed unable to get the words out.

"Do you want the youngest dragonrider to join us before you read the message from the Elfin Council?" Mama Jamba asked.

"No!" Hiker boomed at once. "I'm not calling Sophia up from the dining hall or away from the Expanse or from whatever mission she's on to hear this."

"Oh, but son," Mama Jamba began casually, "she's outside the door."

Sophia tensed on the other side of the wall and thought of running. She suddenly felt like an invader.

Hiker hiccupped and looked at the Dragon Elite globe. "Of course she is. I knew she was home." When he said the last word, he sounded relieved. "Sophia!" he boomed.

She straightened against the wall, feeling like she was playing the world's stupidest game of hide and go seek with the best finder, and was doomed no matter what. Sophia pressed her eyes shut and pretended like she wasn't there.

When she peeked through one eye, she knew the game was over. There between the crack of her lids, staring at her from his office door, was none other than the leader of the Dragon Elite.

"Hey, sir," Sophia said when she saw Hiker Wallace.

"Get in here," he ordered while looking at her hiding place outside his office.

"Yes, sir," she replied as he marched back inside.

Once in his study, Sophia found Mama Jamba arranging sunflowers and whistling like there was nothing else of consequence going on in the world. "Well, isn't it better in here with us than spying in the corridor?"

"I wasn't spying," Sophia began, but decided there wasn't any point. "Honestly. I was about to knock."

"Doesn't matter anyway. Now Hiker can stutter through the message that's been getting the better of him for an hour or more," Mama Jamba interrupted.

"It hasn't," he argued, but didn't seem that adamant about. "Anyway, it's nothing. It's a message from Ainsley."

"Ainsley?" Sophia was excited to hear the elf's name. "How is she? What's she up to? What did she say?"

All the questions fell out of her mouth without her permission, and now she stood there looking excited and young as she stared at the two and felt dumb. But Mama Jamba simply cut the stem to a sunflower and smiled. Hiker sighed and looked at the message in his hand, then sighed again.

He began, "It says that Ainsley is gaining insights at the council and getting more intel on things that could become of interest to the Dragon Elite. Resources we could use to our advantages in the future if we forge certain alliances." Hiker suddenly snorted. "It's like in the old days. She wants us to create partnerships."

"What's wrong with partnerships, son?" Mama Jamba tried a large sunflower in a position and changed her mind.

"It's not the way it was designed," he answered. "We're in charge. If we sign on for that, then that's what we're seen as. Partners. I won't bow."

Like he was being challenged, Mama Jamba nodded in appreciation. "Right you are, son. Hold your ground. Don't bow."

"But can you find a common ground where they still have to stretch?" Sophia offered. "Something that's out of their territory? Something that's out of their normal? Then you seem like you're still in the right and have the supremacy, and create the partnership but with higher ground? However, you're in their territory."

Mama Jamba indicated her with a sunflower. "See why I chose her?"

Reluctantly, Hiker nodded. "Why were you snooping?"

"Just trying to help, sir," Sophia offered.

Whether Hiker knew that Sophia had witnessed the intimate moment with Ainsley or not was unclear by the expression in his eyes, but what was clear was the regret. It seemed like he was waiting for someone to rescue him. Like there was a dragonrider out in the sky waiting to swoop down and fix his problems. Ironically, the only one who could save Hiker was probably him, and it would only happen if he allowed it.

After a long moment, he strode for his desk. "Well, there's lots you can help with. The strangers—"

"The men are on that, sir," she answered.

"Well, then go to the Elfin Council—"

"That's for you, son," Mama Jamba interrupted. "But not yet."

Hiker turned his chin and gave Mother Nature a long, cold look. Finally, he glanced back at Sophia. "And the sheep?"

"I'm on it, sir. I think I know exactly who can help."

CHAPTER THIRTY-SIX

F airy Godmother College looked different.

Not bad. Not scary. But definitely different.

It put Sophia on edge and made her pull Inexorabilis when she stepped through the portal created from the bite of macaroon.

It wasn't large monsters or fire or rapid winds that put Sophia on guard. Instead, to her surprise it was something small that buzzed through the air and streaked past her at lightning speeds, making her jerk from side to side.

"Are those bugs?" she asked aloud to no one at all.

"They're robot spies," a voice at her back answered dutifully.

Sophia whipped around, sword held at the ready, and found a familiar face although one she hadn't seen in a long time. It was Amy, the math professor Sophia had chanced upon once before.

"Oh, a robot...spy," Sophia repeated. Then added, "Why?"

The professor strode up next to Sophia and shrugged while holding out her hand as a bug—or what the dragonrider had thought was a bug—landed on the palm of her hand. Its wings flapped and showed their metal workings as it landed. "They give us intel on our Cinderellas and Prince Charmings. More for our knowledge than anything else. They help us to know how to help them."

"By help, do you mean intervene?" Sophia asked.

The professor simply smiled. The look seemed to say, "Fill in the blanks as you wish."

"I'm looking for Mae Ling." Sophia glanced around the always pristine grounds of Happily Ever After College through the swarm of strange robot spy bugs. She never seemed to know where to start at that place because the grounds went on and on, but she was always inspired by the college's beautiful environment.

"When you're looking for your fairy godmother, you have to know that she's always looking for you," Amy answered with a smile.

Right on cue, the short, unassuming woman known as Mae Ling materialized beside the two with a studious expression on her face as she appraised the robot bugs buzzing around. She shook her head. "I never much liked the spies. I think there are better ways."

Amy considered this and shrugged. "There are always different ways, that's for sure."

Like this had been a constant topic of conversation, the two simply exchanged looks that said, "We will talk more about this later."

"You need to see me about something," Mae Ling stated, no question in her voice.

"Yes." Sophia split to the right as Mae Ling veered on the path and left Amy to amble toward the college on her own.

Sophia waved to the professor as she continued with her fairy godmother. "I need help with the exploding sheep at the Gullington."

"I would say more than just you needs help with that," Mae Ling stated, like this preexisting problem wasn't news to her—which it most certainly wasn't.

"No, Quiet doesn't seem to understand what to do about the problem, which is rare," Sophia offered. "Like, why would they suddenly start exploding? And how? And poor little sheep, not that their fate of getting eaten by a dragon is that much better. The whole thing is quite the conundrum."

"I like that word." Mae Ling smiled. "Conundrum sounds like what it is. Most words aren't like that."

Sophia mused on the notion for a moment and grinned too. "Yeah,

I think you're right. It is a good word. Anyway, there are many strange things happening at the Gullington. A place that's supposed to be unaffected by the outside world seems to be affected by everything lately."

"It's important to remember that nothing is removed from the world at large," Mae Ling imparted. "We are all a part of everything. We are all connected. Move away and distance yourself, and you'll still find your life is affected by the current affairs of the world. There's no avoiding it."

Sophia nodded. "Yeah, I guess that's true. It's just that the Gullington has the Barrier, and no one is supposed to be able to enter it unless they serve the Dragon Elite or are one of us. And now we've got strangers strolling around the Castle and sheep were exploding. It's all a big mystery."

"I can't help you with the visitors in the Castle, but I trust you'll find out who can and discover the reasons behind it," Mae Ling offered sympathetically.

"Yeah, I'm sure it's because the Great Library has been moved," Sophia stated. "Hopefully when the paint dries or whatever, then all that strangeness will stop."

Mae Ling giggled quietly. "I'm certain that it will simply be replaced by new strangeness."

Sophia laughed too. "You know how my life goes."

"As far as your sheep problem goes, I have some ideas of ways to fix them, but it will take more research on my part," Mae Ling explained. "This is a very complex problem, and also sensitive. The wrong solution could make things worse."

Sophia grimaced. "Our food supply for the dragons is exploding. Let's not get any worse."

"Yes. You might not be aware, but the problem is widespread all over Scotland, so it appears that it's not confined to the Gullington."

"That does make things more complex. I'm grateful for any insights you can provide."

Mae Ling smiled. "You always are. In the meantime, you need to focus on having armor made for you and the other Dragon Elite."

Sophia paused and tilted her chin to the side. "Armor? We have that."

"You do, but you need something better. Stronger." Mae Ling continued to stroll. Sophia hurried to catch up with her.

"Stronger," Sophia stated. "Like, better than the steel top that I wear in most battles?"

"Yes, and much lighter and flexible," Mae Ling answered. "Oh, and something for the dragons too."

Sophia glared at the secretive woman. "I don't suppose you're going to offer up the reason that we need this new armor?"

Mae Ling's brown eyes dazzled when she smiled. "Find someone who can make you this armor. The reason will become clear later. No need to worry about a battle before it's here. Spend your energy preparing."

Sophia let out a breath and nodded obediently. "It's easier than it used to be to shove the worries of upcoming dangers out of my mind and focus on the present moment."

Mae Ling gave her an appreciative expression. "That will serve you well all your life. Try and always be in the present moment. No need to time travel into the future or the past. One is set and the other is constantly in motion, so the best place for a sane mind is in the here and now."

Sophia found herself laughing. "I'm not sure I have much of a sane mind anymore or ever did, but I'll still follow your advice."

"And that's why I keep giving it to you freely," Mae Ling stated. "Although you're never obligated to do so. I'm simply a guide."

"I'm not sure why anyone wouldn't follow their fairy godmother's advice," Sophia imparted.

"Well, it happens all the time for various reasons," Mae Ling explained. "Sometimes people need to figure things out on their own. Or they don't want things to go right. Or they would rather break the world than fix it. You are rare, Sophia, in that you seek the best for yourself, your own and your world."

This made Sophia shake her head. "I have a hard time believing that most don't want solutions or a better world."

"And that's exactly why you're in the position that you are," Mae Ling said with confidence. "You believe in a world that doesn't yet exist, but I'm certain if people like you keep coming into power then it could. I hope it does one day. It would make our jobs as fairy godmothers easier."

Sophia and Mae Ling walked in silence for a long moment. The dragonrider found the experience very calming. It was exactly what she needed as she tried to wrap her mind around the new problems at the Gullington. The robot spy bugs buzzed by them every so often. After a while, Sophia sighed, realizing it was time she left.

"You'll let me know when you have information on the sheep?" she asked Mae Ling.

"Of course," the small woman answered. "And you know where to go for this armor?"

Sophia smiled. "Yes, I know exactly who to ask. Let's hope he can fit it into his busy schedule."

Mae Ling flashed her a knowing look. "One day, you're going to realize how important you are and that anyone will drop anything to help you."

"I hope I don't," Sophia said honestly. "That doesn't seem very humble."

The fairy godmother nodded. "Never change, Sophia Beaufont. You were created perfect and somehow keep getting better."

CHAPTER THIRTY-SEVEN

Roya Lane was bustling with life when Sophia stepped through the portal. She made a beeline for Silk Armor, but the universe obviously had other plans for her than seeing Jeremy Bearimy right away.

As Sophia strode down the busy street, she watched as a familiar figure stuck out their leg as if trying to trip her. She halted right in front of the baker assassin propped up against the brick wall and rolled her eyes.

"Lee, is that seriously your attempt to try and trip me?" Sophia glared at the woman.

"It wasn't a real attempt or you'd be on your back." Lee pulled her leg in and stood straight, towering over Sophia. "I was messing with you. Believe me, if I wanted to, I would have swept your legs out from under you."

"I invite you to try on our next meeting," Sophia challenged.

"Okay, but I'm not dragging your butt to Magical Urgent Care," Lee stated. "I'm not allowed in that place after what happened in there the last time. Well, and the time before that. And before that."

"Did it involve bringing your wife in there with multiple injuries that looked strangely like you were trying to murder her?"

Lee nodded. "Can I help it if that woman is a complete klutz? I swear, sometimes I think she throws herself down the stairs just to make others suspicious."

"Weren't you putting an extra coat of wax on the stairs the last time I was at the Crying Cat Bakery?" Sophia asked.

"I like them shiny," Lee stated. "And that's what the railing is for. If Cat simply held onto it instead of clutching a glass of wine and a cigarette, then she'd catch herself."

"Although this conversation is intriguing, I need to be on my way." Sophia eyed the other side of the lane where the seamster' shop was located.

"Yeah, I don't have anything else going on today either," Lee said, like she hadn't heard her at all. "Want to go get drunk?"

"No, and I'm working," Sophia answered.

"That's what I told Cat when she assigned me chores," Lee stated. "So should we rob someone? Maybe a gnome? Or we could go and get matching foxes. I want something to follow me around. You could name yours This and I'll name mine That. Or something equally as cute."

"I don't think a fox will follow you around," Sophia argued.

"That's why we'll keep a dead rat in our pockets," Lee offered.

Sophia grimaced. "That's gross."

An embarrassed look crossed the woman's face. "Oh, it is? You can't smell anything weird on me, right?"

Sophia closed off her heightened senses, just in case. "Sorry, no time to get matching pets today. Maybe on another occasion."

"I'm holding you to that," Lee stated. "Oh, and I made arrangements for King Rudolf Sweetwater's triplets' birthday. It's going to be special, even for the children who have everything."

"Thanks," Sophia responded. "That was really nice of you."

Lee's eyes bulged as she whipped back and forth. "Are you insane? Keep your voice down. What if someone heard you say that?"

Sophia laughed. "Then your reputation would be ruined, wouldn't it?"

"I swear if it gets out that I've done nice things, I'll have to do some bad stuff to undo people's perception."

"Like murder people?" Sophia asked dryly.

Lee shook her head. "No, something really bad, like litter."

Sophia lowered her chin and gave the assassin a confused look. "That's worse than murder?"

"Of course it is," Lee replied. "Most won't miss the blokes I take out. It's more of a community service than anything. But messing with Mother Nature, now that's awful."

"Well, I won't let it out that you've done anything nice. Therefore, you can refrain from littering," Sophia offered.

"Deal," Lee said proudly. She pulled a card out of her pocket and handed it to Sophia. "There's the details on the arrangements I made for the Captains. Pass it along to the king, but don't let it slip that I set it up."

Sophia glanced at the card, her eyes widening. "Is this experience what I think it is?"

Lee nodded. "Yep. A once in lifetime opportunity. They only open for exclusive people and even the king of the fae didn't qualify, but I pulled a few strings."

"Wow, that's so ni—I mean, you're a horrible person and do the most detestable things, Lee," Sophia said the last part loudly.

Her friend puffed out her chest and lifted her chin as a group of elves glanced in their direction. "Why, thank you. It comes naturally."

CHAPTER THIRTY-EIGHT

To say that being outside the Gullington after so many centuries was nerve-wracking was a serious understatement for Ainsley Carter. The elf knew that it was finally safe for her to be outside the Barrier. She could rely on S. Beaufont to have delivered her a cure that worked. However, her chest carried a permanent ache like her heart had trouble beating. Her hands shook when she lifted tea cups to her mouth, and sleep hadn't been a thing since she left the Castle.

Ainsley reasoned that without the Castle there to put her to sleep or heal all her ailments, her body had to do a lot on its own that it wasn't used to. However, she knew that wasn't altogether true. There were many emotions lying across her heart and weighing down her mind that she knew caused the aches and pains. She just didn't know exactly what to do about it.

"Madam, would you like anything else?" the servant asked from the door while holding the tray of fine china.

Ainsley glanced up from the book she'd been trying to read with no luck. "What's that?"

"Would you like anything else?" The woman curtsied.

Ainsley shook her head. "No, I'm quite all right."

"You didn't eat much," the servant known as Mary stated, and nodded at the tray of untouched food. What she meant to say was that Ainsley hadn't eaten a single bite of her dinner.

"I wasn't hungry," Ainsley replied. She was never hungry since leaving the Gullington. Never sleepy. Never anything except in a perpetual state of confusion.

"Well, I'll have sandwiches ready if you get hungry later, Madam."

"Thank you." Ainsley blushed. It was weird after all this time to be waited on by someone when it had been her serving the Dragon Elite for so many centuries. She had a new respect for the staff who took care of her at the Elfin Council in Ireland.

Mary left without another word, although a look of concern was evident on her lined face.

Falling back into her former role as a delegate for the Elfin Council had gone much smoother than Ainsley would have imagined. Since elves lived so long, being gone for several centuries hadn't been that big of a deal. Many of those that Ainsley had known at the Council were still in command. The old politics was the new one, and she found herself at the heart of many negotiations, once more trying to get the crusty old elves to think with new thinking.

This was something she'd admired about S. Beaufont. That dragonrider used innovative and strategic thinking to accomplish things that brute force could never accomplish. She was solutions-oriented, rather than constantly looking to secure power.

Still, many found Ainsley's absence to be disconcerting and thought that she had a bias toward the Dragon Elite. She couldn't blame them even after explaining that she'd been held hostage at the Gullington to preserve her life rather than choosing to stay there all these years.

Ainsley sighed as she grabbed the time-ball that Mama Jamba had made for her. She hadn't dared to use the powerful magical object yet, almost afraid of what she'd see. Apparently, the device would allow her to make different choices in the past and see how they would have played out. It was obvious what she was supposed to do with it. She was supposed to figure out her relationship with Hiker, which was currently at the pinnacle of her regrets.

Ainsley constantly wondered that if she had been given the choice, would she have stayed at the Castle with the leader of the Dragon Elite? Or would she have fled, tired of experiencing his cold ways and unrequited love?

She didn't blame Hiker Wallace, especially now that she had some perspective. He had always said that the Dragon Elite came first. That had never changed. Then Ainsley became pregnant and he didn't know because she couldn't tell him, knowing it would impact his choices. But more than anything, Ainsley wondered how it impacted her choices. Would she have sacrificed herself for Hiker if he weren't the father of her unborn child?

She closed her eyes and focused the way that Mama Jamba had instructed her to, and saw a new reality in her mind. In this one, so many centuries ago, Ainsley wasn't pregnant. She was still the main delegate for the Elfin Council. And she was an ally to the Dragon Elite. But more than anything, she wasn't with Hiker Wallace either secretly or outwardly. Ainsley was simply a shapeshifting elf that had accompanied the Dragon Elite to the battlefield where they'd meet Thad Reinhart's army. The place that would become the first fight of the Great War—the one that changed everything for everyone worldwide.

Ainsley held the time ball in her hands and kept her eyes pressed shut. She watched in her mind's eyes as a new reality unfolded before her vision. It was what would have happened if things were different. If she didn't love Hiker Wallace. If she hadn't been pregnant. If her life weren't tied to his.

When Thad Reinhart shot up his hand and sent a curse meant to kill his brother, the Ainsley from the past did something surprising. Like in the reality that came to pass, the elf jumped in front of the assault to protect the leader of the Dragon Elite. Although she wasn't in love with him, she sacrificed her life for Hiker Wallace's.

Over and over again, Ainsley manipulated the details of the past in her mind and watched that same scene play out. No matter what she did, Ainsley always threw herself in front of the killing spell, making it so that she was tied to the Gullington for the next several centuries.

No matter what, Ainsley was destined to sacrifice her life for Hiker's. Which meant that she was always supposed to lose her memory and be confined to the Gullington. There was no changing the last several hundred years.

Ainsley Carter was meant to serve the Castle all along. There was suddenly no blame, no regret. No wondering. The life that Ainsley had lived was meant to be. And what came next felt easier as she came to terms with the emotions lying across her heart.

CHAPTER THIRTY-NINE

The Silk Armory had seen better days. From Sophia's perspective, any day had to be a better one for Jeremy Bearimy, the shop's owner.

The giant tarantula was understandably in a sour mood when Sophia walked into his seamster store to find the place totally ransacked. She tensed, worried for many different reasons, and also had the fleeting thought that the large spider might be angry enough to eat her by the look in his beady eyes.

"Is everything okay?" Sophia looked around the store where silk fabrics were strewn across the floor, and completely covered it. Shelves were toppled over in all directions and supplies had spilled out, littering the place with sharp needles and measuring tapes and various other things. "Were you robbed? Are you hurt?"

"Robbed?" Jeremy Bearimy turned to face her, hovering high above Sophia. "You mean burgled?"

"I think I mean burglarized, but I feel like we're having a conversation over semantics rather than the obvious concern."

The hairy creature shook his round head. "No, I haven't been burglarized or robbed. Juergen happened."

"Oh." Sophia heard a shuffling sound coming from the back of the shop. She'd met Jeremy Bearimy's assistant on the few occasions that she'd been there. He wasn't the most graceful on his feet, but there was something strange about the character that she'd yet to put her finger on, as if a weird competence lurked under the surface. It was like King Rudolf. He seemed dumb as a brick, but then too often he surprised everyone by saving the day and being the most valued person in battles.

"He dropped a thimble." Jeremy Bearimy sighed and looked around at the disheveled shop.

"By thimble, do you mean a bomb?" Sophia had to ask.

The tarantula shook his head. "When he bent over to get it, he hit his head on a stand and that spooked him so he fell back into the shelves and knocked all of them down. But then, against my pleas, he tried to catch them, which sent all the bolts of stacked fabrics tumbling to the floor. Inside of ten seconds, he'd created this mess."

Sophia offered a sympathetic expression. "Do you want my help cleaning it all up? I could have everything back in place in seconds." She held up her hand, ready for the command.

"No, but thank you," Jeremy Bearimy answered. "Actually..." He glanced down at the floor and picked up a small brass button that should have been lost in all the mess. "This is quite fortuitous. I've been looking for this button for over three decades. I'd nearly given up hope, and here it is!"

The excitement in the tarantula's voice grew as he held the small button up to the light, his eyes sparkling with sudden joy.

"That button..." Sophia studied the small item, but didn't see what was so special about it. "That's a long time to look for something like that." What she didn't ask was the obvious question of "Why?"

Jeremy Bearimy snapped his hairy leg back down while still clutching the button. "Oh, but my efforts were for a good reason. This isn't any button."

"I would hope not," Sophia stated.

The tarantula leaned closer to her, his pincers dangerously near her face, making her tense. Sophia knew that Jeremy Bearimy wouldn't hurt her, or at least she hoped that, but being so close to a large tarantula was still unsettling.

"This button, well, it has incredible magical properties," Jeremy Bearimy began in a conspiratorial voice. "I can spin silk that can withstand fatal blows and create the best protective armor in the world. However, this button...well, I'm not sure I can disclose what it does to you or anyone. It's that valuable."

"I'm not sure my interest will allow me to leave without knowing after that buildup," Sophia stated matter-of-factly.

The seamster considered this for a moment, then added, "Well, I'll tell you this much. One would never want for anything if this button was sewn on their clothes."

"Want for anything?" Sophia thought this was too broad a description and tried to pull the real details from Jeremy Bearimy. "Like riches?"

"Like food, water, heat, coolness, comfort, joy... Do you get the idea?"

Sophia's mouth fell open. "So wearing that single button makes it so the person is never hungry or tired or cold or anything?"

"You're always perfect with this," Jeremy Bearimy stated with satisfaction, still clutching the item. "It makes the wearer as fit as a button."

"Wow, that's pretty impressive," Sophia stated. "So who gets to wear it?"

Jeremy Bearimy shrugged. "I lost it a long time ago, so I don't know. It's not right for me, but I'm sure someone will come along who will need it. Until then, I will allow Juergen to wear it since he is the reason that I found it, after all."

"But what if he loses the button?" Sophia asked.

"Oh, he never loses a thing," Jeremy Bearimy answered. "Juergen is my finder. This button proves it. I couldn't find a thing without him. It turns out that he usually destroys the shop in the process, but sometimes we need chaos in our lives to create order. It is the winds of a storm that knocks the loose branches free from the trees, after all."

Sophia smiled, enjoying the sentiment. "That's a lovely phrase."

"You may borrow it," Jeremy Bearimy said good-naturedly. "Now, you came to see me for a reason, correct? Is it the dress I made for Ainsley Carter? Did it work out all right? Do you need me to make alterations?"

Sophia felt a pang of grief, missing her friend the elfin shapeshifter. "I don't know. I haven't had a chance to ask her, but I'm sure that it's perfect and she loves it. Thank you."

"Oh, good," Jeremy Bearimy stated. "Then you're here for something new."

"Yes, and I'm afraid it will be a large project," Sophia began. "I'm not sure if you'll have time, but I've been told that the Dragon Elite needs armor, both for the riders and the dragons."

"That is a very large project." Jeremy Bearimy suddenly looked overwhelmed.

"I understand if you can't fit it in," Sophia responded at once. "It's just that—"

"Not fit it in?" the tarantula interrupted. "Do you think I'm mad?"

This had to be a trick question. Sophia tilted her head and drawled, "Nooooo..."

"Of course I'm not," Jeremy Bearimy chirped. "I'd have to be to not outfit the Dragon Elite and their trusty steeds with armor at your request. It sounds like you'll be going into an important and deadly battle. What do you know of it?"

Sophia pursed her lips. "Not a thing. I was told by a very reliable source that we'd need armor."

"Oh, I can't imagine how you sleep knowing that you'll face an unknown danger."

Sophia laughed. "Usually with the fan on."

"What's that now?" Jeremy Bearimy looked confused.

"Oh, I was saying that I sleep with the fan on," Sophia imparted, still laughing. "It's pretty easy to go about my business knowing that in the future I'll encounter some serious danger."

"Right you are," Jeremy Bearimy stated proudly. "Embrace the uncertainty in life. Therein lies the true power for those who want great adventures and therefore great achievements."

"So you will make the armor?" Hope laced Sophia's tone.

"Absolutely." He glanced toward the back of the shop. "Juergen, I need the magic-measure-o-meter."

"Coming, sir," the assistant called, sounding winded like he'd been running around. A moment later, the man sped into the front of the shop and nearly tripped on the fabrics and other items strewn across the floor. He held up a single yellow roll of measuring ribbon. "Here it is, sir. I had to look everywhere for it, but I found it."

"That was you looking everywhere?" Sophia questioned. "You turned up with it seconds after he requested it."

Juergen bowed. "And I'm sorry to keep you waiting, sir. My deepest apologies."

Sophia shook her head. Her life and the people in it were so bizarre. She wouldn't change a thing about them or her life.

"That's quite all right, Juergen." Jeremy Bearimy took the measuring ribbon that he held up and handed it to Sophia. "You'll need to take this and wrap it around the pointer finger of each of the riders you need armor for."

When he didn't elaborate, Sophia prompted, "Then what?"

"What do you mean, then what?" Jeremy Bearimy asked, confused.

"Where else do I take measurements?"

"That's it," the tarantula answered simply, like this should be obvious. "Wrap it around their finger, and all their measurements will be reported to me. For the dragons though, you'll wrap it around their tails. I hope that won't be a problem."

Sophia smiled, impressed. "No, it shouldn't be at all. That's amazing."

"Quite," Jeremy Bearimy stated. "Now, I'll make this a chief priority, but still, it will take some time. I'm guessing you don't know exactly when you'll need the armor?"

Sophia shook her head. "No, that wasn't disclosed to me. I just have to be ready for battle at a moment's notice."

The seamster nodded, like that was perfectly acceptable. "Very well, then. I'll work as diligently as I can and have the armor ready very soon."

"Thank you so much," Sophia said with relief. She didn't know what type of battle would require armor for both the riders and the dragons, but as much as she tried to pretend, the foreboding quality of this mysterious battle definitely had the potential to keep her up at night.

"May I make a suggestion?" Jeremy Bearimy asked carefully.

"Of course," Sophia said at once.

"Well, it seems to me that if you require special armor for you and your dragons for this upcoming battle, then you might also need a special weapon of sorts," Jeremy Bearimy mused.

Sophia glanced down at Inexorabilis on her hip. It was a fine weapon, of the highest quality, but the seamster was probably right that they'd need something more. However, how was Sophia supposed to find a weapon to defeat a villain that she didn't know anything about yet?

Although the whole thing was perplexing, she was grateful that she had an option. The only caveat was would the person who could help her, actually do so.

CHAPTER FORTY

"All I'm saying is that smiling wouldn't kill you," Liv said dryly to Papa Creola when Sophia entered the Fantastical Armory.

The two glanced in her direction. Neither seemed surprised to see her.

"You're late," Papa Creola said flatly to Sophia with a punishing look on his face.

She sighed. "Didn't know I was coming here, so for me, I feel like I'm early."

"See, delivering that scolding remark with a smile would have made it all the better," Liv commented to Father Time, which he ignored.

"So you know why I'm here then." Sophia strode over to the counter and stood next to her sister. "That always makes things easier."

Liv laughed. "It's cute that you'd think that."

"You're not here to see me, I know that much." Papa Creola put a strange monocle in his eye and studied a large orange gem in his hands.

"Although I want to believe you're here to see me, I know better." Liv leaned her head on Sophia's shoulder. "How's it going?"

"Good," Sophia chirped. "Looking for a weapon to defeat an enemy that I know nothing about and don't know when the Dragon Elite will face it."

"Sounds about right." Liv straightened.

"But you know you're facing an enemy, and that should be enough." Papa Creola continued to study the gem.

"Isn't he so cute when he squints like that?" Liv asked her sister.

"I still contend it's difficult to know what kind of weapon defeats an enemy or an army or whatever it is that I'll be facing alongside the Dragon Elite," Sophia argued.

Papa Creola sighed. "You two always want information. What am I facing? When? Where?" He shook his head. "For once, just go with the flow, would you?"

Liv grimaced. "When you talk like a hippie, I feel like you're begging me to strangle you."

He nodded. "I think in a way, I am. Put me out of my misery."

"I know you can't help it," Liv stated. "But still, try and refrain from spouting Bob Marley quotes. That really is for the best."

"I like Bob Marley," Sophia replied.

"You're going to regret saying that in a moment," Liv imparted.

"Why?"

"Just you wait." There was a foreboding quality to her tone.

"Subner will be out in a moment," Papa Creola interrupted, and continued to squint as he studied the gem.

Liv sighed. "I'm sorry that he's keeping you waiting, Soph. That's very rude since he obviously knew you two had a meeting, although you didn't."

"He's not late," Papa Creola sputtered. "He'll be here as soon as this repugnant conversation is over."

"If that's your way of dismissing me, then it totally worked." Liv smiled. She pointed at her mouth and grinned wider. "See how this makes a big difference, Papa?"

"No," he said at once. "It does nothing to improve your face."

Undeterred, Liv shook her head. "If you weren't the most powerful entity, I'd give you a piece of my mind."

"Oh, has that been what's been stopping you?" He sounded surprised.

"No, not really," Liv stated. "It's mostly because I'm a people pleaser."

"Is that why I get so many complaints about you?" Papa Creola asked, quite seriously.

"Anyway Sophia, I hope that whatever you've got to fight goes down easily—"

"It won't," Papa Creola interrupted, his attention still on the gem.

"And I further hope that you escape unscathed," Liv continued.

"She won't," Papa Creola stated dryly.

"Well, then I hope your scars make for good stories at dinner parties," Liv offered.

Papa Creola lowered his chin and glared at the Warrior for the House of Fourteen. "Because nothing is more appetizing than yanking up your sleeve at a dinner table and showing your scars."

"Is that why all the invites stopped?" Liv joked.

Papa Creola shook his head. "You are the epitome of class."

"Well, Soph..." Liv put her hand on her sister's shoulder and gave her a meaningful expression. "I want you to know that if you need anything, I'm always here for you. Whatever, whenever, no matter what I'm here—"

"Liv, you're late for that thing," Papa Creola interrupted.

Her eyes widened with alarm. "Oh, hell. You're right." Liv smiled at Sophia and winked. "Catch you later. I've got to go."

CHAPTER FORTY-ONE

As soon as the door to the Fantastical Armory swung shut behind Liv, Subner entered from the back, an expectant expression on his face. He strode straight over to Sophia and simply glared at her.

"Hey," she said casually. "So apparently, I need your help."

"Open your eyes, look within," Subner began, quoting Bob Marley. "Are you satisfied with the life you're living?"

Sophia groaned. "Oh, I get it now. You're stuck again, aren't you?"

"Emancipate yourselves from mental slavery," he went on. "None but ourselves can free our minds."

Sophia glanced at Papa Creola. "What is wrong with him?"

The elf shrugged. "It passes. A result of not coming to terms with this form."

"Maybe Liv should kill you so that you regenerate as something else," she offered.

"I wish it were that simple," Papa Creola replied. "I really do. But that isn't a job I want for her, so we have to endure."

"You never know how strong you are until being strong is your only choice," Subner stated, again using the words of the great musician.

"Right." Sophia wondered if this was going to be impossible since the weapon's expert didn't seem to be able to communicate in anything but in Bob Marley quotes. "So I need a weapon or weapons, or I don't know what I need because I don't know what I'm fighting. Can you help with that?"

"Never expect God to do for you what you don't do to others," Subner answered.

Sophia glared at Papa Creola. "Seriously? Can you help here? Otherwise, murder might be my only option."

"Beginnings are usually scary, and endings are usually sad, but it's everything in between that makes it worth living," Subner said in a rehearsed voice.

"It's cute that you have all those Bob Marley quotes memorized, but…" Sophia turned her attention back to Papa Creola and gave him a pleading expression.

"You can fool some people sometimes, but you can't fool all the people all the time," Subner stated, his tone airy like he was high on drugs.

"Yeah, you know what, never mind." Sophia threw up her hands. "I don't need a weapon that badly. Hopefully this mystery evil puts me out of my misery."

"When one door is closed, don't you know that many more are open?" Subner asked, her with a curious expression on his face.

"There's a famous psychiatrist who might be able to help Subner," Papa Creola offered. "This has been an ongoing problem since we regenerated. I know that you helped him before, but the issue keeps resurfacing and I think it's because there's a schism in his personality. He didn't completely assimilate into the elf form."

"Because being hippie is a horrible thing and he can't come to terms with it?" Sophia asked.

"Pretty much," Papa Creola stated dryly.

"But I've met elves that weren't hippies." Sophia thought of Ainsley and Renswick, an expert on demons who Liv had worked with.

"That's true, but they are a rarity," Papa Creola argued. "All the races have a core component for the main part. Magicians are practical as a whole. Giants are reclusive. Gnomes are sullen. Fae are wasteful, overly lavish, flamboyant, brainless—"

"Why don't you tell me how you really feel about them," Sophia interrupted with a laugh.

Papa Creola shot her a repulsed expression. "They aren't my favorite of the races."

"Complaints are prayers to the devil," Subner offered.

"This psychiatrist," Sophia began while looking at Father Time. "Where do I find them?"

"In the mortal world," Papa Creola explained. "She's a mortal, but I need you to bring her here to Subner. I believe she's the only one who has the ability to help him."

Sophia crossed her arms in front of her chest. "Why does this sound too easy?"

"Although some mortals can enter Roya Lane," Papa Creola began, "those are rare exceptions. There are wards here that are meant to prevent mortals from coming here. It's safer for everyone if they don't enter this place."

"So Subner goes with me to find this lady then," Sophia offered.

"If you don't start somewhere, you're gonna go nowhere," Subner quoted.

"Actually, I can see that going very poorly," Sophia said dryly.

"Tiffannee Freud needs to come here to see Subner," Papa Creola explained.

"That name...she isn't..."

"Yes, she most certainly is," Papa Creola answered.

"I can't believe it," Sophia said in awe.

"Well, you should," he stated. "Some people make bad decisions when naming their children."

"Wait, what?"

"Tiffannee," Papa Creola said. "And yes, it is spelled with two fs, two ns and two es. Very wasteful and unnecessary."

"Okay, that's ridiculous, but that's not what I was referring to." Sophia laughed. "Is this psychiatrist related to the famous neurologist, Sigmund Freud?"

Papa Creola shrugged. "How am I supposed to know?"

Sophia rolled her eyes. "Because you know everything."

"So I do," he said rather smugly. "And it's not really of importance. She's a master in her field of hypnosis, dream interpretation and various other mental health techniques. I think she's the only one who can help Subner."

"Don't live for your presence to be noticed," Subner drawled on, "but for your absence to be felt."

"A gag might also help," Sophia offered.

Papa Creola shook his head. "As I was saying, to get Dr. Freud onto Roya Lane will be tricky."

Sophia giggled. "Dr. Freud."

He grimaced at her. "I don't get it."

She shook her head. "Anyway, what do I have to do to get her here, and where do I find her?"

Papa Creola shrugged. "I can't say where to find Dr. Freud. And as far as getting her here, can you think of any other mortals you've seen on Roya Lane before?"

This was a test and Sophia knew it. She thought hard, trying to recall when she'd seen a mortal there. It dawned on her, and her mouth popped open. "Serena Sweetwater."

He nodded. "And why do you think she could come through the portal to Roya Lane?"

Another test. "Because she doesn't have any brain cells left to lose?"

Papa Creola didn't appear impressed. "Try again."

"Is it because she's married to the king of the fae?"

"Love the life you live," Subner stated. "Live the life you love."

"That's exactly why," Papa Creola affirmed, ignoring his assistant.

"Well, I guess the king of the fae can marry multiple people," Sophia said mostly to herself, trying to work this all out in her head.

"It's not so much about marrying royalty as much as marrying someone from a magical race," Papa Creola corrected, strangely being direct and somewhat helpful.

"Oh, cool," Sophia said dryly. "So I need to find this lady and ask her to marry a magician or elf or something so that she can visit Roya

Lane and fix Subner before I kill him. I look forward to explaining this all to a stranger who will no doubt put a restraining order on me right away."

Papa Creola nodded. "Good. Glad you have a plan."

"True friends are like stars," Subner said, "you can only recognize them when it's dark around you."

"Friends..." Sophia thought, trying to figure out which one of hers she could ask to marry this mortal.

"The truth is, everyone is going to hurt you," Subner went on. "You just got to find the ones worth suffering for."

"You're causing me a great deal of suffering," Sophia joked.

"Some people feel the rain," Subner stated. "Others just get wet."

"Can you make this a priority?" Papa Creola asked, the irritation heavy in his tone.

"Yes, I'll devote my attention straight to it." Sophia made for the door. "I think I know how to track down this doctor, but I don't know who I'll chain her to yet."

"Every man gotta right to decide his own destiny," Subner sang as Sophia sped out of the Fantastical Armory.

CHAPTER FORTY-TWO

A figure went down Roya Lane with a crazed expression on his face as he whipped his arms back and forth to propel him faster.

He weaved around larger groups and slammed into a cart that sold "unlosable" keychains. They clattered to the ground and made a series of chiming noises as they fell.

Sophia would have ignored the commotion, bent on getting to the Brownie Official Headquarters as fast as possible since Father Creola expressed how important it was to help Subner. However, tucked under one of the madman's arms was a small figure that Sophia recognized, although he was moving at almost a blur.

And if she didn't think she recognized the little Brownie, she definitely knew Ticker's voice as he yelled, "Melp he! Melp he!"

Sophia darted forward, racing after the criminal who had abducted the little guy who belonged to Mortimer and Pricilla. She planned on running straight into him, halting his progress and grabbing the Brownie from his grasp. However, the offender caught sight of her and veered suddenly down a narrow alleyway off the main lane.

"Damn it!" Sophia yelled while pushing past elves and gnomes who didn't seem to have anywhere to be and clogged up the area in front of her. They were all lollygagging like they didn't have a care in the world or notice that a crazed lunatic was carrying a Brownie and darting through the roads.

"Move aside!" Sophia screamed and made a broad sweeping motion in front of her, using magic to help encourage the obstacles of people out of her way.

Gnomes, who never liked to be told what to do, stubbornly stood in her path with their hands on their hips or crossed over their chests. They weren't being budged by her magical attempts to get them out of the way. This was one of the ill-timed opportunities where they chose to exert their independence.

"Oh for the love of the angels," Sophia complained, sliding around a group and then leaping over the next. She sprang high enough in the air to clear the heads of the gnomes she jumped over, but barely.

Like a pole vaulter, Sophia's arms and legs pistoned through the air as she soared. The heel of her boot grazed the top of a gnome's head, and he yelled in protest.

"Well, move then!" Sophia shouted as she landed in a crouched position on the other side of the stubborn group of gnomes. She kept moving and swung around the corner of the narrow alleyway where she saw the villain turn down.

He was already to the far side, and whipped his head around to look at Sophia's pursuit over his shoulder.

"Bophia Seaufont!" Ticker yelled with his head pressed between the guy's arm and side. His little voice pained Sophia, thinking that the criminal could be hurting the little Brownie.

Sophia darted a to halt and removed her grappling hook from her cloak, which thankfully she'd remembered to bring with her, although at the time she didn't know why since she was only coming to Roya Lane. Just showed that she needed to be prepared for a battle or a pursuit no matter what.

If she were simply trying to take down a bad guy, she would have fired on him. However, Sophia was acutely concerned about not harming little Ticker in her process. That's why she refrained from throwing anything at the guy that could stop him but might indirectly hurt the Brownie.

He was moving fast and nearly to the far side of the alleyway, which she knew spilled out into a very large area with tons of hiding places. If the madman got there, then finding him might be a lost cause. And more importantly, getting Ticker back safely would be next to impossible. That was unacceptable.

Therefore, Sophia aimed at the building on the far side of the alleyway and fired the grappling hook. It zipped through the air and stuck into the wood of the building, then instantly yanked Sophia in that direction. She clenched her teeth together as she sped through the air, racing toward the solid building.

The guy didn't seem to know what was happening—all the events took place so quickly before his eyes.

When Sophia was on the other side of him and before she hit the building, she let go of the grappling hook and dropped straight in front of the guy, which made him halt suddenly.

He backed up and nearly tripped on his feet.

"Hand over the Brownie and you won't get hurt," Sophia warned while holding up both of her hands to try and make the guy surrender.

He apparently wasn't the surrendering type. Up close, Sophia could see that he had piercings all over his face and neck tattoos and dirt caked under his fingernails. He was a magician down on his luck by the look of his torn and stained clothes. He whipped around and looked at the alleyway where they came from.

Apparently the guy wanted to get hurt because he didn't release Ticker but instead, took off back the other way.

Sophia rolled her eyes, realizing she was going to have to get dirty taking this guy down. And right when she thought she had an easy case where she only had to fetch some mortal.

She darted forward and caught up with the guy within a few strides thanks to the chi of the dragon. Sophia slid forward, brought her leg around, and swept the guy's legs out from under him.

In a swift, clean movement she kicked out his feet and made the guy fly up, his back horizontal to the ground for a moment. Sophia jumped up, seized her opportunity and snatched the Brownie from the criminal's hands, then tossed him over her back where he held on tightly around her neck. Back there, he would be safe from an attack if the guy tried. However, the man landed hard on his back and appeared to have the wind knocked out of him.

Still, Sophia stayed tensed in a fighting position, ready for his next move.

He groaned and rubbed the back of his head that had smacked into the pavement. Not wanting to risk him getting away, Sophia sent a binding spell at the madman that tied up his wrists and feet, and made it impossible for him to get up.

"Oh, come on!" he complained.

"Be grateful I didn't break something of yours," Sophia challenged.

He tried to roll over, but with his hands pinned tightly in front of him, it appeared impossible. "I think you did."

"Mad ban," Ticker said in a low voice in Sophia's ear.

"What did you want with Ticker?" Sophia watched the guy squirm.

"Nothing," he lied and kicked his feet, which were bound too.

Sophia sighed. "Guess how much worse your life can get?"

He growled. "Not much! I'm out of money and have debts to pay or I'll be paying with my life."

"So?" Sophia challenged.

"So, Brownies know where treasures are!" he yelled. "They know where everything is!"

That was true. Sophia had been on her way to see Mortimer when she ran into the guy fleeing with Ticker. She hoped that the head official for the Brownies would be able to tell her where to find Tiffannee Freud. They didn't know everything, but they did have eyes in many places and knew a lot. One of those things was undoubtedly the location of treasures.

"You were going to have Ticker tell you where to find money and valuables, then," Sophia guessed. "And steal... Your problems can't be that bad."

"How would you know, rich girl?" the guy whined.

Sophia shook her head. "You know, having money doesn't fix all your problems. There are some things in the world bigger than that."

He laughed, but the sound contained no joy. "How would you know?"

Sophia thought about the upcoming battle where the Dragon Elite would need the best armor in the world and a mysterious weapon. A cold chill ran down her back. "Believe me, I know."

She pulled out her cell phone and messaged Liv. It read: "You still on Roya Lane? I have a present for you."

CHAPTER FORTY-THREE

"You and I need to discuss what qualifies as a present." Liv eyed the criminal who was giving her a scared stare.

"Please, please don't leave me with her!" he begged. "Kill me now. Put me out of my misery. Take me to your authorities. Just don't leave me with that woman!"

Sophia laughed. "Sorry, you fall into her jurisdiction, magician. And my authorities would roast you...quite literally."

"Oh, Jock." Liv shook her head and clicked her tongue. "You missed me, didn't you?"

Ticker had climbed over Sophia's shoulder and was now cradled in her arms, perched up high and watching everything with wide eyes.

"Liss Miv!" The little Brownie blinked at Liv with an endearing expression.

"Aww, I missed you too, Tick," she gushed. "We need to go on another mission together."

"Yes, but right now I'm going to get this little guy back to his parents," Sophia stated. "I bet they missed him and are worried sick."

Liv nodded. "Although they know he can take care of himself. I would have felt sorry for Jock if he thought that Ticker wasn't going to get away and in the process make his life hell. You picked the wrong Brownie to nab, Jock."

The guy gave Sophia an urgent expression. "I don't know who you are but please, take pity on me. Don't leave her with me! She's horrible."

Sophia laughed. "She's my sister."

Jock groaned. "Oh, kill me now."

"Wow." Sophia shook her head at Liv. "What did you do to this guy the last time?"

"I thought we had a great time, Jock," Liv joked. "You didn't like my singing?"

"She didn't stop for hours," Jock said like it was the most horrifying experience. "And then her and the demon hunter used me as target practice."

"No," Liv corrected. "If Stefan and I used you as target practice, then there'd be holes in you. The objective was not to nick your pretty little face. Did we?"

"Multiple blades grazed by my face!" he boomed.

"But they didn't cut you, now did they, Jock?" Liv hauled him up to his feet and looked him over. "Wow, you look like crap. What have you been doing, living on the streets?" She reeled back. "Yeah, you smell like you've been living in a cardboard box."

"What else am I supposed to do?" he complained. "You shut down my business—"

"Selling illegal magical devices to underage magicians," Liv interrupted.

"They're harmless," he argued.

"They help them cut school and cheat on their exams," Liv countered.

"And I still owe those thugs for the merchandise, which you all confiscated," Jock stated.

"Maybe we've learned to stop doing business dealings with thugs, then?" Liv asked. "I mean, I shouldn't have to tell you that when your business associate is named Blood Stains, that you probably don't want to work with him."

"It was supposed to be easy money," Jock griped. "Now I owe him a ton of money, and if he finds me, I'm dead."

"If I catch you doing anything illegal or anywhere near the Brownie Official Headquarters, then you'll be begging Blood Stains to take you out," Liv threatened. "I can promise you that my punishments are a lot more creative, and will leave you with nightmares."

He visibly shivered in her grasp. "I know from experience."

Liv gave Sophia a sideways expression. "Thanks for taking Jock down. He'll be safe with me."

He shook his head adamantly. "I won't. She'll keep me alive, but I promise I won't be safe."

Sophia laughed. "How did you get into the Brownie office?"

Liv sighed. "Jock is pretty clever." She gave him a pursed expression. "Imagine if you used your talents for good?"

"What are you going to do with him?" Sophia watched as Liv led him off.

"I'm going to give Jock one last chance to turn it around," Liv stated, not using as much force with the guy as if she loathed him. Knowing her, she was going to bail him out and try and reform him so he quit doing illegal stuff and contributed to society rather than was a drain on it. "But I'm probably also going to give him matching black eyes and some scars to remember me by."

Jock shook his head, his eyes wide as he looked over his shoulder. "Please help me," he begged Sophia.

She simply laughed and squeezed Ticker tightly, grateful that he was okay. "Good luck, Liv. Chat soon."

"Yeah, I'll catch y'all on the flip side." She waved as she led the criminal away.

"Lye Biv!" Ticker waved back, smiling wide.

CHAPTER FORTY-FOUR

"Ticker!" Pricilla exclaimed and threw her arms around the little Brownie when Sophia crawled through the small door. She didn't know how Jock got out of there so fast since he was larger than her, but like Liv said, he was very clever. Hopefully he went on to use his brains for something good rather than illegal.

"Mi Homma." Ticker smiled wide, not at all looking flustered from his adventure. He was a tough one and Liv was right that he probably would have given Jock a world of trouble if he'd tried to use him to find treasure.

She held him out and looked him over. "Are you okay, son?"

"Fep, yine!" he answered, smiling.

Mortimer rushed in from down the hallway where he'd been in his office. "Ticker! You got him!" His gaze ran over his son, then to Sophia. "Thank you. I should have known that we'd have the opportunity to thank a Beaufont for rescuing our kiddo."

Sophia beamed. "I was in the right place at the right time."

"And humble like your sister," Mortimer added, smiling wide.

"I'm gonna take Ticker to get some food after the commotion." Pricilla made for the door.

Mortimer nodded. "Yes, please do. You two rest up and I'll see you when you return."

Ticker waved, then took his mother's hand and hurried for the door. "Dye Bad!"

"Bye, son." Mortimer waved back at his son. When they'd left, he sighed in relief. "I can't thank you enough for helping to save Ticker."

She waved him off. "I'm certain he would have been okay without me, but I'm grateful that I could intervene."

"Well, not that I wouldn't help you otherwise, but I'd like to return the momentous favor," Mortimer stated.

"As luck would have it, I need some information on a mortal and was hoping that you could help me," Sophia began.

Mortimer lowered his chin and gave her his full attention. "If there's a mortal you need to find out there, then I'll make it my top priority. Just give me a name and I'll locate them."

CHAPTER FORTY-FIVE

"You want me to do what?" Evan slathered raspberry jam on a scone.

"It's no big deal," Sophia said in a convincing tone, and gave Hiker a tentative expression. "I just need you to marry this mortal."

"Why me?" Evan narrowed his eyes, a skeptical expression on his face.

"Because you're an eligible bachelor, and who wouldn't want to marry you, even if it's for show?" Sophia argued.

"Wilder could marry her," he stated and pointed at the other dragonrider.

"He can't," Sophia said at once.

"Because?" Evan challenged.

"Because I'd kill him," Sophia replied matter-of-factly.

"It's for show though," Evan countered.

"It's still marriage." Sophia was aware that Wilder was smirking at her, seeming to enjoy this.

"And Wilder has a mission," Hiker stated with confidence as Trin brought out a platter of sausage.

"And Mahkah?" Evan questioned.

"You're given the easiest, best mission possible, and you're objecting," Mama Jamba stated.

"Mahkah needs to help with the dragons," Hiker imparted.

"Fine," Evan said with a dramatic sigh. "I'll marry this mortal, but only if I can seal the deal, if you know what I mean."

Trin dropped the platter in front of Evan, which made grease splatter on his front.

"Hey!" he complained, then pushed back from the table and ran a napkin over his shirt. "Watch it!"

"Oops," The cyborg trotted back toward the kitchen, but didn't look at all apologetic.

"What's her problem?" Evan sounded offended.

"She's still adjusting," Hiker said.

Sophia eyed the kitchen where Trin had disappeared and wasn't so convinced she'd dropped the breakfast meat because she was still adjusting to things at the Castle.

"And there will be no sealing any deals," Hiker went on. "You're to marry this mortal, get her into Roya Lane, and do whatever Sophia needs you to in order to secure this weapon or weapons or whatever we need to fight this unknown danger."

Sophia had explained to Hiker about the armor from Jeremy Bearimy and the weapon that Subner might be able to help with if he was fixed. Hiker wasn't as worried as she would have thought. He said that getting armor for the riders and dragons from the esteemed seamster was probably overdue.

The mysterious villain or villains also didn't seem to bother him much. Hiker appeared very preoccupied, like there were bigger worries for him in the world than having to face something where they needed special armor and weapons from none other than Subner —the weapons expert.

"Then what?" Evan asked. "I divorce this woman? Leave her heartbroken and longing for what she can't have?"

"Or relieved," Wilder offered with a laugh.

Evan huffed. "Not to mention that you're sullying my reputation, Pink Princess. What do I say when some dame asks me if I've ever been married? I'll have to say yes and they'll think my goods aren't any good anymore."

"That's not why they'll think that," Wilder teased.

Trin had returned with a bowl of fruit. She narrowed her eyes at Evan. "There's nothing wrong with being divorced." There was an edge to the cyborg's voice. This was personal for her.

"Of course there isn't, dear," Mama Jamba stated with confidence.

"Fine, since I'm the only bachelor here who can entice a stranger to marry me, I'll do it." Evan stretched his arms over his head as he leaned back in his chair.

Trin strode for the kitchen. Her foot kicked out the back legs and made Evan tumble over backward—a trick the gang took turns playing on him. He tumbled to the floor with a yell.

"Oops," Trin said again and disappeared into the kitchen, again not sounding at all apologetic.

NO10JO yelped from the entryway, concerned about Evan after his fall.

"I'm all right, boy." He pushed up and wiped the dust off his pants. "It appears someone is very klutzy today." He narrowed his eyes at the kitchen where Trin was making lots of racket.

"Do you have the location for this mortal?" Hiker asked.

Sophia dared to pull out her phone at the table, since it was for work and Hiker had asked. She noticed then that the message from Mortimer had just come through.

She smiled victoriously. "Yep, I've got a location." She gave Evan a playful look. "Ready for a Las Vegas wedding?"

"You know it," he answered. "The less classy, the better!"

CHAPTER FORTY-SIX

"Is it me, or did Mama Jamba forget to turn the heat off in Baton Rouge?" Evan asked after the pair stepped through the portal.

"I think the thermostat in the south is permanently broken," Sophia replied. "If it makes you feel any better, the sweltering heat gives you a nice glazed donut look."

"Yes, what every man wants to look like on his wedding day—a fried pastry that makes you fat," Evan grumbled.

"Well, not you or me since we're magicians, but your bride is a mortal," Sophia teased.

"Oh, to not be able to eat your weight in fried foods and not a gain an ounce," Evan said in mock sadness. "The woes of the mortals."

Sophia nodded and looked down the busy street in downtown Baton Rouge—the capital of Louisiana. To say that the two dragonriders looked out of place with all the mortals striding by in business suits was a gigantic understatement.

The long black cloak that Sophia wore did little to hide the fact that she was wearing light armor, knee-high boots and a sword. Evan was less conspicuous in his usual getup of a gray armored top and matching leather pants—his trusty axe strapped to his back.

After receiving a series of curious and cautious expressions,

Sophia considered glamouring their appearances. However, Hiker hadn't encouraged this approach, wanting the Dragon Elite to be visible when out in public. It was just that mortals weren't used to seeing dragonriders carrying ancient weapons in city centers yet. It all made Sophia feel like she'd stepped out of a time machine and she was the medieval warrior bumbling around in the modern world.

"Do you get the impression that you've got spinach in your teeth or a booger hanging out of your nose?" Evan asked in a low voice at Sophia's shoulder.

She laughed. "Maybe you do. I feel more like an actor from a Renaissance fair that's lost their way."

"Are Renaissance fairs a thing?" Evan asked, surprised.

She nodded. "Yeah, people dress up and eat turkey legs and watch men joust."

"Just shows the past always seems more appealing than it really was," Evan related.

Sophia laughed. "You're not old enough to remember the Renaissance era."

He pressed his hand to his chest. "I, Pink Princess, am timeless. But no, I'm still a youngun'. Hiker would be close to that time period, but still a wee lad then. Quiet would have had a good romp during the Renaissance though. Your friend Rudolf, too."

Sophia nodded. "Yeah, I've got some old friends, it seems. I guess it will come in handy if I need to do a history project for college or something."

Evan shook his head. "Your mom goes to college."

"Shush it," she warned and tried to get her bearings. "Dr. Freud's office is that way."

"I hope she's pretty." Evan strode after her. "I don't want to marry no Miranda."

"Her name is Tiffannee," Sophia stated. "With two fs, two ns and two es."

"She sounds high maintenance as f—"

"Watch your mouth," Sophia interrupted.

"As fancy tea with the queen," Evan corrected. "Gosh, what did you think I was going to say?"

"Your references are weird," Sophia offered.

"You're weird," he countered. "And for your information, a Miranda isn't real easy on the eyes, if you know what I mean."

"I think I do," Sophia stated. "You've been chatting with Lee from the Crying Cat Bakery, haven't you? She doesn't like Mirandas either."

"It's not an *us* thing," Evan stated. "It's a *them* thing. We can't help it if we just collectively noticed that they are all a bunch of—"

"I think we need to go up there." Sophia pointed to the lobby of a skyscraper.

"All right, but how do I look?" Evan tilted his head and gave her a very debonair expression.

"I only mildly want to throw up."

He nodded proudly. "That will do."

CHAPTER FORTY-SEVEN

The air conditioning in the building with shiny marble floors and banks of polished windows was a welcome relief.

Evan mopped his forehead when they were in the elevator, and flicked the sweat on the floor.

"Classy," Sophia muttered as the elevator traveled up to one of the top floors. It was taking its time and the mortals that were crammed in next to them didn't at all appear relaxed about having to share the space with them.

"Well, someone didn't tell me about the weather in this place on the other side of hell, and I didn't dress appropriately," Evan quipped, which earned a rude stare from a woman with a pinched expression and who wore too much red lipstick. He pretended to smile at her. "I meant other side of paradise. Do you know a good real estate agent? I'm thinking of getting a summer place here. I'm really into the, 'feels like I'm wearing a wet, hot blanket' climate."

"Please ignore him," Sophia stated. "I'm taking him to see a psychiatrist right now because you know…"

The woman nodded curtly because obviously she did know.

Evan rolled his eyes and looked around at the mortals wearing starched dark suits and carrying briefcases. After a short stop at the tenth floor, he cleared his throat. "Well, thank you all for joining me here today. I've got some exciting news—"

Sophia slapped him across the chest and interrupted him. All eyes whipped around to look at them. "Would you shush it? I get that you're starved for attention, but now isn't the time." She smiled politely at the many curious stares. "Sorry, he's off his meds."

Many of the mortals glanced at the axe on Evan's back, and horrified expressions sprang to their eyes.

"He's still totally safe though," Sophia said in a rush, realizing her mistake.

"Depends on who you are," Evan amended. "I messed up a gang of deranged gargoyles the other day. They wouldn't allow me access to this building, so their heads had to go."

Sophia leaned in close to Evan and whispered, "I'm trying to make the mortals feel safer in our presence, not like running wildly from the elevator."

Evan scoffed. "You all know the Dragon Elite is the bees knees and you can rely on us to keep you safe and the globe spinning on its axis, right?"

"What they can't rely on is for you to make a reference from this century," Sophia joked.

When the elevator opened on the next floor, whether it was all the mortals' destination or not, they rushed off, pushing each other to get out of the compartment and away from the dragonriders.

The doors bounced shut and Evan smiled. "Well, that went nicely."

"Never go into the hospitality industry," Sophia warned.

"Right, because if this dragonrider thing didn't pan out, my goal was to become a concierge at some posh hotel," Evan joked.

"With you, I never know," Sophia stated, as the elevator stopped on their floor.

It was time to demand a mortal marry Evan and fix the Protector of Weapons so that they could enhance their chances of defeating an unknown danger.

I freaking love my job, Sophia thought. *Never a dull moment.*

CHAPTER FORTY-EIGHT

In the waiting room to Dr. Tiffannee Freud's psychiatrist's office, there were many strange characters who sought to make Sophia and Evan look normal.

Sitting on the floor and counting the pages of a magazine as she flipped them was a woman with carroty orange hair and a face full of freckles. She was probably in her forties, but had the demeanor of a child.

In the corner was an older man with a comb-over who was mumbling to himself and playing with a red stapler.

And sitting next to the only two open seats was a mostly normal looking woman wearing a pencil skirt and a smart blazer.

Sophia pointed to one of the open seats. "Sit. I'll be right back."

Evan scoffed, but took the seat dutifully anyway. "So demanding. How does Wilder put up with you?"

"With a smile," she retorted as she strode up to the receptionist. Sophia didn't want to spell the woman into letting them in to see the doctor, but she might have to. What she apparently couldn't do was spell Dr. Freud into marrying Evan because then it wouldn't be official and she couldn't enter Roya Lane. So many obstacles, it seemed.

"So you come here often?" Sophia heard Evan ask the only normal-appearing person in the waiting room.

She made a note that she should have told him not to talk to strangers, but that probably would have just made things worse.

Clearing her throat, Sophia offered the receptionist a polite smile. "Hi there. We need to see Dr. Freud. It's important and—"

"You don't have an appointment," the woman interrupted.

"That's right, but we're—"

"Without an appointment, I can't help you."

Sophia kept the pleasant smile on her face. "Right. I understand. But you see, we're with the Dragon Elite and—"

The woman gave Sophia a sympathetic expression as she nodded. "Of course you are. And a fine dragonrider you are, but without an appointment, I can't help you."

Sophia had to walk into a room full of crazies and state she was a dragonrider to the one person who was probably told all sorts of strange things all day. The receptionist didn't believe her.

She sighed and discreetly twirled her finger while silently creating a spell on the woman. A moment later, the receptionist robotically picked up the telephone. "I'll clear Dr. Freud's schedule. She'll be out to see you in a minute. Please have a seat and wait."

Sophia nodded and strode back over to where Evan was chatting with the woman in the blazer. When she sat, he slid low in his seat. "This lady scares me."

Sophia leaned forward and looked the seemingly normal person over. "Hey," she said, when the woman noticed her.

"Hay is for horses," the woman grumbled as she moved back and forth, her brow pinched. "You a horse? If so, that would also make you an alien. You know that your kind are from the planet Ronin, right?"

"I didn't." Sophia tried to keep the surprise out of her expression.

"See what I mean," Evan whispered.

"This is how everyone always feels when around you," Sophia stated.

"If you need a ride home, I'll give you a lift on my spaceship," the woman went on to say, butting into their conversation. "We'll have to stop at one of the space stations to refill, but it only takes a few hundred light years and we're eternal beings."

"Thanks for the offer," Sophia said carefully.

"You're welcome," the woman chirped. "Bring gas money. I'm almost out of plutonium and spaceships don't fly themselves." She laughed abruptly. "Well, not yet they don't. Give it a few centuries."

The door to the office opened and a woman with long brown hair and a confused expression poked her head through. "I'm ready to see Sophia and Evan now."

Evan bolted upright and hurried away from the crazy woman. Sophia rose, waved to her, and felt sorry that she was so out of it. Or maybe she wasn't and they were the crazy ones who didn't know the truth about alien horses and spaceship travel. Anything was possible in her world.

CHAPTER FORTY-NINE

"Do you want to tell me what's going on?" Dr. Tiffannee Freud said to them when they filed through the door into her office. She stood inside a large warm study, her hands on her hips and an angry expression on her face. To Sophia's surprise, she was quite young, around her mid-thirties.

"Oh good, she's not a dog," Evan said with relief.

This did little to improve the angry expression on Dr. Freud's face. "I had a fully booked schedule of clients. Then suddenly, Miranda tells me that all my appointments have been cleared and I'm to see you two. What's that about?"

Evan laughed. "She totally looked like a Miranda."

Sophia snapped her fingers in front of his face. "Focus, would you?"

He shook his head like a dog after a bath. "I'm trying, but wedding day jitters."

Dr. Freud narrowed her eyes. "You two are getting married today? Is that why you're here? You're magicians, aren't you, and you spelled Miranda?"

"No. To rock your world and yes," Evan replied to all her questions. "But I'm not sure there's a spell to fix Miranda. She could try a hat maybe. Something with a veil, possibly…"

Sophia almost slapped her friend. "I'm sorry, but we need your help so I had to spell your receptionist into allowing you to see us."

Softening, but barely, Dr. Freud looked them over. "You're one of those dragon people, aren't you?"

"Dragon Elite," Sophia corrected.

Evan shuddered. "Dragon people makes us sound weird."

"You need no help in that arena," Sophia quipped before she turned her attention back to the doctor. "I know this is going to sound weird, but we need your help with a friend of ours. He's losing his mind off and on. I thought I fixed him a few times or that he'd snap out of it, but the problem appears to be much deeper and without his wits about him, well, there are bigger issues that could arise."

Dr. Freud nodded. "Mental health is of supreme importance and can have devastating effects on families." She looked Evan over. "How long has he been suffering?"

A laugh burst out of Sophia's mouth. "Oh, that one is crazy all right, but he's not the one we need help with. And the problem won't affect just a family if it continues."

"It won't?" Dr. Freud asked.

"Well, when you think of family, think of everyone you've ever known," Evan offered. "Like the whole world family."

Deciding it was probably best to be direct, Sophia explained all about Subner. When she was done, Dr. Freud looked as bewildered as one of her patients in the waiting room. "So you want me to do mental counseling for Father Time's assistant?"

"Well, and he's also the Protector of Weapons, which is what we need him for," Sophia stated.

Evan shook his head and elbowed Sophia. "You just use people, don't you?"

"Okay, well, I guess this does seem important," Dr. Freud said. "I'm okay with the fact that you interrupted my entire day for this, and I'll agree to help."

"Just you wait until you hear how much we're going to interrupt your life," Evan said with a laugh.

CHAPTER FIFTY

"You want me to what?" Dr. Tiffannee Freud exclaimed, her eyes wide.

Telling the mortal that they needed their help to repair a schism in the personality of Father Time's assistant went over pretty smoothly. However, when Sophia informed her that she'd have to marry Evan to get to the place where Subner was located, all of a sudden she was in shock.

Glancing at her hand, Sophia sighed. "Oh, good, you're not already married."

"I can't marry him." She pointed at Evan. "I don't know him."

Evan nodded. "A traditionalist. I approve. But let me give you the quick lowdown. I'm a Taurus. I loathe long walks on the beach, sand always gets everywhere. My dragon's name is Coral and she won't like you—she doesn't like anyone. Well, except me and not all the time. I have a cyborg dog name NO10JO. He has to sleep in the bed, there's no negotiations on that one, sweetheart."

"I'm not sleeping in your bed," Dr. Freud stated.

"Of course not," Sophia assured. "I'd never expect you to do something so horrible."

"Hey now!" Evan complained. "This marriage thing is an honor."

"It's a technicality," Sophia corrected, and glanced at the doctor. "You can't enter Roya Lane unless you're married to someone from a magical race and unfortunately, Evan is the best I can do. But after you help Subner, then we'll annul the marriage and it will be like it never happened."

"Why didn't you spell me to marry him?" Dr. Freud asked.

Sophia nodded. This one was a critical thinker. "It wouldn't have worked. The marriage has to be entered into by both parties willingly, otherwise you can't enter Roya Lane. So if you're willing, then I can perform the ceremony here and we can be on our way. I don't want to take up any more of your time than we have to, especially after asking you to do something so awful."

"I'm standing right here!" Evan protested.

"You can perform the ceremony?" the doctor asked.

"Yes, I got ordained online right before this in preparation," Sophia stated.

Evan shook his head. "The modern world has abolished all that is holy."

"Oh, because you had strong feelings on this subject before, huh?" Sophia asked.

"I'm technically Catholic and should be married in a church by a—"

"A wedding and a funeral today," Sophia interrupted, pretending to be cheery. "What a momentous occasion."

"Fine," Evan acquiesced. "I'll get married in a psychiatrist office to a woman I hardly know, but this isn't exactly how I saw this day going."

"But you saw it going this way?" Sophia questioned.

"Well, I try and keep an open mind about these things," he spat.

Their banter seemed to be making Dr. Freud more comfortable, to Sophia's relief. She smiled at her. "So, what do you think? Can you please help us?"

Dr. Freud seemed to consider her options and then nodded. "Okay, well, this seems like a very worthy cause and it's not every day that I'm asked to help an important magical figure. I'll do it!"

"Good choice," Evan stated. "I'll make you the happiest wife for like a whole hour or two. Then I'm kicking you to the curb, darling. This man can't be tied down."

Sophia gave the doctor a bland look. "I know, you're shocked that he's still single, right?"

CHAPTER FIFTY-ONE

"Oh, good she didn't combust!" Evan exclaimed when Doctor Tiffannee Freud stepped through the portal onto Roya Lane.

She halted and gave Evan a horrified expression. "Was that the risk if it didn't work?"

He shrugged. "I don't think a mortal has survived it to tell the tale, so we have no clue."

This did little to make Dr. Freud appear at ease. Apparently she wasn't counting herself lucky that the whole thing worked and she was a rare mortal who got to stride down the magical road, lined with one-of-a-kind shops and filled with various magical races.

"I was confident there wouldn't be any issues." Sophia gave her a comforting smile.

The ceremony had taken less than a few minutes, no thanks to Evan wanting to recite his own vows which he obviously had written beforehand. They didn't relate to the psychiatrist at all since they often included phrases like brown or blonde hair or insert description here. Still, Sophia's online ordained status appeared to work and the two were in fact married. Evan had wanted to delay, saying that it wouldn't be real unless they had a quick honeymoon, but when it appeared to be a tossup over who would put him in a headlock first, Sophia or Tiffannee, he let the whole thing go.

The mortal was understandably overwhelmed when she strode down Roya Lane. It didn't help that the magical road seemed busier than usual, probably due to a crazy autumn sale that was going on across most of the shops.

The Rose Apothecary was having a buy-one-get-one-free sale on cauldrons, and Crying Cat Bakery was apparently giving away free samples.

"I want one!" Evan stated.

"Nothing in that store is free," Sophia warned. "It always comes with a price, whether you realize it or not."

"But we need a wedding cake," he argued.

"You need a padded cell," Sophia replied.

"I can arrange that," Dr. Freud nodded at the notion.

Sophia flashed her a smile, seeing that she was more at ease and joking about her new husband.

"It's this way." Sophia led them toward the Fantastical Armory. Once inside, they found Papa Creola and Subner standing in the middle of the shop, no doubt waiting on them.

"You're late," Papa Creola said in a punishing tone, his arms crossed on his chest and a scowl on his face.

Sophia glanced sideways at Evan. "I think we should have stopped off at the bakery at this point since I'm in trouble for an appointment time I didn't know about."

Evan strode past her and over to a case full of knives and axes. "Our tardiness is all Pink Princess's fault. She was lollygagging when I was trying to get the job that you assigned us done."

"The more you live, the less you die," Subner said in a mechanical voice.

"Oh, so he's moved onto Janis Joplin lines?"

"Yes, after he said every single one of Bob Marley's and ran out," Papa Creola droned on, his patience obviously at its lowest. "And I know that you all are late because of you, Evan."

"Hey, when in Louisiana one needs to get a beignet," Evan complained.

"Lead a life of greatness," Subner quoted.

"That's what I'm saying, my man!" Evan cheered, then leaned closer to the case and studied the various weapons. "How am I supposed to do that without stuffing a beignet in my face?"

"Sophia was under strict orders to be as efficient as possible—making quick work of her time," Papa Creola told Evan.

"I get it, but when in Rome… And we did what you asked." He held his arm out, presenting Dr. Tiffannee Freud.

"He gets that you weren't in Rome, right?" Papa Creola asked Sophia.

"I'm not certain he knows what year it is," Sophia joked.

"Why should I hold back now and sound mediocre just so I can sound mediocre twenty years from now?" Subner asked, a sincerely curious expression on his face like he was expecting one of them to answer him.

"Dude, I'd lay off the herbs, if you know what I mean," Evan imparted.

"My business is to enjoy and have fun and why not, if in the end everything will end, right?" Subner stated, quite seriously.

"Amen, my brother," Evan commented. "I can't argue with you there." He flashed a smile at Sophia. "Maybe this guy doesn't need to be fixed after all. I like his attitude."

"He needs to be fixed," Papa Creola insisted.

Sophia nodded. "And it's not his attitude. It's the words and thoughts of Janis Joplin."

"Being an intellectual creates a lot of questions and no answers," Subner mused.

Dr. Freud had simply been observing, not saying anything up until then. "This is very interesting. What a fascinating disorder."

"I'm one of those regular weird people," Subner said in an airy voice.

"Can you help him?" Sophia asked in a hopeful voice.

"It's hard to say," Tiffannee answered. "It might take some time."

"It will take roughly three days, eight hours and thirty five minutes," Papa Creola stated dryly.

"Roughly," Sophia joked with a laugh.

"You're the Father of Time?" Dr. Freud asked in amazement.

"Yes," he stated calmly. "And I'm not a patient man, so you should get started."

"Don't compromise yourself," Subner stated. "You are all you've got."

Dr. Freud nodded. "We will need a quiet place for me to start my full assessment."

"You can destroy your day now worrying about tomorrow," Subner imparted.

"You can use my office downstairs." Papa Creola ignored his assistant and gestured at the door at the back of the shop.

"Freedom's just another word for nothing left to lose," Subner stated dryly.

"That's right," the doctor said sensitively as she strode forward and led Subner toward the door to Papa Creola's office.

"I just want to feel as much as I can, it's what soul is all about," he said with a dreamy expression on his face as they walked away.

"I'm gonna miss that guy," Evan commented and pushed away from the glass counter.

"I'm not," Papa Creola stated. "And you should go ahead and get that." He pointed at Sophia's cloak.

She gave him a confused expression. "Get what?"

"Your phone," Papa Creola answered. "Hiker Wallace doesn't know how to message you so that it activates the volume on your phone when it's on silent."

"I'm surprised he knows how to send a message," Evan stated.

"He's coming along." Sophia retrieved the phone from her pocket. Then her eyes widened at the message from the leader of the Dragon Elite.

It read: Get back to the Gullington. We have an emergency.

153

CHAPTER FIFTY-TWO

"You're so lucky to have me as a friend," Evan remarked as he and Sophia hiked across the Expanse.

She sighed. "Although I'm certain that I'd disagree with you, why is it that you think that?"

"Because who else would marry someone for you?" he answered.

"Well, it's so we can fix the Protector of Weapons, so that he can outfit the Dragon Elite with a proper weapon to fight an unknown evil so that we don't die."

He shrugged. "I get that it's difficult for you to say thank you. You're welcome anyway."

Sophia hurried, worry buzzing in her chest over what could be wrong that Hiker pulled them both back to the Gullington. "I like to think that I have some pretty good friends who would marry a mortal to help out."

"Yeah, but will they also later help you hide the body?" Evan challenged.

She shook her head. "Why would you need to do that?"

"Well, because our romance maybe turned bad," Evan explained. "I mean, you saw that my wife strode off with another guy, right?"

"You mean Subner, who has lost his mind and is the reason that we recruited the doctor?"

"Don't make excuses for them," Evan stated.

"You're very strange."

"I'm a regular Casanova. When I love, I love deeply—passionately. That's why I'm such a good friend."

"You're the friend who fills me with multiple regrets," Sophia teased, grateful not to find the Castle on fire or any other noticeable dangers on the grounds of the Gullington.

She sped up, even more curious about what could be wrong if there wasn't a battle going on there. Sophia half-suspected that more strangers might have come through the portal from the Great Library.

She rushed up the steps to the Castle and burst through the door, expecting to find a commotion in the entry way. There wasn't. It was strangely quiet, but her enhanced senses told her that Hiker was in his office, thundering back and forth—worrying his way across the floors as he usually did when upset.

Sophia took the steps two at a time and did her best to keep up with Evan's long strides. He gave her a mischievous glare, and she knew it had suddenly become a race to the finish.

Increasing her speed even more, Sophia bolted forward, but was reminded that she wasn't playing with someone who fought fair. Evan pushed her into the railing at the landing to the stairs, took the lead, and rushed into Hiker's office.

She darted in behind him, but Evan was already lounging on the sofa with his legs propped up and lying in Mama Jamba's lap. She didn't appear to care or much notice as she sketched something on a pad of paper. Wilder and Mahkah were stationed behind the sofa, their hands pinned behind their backs and astute expressions on their faces.

"Gosh, Sophia," Evan complained. "Way to keep us waiting. I thought that our esteemed leader pressed the importance of this meeting."

"Sorry, sir," Sophia said to Hiker, and caught the look of stress on his face. "I got here as soon as I could."

He nodded. "Evan, is that powdered sugar on your armor?"

Evan glanced down at his shirt and rubbed the stain before licking his finger. "Cocaine, sir. I had to drag Sophia out of this drug house in Baton Rouge."

Hiker let out a breath, and to Sophia's surprise nodded. "As long as you weren't dawdling at a pastry shop again."

"Sir, I would never." Evan put his hand to his chest and looked offended. "I didn't get a wedding cake after getting married although Sophia kept begging for us to stop." He glanced back at Wilder. "This one and her sweets. Good thing she's a magician or you'd have to buy her two airplane seats."

"Can we focus?" Hiker growled.

Evan nodded. "Of course, sir. I'm sorry that Sophia keeps derailing this meeting."

She rolled her eyes and focused on Hiker. "What is it, sir? Is everything okay?"

"Yeah, Pink Princess," Evan remarked. "Hiker always sends messages saying that there's an emergency when everything is all right."

"I've become aware of a serious danger," Hiker began. "And defeating them will require all your efforts."

CHAPTER FIFTY-THREE

"A serious danger?" Evan sat up. "I'm not sure about my participation, sir. I'm a married man now and need to think about my wife."

"There are other dangers lurking very close," Wilder said, a mock menace in his voice.

"Don't throw your empty threats at me," Evan spat. "What if something happened to me? How would my wife deal?"

"Probably with a party," Wilder replied.

Hiker didn't appear too keen to cut off the banter, having halted his pacing in front of the Elite Globe. When he was quiet for a long moment and the guys had stopped teasing each other briefly, Sophia dared to try and get the leader of the Dragon Elite's attention.

"Sir," she began, "When you're ready, will you please elaborate on what we'll be facing? Or is this the unknown evil that we don't know anything about?"

He spun around. "No, I don't believe it's that. For one, the armor isn't ready, right?"

"No, I think it will be a while for that much armor," Sophia answered.

Hiker nodded. "That's what I thought. And you all also don't have the weapon you'll need from Subner."

"It will be at least three days for that," Sophia imparted.

"And eight hours and thirty five minutes, if you were listening to Father Time, like me," Evan teased.

Hiker ignored the quip. "I don't think that this evil will present itself until you have what you need for the battle. Too many powerful and all-knowing entities have presided over the events for it to come up before you're ready."

"But being prepared won't guarantee success," Mama Jamba advised, continuing to sketch out something on the pad of paper.

"Obviously." Hiker ran his hands through his hair. "Mama, what can you offer on these strange monsters who have sprung up in the Mediterranean Sea?"

"They aren't my creations," she stated, seeming to be shading her drawing with the side of a pencil.

"No, they're definitely magical creatures," Hiker grumbled.

"I'm a magical creature and you created me," Evan argued.

"You're an anomaly that Mama Jamba found in the proverbial dumpster in the alleyway of the Earth," Wilder joked.

Evan rolled his eyes. "This planet doesn't have a back alley."

"That's what you're choosing to argue with out of what I said?" Wilder asked.

Evan sat up and pulled his legs off Mama Jamba. "I'm a mature married man now. I don't have time for your games and antics anymore. You'd know what I mean if you made Sophia an honest woman."

"No one else is getting married," Hiker ordered.

"Not your call, son," Mama Jamba sang.

"Anyway, as I was saying," Hiker continued, "there's a danger in the Mediterranean sea off the coast of Turkey. It's already taken down a ship and a plane in that area, and I fear more mortals will be threatened unless we intervene soon."

"What kind of monster are we facing, sir?" Mahkah asked, his chin held high and his eyes focused.

"Monsters," Hiker corrected. "No one knows where they came from, but there's suddenly two monsters creating havoc in the sea. One is in the water and is known as a leviathan—"

"Nasty little creatures." Mama Jamba clicked her tongue and shook her head.

"Little isn't a word I've ever heard to describe a leviathan," Hiker stated.

"What exactly is a leviathan?" Evan asked and then quickly added. "I mean, I know, of course. But from the dazed look on Wilder's face, I'm guessing he needs an education on the subject."

Wilder laughed. "Leviathan is a sea serpent of sorts, closely related to that monster that lives in the Pond. I had the pleasure of being real up close and personal with it before."

Hiker nodded. "That's correct. This leviathan is reportedly much larger than any other sighted. It is apparently bigger than Lunis at his largest at this point."

Lunis was the largest dragon at the Gullington when he did his supersized stunt, but that was usually only during a full moon. Otherwise it was very draining for him and not worth the risk.

"Wow, we're going to have fun putting this beast into submission," Evan said with an excited laugh.

"That's what your wife said," Wilder teased.

"It will be a handful, I assure you," Hiker stated. "And one leviathan would be enough to keep you all busy. However, there's another monster in the sky that will also pose a real challenge."

"A pesky little thing," Mama Jamba said, then started humming.

"Again, little isn't an accurate description," Hiker stated.

"I like that you use terms like pesky to describe these monsters who could end us, Mama Jamba." Wilder smiled down at the small woman.

"Well, those birds are a real nuisance," Mother Nature related. "They've been impersonating my beloved phoenix for ages, although they have all the flair and none of the benevolence, if you ask me."

"We're not, unless you're giving us a shortcut and telling us how to end them quickly," Hiker said dryly.

"I'd recommend a giant sling shot," Mama Jamba offered.

"Oh shucks." Wilder chuckled. "I left my slingshot in my tree house."

"Poor planning on your part, bro," Evan stated.

"So what exactly is this bird we're facing?" Sophia asked.

"It's called a simurgh," Hiker stated.

"Easy for you to say." Evan laughed. "Why can't these monsters have easy names like Zot or Zart or Zap."

"Those are easy names for you, huh?" Wilder asked. "Do you prefer things that start with a z?"

"I prefer when you're quiet," Evan stated.

"The simurgh appeared at exactly the same time as the leviathan," Hiker informed them. "No one knows where they came from, and they're relying on us to get rid of them. We're the only ones in the position to take them down."

"We can do it, sir," Mahkah said with confidence.

"I hope you're right," Hiker stated in a heavy tone. "Because if those things are left unchecked much longer, then many lives will be in danger."

CHAPTER FIFTY-FOUR

"Do you think she misses me?" Evan asked over the comm they all wore to communicate from their dragons.

"Who?" Wilder's voice asked in her ear.

"My wife," Evan answered as they rode on their dragons in formation over the sparkling blue waters of the Mediterranean Sea—Sophia in the front and Mahkah in the rear.

"What's her name again?" Wilder asked.

"Something, something Freud," Evan answered.

"Sounds like true love." Wilder laughed.

"Doctor Tiffannee Freud," Sophia stated. "And it's Tiffannee with two f's, two n's, and two e's."

"She sounds annoying," Wilder said. "But she's married to Evan so it must run in the family."

Sophia studied the area around them from Lunis' back, looking for signs of the leviathan in the waters below. Mahkah's job was to look for the simurgh in the skies. The other guys were to keep their eyes focused ahead for other potential dangers. They knew there were two monsters, but that didn't mean there weren't more.

It wasn't lost on Sophia that these two dangerous creatures had materialized in the same spot at the same time. There had to be someone behind this. Maybe someone who wanted to create havoc and harm many. Maybe someone who knew the Dragon Elite would come to the rescue and want to take them down. Definitely someone evil was behind this. But they'd have to research that more later. Right now the biggest concern was stopping the beasts before they did any more harm.

In the distance, Sophia spotted some of the damage created by the leviathan. A ship was overturned, debris from it floating in the choppy waters.

It was hard to discern what belonged to the small vessel and to a single engine plane that the simurgh had taken down. The pair had worked fast, clearing the waters and skies in the coastal region off Turkey.

What's the strategy once we find the monsters? Lunis asked in her head.

Survive and kill them, Sophia stated with confidence.

Wow, the amount of details you've put into the plan is simply overwhelming, Lunis joked.

Sophia didn't usually go straight to the idea of killing, but Hiker had been very clear about his orders. There was no negotiating with these monsters. Taming a leviathan was out of the question. And persuading a simurgh to move on when it had made claim to an area had never happened. Once the two set down anchors, so to speak, they simply expanded their territory until they'd wiped out resources, buildings, and landscapes and of course, slaughtered people and other animals.

Do you have any bright ideas? Sophia asked her dragon as they veered through the sky and the wind rushed through her hair.

I have a ton of them, Lunis stated.

Feeling a renewed sense of hope, Sophia tightened her grip on the reins. *Oh, do tell then? How do you propose we take out these monsters?*

Oh, you wanted bright ideas related to the leviathan and simurgh? Lunis asked. *You should have been more specific. I thought you meant in general. 'Cause I'm working on all these new business ideas, like a prescription windshield for those who always forget their glasses but need to drive.*

That's the worst idea I've ever heard, Sophia stated.

All great truths begin as blasphemy, Lunis retorted.

Please don't start speaking in quotes. Sophia thought it would be weird if her dragon quoted George Bernard Shaw all the time. Well, weirder.

My point is that the best inventions were originally thought to be insane, Lunis said. *I'm like Google or Facebook or Crocs before they were big.*

Crocs are still the worst invention ever, Sophia imparted. *Like, no one looks good in those ever.*

What about Wilder? Lunis questioned.

He's different, Sophia argued. *He looks good no matter what.*

It had been quiet in Sophia's head for a while when Mahkah's voice echoed in her ears. "It's time for us to break formation."

"I believe that's supposed to be Pink Princess's order to make," Evan argued. "She's the power-hungry one who is to boss us around, according to Hiker."

"Okay, then so be it," Mahkah said good-naturedly. "I've spotted the simurgh, and it's directly above us behind a large cloud."

Sophia's head jerked up. The sunlight overhead nearly blinded her for a moment. "Let's break formation. That's an order."

CHAPTER FIFTY-FIVE

I f Sophia didn't know what she was looking for, she wouldn't have seen the simurgh lurking behind a large, puffy white cloud. Its orange feathers blended in with the sunlight that radiated overhead, making it look like part of the afternoon sky.

As they had planned, Wilder and Evan split off from the group on their dragons and streaked in opposite directions. Mahkah held the position below the simurgh, and Sophia and Lunis rode farther away to get some distance.

When she turned, Sophia got a real glimpse of the giant bird. If she didn't know how deadly the creature was, she would have taken a moment to be in awe of its beauty. The bird resembled the fiery-looking phoenix, although it was much, much larger—about the size of a small plane. It had long wings covered in shimmering orange feathers, a white mohawk on its head, and a long tail that streaked through the air like a kite in the wind.

"Maybe it hasn't seen us yet and we can still have the element of surprise," Evan stated over the comm.

The simurgh opened its beak, and a sound that was half way between a murderous scream and a melodic melody ripped from the monster's mouth. Then it shot its head down and stared straight at Sophia, its eyes black and an unmistakable sinister glint in its gaze.

"I think that ship has sailed and the big bird knows we're here," Wilder remarked as he spiraled through the air on Simi, making quick progress.

To Sophia's horror, Howard had a human-like face with cheekbones and slanted large eyes and a chin.

Howard? Really? Lunis questioned. *I think he looks more like a Jeffrey.*

We're going with Howard, Sophia stated as the large bird dove straight in her direction while barely moving its wings. It simply pointed its head downward and shot in their direction with its orange wings spread wide on either side of it.

Lunis sprang into action by diving low as well and speeding toward the shore some miles away. They didn't want to lead Howard toward the others. However, plans quickly changed as the leviathan surfaced, sprang straight up into the air from the Mediterranean Sea, and created a wall right in front of them.

CHAPTER FIFTY-SIX

"Watch out!" Wilder called in Sophia's ears.

"I see it," she replied, suddenly breathless as she and Lunis lost altitude, her ears popping.

"How could you not see it?" Evan replied. "That thing is massive."

Sophia didn't have much of an opportunity to take in the leviathan's size as she attempted to get out of its path. The thing was like a skyscraper that sprang up from the waters and towered above them. Water sprayed out from every direction, and the sea below was dark and suddenly churning violently.

Lunis acted fast and veered in multiple directions, increasing his speed to get out of the sea monster's path. Like Howard, the creature let out a battle cry—this one sounded like a dragon's roar if they were choking on water at the same time.

Water sprang up, blasting with a dangerous force that Sophia knew would blow them off course if they were hit. Thankfully, Lunis weaved around the geysers and narrowly got them a safe distance away from the leviathan before turning around.

That's when they both took in the sea monster's size. Of all the things the pair had seen, the leviathan was by far the most horrifying.

CHAPTER FIFTY-SEVEN

"Holy hell!" Evan exclaimed in Sophia's ears. "Hello Satan, how are you today?"

Sophia bit her tongue, her eyes wide as she took in the massive form. It was the size of a skyscraper, both in width and height. The monster waved in the air as if deciding whether to topple over, and displaced a huge chunk of the sea.

Carl, as Sophia had instantly nicknamed him, was easily the width of a city block and at least twenty stories tall. Long spikes covered various parts of its body and tentacle-like appendages stretched up from its thick midsection, slapping the water like whips.

The monster had a long snout like an alligator and multiple rows of tiny sharp teeth. Its glowing red eyes seemed too small for its head, but still had the ability to evoke fear in Sophia as Carl whipped its head around and stared straight at her and Lunis.

Do you know what worries me about Carl? Lunis asked in Sophia's head.

Besides the obvious fact that it could swallow us whole with very little effort? She asked as her dragon flapped his wings and kept them hovering in place. The leviathan was also simply hovering, seeming to consider its next move.

Overhead, Sophia only caught partial sight of Howard streaking through the air followed by shades of purple, white and brown as the other riders and their dragons "managed" the beast. She was aware of the guy's voices in her ears, but ignored them—focusing most of her attention on the leviathan in front of her.

It appeared that Carl was all hers at this point. *A real David and Goliath story,* she thought.

What worries me is what we can't see, Lunis continued, referring to Carl.

You mean like what's under the water?

Yeah, like a swan, Lunis answered. *You see this elegant bird on top of the water all floating along, but under the surface of the water, its legs are working like mad to propel it along.*

I'm not sure that relating Carl to a pretty little swan gliding along is the right reference. Sophia was having a staring contest with the leviathan. It wasn't splattering the top of the sea with its long snake-like tentacles anymore. Instead they wiggled in the air as the monster swayed, its mouth open wide—a black cavernous space as big as a truck.

My point is that I wonder what's below the water.

I'm guessing fins and a tail and other things that keep it afloat, Sophia stated. *Why does it matter?*

Because there isn't much in the collective consciousness of the dragon ancestors about leviathans, but there is something, Lunis explained.

Sophia tensed and prepared herself for bad news based on the tone in his voice. *And that would be?*

A leviathan's weak spot is on the middle section of their body, which based on my estimates, is under the water's surface.

CHAPTER FIFTY-EIGHT

hy isn't she moving? Wilder thought erratically, constantly
W looking over his shoulder to spy on Sophia far below them.
Focus, Simi encouraged in his head. *She'll be fine.*
Or she won't, he argued. *She's facing a large sea monster...by herself.*
It hadn't been planned that Sophia would face the leviathan on her
own. However, as things often happen in battle, the plans had
instantly changed. Originally, they'd planned that Wilder and Mahkah
would battle the simurgh and Evan and Sophia would take care of the
leviathan. Now judging by the beasts' size, it seemed like a joke for all
four of them to handle it and ironically it was only Sophia.

But Evan hadn't been given a break since the simurgh spied him
after Sophia raced off, trying to flee the leviathan. Now the large bird
was hot on his and Coral's trail, not granting them a moment of relief.
It made the most sense for Evan to help with the sea monster since
Coral's element was water and Lunis' was the moon which controlled
the tides.

As much as Wilder wanted to spring away and help Sophia, he
knew that he and Mahkah had the best chances of defeating the
simurgh. Simi's element was the wind, which would hopefully give
them the advantage they needed over the murderous bird. Mahkah's

and Tala's was the Earth, but his special contribution was that no one understood animals that had flight better than the Native American. It was best if Wilder and Mahkah kept their focus on the simurgh, but what they had to do first was give Evan a way of escaping the chase.

Pressing his heels into Simi, Wilder leaned low.

Let's try something unorthodox, he growled.

What's that? Simi asked.

Let's take the danger off Evan and put it on us.

CHAPTER FIFTY-NINE

The very best thing about Evan McIntosh was his lack of fear in the face of danger.

The very worst thing about Evan McIntosh was his total lack of fear when in the face of danger.

This quality of his had gotten him into his fair share of trouble and had also been the reason for many of his successes, which benefited the world at large.

When Evan had seen the simurgh dart after Sophia and also the leviathan rise from the Mediterranean sea before anyone else, he'd made an impromptu decision to serve as a distraction to get the giant bird's attention off Sophia. If he hadn't, then Sophia would have been stuck when the sea creature sprang from the waters.

But thanks to Evan's quick thinking and bravery, Sophia was safe once more. He made a note to remind her of it later, and often after that.

However, the flaw in that plan was that now Evan had the simurgh hot on his ass with no hint of letting up.

Evan streaked through the air atop Coral, flipped head forward like a swimmer changing directions in the pool, then raced the opposite way. The ocean below them was feeding Coral's speed, but where her advantages came into play was in the actual water, where Evan was supposed to be saving Sophia's butt.

The simurgh screeched like a scorned girl caught in yet another compromising position.

"I'm a married man!" Evan exclaimed over his shoulder. "Get off my butt, or my wife will tear you in two."

This did little good to dissuade the possessive succubus, but it made Evan feel marginally better as he felt the hot breath of the large bird as it called after him, sniping dangerously close to Coral's tail. She snapped it through the air, trying to send the spikes at the end onto the simurgh's head. However, the monster was surprisingly agile for its size and swerved to the left and right, avoiding the attacks.

Evan knew that Coral was running out of steam. They'd been at this for a while now at top speed—even with the ocean aiding her, a dragon wasn't good at long-term sprints. They were known for their endurance in long races or short spurts, but a constant chase would end a dragon sooner than almost anything else.

From the corner of his vision, Evan saw Mahkah with his bow and arrow, trying to get a shot at the large target but apparently afraid that it would hit the dragon and rider. Mahkah was always careful, unwilling to shoot if he might hurt one of his mates. Evan usually liked that about the guy but with the simurgh breathing down his neck, he was grateful for his other, bolder friend.

To Evan's surprise and relief, none other than Wilder Thomson barreled in the simurgh's direction with his sword above his head and a crazed look in his eyes, making a beeline straight for the monster. It didn't take such a suicidal attempt seriously, and continued to race after Evan until it realized that Wilder wasn't going to divert from his path.

The crazy maniac planned to collide with the simurgh, since apparently that's what it would take to get it off Evan and Coral.

CHAPTER SIXTY

Mahkah Tomahawk knew that his friends were bold. Whereas he was patient and careful in battle, Evan and Wilder usually employed more of a surprise attack approach. Sophia often relied on something in between, using strategy along with something the enemy didn't expect. Their different styles in battle had played well for them, but this was the first time that Mahkah worried they simply didn't have what it would take to defeat not one, but two deadly and dangerous enemies.

The eldest dragonrider sat atop Tala, the dragon impressively still as he hovered in the air, so as to not mess up Mahkah's aim. However, no matter how still his dragon was or calm the air around them, it seemed impossible for him to get a good shot with the speed at which the simurgh flew as it darted after Evan.

Mahkah closed one eye and followed the simurgh's path, nearly getting dizzy from its speed. The arrow that he had nocked was enchanted, but still the dragonrider worried that it wouldn't be enough to penetrate through the simurgh's feathers. The creature most likely had a protective quality shielding it. There wasn't much known about the birds.

Centuries ago, they were much more prevalent, especially in the savannah where they had apparently been seen carrying off elephants to feast upon. That had been hard for Mahkah to imagine, but now studying the creature, he could totally see how that was possible.

Although much of the folklore that surrounded the simurgh saw the creatures as benevolent, Mahkah knew that the modern incarnations of the birds were anything but. Many times the animals of the old world were enhanced using magic until they became corrupted and possessed by evil. That was the problem with too much magic. Everything was about balance. The original simurgh might have been a blessing to many lands, and left alone, they brought many fortunes. Then a magician came along, thinking they could make these animals better, but more wasn't usually better—it was dangerous, and this was proof of that.

Mahkah sucked in a low breath. When Evan had some distance on the simurgh, he released the arrow. It spiraled through the air and crossed the simurgh's path a good distance after it passed. He wasn't close to hitting the creature, and Evan was slowing down. Which meant they were running out of options.

He pulled another arrow from his quiver and nocked it, again following the monster's path. He hadn't wanted to call it that before, feeling that was too strong a term for something like this. But he had to admit that it was exactly what the simurgh was. It might have once been good and represented good, however this monster was anything but.

This simurgh was full of evil and it was the Dragon Elite's job to take it down—hopefully before it ended them all.

CHAPTER SIXTY-ONE

How are we going to get to Carl's underside? Sophia asked, the first bit of fear entering her voice.

Maybe we can get it to play fetch and roll over, Lunis joked.

Usually Sophia found relief when her dragon made jokes in battle, but staring at a creature a hundred times bigger than them made the quip seem untimely.

Seriously, Lunis, we don't have a plan.

We never have a plan for the most part and we're still alive, he argued.

That's not making me feel much better since this battle could be our last. Sophia dared to look up at where the guys were intercepting attacks from the simurgh. The large bird appeared to be schooling all three dragonriders in stealthy attacks as it streaked through the air, sent Evan on a chase, gave Mahkah no chance of shooting it and—

"Wilder!" Sophia exclaimed as she watched her boyfriend and Simi race straight for the large bird. It didn't seem to notice their approach, the beast's attention on Evan who was no doubt taunting it into following him.

He'll be okay, Lunis lied.

They both knew that there was little chance that any of them would be okay after this battle. There would be scars if any of them survived it.

We have to help them, she argued and felt Lunis' fire suddenly warm underneath her.

We have our own problems, he stated, his voice tense.

She whipped around. The leviathan had decided to make its move. Or rather, moves.

It bolted forward, and its mouth widened as it roared. The creature blew sea water and monster saliva straight at them, which created a tropical storm of sorts.

Sophia's hair blew violently around her face from the attack. The wind that spilled from the monster's lungs pushed Lunis back. The waters soared in high waves that licked at the dragon's belly. Then the beast's tentacles slapped the water and turned the once somewhat calm scene into total chaos.

The standoff was over. It was time to fight.

CHAPTER SIXTY-TWO

If Wilder survived this and saved Evan, then he was going to regret it. There was no way that the younger dragonrider would ever shut up about it. For the rest of their hopefully long lives, he'd hold it over his head that he'd risked his life to save him. But there were some things worth enduring, and Wilder reasoned that he'd like the bragging rights of saying he was the one who defeated the giant bird— although it would undoubtedly have to be a team effort.

The simurgh hadn't turned when Wilder barreled in the bird's direction on Simi. That must have been how much the creature detested Evan's presence. It simply took over all else and made the beast want to end him first.

I get it, Wilder thought with a laugh.

Simi's wings flapped furiously as she cut through the cold winds and made quick progress. They were only thirty yards away when the monster turned its attention to Wilder. Its black eyes widened at the oncoming attack. Most must not have been so bold as to race straight at something so large and menacing. Wilder usually had better sense, but desperate times apparently called him to do dumb things. He wondered then if Evan thought he was in perpetual desperate times and that was his excuse for all his bad decisions.

The strategy had worked, Wilder realized with both relief and total horror. The simurgh had abandoned its pursuit of Evan and turned and hovered in the air, its attention solely on Wilder.

With the bird finally still, Mahkah took his opportunity and fired several arrows. They all rebounded off the simurgh's feathers, which were obviously protected by strange magic.

"Thanks for that, mate," Evan stated with relief as Coral halted in the air, probably to draw on her reserves. "I'm gonna dart down to Cyprus and get a drink. There's a great bar there I found on my last visit."

"Go help Sophia!" Wilder exclaimed while watching the beasty bird facing him. It moved methodically, but he knew that was about to change dramatically when the monster took off after him. Unlike Evan, Wilder had no intention of playing a game of chase with the creature. The only way to end things was with direct combat.

"Sophia?" Evan asked breathlessly over the comm.

"Evan!" Wilder yelled, suddenly feeling frantic with worry.

"Oh, the one about to get eaten by the sea monster," Evan said in a rush. "Why didn't you say so?"

Wilder noticed three things simultaneously. Evan darted into action as Coral plummeted toward the ocean where the leviathan was throwing an awful fit. Mahkah nocked another arrow on his bow. The simurgh shot forward and raced at Wilder as he and Simi closed the distance between it.

CHAPTER SIXTY-THREE

T he relief of not having to dart away from the pursuits of a crazed lunatic bird was instant for Evan. Then it was followed by total terror as he realized he was racing toward a huge angry sea serpent that was thrashing around in the ocean and making it their bitch.

Salt water sprang up from the Mediterranean and made it seem like they were in a hurricane of sorts. But around the chaos, the coastal area was clear. They were in the storm. The monster was the eye of it.

"Don't worry, Pink Princess," Evan called over the comm. "I'm coming to the rescue."

"Thanks, but I think worry is still going to be a part of the equation," Sophia stated, breathless as she and Lunis darted around the many attacks unleashed by the leviathan as its tentacles whipped through the air. They were doing a surprisingly good job of avoiding getting hit, although like Evan trying to evade the simurgh, it was impossible to keep it up for too much longer.

And the leviathan had surprising speed for being so large. The ends of its tentacles were tiny, like ropes, but grew in width closer to its body and created quite the effect on the water's surface.

As Evan approached, the monster caught sight of him and twisted in the air. Its mouth chopped at them, looking for a little appetizer, which was exactly what Coral and Evan would be for the gigantic monster.

"I'm glad you're here." Sophia and Lunis rode to the creature's backside.

"I'm married," Evan said dryly, always able to keep up the pretense, even in battle.

She sighed, but still laughed over the comm. "We know how we need to defeat this monster."

"Cool, then I'll just pop off to Cyprus, which isn't far from here," Evan replied, still racing toward the scene of chaos. "Awesome tiki bar, and I once met a waitress there who—"

"You're going to have to do it," Sophia interrupted.

Because no one ever taught her manners, Evan thought. "Continue."

"We'll serve as the distraction," Sophia stated with authority. "You need to get to Carl's underside."

"Carl?"

"This monster with a bad temper," she explained.

"Oh, he's a total Carl." Evan laughed. "And this underside?"

"According to Lunis, it's underwater," Sophia stated. "He's not sure what you're looking for, but you'll know it when you see it. Or more likely, Coral will."

"Oh good, so you can't offer many specifics." Evan swerved to the side as a tentacle tried to shake his hand—and by hand, he meant his face—right off.

"Can you do it?" Sophia asked, hope in her voice.

"Distract Carl," Evan ordered. "I'll go swimming with the fish."

CHAPTER SIXTY-FOUR

Shooting at the simurgh hadn't worked, Mahkah realized with a rush of disappointment. He had suspected as much, but had held out hope.

The dragonrider wasn't out of options though. In battle, it was a series of eliminations. When one attack didn't work, the warrior had to be agile enough to change their approach and hope that time was on their side.

For Mahkah, time was running out.

For Wilder, time was speeding by him.

Racing away from the simurgh's pursuit had been Evan's attempt to stay alive. Shooting at the monster from a distance was another option. There were a few other attacks that Mahkah was considering. Racing straight at the giant simurgh hadn't been one of them.

The creature was massive and although Simi was a good-sized dragon, as she approached, she looked more and more like a small bird racing toward the zeppelin that had attacked the Gullington under Trin's command. That airship had been huge. The dragons had kept their distance from it and shot fire from afar. Wilder had thrown all those cautious measures away and was now dangerously close to colliding with the gigantic bird.

Mahkah almost wanted to shut his eyes and not witness what would happen next. He was powerless to help as Wilder neared the simurgh. Even if he enchanted the arrows, he couldn't fire an attack with his friend so close to the bird. All Mahkah could do was watch. And watch he did, knowing that when the time presented itself...if it did, he would swoop in and help, hopefully before his friend got himself killed.

CHAPTER SIXTY-FIVE

Having Carl's attention momentarily distracted by Evan and Coral racing in its direction was a welcome relief after having to dodge its many attacks. The splattering seawater and roar of the monster was enough to contend with, but having to dart away from its tentacles and snapping jaws made everything a lot more intense.

However, Sophia recognized that they would have to act fast because the monster wouldn't be distracted for long. This gave Sophia and Lunis enough time to get to the backside of the beast and plan a distraction, which hopefully worked to allow Evan the opportunity he needed to get into place...whenever that was.

Lunis hadn't been able to offer more on Carl's vulnerable side—only that it was underwater. That, and as much of the leviathan as they saw above the surface, more stretched under the sea.

Sophia didn't know what kind of magic had created this beast, but she didn't think the world would miss something so large and destructive. More perplexing was the question of where the monster came from. Hiding something this large or manifesting it would be complex. The leviathan's presence brought up a lot more questions than it answered. But those would all have to wait.

"Anytime you're ready, Pink Princess," Evan called. A rush of wind and splattering rain echoed in the comm.

"I'm almost in place." She steered Lunis around the monster's backside, which was expansive. There were spikes and more tentacles on the back, like the creature preferred a multi-pronged approach.

Thankfully, Carl didn't have eyes in the back of its head and the tentacles moved with less precision, more like flags in the wind than enacting actual attacks. This gave Sophia and Lunis a chance to get into position, hovering in a place at the monster's back that was less covered in thick spikes and appeared somewhat vulnerable.

"We're ready," Sophia announced over the comm.

"About time," Evan huffed. "And thanks. Once we take the plunge, communications will end."

"Then stay safe and be fast," Sophia responded with a strange fondness in her voice.

"You got it boss," Evan chirped.

"And also," Sophia added. "Don't die."

"Roger that."

CHAPTER SIXTY-SIX

W ilder had done a lot of crazy things in his two hundred years. Most of them didn't matter because if something happened to him, he didn't much care. But recently, things mattered more. His life meant more than it used to.

The Dragon Elite had a purpose after several centuries of being stagnant. Wilder had the chance to save the world again and again for many years to come. More importantly than that, he had someone worth saving the world for. Even better, Sophia Beaufont didn't need Wilder to save the world for her. In most cases, she would be right by his side and saving it with him.

It was that reason that made Wilder momentarily doubt his rash decision to race toward the giant bird and make himself more vulnerable than ever before.

He felt Simi doubting his decision as well as they approached the monster, which opened its beak and screamed across the lone ten yards that divided them. The simurgh extended its talons as it righted itself in the air, its large wings flapping in the wind.

Wilder smiled despite the rush of adrenaline seeking to steal his breath. *We're not out of options,* he said to Simi in his head.

He gathered his strength and lifted his hand into the air, although the force rushing at him would usually have required both hands for balance. He'd sheathed his sword, but only for the moment. There would be a time for that—if the next part didn't kill him.

Wilder sent out a shockwave of wind, and forced all his gathered energy combined with Simi's elemental power at the simurgh. The gust hit the bird like a wall and made it tumble backward into a series of flips. Its neck jerked back at an odd angle and the creature lost height as it shrieked with real pain in its voice.

Wilder would have felt bad for the monster if he hadn't witnessed how cruel it could be if left unchecked. It was better for the world if they rid the Earth and its peaceful skies of such an unreasonable beast.

The gust of wind sent the simurgh back several dozen yards, but it recovered too quickly, then flapped its wings and rose level with Wilder once more. Although its feathers were disheveled and its eyes flustered, the monster wasn't harmed. It only appeared angrier, which would make the next part more interesting.

Wilder had played his card. Now he couldn't rely on his elemental power. It was time for brute force.

CHAPTER SIXTY-SEVEN

The blast of fire when Lunis opened his mouth radiated off the leviathan, and cast its back in a glow of sparks and flames. The beast screamed its protests, and its head shot up toward the heavens.

Evan knew that he couldn't wait around to see what happened next. This was his and Coral's opportunity to end things, and hopefully on their terms.

He whipped his axe out of his sheath and sucked in a gulp of air. With Coral's elemental magic, he could last underwater longer than most. They had enhanced strength and speed in the waters, much like the sea monster. But the sea they were entering was unlike any other.

Evan had no idea what they'd find in the Mediterranean waters. The dangers would no doubt be vast. Whatever happened had to be fast because it was unlikely that Sophia could distract Carl for long.

The beast wasn't looking, its attention stolen by the attack on its back. This was their chance to end things on their terms. Hopefully they killed the monster before it ended them, and went on to destroy the world.

Evan held his breath before Coral plunged into the undulant waters of the sea.

CHAPTER SIXTY-EIGHT

What happened next between Wilder and the simurgh wasn't what Mahkah had expected to witness. He'd expected his fellow dragonrider to use his elemental wind magic to weaken the monster. He thought the attack would be devastating for a creature who relied on the wind. However, he didn't think the giant bird would recover so fast.

Not only that, the animal looked enlivened by the attack, like it was what it needed to feel charged about killing the dragonriders.

Wilder didn't appear deterred though, to Mahkah's surprise. When the beast sped forward, Wilder and Simi did too, flying toward the open talons of the simurgh as it let out a piercing call.

Mahkah never believed in anyone like he did his friends in the Dragon Elite. They were his whole life now, and he didn't want it any other way. However, he knew acutely that they were all in danger of extinction. One false move, and these beasts would swallow them whole with little effort.

Whoever had unleashed these monsters on the Earth wanted one thing, and it was very clear at that moment—the destruction of the Dragon Elite. They were the only ones in a position to take down forces like these. The Warriors for the House of Fourteen wouldn't stand a chance, as powerful as they were. A magitech army wouldn't survive very long. No, the only way to take down a simurgh and a leviathan like this in close proximity was with the chi of the dragons.

However, that was still asking a lot. That's why Mahkah started the work on his spell, enchanting the arrow he had nocked into the bow. Wilder didn't have long once he collided with the simurgh. After that, none of them would have long.

The seconds were counting down for the Dragon Elite.

It was do or die.

CHAPTER SIXTY-NINE

Planning the distraction had been easy for Sophia and Lunis. Maintaining it had been exponentially more dangerous.

As soon as Lunis fired on the leviathan, it spiraled around and sent attacks at them. All its tentacles whipped in their direction, which made Lunis have to stop firing on the beast. However, Sophia had quickly spied that it had given Evan the chance to slip into the waters around Carl. All they had to do at this point was maintain the distraction, which pretty much meant darting around and avoiding near death.

Unsurprisingly, the monster didn't like fire. It appeared to like Sophia and Lunis even less, and swatted at them like they were pesky houseflies instead of a regal dragon and rider streaking through the air in front of its face.

Taunting the beast seemed like the best way to keep its attention off the fact that Evan was swimming somewhere underneath it.

Sophia desperately hoped that Evan was quick with whatever he had to do. However, communicating with him wasn't an option anymore. The dragons could technically communicate amongst themselves and therefore with their riders. However, this required energy that none of them wanted to expend in battle. That's why they'd instituted comms.

Too many times, Lunis had nearly been swatted across the seas. Sophia held her breath when the beast swung to the side and used its head, the largest target, to try and take them out. Lunis had to dive and roll across the surface of the roiling seas to avoid being assaulted.

Sophia swallowed a ton of water as she clung on for dear life, afraid of getting sucked into the turbulence. Thankfully, Lunis sprang straight back into the air, moving faster than the large monster who seemed to be losing steam.

Her chest burned as she coughed up the saltwater in her lungs and tried to suck in a breath. She thought she'd double over and fall off Lunis as he soared higher into the air. However, Carl stole her attention by glancing down with alarm at the waters around him. He knew that Evan was under there. That wouldn't do.

We've got to distract him, Sophia said in Lunis' head.

I'm on it. The undeterred dragon sped in the direction of a tentacle that was stuck straight into the air, obviously frozen from speculation as the leviathan tried to determine what was happening underneath him.

Good thing I forgot to eat earlier. Lunis opened his mouth wide. *Also thankfully, I'm in the mood for seafood.*

Sophia shook her head and watched as her dragon brazenly streaked by the tentacle that could whip to the side at any second and take them both out. She held her breath and prayed to the angels as Lunis took a bite out of the appendage and made Carl howl with sudden pain.

Thankfully, the beast's attention was no longer on Evan under the water. Unthankfully, it was solely on Lunis and Sophia.

CHAPTER SEVENTY

Simi nearly halted in the air right before colliding with the simurgh. It was a surreal moment where time seemed to slow for Wilder. His life didn't flash before his eyes and he didn't pray, but he did suck in a breath and tighten his grip on the reins. There was nothing left to do at that point except to rely on his training. Thankfully for him, he had more than most since he'd spent a couple of centuries doing nothing else at the Gullington.

The air around the dragon and the simurgh stilled. The beast simply eyed him from a short distance away, a deadly expression in its soulless eyes. Nothing happened for a moment as the dragon and rider and beast faced off in the air, hovering only feet apart.

Then, as if magnetized to one another, Simi's claws gripped the simurgh's and the two were intertwined. Her tail wrapped around the bird's body and squeezed, but as large as she was, the dragon was so much smaller than the monster. Still the bird's eyes bulged when Simi attempted another squeeze.

Wilder held on for dear life, knowing that he was still steering. Simi's talons and tail might be wrapped around the monster, but her life was still in her rider's hands. What he did or thought next would keep her alive or end her very fast.

The trio spiraled through the air and quickly fell toward the ocean below with nothing to stop them as their wings flapped against one another in ongoing assaults.

They must have looked like a strange ball of white and gold in the air as they plummeted one over the other. The simurgh pecked at Simi and got in a few good attacks that pierced her dragonhide, but she wasn't deterred and held tightly to the monster's talons, which kept it from moving properly.

The rush of air and screams of the monster and roar of the dragon cut through Wilder's head, but he tried to maintain focus. This wasn't the way to end the beast. He knew that instinctively. They were outmatched. This was only a diversion. Another attempt to disarm the creature.

Everything in the magical world was about energy. Take down one defense and you leave an enemy vulnerable. He looked up to the skies where his friend would be watching and hoped that he'd bought Mahkah enough time.

It was all up to him now.

With a hard tug on the reins, Wilder told his dragon it was time to pull away. Simi responded instantly by unlocking from the simurgh and flying away at once, employing the last of their magic to make a quick getaway.

CHAPTER SEVENTY-ONE

T he water streaked by Evan and Coral as they plummeted into the cold sea. Water bubbles sped by Evan's face but he tried to see through them, not knowing what he was looking for.

According to Sophia and Lunis, there was a weak spot on the leviathan. He'd questioned Coral on this but she didn't have any more information from the collective consciousness of the dragons than that. There wasn't a lot known about these sea creatures, so they'd have to venture into the new and mysterious territory.

Evan liked that he might be one of the few to take down such a large beast. He couldn't wait to tell his wife the story. She would undoubtedly be impressed.

The monster was massive under the surface. It was surprising that there could be more of the creature under the sea than above it since it was so gigantic.

Someone needs to go on a diet, Evan thought, not earning a reaction from Coral. That was typical. Most dragons, excluding Lunis and some of the new generation, weren't prone to humor.

It was hard to tell the various parts of the sea monster until a tentacle nearly slammed him in the face. Then Evan started to make out parts of the beast. He wasn't sure what Sophia and Lunis were doing in the air, but it appeared to make the creature very angry based on the way it thrashed around.

If Evan had the comm to communicate with, he would have told Sophia to read the monster a bedtime story. Instead, it appeared that she was sticking it with needles, irritating it enough to react but not disable the beast. The whole thing was making it harder to locate this mysterious vulnerable spot. And searching for something like that on a creature the size of a battlecruiser was laughable at best.

Evan was grateful that at least he could rely on his excellent humor to aid him when he realized that Coral was running out of air, which meant that he would soon as well. They'd have to surface soon, which Carl would no doubt notice.

This might not be a fight they could win, he realized with a heavy heart as he pulled his dragon up to the surface of the water, knowing if they stayed under too much longer that they'd drown. And then, that's when he saw it.

Something red. Heart-shaped. And glowing on the side of the leviathan.

It was only a guess, but Evan strongly suspected that he'd located the monster's weak spot. Now he had to make an important choice: risk going for it when in plain view, or die kicking up to the surface. Either way, he might die trying.

CHAPTER SEVENTY-TWO

Mahkah wasn't the expert when it came to weapons. He knew magical creatures better than any of the dragonriders and specifically winged creatures thanks to his time studying the dragons.

For that reason, and solely because of that, he thought he'd know something about the simurgh. Something that would either save Wilder and him from the monster or make it so terribly angry that it didn't stop until it killed them and their dragons.

Sometimes, when in battle, a warrior comes so far that they simply have to rely on hope. That's exactly where Mahkah was at that point. Reason wasn't going to help him. Delaying would only make things worse.

The time to act was then.

He pulled back his arrow laced with all the magic he could funnel into the small object. Instead of aiming at the body of the beast, the largest of targets, Mahkah pointed the tip at the smallest part of the creature—one of its black eyes.

He let it go as the simurgh realized that Simi had fled. It didn't waste any time, and that's why Mahkah laced another spell on the arrow that made it follow the eye of the monster. Hopefully, it would find its target, and that's what would be its demise.

Otherwise, the Dragon Elite might be done for.

CHAPTER SEVENTY-THREE

Sophia knew that complete chaos was happening all around her and Lunis. And yet, she felt strangely Zen in the moments that followed.

Carl was shrieking from Lunis' assault on its tentacle. For being such a big fellow, he was undoubtedly a little baby.

It's always that way, Lunis related as they streaked away from the many tentacles now seeking to take them out.

Does that make you a baby? Sophia hunkered low as they flew out from the barrage of attempts on their lives.

The biggest, Lunis admitted.

Sophia caught sight of a battle between Wilder and Simi and Howard overhead. The dragon and rider looked so small when compared to the giant simurgh. Still, Sophia didn't worry—or rather, overtly worry. Her attention was focused on her battle. She had no time for anything else at that point.

Knowing that she didn't have an option after angering Carl so badly, she encouraged Lunis away. Either their attempts at distraction had worked, or they'd have to try another approach. Sophia also knew that Evan and Coral should be close to out of air soon with as long as they'd been underwater.

She pulled Lunis high enough in the air that they were out of Carl's reach and far enough from the battle with Howard and simply watched while waiting for Evan and Coral to materialize. If they didn't soon, then she and Lunis would have to do something.

Sophia held her breath. She didn't know what Plan B was going to be, and with each passing second, she worried that her friends were trapped underwater and not coming back up, which presented a multitude of problems.

CHAPTER SEVENTY-FOUR

Simi was hurt. Wilder had known that was a part of the risk. He'd expected that. Still, that didn't make it any easier to accept.

It was hard to judge the severity of her wounds from the air. She was able to keep flying and that was something, but they were both surviving on adrenaline at this point. When that waned, Wilder didn't know what to expect.

That's why he turned his dragon around to decide his next option. He didn't want to leave his team. Abandoning the woman he loved wasn't an option either. But if he and Simi became a liability and plunged into the ocean, then they wouldn't be helping but rather harming the Dragon Elite.

Her breath labored, Simi spun and showed Wilder the view that had been at his back. He caught sight of Mahkah not too far off, his stoic gaze directed at the simurgh in the distance.

And to Wilder's astonishment, a fiery arrow coated in magic raced through the air. He expected for it to hit the creature in the midsection and rebound off like before, but instead, it stuck straight into the large bird's eye and made it scream in obvious pain.

The sound echoed all around them, and the air seemed to shake.

Wilder held the reins tighter, thinking he'd be thrown off from the blast.

Then, to his astonishment, the monster spiraled head over feet through the air like the tiny arrow had been a death missile and hit the creature's only vulnerable spot.

And it had, Wilder realized. The genius who was Mahkah had found the one magically unprotected part of the simurgh and had struck it using a spell.

The giant bird tumbled through the air for what seemed like eons before it fell into the waters of the Mediterranean Sea and made a huge splash. The water rushed into the air and billowed high like an upended freighter before the bird sank, its calls of pain drowned out by the water that covered it.

One tiny arrow had defeated the massive bird. It was a good lesson for Wilder. The strongest and best were always taken down by something small. Guard your weak spots for once exposed, death is imminent.

CHAPTER SEVENTY-FIVE

Going up for air would ensure that Evan and Coral lived longer. Maybe not that much longer since Carl might take them out straight away, but staying down longer and piercing the leviathan's weak spot would ensure that the Dragon Elite members were safe.

Somewhere over the surface of the water, Sophia and Lunis were endangering their lives trying to serve as distractions. Wilder and Simi were fighting a deranged bird. That crazy guy had raced at the simurgh, all to get its attention off Evan. Then there were Mahkah and Tala, doing something strangely brilliant and strategic.

Yes, Evan and Coral could come up for air and preserve their lives, but the chances of finding the small vulnerable spot on Carl again were unlikely. Sometimes there were things more important than preserving oneself, and right then was one for Evan McIntosh.

Evan's mouth absentmindedly opened as he brought up his sword and used his last bit of magic to propel it through the water. It spiraled forward until it connected with the red heart-shaped glow on the leviathan.

The dragon and rider didn't see what happened next because they passed out, overcome by the churning seas. Even those empowered by water could be taken out by it.

CHAPTER SEVENTY-SIX

I t didn't surprise Mahkah to watch the giant bird's demise, but it did fill him with a great deal of relief.

What surprised him was when the leviathan shrieked in obvious pain, and all of its tentacles reached straight out in a weird formation.

Then he heard Tala's familiar voice in his head.

Coral, the dragon exclaimed. *Evan. They're in trouble. Just to the ten o'clock of the leviathan.*

Mahkah didn't hesitate. He darted straight for the area his dragon had indicated. The others had noticed too because he saw Sophia come around the side of the creature, which now writhed in pain. Whatever was happening to the sea monster was part of its demise.

Still, Mahkah streaked in the direction of a billowing shape that was rising to the surface as the monster sank low. There was so much happening at once that it was hard to discern what was monster and what everything else.

Sophia shot him a look as they neared and they both laid eyes on what was unmistakably Evan and Coral in passed-out form. Tala, who hadn't been through the same events as the others, reached down and picked up Coral with the half-conscious Evan clutching her.

Sophia knew what needed to happen next and opened a portal

using what had to be the last of her magic. To Mahkah's relief, Wilder had followed her and wasn't far behind.

Tala carried Evan and Coral through the portal that led to right outside the Gullington, where the Dragon Elite would be safe once more. The others followed. All of them found solace on the grassy lawn where they passed out, huddled together and protective of one another after the battle that had nearly ended them all—but hadn't, because they'd have other important battles to come.

CHAPTER SEVENTY-SEVEN

Nevin Gooseman watched from the only cloaked magitech plane he had left as his leviathan and simurgh sank to the bottom of the Mediterranean Sea. The Dragon Elite might have defeated him again...

Nevin ground his fist into his knee. He was livid, thinking this would be a bigger battle. However, he wasn't out for the count.

The politician knew better. He hadn't expected this to take the dragonriders out. He'd learned from the past and knew not to discount them.

What he hoped was that they were injured. Scared. Not prepared for what was coming next.

If the Dragon Elite thought that these monsters were sizable, they had no idea what was coming for them.

This had been Round One. None of them would survive Round Two.

CHAPTER SEVENTY-EIGHT

"What are you sketching?" Hiker asked Mama Jamba as they all sat at the breakfast table and waited for Trin to bring their food.

"Things," she said simply and kept her attention on the pad of paper in her hands.

He sighed before turning his attention to the bruised and battered Wilder, Evan who didn't appear much better, and Mahkah and Sophia. "Good work out there. I hope you all got some rest."

"I slept fitfully," Evan admitted. "Without my wife, I just can't sleep."

Quiet mumbled something from his place beside Mama Jamba. She nodded in reply.

"Try telling him that though," Mama Jamba replied to the gnome.

"Tell me what?" Evan asked at once.

She pursed her lips. "How do you know we're talking about you?"

"I know." Evan looked toward the kitchen. "Do you think Trin will come through with food any time this century? I'm starving."

Hiker, who would normally tell him that he was exaggerating, glanced back at the kitchen. "Trin?"

The cyborg didn't materialize. He shook his head and returned his attention to the riders.

"Any luck on finding out where those monsters came from?" Wilder sipped his water and sucked in a breath. His busted lip was much better thanks to the Castle, but he was still pretty bruised. It would take a few more hours until he was all better. Simi and the other dragons were all recovering in the Cave.

"I still need to do more research," Hiker answered. "Someone is trying to harm us, that's for sure. But if they think the Dragon Elite will hide away while they send dangerous creatures out to harm the mortal world, they're wrong."

"That's right," Evan cheered. "We'll go out and fight those fights. You lead the way."

Sophia shook her head. "I'll lead the way. Sir, I know you need to maintain vigilance here."

"Of course you do, Pink Princess," Evan retorted but winked at her good-naturedly.

The truth was that Hiker Wallace was much more valuable as a trusted leader at the Gullington than out in the field. There was a place for him and another for a combat specialist. Sophia had found her calling in a way, and it was out fighting battles with the others. It felt natural to give orders when things were at their worst. She didn't feel pressure but rather the adrenaline of the moment, and that aided her.

Trin exited the kitchen, holding a huge tray that overflowed with a bounty unlike anything she'd served thus far. She set it down between Sophia and Hiker and attempted a smile, which always appeared strange on the cyborg's face, but still nice.

"Welcome back, S. Beaufont and the others," Trin said, seeming to mean it.

"Thanks, T." Evan reached for a pastry on the end.

The cyborg reached out and slapped his hand. "Not you. Your wife can make you breakfast, if that's what you want."

She then turned and strode for the kitchen again, her hips swaying back and forth.

Sophia's eyes widened, and she exchanged a look with Wilder that said it all. They both knew what was going on, but based on the offended expression on Evan's face, he had no clue.

"Wow, how rude." Evan looked at his hand like Trin had left a mark. The cyborg was stronger than most and probably could have, but her slap had simply been a warning instead.

"So, your wife," Wilder began and took a piece of bacon from the platter. "How is she?"

Evan shrugged. "How am I supposed to know? I can't have that one weighing me down. I'll pick her up when it's time."

"When will that be?" Hiker asked Sophia.

She glanced at the grandfather clock on the far side of the dining hall, knowing it told more than time. "In a couple more days."

Hiker nodded. "Then it seems we have more time to rest up and prepare for the next battle."

Sophia grabbed a scone off the tray and took a bite, enjoying it plain. A few more days. Nice. She needed that. They all did. They'd survived and been victorious, but the next battle appeared to be more momentous based on what others thought they'd need. Armor. Weapons. Special advantages.

That was fine. Sophia would be ready when the mysterious danger presented itself.

"Sophia, can you help me with the dragonettes this afternoon?" Mahkah asked while buttering a roll. "Lunis has promised to assist with their training."

Quiet mumbled something inaudible.

"That's true, the sheep are still a problem," Mama Jamba replied to the gnome.

"I thought you were going to take me shopping for my belated wedding present," Evan wheedled.

Sophia smiled. "All of that except for you, Evan. However, the sheep have gone long enough. I will help with that soon. I promise. And I'm happy to assist with the dragonettes too. But I've got something else I promised to do first. It won't take long, but I need to devote my attention to it before anything else."

"A deathly mission to fight deranged house elves?" Evan asked.

Sophia shook her head. "No, house elves are awesome and never deranged."

"A mission to buy me the best anniversary present ever?" Wilder chimed in.

"Our anniversary is coming up?" Sophia questioned seriously.

"A mission for the Dragon Elite, right?" Hiker speculated.

She shook her head. "None of that. Sometimes you have to know when to celebrate the little things, the ones that mean a lot to others because later, they will mean a lot to the rest of the world. Or at least, I suspect they will."

CHAPTER SEVENTY-NINE

"Happy birthday to me," King Rudolf Sweetwater sang and clapped his hands. "Happy birthday to me!"

Liv slapped a hand over his mouth. "It's not your birthday, Ru."

He apparently licked her hand, making her jerk it away. "I thought that when children had a birthday, that parents got to pretend it was theirs too because we went to so much work to bring them into this world."

"What did you do?" Liv questioned.

"I gave up multiple naps," he declared.

Sophia shook her head, but smiled and watched as the Captains toddled around in their pretty little outfits on their birthday. "I think that the triplets having to share a birthday with each other is quite enough."

"Thanks for arranging this," Rudolf said, quite sincerely as he looked around at the Build-A-Bear workshop that was different from the one in the mortal world that most were used to.

Sophia had agreed not to tell anyone, even King Rudolf, that Lee from the Crying Cat Bakery had made the arrangements, at the assassin baker's request. Apparently being thoughtful would be the worst thing in the world. So instead, Sophia had to take the credit. She nodded. "You're welcome. I hope they enjoy it."

The triplets waddled over to the shop attendant who began leading them in the activity, which included assembling all parts of a bear that would in fact come alive at the end and be a lifelong companion if they so desired. Getting into the Magical Build-A-Bear workshop wasn't easy, but Lee had connections and it was truly a fun experience for Rudolf and Serena and the triplets, who were used to having everything.

Sophia smiled. She felt that even the privileged deserved the best. It wasn't Rudolf's fault that he was filthy rich or handsome or strangely lucky. At the end of the day, no one had a bigger heart than the king of the fae. He would do anything for his people or magicians or the Dragon Elite. Those people deserved to be rewarded, and so did his lovely halflings, who Sophia truly believed were destined to go on and do great things.

"Oh, don't choose that outfit for your bear, Captain Morgan." Rudolf pushed Sophia back to get around her. "Something short and scandalous. Don't take after your godmother Liv."

Sophia laughed and slapped her sister on the arm. Liv smiled at her.

"This is fun." Liv looked around as Queen Serena helped Captain Kirk and Captain Silver pick out accessories for their bears.

"Life is fun," Sophia stated.

"And full of adventure, based on the marks on your face," Liv added.

Sophia brushed her hands over her cheeks, realizing that some of her battle marks were still there. "Well, you know how it goes."

Liv nodded. "That I do. And I wouldn't have it any other way. How about you?"

Sophia thought for a moment. "Every day is an adventure. It's exhausting and terrifying and often heartbreaking, but you know what? I want to be the one who saves the world so the rest of the population can sleep in. Even after coming off a battle, I look forward to the ones of tomorrow and I know there will be more because evil never takes a day off. So no, I don't want a do-over or a different job. I want to keep doing this for the rest of my life, which I hope will be very, very long."

Liv wrapped her arm around her sister's shoulder and hugged her tightly. "I have a feeling that you, Sophia Beaufont, will outlive us all. Or at I least hope you do. Because you're the absolute best of us all."

Sophia smiled at her sister. She didn't know about that, but she hoped that tomorrow wasn't her last day...or the next. She had exploding sheep to fix, bad guys to take down, and a whole list of things she needed to do—and that was all before the epic battle that approached, full of unknown evils.

However, after fighting the giant bird and sea monster, she wasn't scared anymore. Whether her enemy meant it or not, sending something huge to try and take down the Dragon Elite only made her braver...tougher.

Sophia was ready for the next challenge. And she was hopeful that she'd defeat it.

The world depended on it.

CHAPTER EIGHTY

A guttural howl echoed from the horned creature's mouth. It sounded both like a bitter threat and a promise of bad deeds yet to come.

Nevin Gooseman watched his "pet" from the safety of the box office at the top of the abandoned stadium in Dallas, Texas.

The tarrasque had grown considerably and was now threatening to break free of its restraints. It was more important than ever that Clyde Jackson, its handler, kept it subdued when the monster wasn't eating. The magically enchanted chains kept the beast from demolishing the stands and trampling through the streets of Dallas.

That time would come very soon though, Nevin thought with satisfaction. However, the timing had to be perfect. If they released the tarrasque now, it would be easy enough for the Dragon Elite to take it down, based on how they handled the simurgh and the leviathan. Nevin had to give it to them—the dragonriders shouldn't be underestimated. But they weren't invincible, and he thought he'd found their match. Something that would overpower the dragons and outsmart the riders.

However, when Nevin released the tarrasque, it would be because it could no longer be contained. Then there would be no stopping it.

Technically, Nevin had no plans to release the monster. He would simply allow the handler's magical wards that kept it asleep to wear off. Overwhelmed by hunger, the beast would break free of the abandoned and rundown sports stadium. Then it would feast on mortals until the Dragon Elite undoubtedly showed up and finally met their match.

It wouldn't be much longer now. The tarrasque was as big as the football field. Soon it would fill up the entire space, including the stands. The spikes on its back were already close to the domed ceiling. When it was allowed to sober up completely, all the monster would have to do was rock back on its heels, then it would bust free of its confines.

Nevin Gooseman would be long gone by then.

A tarrasque had never been allowed to get as big as the one he had Clyde Jackson rapidly maturing. This was the last one in existence, and it wouldn't live long after breaking out due to all the magical enhancements they'd used to make it grow, but it would live long enough. According to Clyde Jackson, the tarrasque would live at least a month before its heart gave out. That was more than enough time for it to do massive damage. Nevin thought that the beast would take down the Dragon Elite within minutes. Then, left unchecked, it would further destroy the city and probably all the military forces that came after it.

The tarrasque's armored skin was impenetrable by most weapons, and like diamonds, its claws and teeth could tear through just about anything. The Dragon Elite wouldn't be prepared for this. There was no way that they could be.

The simurgh and leviathan should have been more of a challenge for the dragonriders. They had, after all, been enchanted to be extra difficult to fight and aggressive. However after watching the battle, Nevin was hopeful that he'd at least injured the Dragon Elite. That was the plan all along. It hadn't been hard for him to locate the beasts with Bermuda Lauren's unknowing help and aided by Clyde Jackson's expertise.

The creatures had been in hiding, but it was easy enough to draw them into place and create a disturbance that would get the Dragon Elite's attention. As Nevin suspected, the do-gooders came running right on cue.

Imagine when the Dragon Elite learn that the city of Dallas is under attack by a giant dinosaur creature. They won't think first. They'll simply run so fast into battle with their smug attitudes that they'll be picked off within a matter of minutes.

Then the tarrasque could overrun the city, and mortals would get the punishment they deserved for taking Nevin Gooseman for granted.

Nevin smiled with satisfaction at the beast that would be the Dragon Elite's final demise. Without them, he could destroy the other dragons and eggs. It was all coming together. Soon, he'd have the revenge he was so hungry for.

CHAPTER EIGHTY-ONE

"Would you scooch over?" Evan pressed his feet under Sophia's butt on the leather couch. "You're taking up too much room."

She took up hardly any space on the oversized sofa—less than three-quarters of the space where Evan was stretched out with his head on the arm rest.

After tucking her legs up to her chest, she shook her head. "If you don't stop, then I'm going to chuck you out the window."

Evan laughed at her threat. "You mean throw me into Lunis."

Sophia looked up to find her dragon striding in the direction of the sitting room's open window. It wasn't raining at the Gullington for once, but all the dragonriders had congregated in the room that was hardly used, right off the entryway to the Castle. After their battle with the leviathan and simurgh, they all recognized that they needed a break. Hiker had authorized them to have a single day off, to which Evan made a sarcastic remark about how giving he was after they'd risked their lives to save the world.

"Hey, Lun." Sophia smiled as the blue dragon stuck his head through the open window. He winked at Sophia before turning his attention to Wilder sitting in the oversized armchair beside the window.

"What are you watching?" Lunis glanced down at the tablet in Wilder's hands.

"Zefrank," Wilder answered. "He does all these nature videos on animals on YouTube, but teaches nontraditional information on them."

"Sounds intriguing." Lunis watched the screen. "What's this one on?"

"Marsupials," Wilder explained and held up the iPad so the dragon could get a better look. "Did you know that koalas don't have those folds in their brain, also known as the 'thinky-thinky parts'?"

"Makes sense if you've ever met a koala," Lunis stated. "They're happy no matter what."

"Are you inferring that happiness is linked to intelligence, or lack thereof?" Evan asked absentmindedly, his attention on the device in his hand as he played Animal Crossing.

"If that were the case, you'd be as happy as a lark," Wilder joked.

"Studies have proven that there isn't a correlation between intelligence and happiness," Mahkah explained from his place sitting cross-legged on the floor. He was also using an electronic device—a Kindle e-reader. "However, it's important to note that those with higher IQs have more avenues for finding and maintaining happiness. They have the ability to find coping mechanisms when things are hard. There are many factors to consider, like the fact that higher intelligence usually results in better health, which would lead to better life satisfaction."

"Would you stop reading Psychology Today?" Evan teased, still playing his game.

"You make some excellent points, Mahkah," Mama Jamba said from her place on an elegant chaise lounge next to the roaring fire on the opposite side of the room. "Many believe that ignorance is bliss, but that's not usually the case. Less knowledge means fewer options." She went back to sketching on her notepad, which was always with her lately.

Trin strode into the sitting room and paused in the doorway at the sight of all the dragonriders lounging and playing on devices. At her heels was the cyborg dog, NO10JO. "I brought you all some refreshments."

"Thank you." Sophia stretched and put down her phone.

Trin's gears made noise as she set the tray of finger food down on the coffee table.

"Oh, let's watch the video on angler fish," Lunis said with his head still hovering over Wilder's shoulder.

"Trin, if Sophia would move over, then you could take a break and play games with me," Evan offered as he stretched out and took up more of the sofa.

Sophia shot him a scowl. "I couldn't take up any less space here, Dork Face."

Trin shook her head. "I prefer not to use devices."

"Oh, because you have one in your head and all?" Evan insensitively asked.

Sophia slapped his leg. "Show some respect, would you?" She knew that the cyborg was still—always—sensitive about the fact that she was mostly composed of wires and bolts and magitech.

"I am showing respect," Evan stated. "I'm pretty certain that Trin knows she has iPhone technology in her as well as other handy-dandy stuff."

"They aren't as handy as you think," Trin said dryly.

Evan straightened and pulled his feet off Sophia. "I think it's marvelous. You're way cooler than the rest of us." He patted the couch, automatically calling NO10JO over. "I mean, look at this guy. He's the best dog in the world. Not boring like all those other animals who can't do cool stuff." He affectionately patted the dog on the head, and a moment later, NO10JO transformed into a foot stool.

Evan let out a howl of satisfied laughter. "See what I mean! He's awesome and thoughtful." He glanced at Sophia. "He knows you've been hogging all the space on the communal couch and is trying to help out. Isn't that sweet?"

"He is thoughtful and knows that I'm about to cut you if you put your feet on me one more time," she threatened. "That dog is trying to keep you alive."

Evan nodded and redirected his attention. "It's okay though, boy. I would rather have you than the convenience of a place to put my feet up."

With a poof of sorts, NO10JO shapeshifted back to his usual form with bolts and metal plates and wires.

"That's nice of you," Trin said, her voice suddenly sensitive.

"Well, I'm nice," Evan stated smugly. "Just ask my wife. She'll tell you that I'm the best lover in the world. Very giving."

Wilder laughed. "You haven't seen her since your wedding day when you got married and left her on Roya Lane five minutes later, according to Sophia."

"But we sealed the deal with a passionate kiss," Evan argued.

"It was a handshake," Sophia corrected.

When Evan reached for a cream cheese and cucumber sandwich, Trin's robotic hand stretched across the several feet separating them and slapped him. He pulled his arm back and gave her a look of offense.

"What did you do that for, woman?" he asked, his eyes wide.

Her gaze took on one of surprise. "Oh, well, you didn't wash your hands first."

Sophia eyed the housekeeper and read something else under her expression.

"Evan hasn't washed his hands in three decades," Wilder stated flatly. "How is today any different than any other?"

"Ha-ha," Evan said with no humor. "And my hands are plenty clean." He gave Trin a careful look as he reached for a sandwich again. This time she didn't slap him, although the look of irritation was still heavy on her face.

"Oh, there's a new branch of Amazon that's come out of Roya Lane," Sophia said while reading a press release from the House of Fourteen.

"Like you need anything to further your Amazon addiction," Evan teased and put his feet back on the couch, taking up most of the space again.

"I do," Sophia stated. "And this will make impulse buying even better. Wild, didn't you say you needed a new pair of shoes?"

He glanced up, obviously engrossed in whatever he and Lunis were watching on YouTube. "Yeah, what are those cool shoes that all the kids are wearing? Didn't you call them Converse something or another?"

"Yep," Sophia stated. "They're Chuck Taylors. What size are you?"

"You should know that about your man," Evan quipped.

"Your wife doesn't know what your last name is," Wilder insulted.

"Well, she knows the important stuff," Evan countered.

"Like to stay far away from you, as evidenced by the fact that you haven't heard from her since the wedding done for purely logistical reasons," Wilder stated.

Trin let out a high-pitched, sudden laugh that was completely uncharacteristic for her. When everyone, including Mother Nature, gave her strange looks, her face turned red and steam spilled from her ears. She rushed from the room while muttering something about smelling something burning.

"Anyone else sense that something isn't right with Trin?" Wilder asked.

"Or everything is right with her and she's dealing with things the way humans do," Mama Jamba offered.

"By having steam shoot out of our ears?" Evan asked. "That seems more like a way that a dragon deals with things."

"These are nostrils," Lunis stated, then huffed and made smoke issue from his.

Wilder waved the smoke away while coughing. "Hey, buddy. Can we not do that when we're sharing screen time?"

"Sure thing," Lunis agreed. "Let's watch the Zefrank video on hummingbirds. I can imagine the weird facts we'll learn about their mating habits and killer ways with their knife beaks."

"You bet, buddy." Wilder looked up at Sophia. "And to answer your question, I'm a size ten in shoes."

"Oh, wow, I knew you were little but—"

"Size ten shoes." Sophia tapped on her phone. A moment later—only a few seconds—a Converse shoe box appeared on the coffee table.

Evan and Mahkah both straightened with surprise. Sophia smiled. Wilder's eyes widened.

"Are those my shoes?" Wilder asked.

Sophia nodded proudly. "The new service for those who qualify is called Instant Amazon. It can deliver to the Gullington, as you've all witnessed."

"How do you qualify?" Evan swiped through his phone.

Sophia shook her head. "You don't. The first thing you have to have is good credit and since you have none, you don't qualify. You also have to pass a series of personality tests that show you won't abuse the service, and aren't prone to immediate gratification."

Wilder sighed. "Maybe in your next lifetime, Evan. But Mahkah, you're perfect for that kind of thing."

"I would be interested in checking it out," Mahkah stated, then returned his attention to his Kindle book.

"Well, Sophia can you pretty please buy me some shoes?" Evan batted his eyes at her. "I'm a size thirteen, which I know is totally blowing your mind."

"It's not," Sophia stated. "And I got those for Wilder as a gift, but I'm not allowed to order too many things for other people."

"How about a new track suit for me?" Mama Jamba asked. "I got orange marmalade on my white one and the stain won't come out."

"First of all," Evan began, "why does the queen of the Earth have to order anything? Why can't you poof whatever you need?"

"Because it keeps me humble," Mama Jamba answered simply.

"And why can't you just magic out the stain?" Evan asked.

"Because I'm horrible with domestic stuff," Mama Jamba replied. "I don't know how to do laundry. I've never, ever done it, if you can believe it."

"Me either," Wilder stated.

"Nor me," Evan chimed in.

"Why am I not surprised?" Sophia asked.

"Hey, we're in good company," Evan argued.

Sophia made a series of swipes on the phone and a moment later, a brown box that said Chanel on the side appeared at Mama Jamba's feet on the chaise lounge.

"Why thank you, dear," Mama Jamba exclaimed.

"Why can't you gift me something?" Evan asked, pouting.

"Because you're you and I'm me," Sophia stated.

"But you didn't get me a wedding gift," he argued.

"It's in the mail," Sophia replied.

She was going to elaborate, but they were interrupted when Hiker Wallace stormed into the room and looked at them all with great offense on his face.

They all directed their attention to their screens and pretended to ignore the lurking Viking. After a moment, he sighed. "This electronic thing has gone too far."

"When you gave us the day off sir, did you mean the hour, and that you'd spend the rest of the day berating us for our choices?" Evan wisecracked.

"And there's why I'm not getting you anything," Sophia said to the dragonrider on the other side of the couch before she glanced up at Hiker. "Hello, sir."

He nodded and thundered over to Mama Jamba. "What are you working on?"

"Why do I have to be working on anything, son?" she asked in reply.

"Oh, did you take the day off too?" he countered.

"A day off," she mused. "I wonder what that would feel like?"

"The world would go to hell," Hiker answered.

She shrugged. "Well, a girl can dream." Mama Jamba looked up at the Viking and smiled sweetly. "Since you must know, I'm still working on the way to track down the demon dragons. It's not going to be easy."

ADAPT OR BE CRUSHED

"I thought you were drawing me a pretty picture," Evan teased.

Hiker spun around. "You do realize that she can make it so you never existed, right?"

Evan gulped. "But you won't do that, will you Mama Jamba?"

"Not today, I won't," Mama Jamba answered in a sing-song voice and continued to sketch something on her pad of paper.

"I'm not having any luck tracking down where the leviathan and simurgh came from," Hiker announced with frustration in his voice.

"I'm not having any luck pronouncing either of those terms," Evan stated. "Why couldn't they be called something easy?"

"Like Evan One and Evan Two?" Wilder propped his iPad on the arm of the chair so Lunis could continue to watch animal videos while he opened his new pair of shoes.

"I can look into it for you, sir," Mahkah offered.

Hiker nodded. "Thank you. That would be helpful. And Evan and Wilder—"

"Sir, it's still my day off," Evan interrupted. "And although I'd like to take orders from you, we both know that I need my reserves filled after single-handedly killing that giant sea monster while the rest of these slackers swam around in the Mediterranean."

For some reason, Hiker didn't appear motivated enough to argue. It was true that Evan was the reason they defeated the leviathan because he could swim in the sea and find its weak spot. However, the entire battle had been a group effort.

"Yeah, fine," Hiker stated. "But tomorrow, I'll have missions for all of you."

Sophia eyed the leader of the Dragon Elite and spied the tension hiding behind the surface. None of them had spoken about Ainsley in quite some time, but that didn't seem to make things easier for Hiker. She secretly knew that with each passing day that they didn't hear from her, he worried more and wondered if she'd ever return to the Gullington.

She was going to mention something about the previous house-keeper to test the waters when she was interrupted by a message on her phone. It was Mae Ling, her fairy godmother. Sophia sat bolt upright, and gained the attention of everyone in the room with her sudden movement.

"What is it?" Wilder asked, one of his black Converse shoes in his hands.

"It's about the exploding sheep problem," Sophia answered as she read the message. "It looks like we might have a solution."

She stood at once and looked around for her boots.

"What does it say?" Hiker asked.

"Nothing much," Sophia answered. "My fairy godmother says for me to get to Happily Ever After College right away."

"Did you tell her it was your day off?" Evan stretched into the place that Sophia had abandoned on the couch.

She shook her head at him. "No. This is important. I'll leave right away."

Hiker gave Evan a punishing expression. "See that work ethic? Learn anything from it?"

Evan nodded. "Yeah, that's one surefire way to burn yourself out. Learn from the masters, young one."

Sophia dismissed him. "Also, Mae Ling reminded me that you all need to get your measurements done for the suits of armor that Jeremy Bearimy is making for us, if you haven't already."

"I've done mine," Mahkah stated.

"Me too," Wilder added.

"It's my day off," Evan said.

"Do it now," Hiker ordered.

"Of course, sir," Evan stated at once, urged on by the authority in Hiker's voice.

"And we're supposed to get this armor because?" Wilder asked.

"For an upcoming battle." Sophia pulled on her boots and cloak. "I don't know anything more. But also, we'll need some special weapons. I'll check on that too after figuring out the sheep situation."

"And I'll be right here." Evan continued to play Animal Crossing.

"When you need someone to test out the exploding sheep solution, I'll gladly offer Evan," Hiker stated.

Sophia laughed and made for the entrance. "Okay, I'll see you all as soon as I've got more answers."

"Size thirteen, Sophia," Evan called after her. "Surprise me with colors, but be sure my new shoes match my green eyes."

CHAPTER EIGHTY-TWO

The last time that Sophia was at Happily Ever After College, she'd thought something was wrong when she stepped through the portal. This time she knew it.

Before, it had been tiny robotic bugs flying through the air that had set Sophia on edge and made her think that there was a new pest at the fairy godmother college. Those had turned out to be seemingly harmless spies used on Cinderellas and Prince Charmings in the field.

However, what Sophia encountered after stepping onto the grounds of the college wouldn't be confused as ambiguous. The invaders were definitely trouble—no doubt about it.

Sophia automatically pulled Inexorabilis from its sheath and connected immediately with a stone statue that lunged at her upon arriving. She had little time to react to the attack. Sophia recognized the statue as one that stood in the gardens on the eastern side of the main building. It was of a man holding a book in one hand and pondering while stroking his chin with the other.

Now the statue was moving and trying to assault her with the book and the free hand. Sophia darted under his next attack and nearly got hit in the forehead by his arm as it swept over her. She spun at once and brandished her sword when the next swing came her way.

It connected with the mad statue's forearm and prevented it from coming down on her. But the now-living statue's strength was fierce, and Sophia knew she couldn't hold him that much longer. He was much taller than her and made of stone, which made the whole act of keeping him from knocking her to the ground more difficult. Sophia gritted her teeth and rolled to the side, which made the statue tumble to the grass from the momentum.

Sophia took the opportunity to throw a disintegration spell at the man while his back was to her. It was something usually used to dissolve rock walls, but she thought it would be the most effective offensive attack in this circumstance. To her relief, it hit the statue square in the back and made him arch dramatically. His head shot back and his mouth opened wide. Then he crumbled to dust and made a neat pile on the ground where he had been seconds before.

Sophia didn't get a moment of relief. With the statue gone, she became aware of the chaos all around her on the usually peaceful grounds of Happily Ever After College. All over the place, sculptures of animals and magicians and fairies and many other magical races had come alive and were anything but happy about their new state of being.

Like the man with the book, the statues appeared enraged and fought the fairy godmothers with a vengeance. In the distance, Sophia caught sight of her fairy godmother Mae Ling battling a statue of a centaur. She appeared to be doing okay, but the beast was relentless. It alternately kicked out its back legs and reared several times, trying to kick the small woman.

It was probably to Mae Ling's advantage that she was so small since it made it easier for her to dive out of the way. When she had a clear opening, she shot a spark of red at the angry centaur that made him freeze as he attempted to charge in her direction.

On the other side of the grounds, Sophia caught sight of Professor Amy, the math instructor, fighting a gnome statue that held a broom. She recognized the figure from the front steps where it always looked to be greeting the students while also wearing an expression that said, "Wipe your feet before entering this school. I just swept."

Behind Professor Amy was a woman Sophia recognized as the Head Mistress named Willow. Her long brown hair flew out behind her as she battled two statues, one of a large jackrabbit with fierce teeth and another of a goat. Never before had Sophia thought of goats as deadly, but right then she was terrified of the creature that jumped around and tried to ram its horns into Willow.

Sophia yanked her attention off the professors fighting statues when she caught sight of a gray figure striding in her direction. It was the largest one she'd seen on the grounds of the college, and it appeared angrier than all the rest as it moved toward her.

Sophia backed up while trying to figure out how she could fight a full-sized giant made of stone that held a sword bigger than her.

CHAPTER EIGHTY-THREE

S ophia shot a disintegrating spell at the giant right away, but he was too fast. He yanked up his sword arm and held up the metal shield in his other arm. The spell ricocheted off the shield.

Of course, the sword and shield were the real deal on the statue, Sophia thought bitterly.

The giant, who was taller than any she'd ever met, lumbered in her direction. He wore traditional giant attire and reminded her of Hiker, who was often in clothes reminiscent of Vikings.

Easily over seven feet tall, the giant's strides brought him in Sophia's direction quickly and made her stumble backward to keep her distance from him. He moved so fast that it was impossible to throw another disintegrating spell at him, and she worried that he'd deflect it again and waste her use of magic.

She felt like David facing Goliath again, like when she battled the leviathan in the Mediterranean Sea. Sophia took that moment to wonder why it was that she couldn't pick fights with anyone her size. It always had to be beasts that towered over her and had the advantage.

The angry giant had backed Sophia up against a large oak tree, but she didn't realize it until her spine collided with it. The only good thing about hitting the dead end was the tree's low branches obscured the giant's line of sight and made him use the sword to cut down the limbs.

Like he was a tree trimming service, the giant made quick work of the gnarly branches and sent them to the dirt below. Many tumbled down in front of and beside Sophia and blocked her path. She nearly tripped while trying to get over the thick limbs and around to the other side of the tree.

The giant swung his sword at her, but she dove through a thicket of fallen leaves and twigs just in time. The blade cut into the trunk of the tree and immediately got stuck.

Sophia instantly brought up Inexorabilis as the giant tugged on his sword's hilt and tried to free his weapon. His strength had disadvantaged him and made his assault cut deep into the wood. Sophia thought he would have released the sword if he could, but it was part of him and melded into his stone hand like the shield.

After charging her blade with a combat spell, Sophia brought it around as quickly and with as much force as she could muster, straight into the giant's side. He howled from the assault and jerked backward. Unfortunately, the motion was enough to yank the sword from the trunk. The attack was also enough to enrage the already mad giant.

He barreled in Sophia's direction. She ran backward, not watching where she was going. Nothing she ran into could be worse than being bowled over by the stone giant.

The giant lowered his shoulders and ran at her. Sophia had no choice but to dart to the side and jump behind another tree trunk. She momentarily disappeared from view but swung around the other side as the giant pursued her. For a moment, the two ran around the large tree like a silly game of cat and mouse, with Sophia the tiny creature trying to escape the towering feline's claws.

Sophia knew this strategy wouldn't last long, so she pushed herself to move faster until she caught up with and was directly behind the giant since the low branches again made his pursuits more difficult.

With a clear shot at his back, Sophia lifted her hand and pointed at the giant, then shot him with a disintegrating spell.

He froze, threw up his hand with the sword, and knocked the shield hard into the tree. Then, as if he'd never existed at all, he evaporated from view and settled on the ground in a large pile of dust. The metal sword and shield clanged to the dirt as they fell into the giant's remains, where they suddenly appeared a lot less intimidating lying next to a green patch of grass.

CHAPTER EIGHTY-FOUR

A fter assessing that no other statues were charging after Sophia or anyone else on the grounds of Happily Ever After College, she doubled over and pulled in large gulps of oxygen. Sophia's adrenaline had spiked when she arrived at the fairy godmother institute, and she hadn't taken a proper breath since.

With the threats eliminated, she took a moment to rest as her hands shook and her brow dripped with sweat.

"We can't thank you enough for coming to our rescue," Willow suddenly said at Sophia's side. She nearly jumped from the woman's abrupt presence, still on guard from being attacked by angry statues.

"I didn't know I was coming to your rescue," Sophia admitted. "I arrived at Mae Ling's request."

"Which I sent right before the attack started," Mae Ling stated, also unexpectedly right beside Sophia although the dragonrider hadn't seen her approach. "It all happened so fast."

Willow nodded, her hair hardly out of place from her recent battle. Her skin glistened with a faint bit of sweat on the bridge of her nose and cheeks. "Yes, we barely had enough time to get the students to safety."

"What happened here?" Sophia looked around the grounds where statues had been disintegrated, frozen, or broken into large pieces. Thankfully, there didn't appear to be any more ready to fight them.

"I'm not sure." Willow looked around too with a perplexed expression on her face. "As you've just learned, the attack was sudden, and we're still reeling from the events."

"So the statues all over the grounds simply came alive and attacked you all?" Sophia asked.

Mae Ling nodded, seemingly in a daze. "It's a very uncharacteristic thing to happen here at the college. Everything is almost always so peaceful."

Sophia knew this was true about the grounds of Happily Ever After College. The weather was always ideal—not too hot or too cool, with a gentle breeze. The students were mostly in good spirits and the food exceptional, consisting only of dessert. It seemed like the happiest place on Earth, which begged the question of why the statues would all come alive and try to murder them.

"Has anything new happened here recently?" Sophia questioned. "New students? Procedures? Magic? Anything that we can correlate to this issue?"

Willow frowned as she thought. "I don't recall anything. Professor Ling, can you?"

The fairy godmother was still trying to catch her breath. "Not a thing. All is normal here." She sighed heavily and added, "Well, I had to cancel my monthly trip to the Great Library and therefore wasn't able to update the curriculum, but that's such a minor thing. It wouldn't be related."

"Oh, yeah. No one can get to the Great Library currently," Sophia stated. "Not until the location is set once more."

Willow nodded. "Then our portal will work again."

Sophia's eyes widened. "Wait, you have a portal to the Great Library?"

"Well, naturally," Willow answered. "Fairy Godmother College is one of the few places with one because our curriculum relies on having direct access to the library at all times."

"This portal," Sophia nearly stammered. "Where is it?"

"It's in the garden, of course," Willow stated, confusion written on her face.

"The garden that used to be filled with statues?" Sophia questioned.

"Yes." Willow's muddled look deepened.

"Of course," Sophia muttered, mostly to herself. "It's got to be the portal."

"Can you please explain what's going on?" Willow's voice was full of authority.

Sophia hurried toward the garden, having passed it many times on her way to find Mae Ling. The fairy godmothers followed her. "With the Great Library's location not fixed yet, there's a problem with the portals."

"Well, I'd say," Mae Ling related. "When I tried to make the monthly trip, I opened the portal to find the door suspended in the middle of outer space. There were stars all around and distant planets that I didn't recognize. I don't think it was our current galaxy."

Sophia nodded, thinking that sounded about right. "Yes, and I think that with the portal location bouncing around, some strange magic probably seeped through. That would be enough to curse the statues and make them come alive."

"Portal magic is very volatile," Willow offered. She moved surprisingly fast although she wore pink heels that matched her skirt and button-up blouse.

"Yes," Sophia agreed. "At the Castle, we had strangers come through the portal leading to the Great Library. They went into their closets and it put them at the Castle, so we had a different experience but still very perplexing. It took us a while to figure it out."

"And to fix the problem?" Mae Ling asked. "What did you do?"

"We had to close the portal." Sophia was surprised that her all-knowing fairy godmother didn't already see this about her.

As if she'd read her mind, Mae Ling stated, "I don't know everything about you, Sophia. Only that which you need my help with and even then, things aren't automatic and take time for me to see, like your problem with the sheep that you came to me about."

"Which is why I'm here," Sophia stated. "However, let me close your portal first because who knows what the magic seeping through into the college could do next if it turned the statues evil and made them come alive."

The English garden alongside the main building looked quite bare without the usual stone sculptures gracing the space. Many of the rose bushes had been trampled, probably when the statues marched out of the garden and went after the students and professors.

Sophia was going to ask where the portal to the Great Library was, but then noticed an arched lattice arbor in the middle of the space and knew right away that had to be it.

"Are the students allowed access to the portal?" she asked the fairy godmothers.

Both shook their heads. "Only with special permission. They know not to pass through the arbor."

Sophia nodded, grateful she didn't have to worry about one of the college's students floating around somewhere in space in another galaxy.

"My magical reserves are pretty low after taking down that giant," Sophia admitted.

"An impressive feat," Mae Ling stated proudly.

"We will loan you ours," Willow said confidentially and threaded her fingers through Sophia's at once.

On the other side of her, Mae Ling did the same thing.

Sophia nodded and directed her attention to the arbor in the middle of the garden. She hadn't been the one to close the portal at the Castle and had been grateful that Quiet took care of that detail. She was especially glad for that when she started the spell that she thought would seal the portal shut at Happily Ever After College. It was complex and incredibly draining. After a few seconds, Sophia felt her reserves deplete and slumped, thinking she might pass out from the effort.

However, Mae Ling squeezed her hand, and she remembered that she wasn't alone. The magic from the two fairy godmothers pooled into Sophia. She welcomed it, then funneled the energy into her spell.

It was complete within a minute, and the arbor glowed brightly before dimming completely like a candle being extinguished.

Sophia let out a breath and forced a smile. "It's done. The college is safe once more."

"Therefore, we must now look after ourselves," Willow stated with conviction. "Let's go to the kitchen where we will refill our reserves and discuss next steps."

CHAPTER EIGHTY-FIVE

The huge chunks of chocolate in the ice cream sundae made every bite better than they would have been otherwise. Vanilla and chocolate syrup were excellent on their own, but when piled high onto a chocolate brownie and layered with chunks of dark chocolate and covered in whipped cream, the whole thing went to the next level.

Sophia was full after finishing only half of the dessert. That earned contemptuous glares from Mae Ling and Willow, who were apparently going to eat all of their sundaes like they were a pile of green beans and spinach.

"Feeling better yet?" Willow's tone was speculative, like if Sophia said no, then she'd get her head dunked into the dessert sitting in front of her.

"Yes, much better," Sophia confessed and licked the chocolate from her teeth. The sweetness made her mouth hurt. She couldn't very well say that to the fairy godmothers without earning annoyed glares though. They would undoubtedly think she wasn't trying hard enough if sweet treats were painful for her to consume. It was just that Sophia, much like Liv, preferred savory and salty things to replenish her reserves. The fairy godmothers had their way of doing things, and they were smart. They ate sweets to refill theirs, but

Sophia could eat more salty chips than chocolate cake, so it was easier for her to eat lots of nachos over desserts.

It was strange being at the college and having it deserted around them. They sat in the empty kitchen with large industrial containers of ice cream sitting out and sweating on the countertop beside them. The students apparently wouldn't return to the Happily Ever After College until there had been a full sweep of the grounds to determine there weren't any other statues alive and hiding somewhere. Fairy godmothers weren't usually taught combat training. They learned many other useful things, like how to make matches or create happy endings or bring peace to the world, but how to fight evil creatures wasn't one of them. That was for Warriors of the House of Fourteen or riders of the Dragon Elite. Everyone had a role in the magical world, and some learned to fight while others studied how to create love.

"So, the exploding sheep," Sophia finally said when they'd been quiet for a long time other than slurping from their spoons and licking their fingers.

"It's the water supply," Mae Ling revealed and pushed an empty dish of mostly melted ice cream away.

"At the Gullington?" Sophia asked.

"In Scotland in general," Mae Ling corrected. "All of the sheep all over the country have this problem."

"I'd heard that, but are we sure the water supply is the problem, and it's that wide-spread?" Sophia asked.

Mae Ling nodded. "I'm afraid so. Whoever was behind this contamination wanted to ensure that it affected the Dragon Elite, so they didn't stop with doing one region, but rather the entire country."

"So we know this person or whoever targeted the Dragon Elite?" Sophia questioned. "Do you know who it is?"

"I don't," Mae Ling answered. "But I think we can guess."

Sophia thought for a moment before the inevitable dawned on her. "Do you know that it's Nevin Gooseman? Do your sources or whatever tell you that?"

Mae Ling glanced sideways at Willow, and they shared an amused look before she shook her head. "We don't have sources. That's not how we work. I'm inferring that the person who has the most to gain by taking out your sheep is the one you almost took down."

"But we're not sure that we didn't," Sophia argued. "We haven't seen anything of Nevin since that battle outside the Great Library. He could have been in any of those aircraft that we destroyed as part of the magitech army."

"He could also be the one who unleashed enhanced magical creatures for the Dragon Elite to go after in the Mediterranean Sea." Mae Ling took a long sip of water.

Sophia's mouth popped open and stayed that way. She suddenly wondered how she hadn't seen it before. It now seemed so obvious. But she'd been so busy trying to help Subner and prepare for the upcoming mysterious battle with an unknown evil. Then there had been the leviathan and the simurgh and exploding sheep. But she suddenly felt so dumb.

She slapped her forehead and nearly knocked herself out from the blow. "Of course, it was Nevin Gooseman all this time. He's the only one who wants to take us down so badly that he'd go to such extreme measures. This has all been about eliminating the Dragon Elite."

"I'm sorry to say that I think you're right." Willow ran her finger over the side of her sundae bowl and licked it. "It is the desperate who will go to the most dangerous degrees."

"And nothing says danger like killing Scotland's entire sheep population," Sophia remarked.

"Not only that, but exploding sheep will take out dragons, farmers, and civilians alike," Mae Ling imparted. "Whoever is behind this, whether Nevin Gooseman or someone else, has little concern or value for lives whether mortal, magical or otherwise."

"What are we supposed to do?" Sophia asked. "How do we fix the water supply in all of Scotland? That seems very complex since it comes from multiple sources, including the sky."

"It will be," Mae Ling agreed. "And I don't have an answer to that."

Sophia deflated.

"However, although I can't offer you answers, I can offer you places to look," Mae Ling said hopefully. "Or rather, people to ask."

Sophia perked up. "Oh? You know of an expert on sheep or water or whatever? I'll search them out. Just tell me where to look."

"I won't have to," Mae Ling began. "Think of the one person you know who has the most knowledge of animals and can maybe share their insights on the monsters you've already faced—helping you fill in the gaps on the leviathan and the simurgh."

Sophia bolted upright and wondered how this notion hadn't occurred to her already. "Of course! You're a genius. How did I not consider this before?"

Mae Ling smiled at Willow before flashing the look at Sophia. "Sometimes the most obvious resources escape us because we're too busy trying to escape death. It takes a familiar voice to remind us of what we instinctively knew on our own."

CHAPTER EIGHTY-SIX

Sophia offered to help clean up and check the grounds of Happily Ever After College, but Mae Ling and Willow refused. They urged her to leave at once, stating that what she had to do was more important than anything else. That filled Sophia with a ton of pressure, but she reminded herself that this was a regular old Thursday at this point.

"Save the world and figure out who is trying to destroy it behind the mask," Sophia said to herself as she stepped through the portal to a world she had enjoyed many times and hadn't seen in a short while.

The noises that echoed from Bermuda Lauren's big top at the magical circus gave Sophia a short pause. She didn't want to enter the tent and get mauled by Venice the winged lion, or whatever creature was currently on exhibit. The giantess had taken on the recent mission to educate the public about various magical creatures to erase misconceptions and create an appreciation for the animals.

"Master Lauren is expecting you, Miss," a squeaky voice said at Sophia's back.

She jerked around to find a small imp looking up at her, his arms full of a couple of heads of green leaf lettuce that looked recently harvested. Fresh dirt flaked off the bottoms.

Sophia recognized the creature with oversized ears, teeth, and hands as Bermuda's assistant at the circus—Goat. She'd always considered imps to be pranksters who couldn't be trusted, but Bermuda had informed her that they were very loyal servants and worked well with magical creatures. This was exactly the reason that Bermuda should be in charge of reeducating the public since Sophia had been raised learning about magic and had her share of misconceptions to rewrite.

"Hi, Goat." Sophia smiled at the creature. "You say that she's expecting me? I didn't know that I was coming here until a few minutes ago."

That was pretty much status quo at this point though, Sophia thought. She was late for appointments with Papa Creola that she didn't know she had, and Bermuda expected her when she didn't think she'd see her anytime soon.

"Yes, she said you would have quite a few things to discuss with her," Goat informed her. "I'll show you into the tent, then get you two some refreshments."

Sophia shook her head, her stomach still full of ice cream sundae. "Thank you, but that won't be necessary. I just ate."

"Then I'll fetch madam some tea if that's okay," he politely replied.

"Thanks, Goat," Sophia replied. "That's very nice of you."

"What's nice is that you remember my name when most simply scowl at me." He strode past her with the lettuce bobbing in his arms and entered the big top.

Sophia had to peel the vinyl flap back further to get through but immediately halted to take in all the strange sights around her. She thought that she'd be prepared for the bizarre and magical creatures that would grace Bermuda Lauren's tent, but it never failed to surprise her. And on that particular day, there was something uniquely perplexing buzzing around at the back of the tent that immediately stole Sophia's attention and gave her a weird urge she couldn't describe or explain.

CHAPTER EIGHTY-SEVEN

Without her permission, Sophia's feet brought her forward toward a collection of hovering lights at the back of the tent. She felt an irresistible urge to follow them. It was impossible to counter it although she was aware of other strange creatures in the big top staring at her.

A large arm reached out from seemingly nowhere and blocked Sophia, stopping her in her tracks.

"Blink rapidly and shake your head, then look away," Bermuda ordered in an authoritative voice.

Sophia felt like someone had splashed her with cold water as if trying to wake her from slumber. She did as instructed, and when she pulled her eyes off the buzzing golden lights at the back of the tent, the urge to go in their direction immediately evaporated.

Strangely, Sophia couldn't describe what she'd seen. Whatever they were, the creatures appeared as lights—similar to lightning bugs. However, there was something much more mysterious and alluring about them.

"What are they?" Sophia continued to blink as she looked up at the giantess.

"They are known by many names, depending on the culture,"

Bermuda began. "You might have heard them referred to as aleya, boitata, La Candileja, luz mala, or brujas."

"I haven't heard any of those names," Sophia admitted, careful to keep her eyes trained on the giantess although she could see a few creatures moving around the tent in her peripheral vision.

"No, those aren't the ones I thought you'd be familiar with. You most likely know them as will-o'-wisps."

Sophia thought for a moment. She knew the term, but couldn't connect it with anything. "What are they, and why do I feel such a strong draw to them?"

"Not to them," Bermuda corrected. "Your draw is to follow them, and it will dissipate as soon as I reveal their secret."

"Which is?" Sophia was suddenly fiercely curious.

"Will-o'-wisps have been found in forests and dark moors for ages," Bermuda explained. "Their job is simple and also completely mischievous. Their only aim is to get weary travelers to follow them, abandon their routes, and inevitably get lost."

"Oh, that's deceitful," Sophia exclaimed in surprise. "Why do you have them here?"

"Well, because like I did for you, I want to tarnish their ability to make mortals and others stray from their path. Go ahead and try looking at them now."

Sophia did as directed. To her relief, she didn't feel the urge to follow the hovering bits of light. "That's remarkable."

"Yes," Bermuda stated matter-of-factly. "Like many magical creatures, when their secrets are revealed, they lose some of their power."

Liv had once told Sophia that Plato's magic worked similarly. If others besides her saw him use his magic, then it would diminish it.

"Why is making others lost their only mission?" Sophia continued to study the lights buzzing in the far dark corner of the tent.

"They're cursed," Bermuda explained. "There's nothing to be done about it. So I keep them comfortable, and they agree to be in the show to educate the public. It's mutually beneficial."

Sophia squinted at the tiny orbs of light and tried to make out what they were exactly, but she couldn't. "Are they bugs or fairies or what? I can't tell."

"They're energy, like the rest of us," Bermuda answered. "They take on the form of light, but to be honest, I've never seen a form behind it either."

"How bizarre." Sophia shook her head, worried that they'd put her under a spell again, but thankfully they didn't. Then her eyes slid to a black goat sitting a few yards from the will-o'-wisp. She was surprised to find such a normal animal in the circus tent. As soon as she thought that, the goat did the most unexpected thing and nearly made Sophia yelp in surprise.

CHAPTER EIGHTY-EIGHT

When NO10JO morphed from his cyborg dog form into an object, it was always surprising. When Ainsley shapeshifted, it was usually very jarring. But watching the black goat spring up into the form of a large black stallion was beyond astonishing.

"Whoa, what's wrong with that goat?" Sophia's eyes were wide as she watched the beautiful horse whinny and scrape its hoof over the ground, kicking up dirt.

"Manx isn't a goat at all," Bermuda stated.

"No, I see that he's a horse now."

"He's neither a horse nor a goat," Bermuda imparted.

"Right," Sophia drew out the word with uncertainty.

"He's a púca," Bermuda explained.

For a moment, Sophia thought that the giantess had let out a modest sneeze, but then she recognized the term. "Those are the magical creatures that shift from goat to horse to cat to dog and hares, right?"

"And also raven," Bermuda added.

Goat, the imp, had strode over to where the stallion stood and held up the heads of green leaf lettuce.

"Go ahead and shift, Manx," Bermuda encouraged the púca.

The creature looked over his shoulder at Bermuda and shook his head with a defiant expression in his black eyes. He stretched out his neck and tried to nibble on the leaves of lettuce. Goat yanked them away.

"Manx," Bermuda chided with a warning in her voice. "What did I say? We're not feeding you in horse form. That will cost more food than is necessary. Remember that it's about being smart and choosing the best form for what you've got to do."

The stallion tossed his tail in the air and whinnied again. However, Manx appeared to have capitulated. He shrank, this time taking on the form of a shiny black hare.

Goat dutifully laid the heads of green leaf lettuce in front of the hare and Manx began nibbling, his pointy ears high in the air.

"Wow, what a brilliant creature," Sophia remarked.

"He's a total pain in the ass, and he knows it," Bermuda said loud enough for the púca to hear. She sighed. "But that's what his type is known for. They are very mischievous and prone to pranks."

"Seems like that's the theme of your current menagerie," Sophia observed.

"Well, I don't know. I think Piper is quite nice." Bermuda held out her hand to a small set of trees nestled among some bushes. At least, that's what Sophia had thought it was, but after Bermuda's words, the tree moved. Sophia watched as a woman's head untucked from the branches. Her face and hair were green and matched the leaves draped like a garland around her neck, arms, waist, and lower half. Her skin was like a human's but also held a wood-grain design, and her bottom portion appeared to be a trunk connected to the bushes beside her.

"Oh, my." Sophia's surprise deepened. "She's beautiful."

Bermuda nodded proudly.

"Why thank you," the woman said. She looked like a human, and also very much like a tree.

"Indeed," Bermuda stated. "Piper is a nymph, and has left the sanctuary of her home to help me to educate the masses this month."

The nymph bowed her head. "It is my pleasure."

Bermuda turned her attention to Sophia. "Piper is a forest nymph, as you have no doubt discerned on your own. There are also freshwater, sea, and mountain nymphs. I daresay you've probably seen all of them dozens of times and not realized it."

Trying not to stare but finding it hard to pull her eyes away from Piper, Sophia nodded. "I can see how they would blend into their surroundings."

"They are their surroundings," Bermuda stated, then turned her attention away. "Well, it looks like we're set up for refreshments."

Sophia spun to find that Goat had disappeared after feeding Manx and quietly set up a table with a full tea service by the entrance. It was elegantly done up with a silk tablecloth and real china. On a three-tiered platter were sandwiches, pastries, and cookies. Sophia wished that she was hungry, but the ice cream sundae had done its job.

"This looks fantastic," Sophia said when she saw Goat by the entrance flap. "Thank you."

He nodded before disappearing outside.

"It does." Bermuda pulled off her flower-adorned straw hat and ruffled her curly hair. "And over tea, I will tell you how I made a grave error that nearly cost the Dragon Elite their lives."

CHAPTER EIGHTY-NINE

Sophia didn't move from her spot as Bermuda, surprisingly gracefully, pulled out the sturdy chair that looked too small for her and perched on the seat's edge. Of all the things Sophia expected Bermuda Laurens to say, an admittance that she made a mistake that almost wiped out the Dragon Elite wasn't one of them.

"Is this about the exploding sheep?" Sophia asked, still standing in place.

Bermuda shook her head. "No, but we'll get to that as well. I heard a rumor about your little problem in Scotland."

"More of a big problem if you ask the grumpy dragons," Sophia pointed out.

The giantess nodded while daintily taking a pastry and putting it on her plate. "They do prefer sheep, and I think it offers them the best results based on their physical makeup and dietary needs."

"What error did you make?" Sophia watched as Bermuda poured steaming hot tea into both of their cups.

"Nevin Gooseman outsmarted the educator in me. At least, that's who I assume is behind this."

Sophia nodded. "I've recently come to that conclusion too. He appears not to have died as I hoped."

"Wishing death on your enemies is never acceptable," Bermuda said with a pursed expression. "We should wish reformation on them. Rehabilitation of ways and flawed thinking. But never death."

"Is that what you did to the magicians who murdered your husband and threatened you and Rory if you exposed the House of Seven?" Sophia asked boldly. She knew it was a risk and was prepared for the giant's wrath, but Bermuda's statement wasn't fair. No, death wasn't the first option when facing enemies, but sometimes it was the only one. Sophia had seen that all too often when battling someone who wouldn't back down from their evil ways.

To her surprise, a spark of amusement flickered in Bermuda's eyes. "Touché, Sophia Beaufont. And no, I wanted the Sinclairs to pay for what they did to our family and my clan of giants. I believe that what they got was appropriate because there was no reasoning with them. But I think that for the most part, we shouldn't stoop to the level of our enemies or one day we'll look in the mirror and find we've become the very thing we intended to stop."

"I don't disagree," Sophia admitted. "It's a slippery slope for sure. Fighting for peace has always seemed counterintuitive to me."

Bermuda smiled knowingly at this. "That's why I appreciate your strategic approach. You don't resort to fighting first thing, but it is sometimes unavoidable."

"Unfortunately," Sophia admitted.

"I was referring to the leviathan and the simurgh, which I learned made a recent appearance in the Mediterranean Sea, and the Dragon Elite had to fight."

Sophia laughed at this. "Made an appearance sounds like they showed up fashionably late for a party and left before the appetizers got cold."

"I suppose it does." Bermuda sipped her tea with her pinky high in the air.

"They wanted to eat us as appetizers." Sophia laughed.

"I'm certain that they did." Bermuda set down her cup and let out a weighty breath. "Now sit before your tea gets cold. It's hard enough for me to admit that I'm the cause of this, and it would be easier if you were sitting."

Sophia wanted to point out that standing, she still wasn't as tall as the giantess sitting, but she figured it was best not to since she'd never seen it be hard for Bermuda to say anything. The woman spoke her mind and said things flatly—albeit usually with an edge of rudeness.

She dutifully sat but didn't go for the tea right away. Instead, she gave Bermuda a careful expression that said, "Go on then."

"You see," the giantess began, "I believe, from what I've been able to deduce, that Nevin Gooseman pretended to be a college student and contacted me about a research paper he was doing on magical creatures. I supplied him with information on the leviathan, the simurgh, and many other animals during that conversation. I thought at the time that his knowledge was pointed and the questions about the creatures' locations were maybe a little too specific, but I always want to educate, and in this case it was my downfall."

Sophia sipped her tea now and shook her head. "So he used you to find the animals? That's smart."

"Deceptive is what it is, but yes, that man shouldn't be underestimated," Bermuda related.

Sophia nodded. "And now I believe he's behind our sheep problem."

This didn't seem to surprise Bermuda. "I do apologize that I unknowingly aided him in finding magical and powerful creatures that you all had to stop. I think he must have done something to enhance the animals because, from the news reports I saw of your battle, they weren't acting in typical ways."

"So he put an angry spell on them, did he?" Sophia asked.

"It appears so." Bermuda took a sandwich and nibbled on it. "And my admission isn't the end of it."

Sophia set her teacup down. "What else?"

"Well, as I said, Nevin asked about many magical creatures when he contacted me," Bermuda explained. "Which makes me think that the leviathan and the simurgh were only the beginning, and he might have something worse that he plans to take the Dragon Elite down with."

CHAPTER NINETY

It was hard for Sophia to imagine anything worse than a giant sea monster with huge tentacles and a horrible temper. Or something more dangerous than a massive bird with a bad attitude and a taste for blood. However, the look on Bermuda's face told Sophia this was serious.

"What other magical creatures did Nevin Gooseman ask about?" Sophia asked.

"He asked about quite a few," Bermuda answered. "I can give you a full list, but I don't think it will help."

"I would disagree," Sophia argued. "Knowing what we could face is beneficial. I've already been told that the riders and the dragons will need special armor and weapons for an upcoming battle, but there's been no information on the actual enemies."

"Armor will be important regardless," Bermuda stated. "And I'm glad you'll be prepared for whatever you encounter, but I can't give you any real clues about what you'll face."

"But all you have to do is tell me the creatures that Nevin asked about."

"And I intend to, but the one that I suspect Nevin is sending your way is not something that I'm aware of." Bermuda paused to take another bite of food, then very properly wiped the corners of her mouth with her napkin. "You see, the reason I became suspicious before I saw the reports on the leviathan and the simurgh was because I realized a memory charm had been placed on me. I have an excellent memory, but when I tried to recall parts of the conversation with the college student afterward, it was quite murky."

"He put a memory enchantment on you?" Sophia asked. "Over the phone? That's impressive."

"Scary is what it is," Bermuda retorted. "And I think he did it retroactively because at one point, I do think I recalled all of the conversation, but much like a dream, the more time that went by and the longer I tried to think about it, the harder certain details were to remember."

"So you're telling me that he blotted out the portion on the actual animal that he's using to fight the Dragon Elite, aren't you?"

Sophia instantly deflated, wondering why things had to be so difficult. Was it too much to ask to know which deadly magical creature they would face on a mystery date?

"That's exactly what I'm telling you," Bermuda stated. "The parts on the leviathan and the simurgh were at the beginning of the conversation, and I remember somewhat, especially after the events with them came to pass. I recall a few other details, but there's a chunk that's missing like I blacked out."

"Because Nevin thought you might figure it out after he released those two and didn't want you to give us a heads up," Sophia guessed.

"Which is what I was going to do," Bermuda stated. "I have to warn you, I've seen many a crafty magician, but Nevin Gooseman shouldn't be underestimated. He's incredibly skillful, and the fact that he was able to find the leviathan and the simurgh and enhance them makes me confident that whatever else he has in store for you will be monumental."

Sophia nodded, already preparing herself mentally for this deadly creature or creatures. Her mind was already going wild with the possibilities. Could it be a swarm of murderous bugs or a flock of crazy birds or an oversized cat? "This is a man who singlehandedly turned the world against the Dragon Elite and sent a magitech army to destroy the most powerful place in the world—the Great Library. Believe me. I'm not at all underestimating him. However, is there anything you can offer about what we could be facing?"

The regret was heavy on Bermuda's face as she pushed her crumb-sprinkled empty plate away. "I'm sorry. I don't think any of the information I remember from my conversation with him will help, but I'll send you the details of what I do know for the purpose of elimination."

Sophia nodded. Nevin must have known that the element of surprise was one of his best weapons, and he was right.

"What I can offer you that will be of use is information on your sheep problem." Bermuda's tone lightened.

Managing a relieved smile, Sophia said, "That would be welcome. You know what's wrong with them and how to fix them?"

"I know that the water supply has been infected," Bermuda stated. "But I don't know how to fix the problem. Poison isn't my specialty."

"So it's something that only affects the sheep," Sophia muttered. "So weird."

"Again, Nevin Gooseman is incredibly crafty," Bermuda reminded her. "I've never seen anything like the tactics he employs. Whatever his reasons for going after the Dragon Elite, he's relentless."

"We've got to fix the water supply." Sophia thought hard but didn't find a realistic solution.

"I agree, but I don't believe that a simple healing elixir like what you and Rudolf are selling will work."

Sophia sighed. "Maybe we give the sheep bottled water." The visual of the sheep on the Expanse drinking Smart Water enhanced with electrolytes in sporty little bottles was quite entertaining for Sophia.

However, Bermuda didn't appear as amused by the idea. She scowled. "I don't think that's a realistic solution."

Sophia was about to tell her that it was sarcasm but then remembered that the giantess didn't favor this type of joke and would probably scowl deeper at her if she did. This was chiefly the reason that Bermuda didn't favor Liv. Well, and also because her sister apparently didn't brush her hair often enough for the giantess' liking.

"Save the world, protect the innocent, and put the guilty away," Liv often said. "And at the end of the day, all anyone cares about is how my hair looks."

"Although I don't know how to fix the water supply or heal the sheep in Scotland of this problem," Bermuda began, "I think I know someone who will."

Sophia brightened suddenly. "A lead would be great. Thank you."

The giantess' face darkened. "Unfortunately, the person I'm aware of who has extensive knowledge of poison is not someone I favor."

"Oh…" Sophia drew out the word. That didn't mean much to her since she suspected that Bermuda didn't favor practically anyone.

"Yes, but they have the right skill set to create an antidote for the poison if anyone will."

Immediately, Sophia thought of Bep, the potions expert at the Rose Apothecary on Roya Lane. It would make sense that she would know how to fix the water supply.

"You'll want to be careful around this person," Bermuda continued. "Not only is she incredibly dangerous employing poisoned baked goods to assassinate people, but she also has a horrible sense of humor."

Sophia smiled wide as her mood unexpectedly lifted.

This produced a disapproving expression from the magical creatures expert. "I don't think you're taking this seriously, based on the look on your face. I must stress the importance of not trusting this person. She is your only option, but absolutely can't be trusted. She will save a person only to kill them later."

Sophia laughed. "Oh, don't worry. I'm taking this seriously. It's just that I've worked with the assassin baker many times and don't fear her at all, although her jokes are truly, truly awful."

CHAPTER NINETY-ONE

To Sophia's surprise, she looked forward to seeing Lee. The assassin had strangely started to grow on her after their many adventures together. It made sense that she was a poison expert, having employed a lot of it in her baking.

After stepping through the portal to Roya Lane, Sophia made her way to the Crying Cat Bakery, but she stopped before she reached it when she passed an elfin man who she didn't recognize. However, a specific scar on his temple made her certain she did know the elf.

"Ainsley?" Sophia grabbed the man by the arm and stopped him as he passed.

He narrowed his blue eyes at her. "I don't know what you're talking about."

Sophia studied the scar, which was curved such that it was unlikely two people could have the same shaped one in the same place. Also, Sophia had learned at the beginning of her time at the Gullington that there was one way to spot Ainsley when she shapeshifted. She could change her hair, eyes, gender, race, and her species.

However, the one thing the elf couldn't do was erase the scar on her temple. All shapeshifters had a mark that showed up when they changed. That was the only way to spot them for those who knew what they were looking for.

The elfin man tried to steer around Sophia, but she kept her grip on his arm and stepped in front of him, blocking his path.

"Nice try, but I know it's you, Ains."

The man growled. "Seriously, S. Beaufont, you had to run into me here."

Sophia sighed, glad that she was right and not about to be assaulted by a stranger. "Why were you trying to fool me?"

The guy sighed heavily, and a shadow of a familiar Ainsley expression flickered on his face. "I don't want anything that reminds me of the past right now. I'm working, and it's easier if I stay focused and not get distracted by emotions."

Sophia studied the man and wished she was looking at Ainsley so she could tell what was going on. Reading her nonverbal cues would be helpful. However, Sophia spied the tension that the shapeshifter couldn't cover while still in elfin form.

"We all miss you." Sophia wanted to hug her friend but felt weird doing it in her current form. It would be like hugging a stranger.

Ainsley worked to keep her expression flat. "All? I'm sure you're exaggerating."

"No, I'm not," Sophia argued. "The Castle isn't the same without you, although Trin is doing a good job. Quiet mopes around a lot and Evan can't find his shoes most of the time. Wilder keeps bringing up what he calls Ainslisms. They're always fun things you've done or said."

"Oh, so not all," Ainsley stated matter-of-factly.

"I wasn't done," Sophia said at once. "Everyone misses you in their way." Sophia knew that the previous housekeeper for the Castle at the Gullington was thinking about Hiker. Still it didn't feel right to share any details about him after witnessing their intimate goodbye. What was she supposed to say, that Hiker was distant and constantly distracted? That was the truth, but no one could connect it to Ainsley's sudden absence, and what if it gave her false hope? Sophia decided it was best to stay out of the already complex situation.

"Well, I miss you," Ainsley admitted. "The rest of that lot, well, we spent a lot of centuries together so excuse me if I'm not pining for them yet. Although I could use a hug from Mama Jamba."

Sophia smiled warmly. "Those are the best hugs in the world. And she picks at her pancakes, obviously not as happy with them since you left."

That made the shapeshifter grin. "Trin will get there eventually, but I will admit I'm happy that I'm not easily replaced."

"It would be impossible to replace you."

The smile faded at once. "For you, that might be true, but I don't think everyone shares that sentiment."

Sophia knew they were indirectly talking about Hiker, but again, she wasn't going to get involved. It wasn't good for her and put her in an impossible situation. So she decided to try a different approach. "Speaking of Mama Jamba, did you end up using that time ball thingy she made for you?"

Ainsley looked away suddenly, like something at the far side of Roya Lane had stolen her attention. "Oh, that thing…yeah, I played around with it, I guess."

"It's such an interesting magical object," Sophia related. "To be able to see your life if you made different decisions. I bet it's a head trip."

"Not as much as you'd think." The elf still wouldn't meet Sophia's gaze.

"So how is your work with the Elfin Council going?" Sophia tried to change the subject, sensing the stress that Ainsley tried to hide.

She shrugged and appeared disinterested. "It's the same old, same old."

Sophia couldn't help but laugh. "Only you would say that about doing international delegate work for a governing body after being stuck at the Gullington for centuries."

Amusement danced in Ainsley's eyes before she shook it away. "The Gullington during the dark ages was interesting. It seemed there was always something going on. I mean, you live around dragons, and it's never a dull moment, but don't tell anyone I said that. It's better if I pretended to loathe it, even back then."

Sophia ran her fingers over her mouth like she was zipping her lips shut.

"Well, tell the others that...no, don't tell them you saw me," Ainsley stated. "Or do and say that I looked better than ever, full of life, and richer than ever. Oh, and somehow let it slip that I'm dating an elfin warlock by the name of Gregor Flamel the Second."

"Oh, are you?" Sophia asked, suddenly curious.

Ainsley shook her head. "No, but he's a devilishly good-looking guy who everyone knows."

Sophia was pretty sure that by "everyone," Ainsley meant, "Hiker."

"I'll let it slip," Sophia stated. "I'm sure the others will be happy to hear you're doing well."

"Maybe," Ainsley muttered, not at all looking convinced. "Well, I'm sure you're busy trying to save the world. I'll leave you to it."

"The Gullington, currently," Sophia admitted, remembering her present mission.

The look of concern on Ainsley's face was immediate. "The Gullington? What's wrong? Is everyone okay?"

Sophia nodded at once. "Yes, it's just that the sheep are exploding. It gave Lunis an awful stomachache at first, but he's fine, and Quiet has secured a different food source for the time being. But I'm here to fix the water supply, which caused it."

Ainsley laughed with relief. "Oh, little bits of wool everywhere. I bet Quiet is livid."

"He's muttering nonstop and definitely peeved," Sophia admitted.

"Well, tell him that I said hello. Then inform Evan that I said to tuck in his shirt. And tell Wilder that his hair is messed up." She laughed. "He'll rush off to fix it, I bet. Let Mahkah know that he's still my favorite, and hug Mama Jamba for me."

Sophia waited, thinking that there was one last message that Ainsley forgot to pass along. However, the elf smiled and said, "That's it. You take care of yourself, S. Beaufont. You hear?"

She nodded. "I will, of course. And you too."

The elfin man backed away, a look of sentimentality heavy in his eyes as he disappeared into the crowd.

Sophia waved at her friend, wishing that she'd have mentioned Hiker at least once. But again, she didn't know where her place was in the assorted affairs between the leader of the Dragon Elite and the delegate for the Elfin Council.

CHAPTER NINETY-TWO

After the reunion with Ainsley, Sophia felt heavier. It was good to see her friend, but also made her wish that nothing had changed. That always felt like the way for her. When she'd come to the Gullington, she missed her family and was torn between them and starting a new life. It was always the good with the bad—progress mixed with painful nostalgia.

That was one of the reasons she hurried to the Crying Cat Bakery. Also, she knew that she needed to get to the exploding sheep as soon as possible and that her friend would probably take her mind off her troubles. She hoped so. Or at the very least, she could ask Lee to slap her in the face, and that would do the trick. The assassin baker would welcome such an opportunity.

When Sophia entered the Crying Cat Bakery, she found King Rudolf Sweetwater leaning over one of the counters with a stack of pictures in his hands.

"You should have seen it," he gushed while sorting through the prints. "The Captains had the best time, and they all built bears that have been eating through the pantry at night, although I suspect it might be Serena since I could have sworn she had Dorito dust on her fingers this morning when we woke up. She said it was because she caught the bears in the act and had to slap them silly, but I'm not sure."

Lee feigned a smile and waved Sophia in as she approached the counter. "Rudolf was just showing me his triplets' birthday celebration."

"It was fun," Sophia said. "Whoever arranged it is nice."

"Sounds like a horrible person who would like to remain nameless," Lee stated with deliberation in her voice, her eyes wide.

"It was Sophia," Rudolf stated, then put his arm around her without her permission and hugged her tightly. "She's always doing the nicest things, like making my wife live a few extra decades—"

"I did that for several million dollars," Sophia argued.

"And saving me from abduction," Rudolf went on dreamily.

"That was to save the Dragon Elite and bring down Nevin Gooseman," she countered.

"And leaving that package of recreational drugs on my doorstep," Rudolf continued.

"That wasn't me," Sophia replied.

He smiled. "Well, still, it's the thought that counts. Your thank-you note for the hallucinogens is in the mail, although because of the previously mentioned drugs, I might have only imagined writing a thank you note and sending it. Only time will tell."

"Can't wait," Sophia said with a fake smile.

"Do you want to see the pictures from the Captains' birthday?" Rudolf shoved the prints in her face.

Sophia shook her head. "I'm good, but thanks. I was there, remember?"

He shrugged. "Not really. That's why I took pictures." Rudolf glanced down at the top copy, which showed a group shot of everyone at the party. "Oh, you were there! That's right. And you kept thinking that the Captains were the same age."

"It was their birthday," Sophia reasoned. "They're triplets."

Rudolf shook his head and looked at Lee. "Explaining how math works to this blonde will be the death of me. Anyway, I'm off to conduct fae business. Someone has to keep the best empire in the world afloat."

"And what will you do all day?" Lee asked as he progressed toward the door.

Without missing a beat, Rudolf waved and smiled over his shoulder. "I was told to stay out of the way by those I employ. They say that on the days I leave the kingdom they get the most amount of work done. So hopefully I've been gone long enough for them to solve our financial crisis and create solutions to the fae educational system because Papa needs a nappy nap."

"Fae educational system?" Sophia had to question, surprised by this. "I didn't know there was a problem with it or that you had one."

"Well, I tried to create one, thinking I'd empower my people, but it didn't turn out so well," Rudolf related.

Lee leaned in and whispered over Sophia's shoulder, "You know how they say that line about give a man a fish?"

She nodded.

"Well, if you teach a fae to fish they all drown, so just give them some wine and don't expect much else from them. This is the race that we're all keeping afloat."

"And in exchange, we offer you all the debauchery that you can handle in Las Vegas," Rudolf added with satisfaction.

"Well, I applaud your ambition to teach your people," Sophia stated. "It's the thought that counts."

"Yeah, and it could have gone worse," Lee imparted. "He could have employed common core to teach simple practices. That would have led to a lot of irate parents who took up drinking to deal with helping with homework."

Sophia didn't know what Lee was going on about, but Rudolf pretended to as he opened the door and waved over his shoulder. "You gals are my absolute favorites. Never change, Susan and Pam. Never, ever change."

CHAPTER NINETY-THREE

"Do you think it's all right if I change my name?" Lee asked Sophia when King Rudolf left. "I've never felt much like a Susan...or a Pam. Honestly, I've always wanted to be a Crystal."

"You're a Lee," Sophia argued. "Through and through."

"So if you're here about the wanted ad, the job for a dishwasher has already been filled," Lee told her matter-of-factly while wiping down the counter with a dirty rag.

"I'm not," Sophia stated dryly.

The baker let out a breath. "You should have applied. How much longer are you going to sleep on your parent's couch and mooch off them?"

"My parents are dead, and I'm a dragonrider for the Elite," Sophia argued, mostly amused.

"Don't try that dead parents thing on me," Lee countered. "I know all too well that your parents don't have to be alive to sleep on their couch."

"Can we move on?"

"You don't want the job washing dishes?" Lee asked.

"I thought you filled it."

"I lied," Lee said coyly. "I was playing hard to get. You know, make you want it and think you couldn't have it."

"I'm good," Sophia replied. "Think I'm going to stick with my day job of adjudicating and saving the world."

"'Kay, well, when that whole thing falls through, you know where to find me," Lee sang and continued to wipe down the counters.

"I'm here because I need your help with something."

In a flash, Lee jumped up on a nearby stool, pushed back a tile in the ceiling, and retrieved a long sword from a hiding spot. She held it close to her chest and grinned. "Who hurt you? How many pieces do you want them in?"

Sophia's eyes widened. "Whoa, do you think it's safe to keep blades overhead like that?"

"Probably not," Lee stated. "But neither is keeping them above my wife's side of the bed, or in the bags of flour here, or between the towels in the linen closet. Do you think that stops me?"

"I'm going to answer with no, Bob."

Lee shot a finger gun at Sophia. "Right-o, you are."

"Anyway," Sophia drew out the word. "I don't need your help with taking anyone out. Quite the opposite."

Lee shook her head. "How many times have I told you that I can't bring people back from the dead?"

"Never," Sophia answered.

"Oh, then that's a very realistic, repetitive dream I've been having." Lee shook her head as if dispelling a strange thought.

"Anyway, I've heard from a source that you might be able to help me with something," Sophia began. "You see, it involves poison."

Lee nodded. "I knew you would come around. Who are we poisoning? That boyfriend of yours? Your sister? Oh, maybe both? That's how it always goes. The ones you love the most are the ones you need taken down at some point."

Sophia's eyes widened. "You are a very warped individual."

"Thank you," Lee said proudly.

"And no," Sophia stated firmly. "I don't want you to poison anyone. Quite the opposite. The water supply in Scotland has been tampered with, and it's affecting the sheep. I need your help with fixing it."

Lee gave her a reluctant look. "I'm not in favor of helping things to live. My job is to take down the world's population, not keep it going."

"Well, the dragons eat sheep, and they help us take down bad guys," Sophia argued. "So if you can fix the water problem, then the dragons will be happy and can massacre large leagues of villains."

Lee leaned forward on her arms, which rested on the countertop. "I'm listening."

"Look, I'm sure we can find a way to compensate you for your time and all," Sophia stated. "Just think what it is that you need and—"

"Accompany me to the Fantastical Armory," Lee said in a rush.

It was such a weird and easy request that Sophia paused and tilted her head. "What? But you've been there with me."

"I know, but I'm too afraid to go in there by myself," Lee related. "You know, it being Father Time's shop and all."

"It's Subner's, but I guess I get it," Sophia stated.

"Well, you see, I've been trying to work up the nerve to go into the shop and ask Father Time for his autograph."

"That's what you want?" Sophia asked.

"Oh, yeah!" Lee exclaimed. "I've got a huge book of autographs. Really famous people like Micky Cocker and Kelly O'Donnell."

"I don't know them—"

"Your loss," Lee stated. "Anyway, it's been a lifelong dream to add Father Time's autograph to the scrapbook. And as a bonus, if Subner, the weapons guy is there—"

"I think he's under the weather," Sophia interrupted.

Lee rubbed her hands together with a satisfied expression on her face. "Even better."

"Wait; what?"

"Nothing," the baker assassin said at once.

"Well, I did need to check on Dr. Freud's progress with Subner," Sophia mused.

"Exactly," Lee stated. "And while you do that, I'll get Father Time's autograph, or you have the old geezer accompany you while you check on Sub-whatever. Either way, I request you accompany me in the Fantastical Armory, or I'm not killing your sheep."

"Saving them," Sophia corrected.

Lee waved her hand dismissively at her. "Whatever, same thing."

"It's not," Sophia argued. "Are you sure that you can help with the poisoned water?"

Lee nodded confidently. "Oh, yeah. It's easy to reverse engineer these things. If you can make a poison, then you can take it out. It's simple science."

Sophia blinked at her friend blankly. "Not for most. If you have such skills, why not use them for good?"

This seemed to be an outrageous idea for the baker assassin. "Why ever would I want to do that?"

"Well," Sophia began, working out the idea. "If you could help others by fixing their poisoned water supplies, for instance, then they would be reliant on you and you could charge them a premium and make a killing off helping them with their problems."

"Then I go around poisoning water supplies and waiting for them to call me to fix the problem," Lee said victoriously.

"Nooooo," Sophia stated firmly. "I was thinking that you went around helping with existing problems. There are enough of them in the world. Then you're rewarded handsomely with tons of dollars. And it's a win-win for everyone."

"I don't like the part where no one dies, but I could warm to this idea," Lee said skeptically. "I like your idea of having lots of money that Cat doesn't know about that I can use to buy a private island where I escape to every weekend."

"That wasn't my entire idea," Sophia argued. "Just the getting handsomely rewarded for using your powers for good."

"Will you stop saying it that way?" Lee grimaced. "You don't know how to sell an idea."

"Fine," Sophia acquiesced. "We'll work out these details later. But in the meantime, you'll help me with my water supply problem?"

"If you take me to the Fantastical Armory right now."

"Sure," Sophia answered. "Grab your autograph book."

Lee patted her pocket which appeared empty except for the shape of something that resembled a knife. "I've always got it on me."

"That seems overzealous." Sophia headed for the door, grateful she was that much closer to helping the sheep at the Gullington and therefore the dragons.

As they exited the Crying Cat Bakery, Lee called to the back, "I'm going to the brothels. I'll be back when I damn well please, woman!"

"Bring me back some cigarettes," Cat yelled back without missing a beat.

CHAPTER NINETY-FOUR

"Why not tell your wife the truth, that you were going to help me with a problem affecting all of Scotland?" Sophia asked as they made their way to the Fantastical Armory.

Lee scowled at her. "You are out of touch, aren't you? I bet you're nice to that boyfriend of yours, always lifting him up and never tearing him down."

"Yeah, usually I tell him that I love him often."

The assassin baker shook her head. "Who hurt you, Sophia? Who hurt you?"

"My siblings always told me that they loved me often," Sophia related while thinking fondly of Reese and Ian. A pang of grief hit her for a moment. "And now, Clark has kept up the tradition. I start to worry that she's fallen into a pit of lava yet again if I don't get an I love you GIF once a day from Liv. It's the way the Beaufonts are. Apparently, my parents believed that you couldn't express love too much."

Lee shivered as if this admission grossed her out. "Can we change the subject? This is all bordering too close to an after school special, and I just ate."

Sophia laughed and led the way to the Fantastical Armory.

"Hey," Lee said with enthusiasm. "Do you want to hear something that will make you want to die?"

"Strangely, no."

"Okay, here it goes. I've been working on some new material." Lee cleared her throat. "If you're American when you go in the bathroom and American when you come out, what are you in the bathroom?"

Sophia cut her eyes at the woman. "What?"

"European!"

"Oh, angels above." Sophia groaned.

"What's red and bad for your teeth?" Lee asked.

"Twizzlers?" Sophia attempted to answer, not sure why she was encouraging the bad joke-telling. Probably because she missed Lunis, she reasoned.

"A brick!" Lee exclaimed with a delighted laugh.

"You should save these jokes for Papa Creola," Sophia offered. "I'm sure he'll love them." She knew for a fact that he wouldn't and his irritation would be palpable, but that would be entertaining for her to watch.

"Do you want to hear a joke about paper?" Lee asked, suddenly quite serious.

"Do I have a choice?" Sophia countered.

Lee waved her hand at her. "Never mind, it's tearable."

"Do you by chance have any poison on you?" Sophia asked. "If so, I'll take a drink."

Lee shot her fist into the air victoriously. "I knew the new jokes were right on the money. And by that, I mean so bad they'd kill."

"You have quite the gift," Sophia agreed while rounding the corner into the Fantastical Armory, where she should have been surprised to find Papa Creola standing in the middle of the store, his arms crossed and his eyes directed at the pair.

"Let's get this over with, shall we?" he asked as soon as they strode into the shop.

CHAPTER NINETY-FIVE

"Am I late for an appointment with you that I didn't know I was going to have until a few minutes ago?" Sophia asked Papa Creola, who wore his usual impatient expression.

"Pretty much," he replied, then turned and strode for the door at the back of the shop.

"Do you want to give me a list of these appointment times so I can put them on my calendar and be on time?" Sophia hurried after him.

He shook his head. "That's not how it works."

Lee had paused at the front of the shop and nervously teetered back and forth with her hands in her pockets.

Sophia gestured at her. "So my friend here—"

"Has to stay in the showroom while we go and check on Subner," Papa Creola interrupted.

"Oh, but she wants—"

"I'm fine," Lee cut in. "You two go. I'll stay here and wait."

"Is no one going to let me finish my sent—"

"No," Papa Creola interrupted again as he yanked open the door and charged through.

Sophia had been down to Father Time's office before, and it was a hundred stories down in a basement. However, the room they stepped into wasn't at all what she expected.

They had entered what appeared to be a psych ward in a hospital. The floors and walls were so white that they made Sophia blink from the sudden brightness. It seemed that they were in an empty viewing room. On the far side was a two-way mirror, and through it, Sophia saw Subner and Dr. Tiffannee Freud.

The Protector of Weapons was lying on a couch with his hands clasped over his chest. Beside him, the psychiatrist sat in a large armchair and scribbled on a yellow pad of paper.

"Now in this dream, what happened next?" Dr. Freud asked.

"Well, I was supposed to take a little boy on vacation with me," Subner began, his voice airy like usual since he'd become an elf, but thankfully he wasn't talking in hippie quotes. "The plan was to meet him at the airport and go from there. It was a charity trip of sorts, and his grandmother was going to deliver him with his suitcase. But when they showed up, they didn't have a suitcase. I called his mother, and she didn't think it was a good idea to take him since the grandmother hadn't prepared him. However, I was sad about disappointing him, so I was naturally torn."

Dr. Freud bit the end of her pen. "That's very interesting..."

"Is it?" Subner sounded confused. "I've had the dream every day for months, since becoming an elf, but I don't get the significance."

"The different characters in the dream represent the three distinct parts of yourself," the doctor stated. "The little boy is your id, the part of your desires that wants what it wants regardless of how practical, or rather impractical it is."

Sophia gave Papa Creola a speculative look, wondering if she should be watching this session that seemed personal and between the Protector of Weapons and his therapist.

He caught her looking at him and said, "We'll stay a little longer. That's all that's needed."

"For what?" she asked, confused.

"Shush," he commanded and pointed at the two-way mirror as the doctor continued.

"The grandmother represents your superego, which is obviously out of balance and forgot to prepare your less governed self," Dr. Freud imparted. "And finally, the mother is your ego, who is realistic, but inevitably has to deliver the disappointing news regarding what is possible."

"What am I to do with this information?" Subner asked.

"The key to balance for anyone is to find balance among the three parts," the doctor explained. "When one is more dominant, then the psyche suffers, as you've experienced by regressing. In your elfin form, your ego doesn't get heard, as you've pointed out, and feels disappointed that your id self wouldn't get to go on the trip because of practicality. And your superego refuses to prepare the id for what it wants. So to achieve balance, you're going to need to—"

"Well, that should just about do it," Papa Creola interrupted, talking over the psychiatrist so that Sophia couldn't hear what she said for Subner to do.

She gawked at him. "Wait; what? What should just about do it?"

"We've been gone long enough," Papa Creola stated and made his way back to the door.

"What are you talking about?" Sophia asked. "You brought me in here to see Subner's progress?"

"Yeah, sure," Papa Creola said dismissively.

"Well, he will get better right?" She looked from Papa Creola through the two-way mirror.

"Yes, he just has to assimilate the parts of himself and come to terms with this form," Papa Creola answered. "He will look different the next time you see him. When you think you see a stranger on Roya Lane, it will be him."

"Okay." Sophia drew out the word. "When will that be? When should I expect to get these weapons that will help me fight this mysterious magical creature or creatures or whatever it is that you won't disclose?"

"When the weapons are ready for you." Papa Creola opened the door to the shop again.

Sophia sighed and followed him through. "You should be glad I'm so patient and have come to terms with being locked in the dark."

"I will be glad if you take that assassin from my shop before she tells me a bad joke," Papa Creola stated while striding back into the Fantastical Armory's main showroom.

Lee suddenly straightened while whistling conspicuously. "I'm not doing anything. I was just standing here."

"Ummm...okay." Sophia looked around suspiciously.

"It's time for you two to leave." Papa Creola pointed at the door.

"Yeah, but first, Lee wanted your—"

The assassin baker grabbed Sophia's arm and hauled her toward the door. "Didn't you hear the man? It's time to leave."

"But you wanted his—"

"Get out, Sophia," Papa Creola ordered.

"Why is it that you two keep interrup—"

"Would you stop blabbering all the time?" Lee cut in. "We're busy people who haven't got the time for your nonsense."

Sophia shook her head at the crazy people and allowed the assassin baker to drag her out of the shop. She waved to Papa Creola as Lee pulled her out the door. "I'm guessing I'll be late to see you the next time. Which will be?"

"You'll find out," Papa Creola replied in a commanding tone.

CHAPTER NINETY-SIX

Once they were out on Roya Lane and not even out of sight of the Fantastical Armory, Lee withdrew a large sword from the back of her waistband with a sigh.

"Oh, that feels much better." She let out a breath. "I never thought we'd get out of that place, you little dawdler."

Sophia froze in place, her eyes wide. "You stole that!"

"I borrowed it," Lee corrected.

"We have to go back," Sophia argued. "You have to return it."

Lee laughed. "Yeah, right. I've had my eye on this pretty thing for a while." She ran her gaze over the blade appreciatively.

"Oh my God, that was all a trick." Sophia put it all together. "You didn't want Papa Creola's autograph. I bet you don't have an autograph book."

The assassin grinned wide. "So you weren't born yesterday. You're cute with your naivety and desire to see the best in others. By the way, would you like to buy a constellation? I have a few for sale."

"I can't believe you!" Sophia's fists balled by her side.

"Fine." Lee groaned. "How about a few stars? I've got a two-for-one special. If you're ever in that area, then you're allowed to camp on your star, but you have to pay a housekeeping fee."

ADAPT OR BE CRUSHED

"You tricked me!" Sophia yelled loud enough that a few gnomes huddled in the shadows of a neighboring building glanced over.

Lee shook her head at them. "Pretty bold move on her part, huh? Yelling at me when I'm holding a sword. Not the brightest bulb, I'd say."

"You can't steal from Papa Creola," Sophia continued.

"Technically, I didn't," Lee argued.

"Borrowed or whatever."

"Technically, I borrowed it from Subner," Lee countered.

"It doesn't matter," Sophia stated. "I have to work with them, and they're going to be pissed when they find out..." She couldn't believe it took her that long to work out all the details. Sophia narrowed her eyes at the pavement, seeing the last set of events she witnessed at the Fantastical Armory. "Papa Creola knew you were going to steal the sword."

"Borrowed," Lee corrected. "I just have no intention of giving it back. Like when I loan my jerk neighbors a book. Wait until they see my new sword." She held the weapon in a fighting stance.

Sophia shook her head. "So Papa Creola knew you were going to steal it. That's why he took me in the other room and said that bit about having been gone long enough. You had no plan of getting his autograph. You were using me."

Lee nodded proudly. "Why would I want that man's autograph? He's the worst. When I'm looking forward to something, time goes so very slowly. When I have to deal with something awful, time all of a sudden slows down. He's the ultimate worst. And don't get me started on time zones and how much I loathe him for that one."

"I was so used." Sophia ambled forward and shook her head.

"You were. Doesn't it feel good?"

"No," she answered at once.

"I know what will make you feel better, or so much worse that you want to end things," Lee stated.

"Please, no more jokes," Sophia begged.

"Did you know that nothing rhymes with orange?" Lee strode up next to Sophia after letting her get ahead for a moment.

"No. No, it doesn't," Sophia retorted.

"Oh, nice way to cut off my joke," Lee said proudly. "Don't worry. Father Time obviously wanted me to have the sword. It's a win-win too because now you get my help with fixing the water supply in Scotland, and I get the sword, which will ensure I don't have to listen to my neighbors watching loud movies at night."

Sophia shot her a punishing stare.

Lee held up her hands in surrender. "Because I'm going to use the sword to cut their cable, obviously."

"Yeah, obviously." Sophia opened a portal to outside the Gullington. "I'm going to take you somewhere that few have seen. Try and be on your best behavior, would you?"

Lee nodded and put one hand behind her back. "I promise."

"Did you just cross your fingers like a schoolchild telling a lie?"

"No!" Lee stated while pulling her hand up and spreading her fingers wide. "See!"

Sophia rolled her eyes.

"Seriously," Lee argued, and held up a pinky. "Look, I'll pinky swear if that will help."

After opening the portal, Sophia shook her head. "You're freaking ridiculous."

"I know you are, but what am I?" Lee countered and stepped through the opening after Sophia.

CHAPTER NINETY-SEVEN

E ntering the Gullington wasn't something that most could do. Sophia had to explain that to Lee.

"You have to want to serve the Dragon Elite, or Quiet won't allow you entry," Sophia imparted.

"I bet y'all have some pretty impressive weapons in there," Lee mused while glancing out at the Barrier she couldn't see, but Sophia instinctively knew was in the distance.

"If you steal anything, then I'll have Liv shut down your bakery and cart you away for petty crimes," Sophia threatened.

Lee's mouth popped open with disgust. "How dare you!"

"Oh, I dared."

"Close my bakery," Lee stated. "Take my wife and lock her up. But send me away for anything less than heinous crimes? Well, that's just wrong, Sophia. I thought we were friends."

"Keep your sticky hands to yourself when we enter the Gullington," Sophia warned.

"Fine," Lee gave in. "Are there any more dumb requests like don't murder my friends or don't entertain me with your incredible wit?"

"Try and murder my friends if you want your wife to be planning a funeral," Sophia stated proudly.

Lee howled with laughter. "Oh, Cat has been planning my funeral for ages. She picked out her dress a few days after our wedding. It's really pretty. I'd say I can't wait to see her in it, but, well…"

"You two are the real deal, aren't you?"

Lee nodded while striding next to Sophia as they approached the Barrier. "Will it hurt when I enter the Gillington?"

"Gullington," Sophia corrected. "I don't think so. Trin seemed all right, but she wanted to serve the Dragon Elite. According to Quiet, our groundskeeper, you have to want to serve us or you won't be allowed entry. I'm not sure what will happen if you're ill-intentioned. Our sheep explode right now, so I don't have high hopes that you'll simply not be allowed to enter. Things tend to happen big at the Gullington."

"Okay, I want to serve the Unicorn Riders," Lee said in a bored voice.

"I don't think that sarcastic attitude will help things," Sophia argued.

"My sarcastic attitude has served me well all my life, Ms. Sophia. So just let me be me, and you be you."

At the Barrier, Sophia passed through as she normally did. She turned and watched as Lee paused, then took a step through. The assassin's eyes widened, either because it hadn't worked or because she could now see the Castle and the Pond and the Caves in the distance. But a second later, Lee sank onto the grass while screaming and writhing in pain.

"Oh, it hurts!" Lee yelled as she clutched her stomach and jerked her head back and forth.

"Lee!" Sophia shot down to a kneeling position. "What is it? What hurts? What can I do?"

Like she suddenly passed out, Lee's head rolled to the side and her eyes closed. Then a smile cracked her lips, and she peeked through one eye.

Sophia growled and jerked to an upright position as Lee howled with laughter.

"You really are twelve years old, aren't you?"

"Twelve and a half," Lee argued and held out a hand like she expected Sophia to help her up.

"So you didn't die entering the Gullington," Sophia stated. "Well, after you fix our water problem, I'll feed you to my dragon."

"It's so cute that you keep up the charade of having a dragon," Lee chimed while nearly skipping on the Expanse as they crossed it, headed to the Pond on the far side of the Gullington.

Sophia pointed at the Castle. "You do see that, which wasn't there before you entered the Barrier, right? And the Caves and Pond, right? Why is it so hard for you to believe we have dragons? They've been all over the news lately."

"I don't watch the news. It gives me nightmares."

The dragonrider laughed and shook her head. "You murder people for a living."

"It's more of a hobby at this point," Lee corrected. "I needed something that was mine after opening up the bakery. Cat has her art projects and books. So I had to find my soul's calling."

"Which was murdering people."

"Yeah, and since then, my soul has sung its song."

"You're the strangest person I know, and that's saying a lot."

"Why thank you," Lee said affectionately, then yanked out the sword she'd stolen from the Fantastical Armory as her entire body tensed. "Get behind me, little one. There's a giant bat headed this way. I'll defend you."

Sophia tensed as well, then turned to find the other half of her soul headed in their direction while gliding through the air, his blue wings like an extension of the sky behind him.

CHAPTER NINETY-EIGHT

"That's my dragon, Lunis," Sophia stated proudly and put a calming hand on Lee to encourage her to put down the sword.

Lee shook her head, pure surprise written on her face. "Dude, I thought you were making up the dragon thing all along."

"Are you serious? You have heard of dragonriders before? We're kind of a big deal. And these missions we've gone on, what did you think those were all about?"

Lee shrugged. "Honestly, I thought they were elaborate escape rooms. So that thing with the evil spirit was real? That's nuts. You almost died."

Sophia nodded. "That's a pretty regular occurrence."

Lunis landed nobly beside Sophia, shook out his wings, and swung his head from side to side. She recognized the little act he was putting on for the company, being regal instead of casually landing like a puppy dog and pretending to lick her face.

"Rider Beaufont," Lunis began in a deep voice. "It has been many moons since you left. Have your travels treated you well?"

Sophia rolled her eyes. "You're ridiculous. You can see everything I see and know that I've been hanging out with this Laffy Taffy, restraining myself from cutting her."

"Wow. You're, like, totally real." Lee ran her astonished eyes over the dragon.

"What did you think?" Lunis asked. "I was all animatronics?"

"Sort of," Lee answered. "And you can talk?"

"Sometimes too much," Sophia related.

"Oooh!" Lunis excitedly said as he dropped the act and resumed his normal way of talking. "Did you hear the rumor about butter?"

Lee didn't expect this strange question. She tilted her head to the side. "No, I haven't. What is it?"

Lunis shook his head. "Never mind. I shouldn't spread it."

Sophia dropped her head, realizing that nightmares did come true in her world.

Meanwhile, Lee howled with laughter and slapped her leg. "Yes, I'm totally stealing that joke."

"Please do," he said proudly.

"Although this is all very entertaining and not at all soul-sucking, we do have a mission for Lee." Sophia pointed at the Pond. "That will be a good place for us to start. Do you need to take readings or do tests or what?"

Lee and Lunis both glared at Sophia, but from the corner of her mouth, the assassin baker said, "Is she always so…"

"Let's save the world?" Lunis supplied.

"Yeah and a stick in the mud too with her responsible attitude," Lee added.

"Always." Lunis also talked from the corner of his mouth.

"I can hear you two dorks," Sophia pointed out.

"I think she knows we're talking about her," Lee whispered.

"Maybe, but if you tell more jokes, she'll ignore you," Lunis offered. "That's how I do it."

Lee nodded. "I like how you do it. Are all dragons as cool as you?"

He shook his head. "None are. The others talk about the days of yore and only eat sheep…well, they used to eat sheep. Now my diet of taquitos and bean dip is looking pretty appealing, I bet."

Sophia crossed her arms and pretended to be annoyed by the two, although they were undoubtedly pretty entertaining and obviously fast friends. "Speaking of sheep, does anyone want to work to save the herd?"

"Again with the demands and always being responsible." Lee sighed. "Is she always like this?"

"Always," Lunis answered.

"Fine." Lee sounded defeated. "Lead me to the poisoned water supply. I'll take a look, but I might need some whisky when we get there."

"For testing purposes?" Sophia asked.

Lee shook her head. "No, to deal with your soul-sucking attitude. I bet you drive many in your life to drink."

Sophia laughed at this. "I can't argue with that."

CHAPTER NINETY-NINE

When the three reached the edge of the Pond, Sophia cautioned Lee with a look of warning. "There's a sea monster that lives in here and protects the waters. So be careful. We can't get too far in."

Lee scoffed at her. "I ate a whole Chilean sea bass this morning for breakfast that was still alive."

"Why would you do that?" Sophia questioned.

"Because we were out of sardines," she answered matter-of-factly.

Lunis gave Sophia a wide-eyed expression. "Can we keep her? Oh, pretty please. I promise to take her out on walks and feed her regularly."

"No, Lun," Sophia answered. "You didn't take care of the last human I let you have."

His face was suddenly covered in embarrassment. "I got hungry."

"I don't taste very good, if that helps," Lee offered. "There was this one time that this bear tried to eat me and I was too wasted on donuts and absinthe from the night before—"

"What a strange combination," Sophia remarked.

Lee nodded. "We were out of Pringles. That would have been the better option over donuts."

285

"Who does your grocery shopping?" Lunis asked. "Or rather, the lack of grocery shopping?"

"I do, but I'm awful at it," Lee answered.

"Obviously," Lunis replied.

"Anyway, this bear tries to eat me while I'm hanging out in Montana," Lee continued. "That's a good story for another time. But the bear takes one bite of my leg and decides I'm not worth it and goes to the river to fish, which was a lot more work than eating me since I was laid out like a Thanksgiving dinner."

"Okay, I'm ready for the story about why you were in Montana." Lunis wagged his tail like an excited puppy.

"No," Sophia cut in. "We have a mission. Water. Remember?"

Lunis sighed dramatically. "You never let me do what I want. When I'm older, I'm out of here!"

Sophia rolled her eyes at her dragon. "You don't mean that."

"Nah, not at all," he said with a chuckle. "Since my life is tied to yours, that would pretty much kill us."

"That's how it works with my wife," Lee mused. "Apparently we're tied together until death does us part, and as far as I can figure out, she's not going anywhere until I die and that will probably be in Las Vegas to put my life insurance all on red."

"Your wife sounds charming," Lunis offered.

"Can we focus here?" Sophia demanded with her hands on her hips. She pointed at the blue water lapping up on the shore. "Water? Lee! Now!"

"Is she always like this?" Lee asked the blue dragon. "All demandy and overcompensating for her runt status with a bad attitude?"

"Always," Lunis stated dryly.

Sophia shot him what most would read as a murderous glare. In her head, she threatened, *I'm considering canceling your Disney Plus subscription now.*

"Nooooo!" he exclaimed out loud, and made Lee, who was bent over the water and studying it jump.

"No what?" the assassin baker asked.

Lunis pointed at Sophia with an accusatory claw. "She threatened to take away my Disney Plus."

Lee glanced up at Sophia since she was hunched low by the water, making her shorter than the dragonrider. "I think you might need to take your dragon to see that psychiatrist. He hears voices, which is normal in my world, but some think of it as weird."

Sophia shook her head. "No, I did threaten him but through our telepathic link."

"Wow, you get to communicate with your dragon telepathically." Lee sighed. "Some people are given all the advantages in life while the rest of us have to settle for mediocre."

Sophia groaned with real annoyance now. "You run a magical bakery on the most iconic road in the world and were recommended by the chief expert on magical creatures as the only person who could fix this water supply problem."

"And yet, I still put my pants on lying down, just like everyone else," Lee related.

"That's not how that phrase... Never mind." Sophia pointed again at the water. "Pond. Fix. Now."

"Someone failed manners school." Lee shook her head and returned her attention to the Pond.

"Speaking of clothes," Lunis began in that voice he used when a bad joke was about to follow. "Do either of you ladies know what a lawyer wears to court?"

"Please...no..." Sophia begged.

"A law suit!" Lunis cheered with a laugh.

Lee's face contorted with confusion. "I don't get it. Why wouldn't they wear a business suit like everyone else? Why does it have to be specific? You don't see me wearing an assassin suit. Or a baker's suit. It's just an apron and a ski mask."

The excited expression on Lunis' face fell away. "Are you serious?" He glanced sideways at Sophia. "I changed my mind. I don't want her."

She nodded. "Told you. A human seems like a fun idea at the time, but then the newness wears off, and they go in the closet with all the other stuff you've lost interest in."

Lee had returned to studying the water. She dipped two fingers into the Pond and sniffed it, her focus to the side as she contemplated it and made her assessment.

Sophia took this rare moment of quiet to look out at the Pond's rippling waters and appreciate its pristine beauty. The Expanse's green hills were such a nice contrast to the blue waters and clear skies, and made Sophia smile from the welcomed meditative experience.

It pained her that Nevin Gooseman had gone after her in Scotland to try and hurt the Dragon Elite. The place wasn't just the home to the Gullington. The cutting winds and sideways rain had become such a strange comfort to Sophia that she always looked forward to returning to the grassy green hills and fresh air at the end of every journey.

"Well, I figured out the problem." Lee stood and wiped her wet hands on her jeans.

"Oh, that was quick," Sophia said with relief. "What is it?"

"The water supply is poisoned," Lee stated matter-of-factly.

Sophia lowered her chin and gave the woman an irritated expression. "Yeah, we already knew that. I was hoping for something more specific."

"You live a charmed life, don't you?" Lee asked, sincerely looking interested in her answer. "You want answers and specifics and some ice cream."

"I never said anything about ice cream," Sophia argued.

"I know," Lee answered. "I just did. Can we have some? You have some up this far north?"

"The water." Sophia tried to steer the conversation back on track.

"Right." Lee clapped her hands on her hips and looked out as if appraising the large body of water. "It's a complex spell that's pretty impressive. It will only work on one type of animal."

"Sheep," Sophia offered.

"Don't interrupt when adults are talking," Lee admonished. "As I was saying, the spell in the water only works on sheep. If my assessment is right, which it undoubtedly is, then it should cause the sheep to—"

An explosion on the eastern hills of the Expanse shot flames and bits of dirt into the air. The herd of sheep quarantined around the small blast scattered and made complaining noises as they did.

Lee glanced out at the disturbance. "You've got neighbors worse than mine. Anyway, the poison will make the sheep explode."

Sophia gave Lunis a look that said, "Kill me now."

"Can you help?" Lunis asked, strangely being helpful, probably sensing that Sophia's patience was waning fast.

"Yes, I most certainly can," Lee answered.

"Finally." Sophia sighed. "Okay, so what do we need to do?"

"Go to the worst place on Earth." Lee sounded ominous.

"Of course we do," Sophia stated dryly.

"Hmmm...let me guess," Lunis began. "Skillman Road?"

"That's very specific." Sophia was surprised.

"Have you been there?" Lunis asked. "The city planner who created that obviously hated this planet and its fellow people."

"No, that's not it," Lee stated. "This place isn't horrible because of its traffic. It's because of its schizophrenic weather. We need to go to Wyoming."

CHAPTER ONE HUNDRED

L ee drew in a deep breath that puffed out her chest upon stepping through the portal into Southern Wyoming. "Smell that?"

Sophia drew in a breath. "Is that cow manure?"

"Probably," Lee answered. "I haven't had my olfactory senses intact since the lobster incident. That's why I was asking. What do you smell? That will help us find our way, so I'm counting on you, Little Bit."

"Don't ever call me that," Sophia warned.

"I need to hear about the lobster incident," Lunis begged after stepping through the portal. He had wanted to come. Not because he wanted to help, but because he seemed highly entertained if confused and intimidated by the assassin baker as if she could out-bad joke him.

"It's a good story for another time," Lee stated. "It involves a bottle of lilac-scented lotion and a guy named Moes. After that, I can hardly smell a thing."

Sophia looked out at the vast wilderness that was rural Wyoming. It was a beautiful country, no doubt, with autumn colors and blue skies. The mountains framed the rolling hills in front of them. "I used to be a curious person. Then I met you. Now I feel better off not knowing things."

"Strangely enough, you're not the first one to tell me that," Lee related.

"Why are we here?" Sophia asked. "What am I supposed to be smelling for? I have enhanced senses so if you tell me I should be able to home in on it."

Lee shook her head. "Again, so spoiled. You get enhanced senses, and I've got a mole in the shape of a stag on my back. Definitely not as cool."

"Can I see it?" Lunis asked, but Sophia shot him a punishing look, and he quickly added, "Later. After the lobster story."

"We're here in Wy-freaking-oming because that's where my specialized water purification system is currently," Lee stated. "It uses reverse osmosis advancements paired with magitech and a secret ingredient."

"So it will work to fix the water in Scotland for the sheep?" Sophia made sure their efforts would pay off.

"Absolutely," Lee answered. "We just have to find the place where I left the device."

"Why don't you remember?" Sophia dared to ask.

"Donuts and absinthe were involved," Lee replied.

Lunis laughed. "Adding that to the story list."

Lee nodded. "In all honesty, I had to leave it with my mechanic here in Wy-what's-wrong-with-the-weather-here-oming. The purification system broke when Cat tried to use it to sift flour. He was getting it fixed up ages ago, and I haven't been back to retrieve it, not having needed it until now."

"Why is your mechanic here in Wyoming?" Sophia watched as a flock of geese crossed the clear skies.

"Because that's where he lives," Lee answered quite seriously.

"I was more referring to why do you have a mechanic in the middle of nowhere?" Sophia questioned.

"I don't know." Lee shrugged. "I can't be responsible for Mike's bad decisions. Anyway, he's the best, so I endure the torture of coming to Wy-is-this-place-so-awful-oming for his services."

"I don't see what you mean about Wyoming." Lunis looked out at the landscape appreciatively. "This seems like a lovely place. Like God's country."

"More like the devil's country," Lee corrected. "Just you wait. This place, much like Sophia, drives me to want to drink...more."

"So where is this guy Mike?" Sophia asked. "What am I supposed to be homing in on?"

"The smell of tagorine-juiceper oil," Lee answered. "It fuels the purification system."

"I don't know what that smells like," Sophia admitted.

"No, you wouldn't because it's a mixture that I invented," Lee stated.

"Can I eat her now?" Lunis asked Sophia quite seriously.

Sophia shook her head. "Let's see if she can recover from this. Since I don't know what that is, can you give us another option for how to find this Mike guy and your water purification system?"

"Fine," Lee huffed. "Let's go that way. It's not far from here, but saying that in Wy-did-Mother-Nature-make-this-place-oming is like saying the weather here is pleasant."

Sophia drew in a breath as a cool breeze laced with grassy smells ran across her cheeks. "I think the weather is pleasant here. Not too cool or too warm. It's nice fall-ish weather."

Lee groaned, and her shoulders slumped as she started forward. "Now you've done it. You've entered into a game with the devil. We better get a move on before we get stuck out here."

Sophia glanced sideways at Lunis and mouthed the words, "What is wrong with her?"

Before he could answer, a dark shadow fell on the dragon's face. Sophia looked up to see gray storm clouds overhead, obscuring all the blue that was once there. A spark of lightning zipped through the clouds, followed by a clap of thunder that nearly made her jump. Seconds later, a torrential downpour drenched the lands and the three at once as they set off across the fields in front of them.

CHAPTER ONE HUNDRED ONE

L unis was crouched low on his belly, crawling across the plains that stretched out between the mountain ranges.

"I had to be the tallest of us as we sludged across flatlands during a lightning storm," the dragon said bitterly.

"I'll open a portal for you back to the Gullington," Sophia offered, nearly having to yell to be heard over the splattering rain. It had started as a downpour and only gotten worse as they crossed with no cover overhead.

"No, give it a minute," Lee advised.

"And what, the rain will get worse followed by more lightning strikes?" Lunis asked as three simultaneous bolts lit up the dark sky that had been pristine moments prior.

"Oh, first-timer, you'll see," Lee sang, her chin high as the rain hit her in the face. "Wy-I-do-whatever-I-like-oming will surprise you."

"I can't wait." Lunis sounded like he could wait, and wanted to be anywhere but there, army-crawling through what had quickly become a swamp. The blue dragon was covered in mud, none of his scales showing through.

"This will cheer you up," Lee began. "What do you call a boomerang that never comes back?"

293

"I'm certain that it won't." Sophia peeked out from under her cloak, which was soaked all the way through and provided little coverage from the rain that seemed to know how to get in everywhere.

"A stick!" Lee exclaimed with laughter.

Lunis shook his head. "That didn't work. Excuse me, but this close to death, with a lightning storm threatening to take me out since I've got horns on my head that make excellent lightning rods, I'm not in the mood for jokes."

"I still remember the last thing my grandfather said before kicking the bucket," Lee fondly said as she looked out at the lake that had formed around them. Soon they'd be swimming.

"What's that?" Sophia tried to do anything to make Lunis feel better.

"Hey, do you want to see how far I can kick this bucket?" Lee laughed at her joke.

To Sophia's relief, Lunis chuckled at that one.

She always wanted to believe that, like the giggle of an angel, that gesture from a dragon had powerful effects. At that moment, she convinced herself it was true because the torrential downpour stopped as suddenly as it had started. As if forced away by a godly power, the lightning and clouds blew away and were replaced by dazzling sun overhead.

"What hell is this?" Lunis straightened and looked up at the clear skies.

"Wy-I'm-the-devil's-home-oming," Lee replied proudly. "Told you this was Satan's land."

Sophia shook off some of the water although she didn't think she'd ever be dry again. "Well, I'm glad the rain stopped. How much farther do we have to go?"

Lee threw her hands up. "Amateurs! Why did I have to be sent out here with a bunch of novices who only want to tempt you, Satan?"

Sophia thought that maybe it had been too long and Lee's meds had worn off. Then something pelted her in the head. She mistakenly looked up and was assaulted in the eye by something cold and round.

Sophia covered her face, tucked her chin, and noticed as little bits of hail fell from the sky all around them, floating in the puddles of water created by the sudden storm that preceded this one.

Lee held out her hand and let the bits of ice gather there. "Oh look, Satan has given us a welcome present. His frozen tears. Yay, he's happy to see me."

CHAPTER ONE HUNDRED TWO

"This is a very strange place," Sophia commented, thankful for the shelter Lunis provided as they strode across the ground, constantly pelted by various sizes of hail. He had extended his wing to make a shelter for Sophia as if she had an umbrella overhead.

"You haven't met the locals," Lee stated. "Also, a word of advice, don't drink the water here unless you want to become one of them. It keeps the population of Wy-would-anyone-live-here-if-they-didn't-have-to-oming going. Otherwise, I don't think there would be anyone in this place."

"Is it ironic that we're here to fetch a water purification system and you think the water spells people into living here?" Sophia asked.

"Irony is the very theme of my life so yes, probably."

"Why don't you use the purification system on the water here and allow the prisoners...I mean, residents to escape?" Lunis asked.

"Because then they'd probably move in next door to me with their goats and alpacas and I'd have to kill them," Lee stated. "Everyone has to live somewhere, and if there aren't folks in Wy-not-oming, they'll clog up other places. I figure they're taking one for the team."

The hail subsided, which made their trek across the vast space easier. When the last of the bits of ice had fallen, Lunis folded his wing back into his body and looked Sophia over. "You okay?"

She nodded. "I've learned my lesson and won't tempt the puppet master again by commenting on the weather."

"You don't have to," Lee replied. "I was only joking about that before. The weather is going to do what it wants regardless, and Satan will have his little fun with us no matter what."

"Well, we've had rain, lightning, and hail." Sophia listed them off on her fingers and shrugged. "That's pretty much the worst of it."

"No, Wy-this-isn't-a-vacation-spot-oming has much more to offer than just crazy weather." Lee pointed into the distance. "Like the local wildlife, who probably hate living here as much as I hate visiting, which is why they're all so angry."

Sophia narrowed her eyes at where Lee indicated, trying to figure out what she was pointing at. Camouflaged into the hillside and puddled Earth were hundreds of small creatures.

Then Sophia's eyes focused on the figures and she realized that they weren't small. It was only that they were far away. But they were on the move. Hundreds of angry buffalo were headed in their direction with their heads down and their feet racing.

"Oh, hell!" Sophia exclaimed.

"Yeah, we got a fun little stampede afoot!" Lee cheered, excitement in her voice as she took off in the opposite direction, running across the plains for the next mountain ridge.

CHAPTER ONE HUNDRED THREE

Sophia's first instinct was to crawl onto Lunis' back and ask him to carry Lee with his feet. However, he must have sensed that idea in her head because he sprinted on the ground, encouraging her to follow his unfolded wing.

"The hail must have frozen my muscles momentarily," he explained as they ran. "I can't fold and unfold my wings to fly properly."

"This is the devil's land," Sophia spat and pushed forward harder, hearing the stomping of hooves at her back.

"Told you," Lee called over her shoulder, having gotten a head start. "And this is Act One. Usually, it gets better the longer you stay."

"And by better, you mean worse, right?" Sophia passed Lee, then hung back not wanting to leave her behind. She and Lunis could no doubt run much faster, but she couldn't allow her friend to get trampled.

"Way worse." Lee laughed.

For having to run for their lives, she sure seemed to be enjoying the whole thing.

Sophia dared to look over her shoulder and saw the wall of charging buffalo closing in, only about fifty yards behind at that point.

They were much faster than she would have expected as they barreled across the plains and kicked up the water that had fallen minutes prior.

The hail had mostly melted, which made the terrain wetter and slippery. The mud they often had to cross seemed to suck her down into the Earth and slowed Sophia's pace.

"Get on," Lunis encouraged as they ran and brought his extended wing closer to her. "Then Lee can too."

"But—"

Sophia's protest cut off when she nearly tripped over stones and mud, her boots squelching in the muck. She decided it was best not to argue with the dragon.

She leapt forward as she ran and caught Lunis' side. Her legs flailed in the wind as she held on tightly and tried to find a place for her feet on the moving dragon. They'd practiced this before, but never while sludging through mud and swamplands.

Sophia's hand slipped and nearly made her fly off where she would have landed in the mud and been trampled.

"No you don't," Lee declared and rammed her shoulder into Sophia while running side by side with Lunis. The motion was rough but did the trick, and shoving Sophia back onto Lunis. Using the momentum, she swung her leg over the side of her dragon and pinned her knees tight around him.

As soon as Sophia was secure, she held out a hand to Lee, who took it at once. The dragonrider yanked the larger woman up with brute force. Lee jumped at the same time and slid backward onto Lunis' extended and locked up wing. She nearly slid off the other side but caught herself with her foot on the front part of Lunis' wing.

With the two magicians on him, Lunis picked up the pace, running much faster than either of them could have on their own.

Sophia looked over her shoulder, startled to see the charging buffalo right behind them. The closest one was about to run over Lunis' tail flying behind them in the wind. However, he kicked up the speed in time and pulled away.

If they had waited to jump onto him a second later, they would have no doubt been trampled. Lunis gained more distance from the racing buffalo, who didn't appear apprehensive about running into a dragon.

They were probably deranged from their time spent in Wy-freaking-oming, Sophia thought and faced front.

The mountain ridge ahead approached, but it wasn't a good option since it would only slow them and the buffalo seemed fine with running straight into the rock walls ahead.

"There!" Sophia pointed at a set of boulders a few dozen yards before the mountains. "Can you jump over those and hide on the other side?"

The set of rocks wasn't high. Even better, the land on the other side was sloped. Sophia thought it was unlikely that the buffalo would climb straight up the rocks. Instead, they'd probably go over them, but there was a chance some would run up them since they were all clustered so tightly together.

"I'm on it." Lunis tried to flap his other wing as much as it allowed. Lee bounced all over the one they'd climbed on, which was luckily straight as a board thanks to being frozen by the hail.

When they were almost to the boulder, Lunis leapt into the air and caught the wind with his wings like a paraglider over land. He soared up, but not high—only enough to clear the boulders.

Once they were on the other side, he folded both his wings into his body. That made Lee drop to the ground, but thankfully it wasn't far.

With nothing keeping them afloat, Sophia and Lunis dropped next to Lee with a *thud.* Sophia's chin slammed into Lunis, and she bit her tongue. She rolled off him to the other side and backed up against the rock wall as much as she could.

Yet again, the timing couldn't have been any better. The buffalo charged around the structure as soon as she and the others were against the rock face. Some ran up the boulders and leapt over the top, but they jumped off far enough away that they didn't land on the three.

It was hard to watch the buffalo tumble ungracefully to the ground and roll into each other, but none seemed seriously injured during the stampede. The herd continued at full speed as they entered the mountain range and kicked up a storm of dust that made it hard for Sophia to see their progress much farther.

After a full minute, the huge herd dissipated and left Lee, Lunis, and Sophia to catch their breath, although that involved breathing in dust and dirt.

Lee turned to Sophia and Lunis and grinned. "Thanks for the ride, dragon, but may I suggest you get some shock absorbers installed?"

CHAPTER ONE HUNDRED FOUR

"This place..." Sophia dusted off her cloak, which was still soaked from the rain storm that seemed like an hour ago but was probably only a few minutes prior.

She was grateful when the sun came out and promised to dry her clothes.

"Which way?" Sophia asked Lee.

The assassin glanced around and shrugged. "Not sure after that detour. Let me get my bearings." She pulled a pill bottle from her pocket and popped a small oblong-shaped pill into her mouth.

"That's how you get your bearings?" Sophia joked.

Lee nodded. "As well as not murder everyone."

"Just some people, right?"

"Exactly." Lee swallowed the pill dry and pointed toward the west. "Mike lives over that way on the other side of those trees. Well, in the woods, but it's not a far walk once we get under the tree canopy."

Sophia didn't want to waste any more time, concerned what Wy-wtf-oming would throw at them next. She started for the trees, which weren't quite a mile away.

The three walked in silence for a while. At first, it was because they were exhausted from all the things this place had thrown at them since arriving. Then it was because Sophia was on guard and constantly looking over her shoulder for killer birds or a tornado or something. But then it was because the sun suddenly became sweltering hot and beat down on them with no relief since they were on the plains with the trees too far ahead.

Although Lunis offered to shade them with his wing like before with the hail, Sophia declined, worried that he'd injure himself again.

To Sophia's surprise, her soaked cloak dried within a few minutes of being in the soul-sucking heat.

"Didn't know that you'd be getting a tan today, did you, Scotland Girl?" Lee had taken off her flannel button-up and fashioned it into a headpiece of sorts.

"What's with this place?" Sophia asked. "How can the weather change so dramatically?"

"You know what they say about Wy-schizophrenic-oming?"

"Don't go there?" Sophia deadpanned.

Lee nodded. "That, and if you don't like the weather, wait five minutes."

"Well, at least we'll be under the trees in a few."

It wasn't one of those dry heats that those in Arizona say is doable because it doesn't feel as hot as it really is. The heat in southern Wyoming was humid and reminded Sophia of when she and Evan had recently visited Baton Rouge in Louisiana. Although Wyoming had the advantage of also having a strange breeze now and then.

Sophia wanted to call that relief, but there was a chill laced into it that seemed weird. She felt something touch her bare arms since she'd removed her cloak and wrapped it around her waist. She held out her hand, and a small white object floated down from the sky and landed on her palm.

"No freaking way." She shook her head.

"Way." Lee looked at the flake lying on her palm that melted immediately. "Welcome to the worst place on Earth."

Sophia couldn't believe it. It was suddenly snowing.

CHAPTER ONE HUNDRED FIVE

C louds had filled the sky that was clear minutes prior. They were the poufy kind that promised snow in Scotland, but these all seemed to have sinister faces in them as well. Within a few seconds, the temperature had plummeted, and snow fell heavily from the sky, covering everything.

"What is wrong with this place?" Sophia shivered from the sudden temperature change. She pulled her cloak off her hips and slipped back into it.

Lee laughed. "It's a geographical anomaly, so I make up reasons that include Satan and it having too many goats per capita or how Mother Nature got bored and decided to make this place a sideshow."

"I'd ask Mother Nature if that were true, but she'd lie or avoid the question," Sophia replied.

"You know all the deities, don't you?" Lee speculated.

"Yeah, but they're all really down to earth."

Lee threw back her chin as she cackled and clapped. "Mother Earth. Down to earth. Good one. You should tell bad jokes with us."

"She's not ready," Lunis said seriously as his feet made large prints in the snow, which was quite thick by this point.

"You're probably right," Lee stated. "Hey, did you hear about what the clock did when it was hungry?"

Lunis shook his head. "I didn't."

"It went back four seconds." Lee howled with laughter.

"Oh, wow." Sophia looked up at the sky. "Where's a bolt of lightning when you need it?"

Her fingers had turned numb much faster than she had expected. Sophia was trying to hide her shivering. It was difficult as the snow piled deeper though. Like the rain, it found the small crevices around her cloak and slipped against her skin, making her colder than she thought possible. Sophia wasn't dressed for cold weather. She hadn't realized that she'd see four full seasons in one hour.

Thankfully, the tree line was up ahead. However, that did little to make Sophia feel better, knowing that there was probably a different danger waiting for them inside the canopy's coverage.

She tensed as they approached the trees and waited for what would come next. Sophia was unsurprised to find that the snow dissipated as they neared.

"Mike's house is on the other side of this shelter belt," Lee informed them.

Sophia nodded, grateful for the warmth that the trees provided. She trudged through the snow, finding the open ground under the trees much easier to negotiate once they got under the canopy.

Then something flew by her head and stuck in a tree at her back. Sophia turned and froze, looking at the arrow that pierced the trunk.

She glanced at Lee, then Lunis. "Looks like we woke the natives."

CHAPTER ONE HUNDRED SIX

S ophia dove at once while protecting her head.

She felt Lunis also cover her protectively, shielding her from the assaults that she heard whizzing overhead.

"Don't worry," Lee stated. "I've got this. I'm used to dealing with these jerks."

Sophia lifted her head and found a spot to poke it out from underneath Lunis' armpit. "Wait; what? You've dealt with these attackers before?"

"Every single time." Lee pulled a small tube from her pocket and put it to her mouth. She drew a quick breath and blew into the blowgun of sorts.

The dart spiraled through the air and stuck in a tree.

"Oh, too bad," Lee stated. "I'll get Mike's kids yet."

"Wait; what?" Sophia questioned again. "Those are Mike's kids shooting at us? You're shooting at children?"

"Yeah, the little heathens like to defend the property," Lee stated.

Sophia took three long, deliberate strides, put her hand on the blowgun, and pushed it down.

Lee glanced up with an offended expression. "Now, why did you do that? I had a clear line at the smallest little shit."

"You can't shoot at children."

"It won't knock them out...well, it won't knock them out long enough, but still..." Lee argued.

"You can't shoot at children," Sophia repeated.

"You can't legally," Lee corrected. "I'm fighting that though."

"Seriously, you can't shoot at these little—"

Four quick shots, all aimed at Sophia's head, nearly took her out. She dropped and ate mud to avoid getting impaled. When she lifted her mud-covered face, Lee was grinning at her with satisfaction.

"I can't what?"

Sophia pushed up and looked at Lunis over her shoulder. "Can you help us out?"

He nodded. "Although watching you take shots from knee-biters with play bows and arrows is much more fun."

"Just create a line of defense," Sophia ordered and pointed as she cleaned the mud from her face.

"Oh fine, but I have to make this worth my while." Lunis held up his wings as he turned his back to the pair.

He looked quite regal with his wings held in the air, shielding the women as he approached on two legs.

Sophia and Lee peeked around his wings. Only when Sophia looked out from the corner of his wing did she spot a few pairs of wide eyes. They paused with bows and arrows in hand as they took in the dragon before them, blocking their attacks. The three blond-haired boys lowered their weapons in unison and walked out from behind their blinds as their childhood curiosity got the better of them.

CHAPTER ONE HUNDRED SEVEN

Is now a good time to scorch the short humans? Lunis asked in Sophia's head.

She gave him a rude scoff but laughed. *Let's wait and see how the discussions go first.* Sophia tried to pretend to be serious as she came out around Lunis' outspread wings.

She had a peaceful smile on her face to appear nonthreatening. Lee on the other hand went for the "You don't intimidate me" approach and brandished the sword she stole from the Fantastical Armory.

"Would you put that away?" Sophia seethed through clenched teeth.

"As soon as the little heathens put down their weapons," Lee replied.

The three kids didn't appear ready to stand down as they faced the large blue dragon with a proud expression on his face. Lunis was always about appearing as regal as possible when he first met those with awful expressions. Of course, he could never keep up the act long and usually laughed and cracked a joke.

The boys were of various ages, probably twelve, nine, and six, and wore camouflage pants and shirts with bandanas wrapped around their messy hair and dirt streaked across their cheeks.

"Hey there," Sophia began in a sing-song tone. Behind the boys were more woods, a few junker cars in different states of repair, and beyond that a house, barn, and fenced area. "We come in peace."

"What are we, aliens?" Lee asked her with a laugh.

"We're trying not to get shot at," Sophia whispered.

"By these little runts." Lee waved her hand dismissively at the kids. "Give me a solid ten seconds with them, and I'll have their weapons and give them a good spankin'."

"Is that a real dragon?" the oldest boy asked.

Lee laughed rudely. "No, kid, it's a fake one. We picked it up at the fake dragon store. It's totally a robot full of bolts and wires."

"Would you not patronize the children?" Sophia groaned.

"Then I'd have nothing to say to them at all."

"So be it." Sophia returned her attention to the boys. "Yes, this is Lunis. What're your names?"

"We aren't allowed to talk to strangers," the middle boy informed them.

"Smart parents," Lee stated proudly. "Kids should be seen and not heard anyway."

Sophia cut her eyes at her. "You don't believe that, do you?"

"I do, which is why I always encourage you to shush your face, child," Lee retorted.

Sophia looked back at the kids and smiled sweetly. "We're here to see a guy named Mike. Is that your dad?"

There was a loud set of clicks, like a gun being cocked. A woman with short brown hair and glasses, also wearing camouflage, stepped out from behind a nearby tree. She held a shotgun that was pointed straight at Sophia. "I believe my children told you that they aren't allowed to talk to strangers."

CHAPTER ONE HUNDRED EIGHT

S ophia's hands shot into the air in the universal gesture that meant "surrender." Lee, on the other hand, sighed as if having a shotgun pointed at them by a deranged country person was a mild inconvenience.

"Well, this is going well," Lunis said dryly, also appearing bored by the recent events.

"Cool," the youngest boy said. "The dragon talks."

"No, he doesn't, kid," Lee lied. "You're hallucinating. Stop drinking the well water."

"Don't you talk to my boy that way." The woman pointed the shotgun at Lee.

The assassin baker nodded. "He doesn't understand English, does he? What age do you teach the children how to speak? After they've learned how to skin a deer and fashion its teeth into a necklace? Or is it after they've taken their first bride?"

"You come onto my property and insult me?" the woman said through clenched teeth. "How dare you?"

"If you think that's bad, you should see what I'm doing when this one isn't controlling me, trying to make me act 'right.'" Lee used air quotes for the last word. "I would have had all your offspring taking a nice nap if she hadn't stopped me from using my blowgun. I still can if you want though. It is nap time for the babies, isn't it?"

"We're sorry for bothering you," Sophia began in a diplomatic tone. "I'm a rider for the Dragon Elite, and this is Lunis." She gestured at the dragon beside her.

The woman cut her eyes at them. "I don't care if you're the queen of England. You step onto my property, and I shoot first and ask questions later."

"You haven't shot us yet," Lee retorted boldly.

The woman swung the gun barrel in the assassin baker's direction. "Why don't you start running and I'll work on my target practice."

Lee yawned loudly. "She's not the queen of England. Don't you watch the telly? That lady wears hats and has dogs, no dragon."

Sophia gave her friend an irritated expression. "Do you have to keep insulting the person holding a weapon on us?"

"Is that a serious question?" Lee fired back.

"Anyway," Sophia said to the woman and smiled at the boys who still had their bows and arrows pointed at them. "We're here to see a guy named Mike."

"There's no Mike here!" the woman exclaimed.

Lee nodded. "That's because he goes by the name Pete."

Sophia rolled her eyes. "Then why do you call him Mike?"

She shrugged. "He looks like a Mike to me."

"You're the strangest person in the world." Sophia glanced back at the foursome. "We need to see Pete, apparently. It's for an important reason. The water in Scotland—"

"Whoa, you're from Scotland?" the oldest boy interrupted, awe written on his face. He slapped the kid beside him on the arm. "The men wear skirts there."

"Kilts," Lee corrected.

"I don't know about my husband helping people who associate with men who wear dresses," the woman stated.

"Look, Sue," Lee began, irritation heavy in her voice. "We don't know any men who wear skirts—"

"My boss does," Sophia interrupted meekly.

"And your boyfriend on special occasions," Lunis supplied.

Lee cut her eyes at Sophia, curiosity written on her face. "What does a Scotsman wear under his kilt?"

"Seriously, can we focus?" Sophia urged. "Poisoned water in Scotland, remember?"

"How could I forget?" Lee groaned. "It's all you ever talk about anymore. You used to be fun. Now you're all obsessed with the water."

Sophia had enough. She spun and dropped her surrender stance. "Well, excuse me for caring about the sheep that are exploding all over the place!"

"They're just little old sheep," Lee argued and turned to face her. "The dragons are going to eat them anyway."

"But they can't because they give them indigestion," Sophia replied.

"And that's from only eating a little one," Lunis complained. "Imagine if we ate a fat one."

Lee laughed. "Then we'd have exploding dragons."

"Ummm...honey," a man said from behind the woman. "Why is there a dragon and two women arguing over there?"

"Something to do with Scotland," the lady replied. "But the one in the long jacket isn't the queen of England."

"And the dragon is real," the oldest boy offered.

Sophia turned to face the family. "Hi, are you Mike...I mean Pete?"

"Who's asking?" the guy with reddish-blond hair asked and crossed his thick arms over his chest.

"I'm Sophia, and this is—"

"Mike, don't you recognize me?" Lee sounded offended.

He narrowed his eyes at the woman and studied her. "No. How do I know you?"

"Oh, that's right!" Lee exclaimed and covered one eye with her palm. "How about now? Last time I had an eye patch."

"Lee!" the man cheered. "Well, I'll be. That is you and your pretty eye. How you been?"

"You know this crazy person?" the man's wife asked.

"Know her?" the guy replied. "I owe her my life."

"And I'll take it if needed," Lee stated proudly.

"Boys, put down the weapons," the man ordered. "We don't shoot at friends."

"Well, you don't," the woman argued.

"You too, Sue," Pete, also known as Mike, commanded. "Let's get them something to eat and show them some Wyoming hospitality."

"Oh good," Lee muttered. "I had a hankering for some Rocky Mountain oysters after being chased by those buffalo."

CHAPTER ONE HUNDRED NINE

"I'm not a big fan of stairs," Lee informed the table.

"Why is that?" one of the kids asked while leaning on his hands, his elbows perched on the dinner table.

"Because they're always up to something." Lee howled with laughter, joined by Lunis, who had his head poking through the kitchen window.

Sue glanced at her husband across the table. "Are you sure I can't shoot her?"

"I'm sure." He pushed his empty food plate away.

They had feasted on chicken fried steak, mashed potatoes, green beans, and rolls—all of it swimming in thick gravy.

"Kirk, will you pass the rolls?" Lee pointed at the basket of bread.

The oldest boy scowled at her. "I already told you that my name is Aaron."

Lee shook her head. "You look like a Kirk. That's what I'm calling you."

"How exactly did this woman save your life?" Sue asked her husband.

"It's a great story," Lee interrupted. "I was supposed to kill him. A hit had been put on Mike's head, and I got the job."

"You're a hitman?" the middle boy Toby asked.

"Hitwoman," Lee corrected. "But I prefer to go by assassin. It sounds classier."

"Because that's the concern here," Sophia muttered, wishing she could eat another bite of the wholesome food, but way past full.

"You invited an assassin into our house?" Sue asked Pete with obvious agitation on her face.

"Yeah, but she's a good one," he argued.

"Because there are good assassins and bad ones," Sophia said mostly to herself.

"Anyway, I'm about to murder Mike," Lee continued. "Then I notice that he's got a catalytic compost figanator."

"What's that?" the youngest boy Nathan asked.

"It's something I'd been looking for," Lee answered. "Magitech stuff."

Pete laughed. "I picked it up at a garage sale and had been tinkering with it for a while. Didn't know what it was."

"So I ask him if he can get it working," Lee explained. "And Mike tells me he thinks so and understands magitech even if he isn't a magician type."

"I think I understand it better because of that," Pete admitted.

"Maybe," Lee stated. "Anyway, we shared a few beers, and I told him I wasn't going to kill him and instead took out the guy who had put the hit on Mike. And he's been my magitech mechanic ever since."

"Who put a hit on you?" Sue asked her husband.

"Some guy I shoved at a bar," Pete answered.

"Oh, well, that narrows it down," Sue said.

"Well, I need that water purification thingy you were working on for me," Lee informed Pete.

He blew out a breath. "It will work for you, but not without some minor complications."

"Minor complications is my middle name," Lunis said with a laugh.

Sophia nodded. "Yeah, that's pretty much how we roll. If it's easy, we don't do it."

"You sure you don't want anything?" Pete asked Lunis. "A goat? An alpaca? A pig?"

"Talk about hospitality," Lunis stated and looked at Lee. "You could learn something from this one."

"I gave you humor, which is the best gift of all," she replied.

"What's the problem with the water purification device?" Sophia asked Pete, struggling to keep the group on task.

"It works, but I fear for a big job, it's probably going to overheat and explode," Pete answered. "I mean, there's got to be a fair amount of water in Scotland, right?"

"Just a smidge," Lunis stated with a laugh.

"But it will work, right?" Sophia pressed.

"Sure, but it's probably going to blow up a sizable area toward the end," Pete stated. "So you'll get your clean water, but probably lose some land."

"Tradeoffs," Sophia muttered and glanced at Lunis. "We put it in the Pond, which feeds into the other water supplies and take a hit at the Gullington. Do you think that will work?"

"It's going to have to," he replied.

"What I don't get," Lee began and nibbled on a roll, "is why you and your camouflaged family live in Wy-pits-of-hell-oming."

"Were we talking about that?" Sue asked, obviously not used to the assassin baker's randomness.

"The voices in my head were discussing it while you all talked about the water thingy," Lee said.

"We got a lot of land to ourselves, which is good because I can't live around people," Sue explained. "I'll kill them if so."

Lee nodded. "I'm the same way, but I do."

"Wyoming isn't all that bad," Pete stated. "There are worse places. We could live in one of those socialist places."

"Like Scotland," Lunis added.

"Or Switzerland," Pete said.

"You know what's the best part about living in Switzerland?" Lee asked the table.

"What?" Toby asked.

Lee shrugged. "I'm not sure, but the flag is a big plus!"

Sue stood. "Well, it seems as though you all should be on your way. We don't want to keep you."

"You're not." Lee held up the half-eaten roll. "These are pretty good. Can I have the recipe?"

"No," Sue answered at once with her hands on her hips.

"You know," Lee squinted at the woman in full camouflage gear. "You look like a floating head. I can't see any of your body with that suit on."

"I feel like you two are even now, Pete." Sue crossed her arms. "You fixed her water device, and she saved your life. No need for further dealings."

"We're friends now," Pete argued.

"That's right," Lee said proudly. "You don't owe me anything anymore."

The scowl on Sue's face deepened. "I don't want the boys around an assassin. The things they'll learn..."

"They shot arrows at us, and you're worried about what they'll learn from Lee?" Lunis questioned.

"Probably just bad jokes," Sophia agreed with a nod.

"Hey, what's another name for an Asian assassin?" Lee asked, her eyes popping wide with sudden excitement.

"Please don't," Sophia begged.

"Chinese takeout!" Lee exclaimed.

"I'm suddenly thinking of going into the assassin business," Sue said dryly.

"Oh, well, then I might have a job for you," Lee began. "I'm gonna assassinate the Prime Minister, and I need help from someone."

Sue lowered her chin and regarded Lee with a silent stare.

"Yeah, so shoot me a PM if you're interested." Lee laughed loudly.

CHAPTER ONE HUNDRED TEN

"I can't believe how fast Sue reached for that crossbow," Lunis said as they stepped through the portal right outside the Gullington.

"I can't believe she keeps it under the table there," Sophia added.

"There was also a box of grenades next to the bread box," Lunis informed them.

"Where else are you supposed to keep the grenades?" Lee carried the large contraption that would hopefully purify the water of Scotland.

Sophia needed to inform Hiker and Quiet that they would have to blow up part of the Gullington for this. "You can wait out here with Lunis," she said to Lee.

The assassin shook her head. "And miss a chance to see the inside of a two-hundred-year-old castle? No way, Jose."

Sophia glanced at the huge castle that appeared when they stepped through the Barrier. "It's more than two hundred years old."

"Anyway, you're embarrassed by me, aren't you?" Lee boldly asked. "You think that I'll embarrass you in front of your little dragonrider friends."

"Your behavior doesn't reflect on me," Sophia retorted. "I'm afraid that you might meet someone who will murder you for your bad jokes."

"Bring this person on," Lee urged. "I'll cut this pansy-ass who can't take a joke."

Sophia gave Lunis a look that said, "She's about to meet her match."

Lee left the water purification device on the stairs to the Castle and entered the large building. She glanced around at the entryway with mild curiosity on her face.

Trin had her legs extended, using the stilt technology built into them, and was dusting the rafters at the top of the cathedral ceilings.

Lee pointed up. "You missed a spot."

The cyborg glanced down at Sophia. "Who is that?"

"She's an assassin baker who is going to help us fix the water supply so the sheep stop exploding," Sophia informed her in one long sentence without taking a breath.

"Well, can she at least wipe her boots before she enters, or is that too much to ask?"

Lee lifted her muddy boots, which were covered in a lot of Wyoming. "You must know my wife. She complains about non-issues too."

"It looks like you'll find multiple people who will murder you." Sophia grabbed Lee by the arm and urged her up the stairs and to Hiker's office.

Once inside the leader of the Dragon Elite's study, Sophia found Hiker, Quiet, and Mama Jamba all seeming to wait for her. It was typical to find Hiker pacing his office, which was what he was doing. Mama Jamba was in her usual spot on the sofa, her legs tucked underneath her as she sketched on her pad of paper. However, to find the groundskeeper in Hiker's office was strange.

He stood inside the doorway, his hands pinned behind his back and a flat expression on his face.

"Oh, and this would be the reason that Quiet showed up and has been stationed here." Hiker said, his gaze focusing on Sophia before sliding over to Lee. "Who would you be, and why are you in my castle?"

"If I told you who I was, then I'd have to kill you," Lee stated. "And I'm thinking of purchasing this pile of rocks. I saw it listed on Zillow. It's small, but I have an excellent carpenter."

Hiker shot Sophia a punishing glare. "What have you brought into the Gullington?"

"She's the one who is going to fix the sheep exploding problem," Sophia stated.

"Her name is Lee," Mama Jamba added, not looking up.

"And apparently she is sincerely going to help, or Quiet wouldn't have let her in here," Hiker observed.

"But I might steal the silverware," Lee threatened. "I didn't make any promises about that."

"You did," Sophia challenged.

Lee held up her crossed fingers. "You can never trust a baker. You should know that by now."

"You think a baker can fix the water supply?" Hiker questioned.

"She's also an assassin," Mama Jamba added.

"You think an assassin can fix the water supply?"

"Yeah, my sources say she's the only chance we have," Sophia stated.

"Which means my price just went up," Lee chided.

Sophia narrowed her eyes at the assassin baker. "You already stole your payment from Papa Creola."

Hiker lifted a single eyebrow. "That's bold. Stealing from the Father of Time."

"Do you know what assassins do when they have nothing to do?" Lee asked.

"What?" Hiker asked because he didn't know any better.

"They kill time," Lee answered with a laugh.

Hiker's eyes widened. "What are you talking about?"

"She likes to make bad jokes," Sophia informed him.

"I didn't think it was that bad," Mama Jamba said.

"I disagree," Hiker stated.

"My jokes tend to go over people's heads," Lee imparted. "Like an attempted assassination."

Hiker closed his eyes for half a beat. "Where do you find these people, Sophia?"

"They usually find me."

"How is your assassin business going?" Mama Jamba asked Lee, not glancing up from her pad of paper.

"It's making a killing." Lee slapped her knee and threw her head back as she chuckled.

"Well, I'm glad you're doing something you enjoy," Mama Jamba informed her casually.

"Mama, have you lost your mind?" Hiker argued.

"Many times," she answered at once.

"You do hear yourself, right?" Hiker asked. "She's an assassin."

"It's a profession like anything else." Mama Jamba looked up and smiled.

"And what other occupation has the word ass in it twice?" Lee grinned proudly.

"Please tell me that you will have this person fix the water and leave as soon as possible," Hiker said to Sophia.

"Yes, but about that," Sophia began tentatively. "We have the technology that will purify the water supply, but there's a reper- cussion."

"As long as the sheep aren't exploding, I'm okay with a small reper- cussion," Hiker stated.

"Yeah, but part of the Gullington is going to explode," Sophia said coyly.

The Viking let out a breath. "Of course. That would be the reason that Quiet is here, then."

"Hey, you're wearing a skirt." Lee pointed at Hiker's kilt as if only then noticing it.

He ignored her and turned to the gnome. "Can you help manage the situation?"

Quiet mumbled something inaudible.

Mama Jamba nodded. "I'm happy to help with that."

Hiker glanced between the two. "What are you two going on about?"

"Oh, son, clean out your ears, would you?" Mama Jamba asked. "That was as clear as day."

Hiker looked at Sophia for backup. "Did you make that out?"

She shrugged. "Sounds like between Mama Jamba and Quiet, they'll manage things."

"See, she heard us just fine," Mama Jamba stated.

"Honestly, I guessed," Sophia admitted.

"It's impossible to know how big an explosion this water purification device is going to cause," Mama Jamba began. "I can only do so much to mitigate the repercussions. Quiet is prepared, but he's limited as well. We have to embrace the uncertainty and be ready for whatever happens."

Hiker nodded. "Let's hope the Castle is still standing after this all."

"Let's hope," Lee agreed. "Or the deal is off, and I'm not buying the place."

CHAPTER ONE HUNDRED ELEVEN

"How does this work?" Sophia asked Lee as they strode out for the Pond alongside Lunis. Hiker, Mama Jamba, and Quiet followed them.

"I'm going to submerge this in that body of water," Lee explained. "Then I've got to put the jinx dial to nine and the pinta dial on sun. We count to zen, then turn around three times. When it reaches circumstance bounty, then it will start working. Make sense?"

"With directions like that, I'll lose my mind in no time," Sophia answered.

Lee nodded. "You understand things as well as my wife. It wouldn't kill either of you broads to get an education. Just because you're women doesn't mean you can't read. This is the twentieth century."

"Twenty-first," Sophia corrected.

Lee tilted her head and gave Sophia a pitying look. "Wow, maybe college isn't the right place for you. But don't worry, I'm sure you can marry well. Well, if that blue lizard stops following you around. No one is going to ask you out with that fire-breather breathing down their necks."

"I'm right here," Lunis said dryly.

"And I'm right here." Lee pointed at the spot in the dirt where she stood. "And Sophia is right there. At this point, we're all going to pass kindergarten."

"Seriously though," Sophia began. "Do you know how big an explosion this thing is going to make?"

"Based on the volume of water it has to purify," Lee mused. "Plus the air density, along with the incredible magical reserves it uses. Add the factors related to the time of day and temperature… I haven't got a clue."

"Well, we better get as far from it as possible," Sophia stated. "Can we set a timer and run like hell?"

"We can, but the water purifier doesn't have one, so you can set one on your phone if you like," Lee offered.

Sophia lowered her chin. "I meant on the purifier."

"Oh, then no," Lee chirped. "I have to set the device and do it manually. Then we run like hell."

"How long do we have?" Sophia waved for Hiker and the rest to stay back. They stopped at the first ridge before the Pond, a good distance away.

"Hard to say," Lee answered. "Probably between five and fifty-five seconds."

"That's quite a range." Lunis chuckled.

"Depends on what you're doing," Lee stated. "But yes, if it only gives us five seconds, then the explosion will most likely take us down. And if it's like the last time, then fifty-five seconds won't give us enough time to get away. That explosion is why I wore an eye patch for a good long time."

"Sounds like a story for later," Lunis encouraged.

Lee stopped abruptly and set the water purifier down. It sank into the water of the Pond immediately nearly covered, but the top with the dials still sticking out. "Okay, I'll just set the stuff, and you all can go and play in your treehouse."

Sophia shook her head. "You get that we're not twelve, right?"

"I don't," Lee said.

"We're not leaving you," Sophia argued. "Maybe you can tell me how to do it, and you can get away. Then Lunis and I can fly to safety afterward."

"Because you so understood my directions before, right?" Lee asked, condescension heavy in her voice.

Sophia hung her head. "I so didn't. Fine, we'll run like hell together."

"It's part of my skill set," Lee bragged. "All good assassins have to know how to get away fast."

"Aren't you supposed to be discreet?" Sophia asked.

"Supposed to, but one anvil takes out the wrong person, and everyone looks at you weird," Lee admitted.

"Please stop using anvils," Sophia encouraged.

"I've tried." Lee returned her attention to the settings for the water purifier. When the motor started and made a loud humming sound, Lee stood back. "I think it's working."

"Because of the loud noise?" Sophia asked.

Lee pointed to a light on the front. "Because of that."

Sophia narrowed her eyes. Next to the light was the word, "Working."

"Right," Sophia chirped. "So now we run?"

"Yes, now you cowards tuck tail and get to safety," Lee ordered. "The rest of us are going to stay to ensure it keeps working. This thing usually needs to be slapped around like an old Nintendo."

Sophia glanced at Lunis and read his response before replying. "Well then, we're staying too."

"Fine, but it's your funeral," Lee sang.

The water around the air purifier bubbled and sent out waves all around it. Steam rose into the air from the water's surface and spread in all directions. There was suddenly static electricity of sorts in the air that made Sophia's hair stand on end as if she'd rubbed it against a balloon.

Her mouth was dry and her pulse quick. In a matter of seconds, the entire atmosphere had changed.

"Do you feel that?" Lee asked her.

She nodded. "Feels like there's electricity in the air, which when mixed with water isn't good."

"Oh, I meant the 'I think I ate a bad burrito' feeling," Lee admitted, her eyes suddenly wide. "The electricity in the air means something else entirely."

Sophia hiccupped on a breath. "What? Is it working?"

"Yes, that means it's working," Lee answered. "And it also means we better run like hell right now!"

CHAPTER ONE HUNDRED TWELVE

All three sprinted away as the ground under their feet began to quake. Sophia nearly fell several times when the rumble made the dirt skip underfoot.

Lunis kept pulling ahead and slowing down when he realized that the others were far behind.

On the ridge, Hiker yelled, and Quiet shook his head. Mama Jamba was still sketching on her pad, not seeming to notice the disturbance. Sophia dared to look over her shoulder as they ran up the hill and saw that water was all simmering and rapidly turning to a boil. That didn't seem so bad, but when she turned back, Hiker was steering Mama Jamba farther away from the water and Quiet had run for the distant hills.

Sophia couldn't figure out what would make those three retreat but then she heard Lee laugh beside her and say, "It's been too long since a proper tsunami drenched me."

"Say what?" Sophia jerked her head over her shoulder and saw a massive wave arching into the air. It rose higher and higher, like a tower growing and promising to fall.

The look in Hiker's eyes when Sophia connected with him looking over his shoulder was what put the fear in her. She had rarely seen that much fright on the Viking's face.

"We've got to get to higher ground," Sophia encouraged.

"Jump on," Lunis demanded while running beside her.

"I can't leave Lee," Sophia stated.

"And I'm scared of heights," Lee disclosed.

"A tsunami is about to take you out, and heights are the issue?" Lunis questioned.

"I'm over seventy percent water," Lee argued. "Not hot air, lizard."

He shook his head. "Be careful what you call me."

"Get into the air," Sophia ordered to her dragon.

"I'm not leaving you." He sounded insulted.

"If a wave takes us out, we'll need someone to recover us," she explained. "You can't do that if you're part of the attack."

He considered this, then nodded. "Fine." Lunis launched into the air, his wings spreading as he soared in the direction of the other three, high up on the hill some distance away.

Sophia immediately missed her dragon by her side but stood by her decision to order him away. She couldn't leave Lee, and she would need Lunis safe to help them if things got worse. On the heels of that thought, Sophia felt a rush of heat in the air and a new level of moisture as if a hurricane was on the way.

She glanced over her shoulder and spied a wall of blue. That was right before the giant wave crashed, knocked her hard to the ground, and covered her in water, seeking to drown her at once.

CHAPTER ONE HUNDRED THIRTEEN

N*o*, Lunis yelled in Sophia's head.
She wanted to tell him that She was okay and not to worry. But that was a lie, and they both knew it. The all-powerful water had its way with her as it threw her to the ground, assaulted her with its impact, and sent her in different directions.

Something hit her head, face, and side. Sophia barely registered knees and knuckles and assumed they belonged to Lee, who was also being tossed around.

Sophia wanted to communicate with Lunis but knew that the effort it would take was beyond her. All her efforts had to focus on surviving the surge of water that sent her one way and another.

Suddenly, Sophia was overwhelmed with the idea of how hard water could be. It was usually so soft when it dripped or sprinkled from the sky. Nothing felt silkier than running a hand through a pool of water. Scotland was known for having the softest water in the world, but right then it felt as sharp as blades as it assaulted Sophia from every angle.

The current pulled Sophia in unknown directions. She couldn't tell which way was up or down, very much like she was in an avalanche. Although she was careful to keep her mouth closed and hold her breath, she knew that her efforts would soon be defeated and she'd suck water into her lungs. Then it wouldn't matter where the water put her.

Oh no, you don't, Lunis said in her mind and picked her up with his claws. *I hear you giving up, and that's not an option. Not like this. Not yet.*

She felt so heavy as he lifted her through the water like a fish caught on a line that resisted being reeled in. But Sophia wanted to be pulled up. She wanted Lunis to save her. She needed him to because she wasn't getting out of this one on her own.

In the recesses of her foggy mind, she was secretly grateful that she'd sent Lunis away because he could never have saved her otherwise. It was a good reminder of why everyone didn't march into battle. Sometimes the heroes were meant to be the ones who stayed behind to swoop in and save the day.

When Lunis lifted Sophia from the rolling waves, she suddenly felt waterlogged. The brightness all around her was too much for her eyes, which had been blanketed by the Pond's darkness.

She felt the rush of wind from Lunis' wings overhead. Her lungs welcomed the air as she sucked in breath after breath. She held onto the claws holding her, not feeling their sharpness but rather their protection.

Sophia was strangely sad when Lunis released her and dropped her on the grounds of what she guessed was the Expanse.

She rolled over on her back, still coughing up spurts of water, and tried to open her eyes, but each assault from her chest kept her lids pressed shut.

It wasn't until she had stopped coughing and caught her breath that she was able to open her eyes. "L-L-Lunis," she stuttered. "Get Lee."

A blurry figure pressed into her line of vision. Sophia could only roughly make out the edges of a familiar figure.

"Don't worry," Lee stated. "Lunis retrieved me first. Guess he's my dragon now."

CHAPTER ONE HUNDRED
FOURTEEN

"You did what!" Sophia stared at her dragon sitting obediently next to her on the Expanse and looking her over with concern.

Lunis laughed when he'd determined that she was okay. "I knew you'd want me to save Lee. And she was in a much worse place than you."

"Yeah, I forgot to mention that I can't swim," Lee admitted.

"Seems like something you should have offered up when we went on this whole purifying water mission." Sophia tried to breathe through the burning in her chest.

"Details." Lee waved her hand in the air dismissively. "Anyway, thanks, Lunis. But I'm not a reptile person, so I don't think it's going to work out. You should probably remain Sophia's dragon. My dog would pee on my bed if I brought you home."

Lunis nodded and pretended to be disappointed before glancing at Sophia. "Is that all right? Will you pretty please keep me?"

She smiled despite the winded feeling in her lungs and the exhaustion seeking to make her collapse where she sat on the Expanse. "Yeah, I guess so. But you were going to let me drown."

"No," Lunis argued. "I saw you quite clearly, navigating the tsunami. Lee was the one who was pulled down and didn't make a single effort to combat the waves. She let them throw her around."

"I pretended it was my wife," Lee disclosed with a laugh.

"I had to choose who to save first," Lunis continued. "And it was you, Soph, who sent me away with the order to help after the impact. I stand by the decision. I had my eye on you the entire time I retrieved Lee and hurried back for you. I think I still had gobs of time to waste. Probably could have hurried a little less."

"Thanks, but when I'm submerged in water and close to drowning, never hurry any less."

"Fine." Lunis smiled at her fondly, obviously relieved that she was okay. He was right to save Lee first. They both knew that the assassin baker wouldn't have survived otherwise. The chi of the dragon protected Sophia, as did her conditioning and training.

It was only then that Sophia took a moment to take in her surroundings. It knocked her breath out of her chest for a second time. The Gullington was unrecognizable.

CHAPTER ONE HUNDRED FIFTEEN

Whereas before the Pond had been vast, and the green hills and slopes surrounded the body of water, now the deep loch was mostly empty with strange creatures wiggling around in the muddy bottom.

The sea monster Wilder had to battle for the first bow laid like an unmoving blob in the center of the dry Pond.

Sophia realized that she, Lunis, and Lee perched high on a ridge, a good distance from the Castle and the other areas of interest. She spied Mama Jamba, Hiker, and Quiet standing on the Castle's backside. They briefly looked at her, and their concern evaporated from their faces before they faced back toward the mostly empty Pond.

Around the Gullington were tiny little ponds. It appeared to be a strange wetland throughout the Expanse.

Suddenly, it all made sense. They'd been caught in the tsunami, which became a rushing ocean of sorts. That's when Lunis had picked Sophia up from the water and brought her to one of the highest ridges, where she'd be safe from any further waves. The Pond's water had settled across the Gullington in the aftermath, rather than in one place like before.

Sophia's heart ached for all the creatures in the Pond that were currently suffering from having their habitat taken from them. But as soon as she thought that, Mama Jamba raised her hands. As small and unassuming as the old southern woman was, the act carried great power with it.

The air around her lit up. Hiker stood back as if needing to give Mother Nature space or pushed back by her strength. Although Mama Jamba's face didn't change from its usual pleasant expression, Sophia spied the intensity behind it.

The ground under them rumbled. Rocks fell from the Castle and tumbled onto the grass. It felt inevitable that another earthquake was imminent. Then the water across the Gullington receded as if being siphoned into the ground.

Sophia stood at once, wondering what was happening and where all the puddles of water making up the new wetlands were going.

Mama Jamba's arms shook in the air, but she smiled. Beside her, Hiker's face contorted with tension. Quiet swayed back and forth. Before Sophia could study the three any longer, she noticed the Pond begin to refill from the bottom up, covering the wiggling aquatic life and blanketing them in sparkling clean water.

The wetlands around the Gullington slowly disappeared as the Pond simultaneously refilled until it was back to the level it had been before the tsunami. Sophia was overwhelmed with relief and turned to smile at Mama Jamba, who helped them restore the Gullington to how it was before.

Sophia's smile faded at once when she saw Quiet sway several inches one way, then the other before he toppled forward and nearly landed on his face. He would have, but Hiker Wallace reached out in time and scooped the passed-out gnome up into his arms.

CHAPTER ONE HUNDRED SIXTEEN

Sophia sprinted toward where Quiet had passed out next to Mama Jamba and Hiker. Her lungs were still taxed from nearly drowning, and her body was recovering on multiple levels. That's why instead of running down the sloping hills, she tumbled several times and rammed her shoulders and knees into small stones.

Still, she sprang to her feet after rolling and continued toward the Castle. However, she watched as Hiker carried the small groundskeeper around the large building and disappeared on the other side.

Completely out of breath and unable to run any farther, Sophia stopped a few yards from where Mama Jamba still stood and looked out proudly at the Pond, which seemed to shimmer with a new intensity.

"He will be okay," Mother Nature sang, not looking at Sophia doubled over with her hands on her knees and her mouth wide open as she sucked in unfulfilling breaths.

"Q-Q-Quiet?" Sophia stuttered.

"Well, you don't think I mean Hiker, do you? We both know that he won't be okay for a long time. Not until he stops being a coward."

Mama Jamba's brazen words made Sophia straighten. She willed her legs forward and strode in Mother Nature's direction. "Hiker isn't okay either?"

It was a stupid question, and she knew it, but the old woman's reply had made Sophia talk without thinking. The look on Mama Jamba's face said as much.

"We both know that man has a lot to come to terms with," Mother Nature stated firmly. "But your current concern was regarding Quiet, isn't that right?"

She'd asked the question, but they both knew that she already knew the answer to it. Sophia nodded and looked out, following Mama Jamba's gaze.

The Pond rippled with activity. The fish and other sea creatures seemed to be rejoicing as they jumped high into the air or skimmed over the surface, grateful to have water and be submerged in the Pond's safety once more.

"You put the water back." Sophia was amazed by what she'd witnessed in the last several moments.

Mama Jamba shrugged. "Someone had to."

Sophia almost laughed. The reality was that no one had to. The Gullington could have stayed like that. All the marine life would have died, but Mama Jamba had done something she rarely did and helped them—saved part of the Gullington.

"Thank you," Sophia said simply. They both knew that she didn't have to help, but she had because they were all in this together. Usually, Mama Jamba wanted to empower the Dragon Elite to save themselves, but that wasn't always an option.

Sometimes they were out of rope. Sophia and the others had gone to great lengths to fix things, but they needed a little something extra.

"And Quiet?" Sophia asked after a long moment of silence.

"He will need time to rest," Mama Jamba stated, still intently focused on the Pond. "He will repair that which needs nourishment after all of this. The Pond, the creatures, the sheep."

"So it worked, then?" Sophia had to ask, although she was certain it had if Mama Jamba and Quiet did their parts.

"I believe so," Mama Jamba answered. "There are over seventy-five thousand miles of rivers, streams, and creeks in Scotland. That's enough to go around my Earth over three times. There are over twenty-five thousand lakes or lochs as the Scots call them. It will take some time for the purification to reach all the areas, but with Quiet's help, things will go along a little faster."

"So the sheep will be okay then," Sophia stated with relief.

"Well, they will until they find themselves on a dragon's dinner plate." Mama Jamba laughed. "But yes, they will live a better life and serve a great purpose."

Sophia looked across the way, where Lunis and Lee headed for the Barrier. It was no doubt time for the assassin baker to return to her other jobs. "I better go and see her off." Sophia pointed at the distant pair.

"You best," Mama Jamba chirped matter-of-factly.

"Thanks again." Sophia moved back in the direction she came. "We couldn't have done this without you."

Mama Jamba shook her head of bluish-gray curls as her smile faltered. "When are you going to realize that I can't do any of this without you? When are you going to figure out that I need to thank you, dear child? You may serve me, but I'm the one who is forever in your debt."

Sophia swallowed, took a step backward, and shrugged. "I think that…will take longer to settle in."

Mama Jamba's blue eyes shone when her smile returned. "Good thing we have some time."

CHAPTER ONE HUNDRED SEVENTEEN

Although Lee tried to act tough, Sophia could tell that she was exhausted after the long set of adventures. None of them had slept in a long time, and it had been one scary storm after another.

At the Barrier, Sophia paused and gazed back at the Castle, her heart feeling tugged in that direction.

"Your friend, that short guy, is he going to be all right?" Lee asked with a rare bit of concern in her voice.

Sophia nodded and glanced at Lunis. "If anyone is going to live to tell the tale, it will be Quiet. I'm certain he'll outlast us."

"Unfortunately, no one will understand the story he tells," Lunis joked.

"True." Sophia returned her full attention to Lee. "Anyway, thanks for helping with this one. Mother Nature informs me that the water supply in Scotland will recover, thanks to your efforts, which means the sheep will too."

"Yum." Lunis licked his lips.

"Oh, so that broad was Mother Nature?" Lee asked. "I knew she looked familiar."

Sophia shook her head. "Yeah, she's the one who keeps things going round and round on this sphere we all call home."

"I should have gotten her autograph." Lee pretended to feel around in her jeans. "Hey, if I find my autograph book, will you get me another meeting with her?"

Sophia laughed. "Yeah, right. That lie has been exposed. Try another one another time."

Lee backed toward the Barrier and smiled broadly as she patted the sword on her back. "That's a promise, Sophia Beaufont. Until our next adventure."

Sophia nodded to her friend and waved while watching her retreat. "Until our next adventure. Try not to get yourself into too much trouble until then."

Lee scoffed. "Where's the fun in that?"

"There is no fun without a little trouble," Lunis stated definitively.

Lee turned and picked up her pace, appearing antsy to get home. Although she wouldn't admit it, Sophia spied homesickness in the woman's eyes. She suspected that the first thing she'd do upon returning to the Crying Cat Bakery on Roya Lane was hug her wife and be grateful that she had another day left on Mama Jamba's planet.

There was nothing like an adventure with Sophia and Lunis to make people thank their lucky stars they were still alive.

"Oh, hey," Lee called over her shoulder as she paused beside the Barrier, which shimmered for those who could see it—those inside the Gullington.

"Yeah?" Sophia perked up through her building exhaustion.

"Do you know why assassins are so good at dating?" Lee asked her.

Sophia smirked and nodded good-naturedly. "Why is that?"

"Because we know how to take someone out."

Sophia and Lunis laughed with the assassin baker and waved, watching as she strode through the Barrier and disappeared through a portal—until the next adventure.

CHAPTER ONE HUNDRED
EIGHTEEN

Sophia spent the next twelve hours in a comatose state. Even when she awoke and told herself that she needed to get up and back to life, dreams sucked her back into the world of sleep where she was its prisoner. Her subconscious wouldn't release her until it was ready. Then she was more than groggy and felt much like a zombie as she made her way to the portal for the House of Fourteen.

During the time she'd been held hostage by her subconsciousness trying to make her body recover from the many recent adventures, Liv had sent Sophia a barrage of messages. Most were probably meant to annoy her with things like:

"Soooooophia!"

Or: "So-what-are-you-doing-phia?"

The youngest sister started to wonder if Liv had taken a page out of Lee's joke book. If so, she was probably in trouble.

However, the latest messages from Liv explained why she was vying for her sister's attention. Plato the lynx had moved the Great Library and was ready for them to "fetch" the new librarian. That wouldn't be like a dog running after a ball, but probably more of a diplomatic mission in negotiations. Sophia wasn't trying to be negative. She recognized that a job done properly for the Dragon Elite, or the House of Fourteen, or any governing agency in the magical world would involve lots of red tape, some bloody wounds, and probably a few or more close encounters with any types.

"Anything else would be boring," Sophia said to herself while stepping into the portal closet that connected the Castle at the Gullington to the House of Fourteen in Santa Monica.

"Talking to yourself is a sign of things…" a familiar voice said in the darkened compartment where Sophia stood and waited for the portal switch to happen and send her into the House of Fourteen.

She would have tensed if she didn't know that standing next to her in the dark was none other than the lynx who had recruited her for this next mission. "Do you make it a habit to hide in dark closets and try to scare unsuspecting people you've asked for help?"

"Habit is such a specific word," Plato stated in the dark. "I happen to be here at the same time as you. It's not like I go around stalking you regularly."

"Don't you?" Sophia challenged.

"Depends on my schedule," he countered.

Sophia opened the portal door when she was certain that the process was complete and stepped into the dim hallway of the House of Fourteen, where thankfully there was no one present. Plato strode through after her, his white-tipped tail flicking above him.

"I happened to be commuting at the same time as you," he continued while looking up at her with his intense green eyes.

It was still perplexing to Sophia that the little, seemingly unassuming feline was probably one of the most powerful beings on the planet, save for Mama Jamba and Papa Creola, of course. That was still saying a lot.

"So what's talking to myself a sign of?" Sophia asked the lynx.

He sat and stared up at her while blinking.

"Probably that you need a friend," Rory Laurens said as he came around the corner of the hallway.

Sophia pointed down at the lynx. "I have friends. I was talking to him."

Rory arched a bushy eyebrow at Sophia and shook his head. "You're as deranged as your sister, talking to that creature."

"But he does talk back," she argued. "You've heard him, right?"

Rory shook his head. "Again, you and Liv suffer from the same hallucinations, it would seem."

"But your mum is Bermuda Laurens, the chief expert on magical creatures. You must know that lynxes can talk, right?"

"I know what I've seen and heard with my eyes and ears," Rory stated, his expression stony as usual.

Sophia glanced down at the lynx. "You make a habit of trying to make us look crazy, don't you?"

"I think you do that all on your own," Rory cut in. "Anyway, Liv mentioned you'd be coming through the Gullington portal about now. She asked me to escort you to where she is."

Sophia groaned. "I'm not nine years old and can find places on my own. She does realize that, right?"

"Probably not," Rory countered. "But I was here and headed that way, so I offered to drop you off, so to speak."

"Oh, are we meeting here in the House of Fourteen?" Sophia looked between Rory and Plato for answers.

"Why are you looking at the lynx?" Rory questioned.

"Well, because he's the one who is assigning us the next mission," Sophia explained, then saw the look of disbelief on Rory's face and sighed. "How are you Bermuda's son, one of Liv's best friends, and a delegate for the House of Fourteen, and you still don't believe in the mega ultra-powers of the lynx?"

"It's more of a 'see no evil' thing," Rory explained as he led the way down the hallway. "If you give credence to the lynx, then he has more power. And his is not a power I trust, not even now."

"Wait, I thought that if you saw his magic, it diminished it," Sophia stated, confused.

"Yeah, that's different than what I'm talking about," Rory said.

"So he's like Santa Claus?" Sophia giggled. "If you don't believe in him he ceases to exist, but if you catch him in the act of delivering your presents, his magic is zapped?"

"Something like that." Rory led them down the stairs. "Liv wants to meet you at a bar and grill down the street."

"So why couldn't she just say that?" Sophia asked.

"Because she's Liv and likes for me to run errands for her," Rory complained. "But also because my mum has a message for you that she wanted only me to give you."

Sophia halted in the corridor, holding her breath suddenly. "Yeah, what is it?"

Rory looked down at her, the giant so much taller than her. Then his eyes slid to the lynx at her feet.

Sensing that he wasn't welcome for the next part of the conversation, Plato strode down the next flight of stairs and disappeared at once. Sophia thought this was ridiculous, even for Rory to buy. He knew enough about the lynx to know that even if he was out of sight, he was always present, hearing any and everything he wanted if he so desired.

After a moment, Rory leaned down. "It's about the memory that Mum believed had been tampered with. She's working on recovering it and wanted me to pass along to you that she's close. Really close, but it will take a little longer."

Sophia nodded, feeling hopeful. "Tell her thank you, and that I appreciate her help with the exploding sheep."

Rory gave her a questioning look. "I don't know what you're talking about, but let's hope you mean that in a figurative sense and not a literal one."

Sophia pursed her lips and gave him a regretful look. "I wished I did. But thanks to Bermuda, the problem has been solved, and the dragons will feast once more."

CHAPTER ONE HUNDRED
NINETEEN

P lato met Sophia at the door to the House of Fourteen without a
word, just flicking his tail back and forth.

"You think that little 'I can't talk' thing is cute, don't you?" she
asked the lynx who refused to speak.

They walked in silence until he led her to a bar and grill where he
disappeared at once.

Sophia sighed and strode into the busy restaurant to find her sister
in the crowded place. Thankfully, Liv had found a booth toward the
back where there weren't many people, and they had some privacy.

"Oh good," Liv exclaimed upon seeing her. "You haven't been eaten
by monsters who were poisoned by friends!"

Sophia accepted the hug her sister offered and dismissed the
people playing pool who gave them strange looks. "You and I have the
same kinds of friends, don't we?" she asked Liv when they both took
seats on opposite sides of the booth.

"I'm afraid we do." Liv hid a smile.

"Your cat is so strange and tried to make me look like a fool earlier," Sophia made the disclaimer right away when they sat down.

Liv nodded without missing a beat. "Good to know that he doesn't show me any favoritism in that regard. So what are we having? The usual one of everything?"

Sophia's stomach rumbled as if trying to reply for her. "That would be great. I woke up, rolled out of bed, and made it here."

"Another all-nighter at the Dragon University then?" Liv asked over the menu with a pursed expression.

Sophia nodded. "Yeah, I spent the day in Wyoming followed by displacing a body of water at the Gullington so I could fix Scotland's water problem."

Liv lowered her menu all the way. "I thought the Scots were drowning in water. What's their water problem?"

"I think the problem is that they have so much of it that if someone infects it, there are far-reaching effects," Sophia answered.

"Oh." Liv drew out the word. "You have enemies like mine. They're crafty and rude and probably never let you have a day off."

"Never," Sophia agreed.

"Well, we eat and leave," Liv stated. "Our enemies can wait until we get back to torture us with their pranks."

"Where are we supposed to go?" Sophia asked. "To find this librarian now that the Great Library has been relocated...which I didn't get the whereabouts of."

Liv nodded. "Me either. I'm on a need to know basis with Plato. He's supposed to be here fashionably late."

"That's weird," Sophia said as the waitress approached to take their order. "He was right with me at the front."

"That's not weird," Liv said under her breath. "What would be weird is if he didn't disappear and reappear as if trying to scare the hell out of us every single time."

CHAPTER ONE HUNDRED TWENTY

Right on cue, as soon as the waitress left with their order, which she didn't believe was for only the two women, Plato appeared with a sly smirk on his face. He was in the far corner of the booth where no one but Sophia and Liv could see him.

"You owe me two hundred dollars for a new bedspread," Liv said to the feline as soon as she set eyes on him, bypassing any pleasantries as she narrowed her eyes at Plato.

"You owe me years of therapy for bringing that thing home," Plato fired back.

Sophia glanced between the two. "What did you do? I'm lost."

"I didn't do anything," Liv seethed, not taking her eyes off the black and white lynx.

"She brought vermin into the house," Plato argued.

"She's a kitten, and she has a name."

Sophia shot a gaze between the two. "Anyone going to tell me what's going on?"

"Well, I was minding my business, trying to be a helpful member of society—"

Liv laughed loudly and cut the cat off. "Try that line on someone who knows you better."

"Anyway, I was doing as I said and Liv brings home this monstrosity of a creature." Plato inched back like he suddenly saw the plague in front of him.

Liv shook her head. "I found a kitten when I was fighting demons in Montreal. I planned to take her to Rory's the next morning, but she seemed so cozy cuddled up on the sofa that I figured what could the harm be?"

"And…" Plato said with obvious irritation in his voice.

"Clark took a liking to her, and now he doesn't want her to leave," Liv said in a rush.

"It appears this is where we part ways, Liv Beaufont," Plato stated matter-of-factly.

"It appears," Liv said absentmindedly. "After you pony up for the comforter of mine that you ruined after said kitten entered the apartment."

"I'm all tapped out or I would," the lynx said smugly.

"Then it appears you can't leave until you've paid your dues," she stated.

"Speaking of dues—"

Plato's words cut off when the waitress trotted over carrying a tray that overflowed with various food platters.

"Your friends not here yet?" The waitress looked around like the sisters had been stood up.

"I'm afraid not," Liv answered. "We'll take the food, and they can eat it cold. Serves them right for being late."

The waitress nodded with a contemptuous expression on her face. "It will. And you show those boys. If they can't be on time, then they don't get their supper hot or you wearing a bow in your hair."

Sophia and Liv exchanged wide-eyed expressions. It wasn't until the waitress left after depositing all the plates on the table, leaving no room for anything else that both sisters let out relieved sighs.

"Bows in our hair?" Liv shook her head. "Is that what's wrong with me? Usually, I barely manage to clean the blood out from under my fingernails before Stefan staggers through the doorway, hungry and tired after hunting demons."

"That's your problem." Sophia laughed and pulled at the nachos, trying to make a perfect bite. "Bow first. Clean blood second."

"When do I empty the bits of ground bones from my boots?" Liv settled back in the booth as a sense of relief fell over her.

"After you throw the kitten off the balcony." Plato reappeared at the table.

CHAPTER ONE HUNDRED
TWENTY-ONE

"You have to take the kitten up with Clark," Liv informed the lynx and dove into the pile of breaded chicken strips. "Oh, hot!" Liv dropped the piece of food and sucked on her finger.

"Orrrr..." Plato said, a devilish quality to his voice.

"Or take it up with Clark," she repeated and went back for the chicken strip, obviously not having learned any lessons from her first attempt.

"What's your problem with kittens?" Sophia smothered guacamole on her chip.

"Besides that they're untrained and don't know how to do anything properly?" Plato asked.

"Yes, besides that." Sophia laughed.

"They're notoriously bad luck and do something to my mojo," Plato answered.

Liv lowered her chin. "Take it up with Clark. He has his heart set on keeping this kitten."

"What he needs is a girlfriend," Plato said dryly and looked at the table of food with judgmental eyes.

"Seems like we should get down to business before you pop off for some mysterious reason." Liv licked her fingers before going for the garlic cheesy bread knots.

"My reasons are never mysterious to me," Plato argued. "And I think we better hurry before you two suffer a heart attack."

"I think someone is jealous that he can do so much, but too much tuna and he barfs all over the rug," Liv teased.

"I didn't have too much! That tuna was old," he stated.

"Then what's your excuse for all the times before?" Liv questioned.

"My stomach hates me," he said irritably.

"Finally," Liv said with satisfaction and grabbed one of the sliders, "a perk to being a magician that you don't have."

"Suck it up while you can," he said smugly. "You have to sleep at some point."

"And that's when you'll barf in my boots again, right?" Liv mocked.

"Can I help it if that's the only convenient place around when my stomach acts up?" Plato questioned.

Liv glanced sideways at Sophia. "And the little lynx never sleeps, so he always has the upper hand."

"I think I'll count myself lucky that Lunis and I can't share a bedroom anymore." Sophia laughed.

"You should," Plato remarked. "This one snores something awful. If I did sleep, it would never happen with someone around."

Liv laughed at this and drained her beer. "Okay, you called us here to sell us on your pyramid scheme. Go ahead, give us your best pitch."

"To recruit the next librarian for the Great Library," Plato stated as if he hadn't heard the joke.

"It's been moved then?" Sophia asked. "Can we open the portals back up?"

"After the librarian is in place and there to protect the magical forcefield," Plato answered.

"What kind of Jedi Master are we recruiting?" Liv picked all the cheese off the garlic bread.

"His name is Paul," Plato informed them.

"He sounds fancy," Liv stated. "Where do we find this bookworm?

Do we bring him nachos? How is it that we need to convince him to take the job?"

"I don't think nachos will do the trick," Plato stated. "He lives on the top of a mountain in a hidden location."

"Cool." Liv sank back in the booth. "I'm liking this mission more and more. Please tell me that he shoots daggers from his eyes and will try and make us explode upon gracing the drawbridge to his lair."

Plato shook his head. "He doesn't have a drawbridge."

"Thanks for clarifying," Liv said dryly.

"Sophia has a map that shows all the hidden locations in the world. She got it for a recent mission," Plato explained.

Liv gawked at her. "Way to hold out, Soph."

She shook her head. "The book is called Hidden Places, and I had to use it to find a way to remove that mark on my soul. But yes, I still have it."

"Good," Plato stated. "You'll need it to find Paul's location, which has been hidden for quite some time."

"Okay." Liv drew out the word. "Why does this sound too easy? We have to find a guy named Paul who lives on a hidden mountain, but Sophia conveniently already has the map for it." She tapped the table. "What aren't you telling us, lynx?"

Plato grinned in reply. "Well, you see, Paul may not want to sign on for this job right away, since it's quite demanding and a lifetime commitment."

Liv rolled her eyes. "Who are these people? I'm a Warrior for the House of Fourteen with zero life insurance, no medical, and a lifetime contract."

"Same," Sophia replied.

"These wimps need to step up to the challenges," Liv stated.

"Others need more persuasion," Plato declared. "And I do think that Paul is the right...no, the only person for this job who is presently alive."

"So why are you delaying in telling us about this mission?" Liv narrowed her eyes at her familiar.

"I've put certain events into place that will hopefully encourage him to take the job without too much persuading on your parts," Plato answered.

"What type of events?" Sophia pushed the plate of refried beans and rice away, suddenly not so hungry.

Plato offered them a sly smile. "Just a tiny volcano…"

CHAPTER ONE HUNDRED
TWENTY-TWO

"Isn't he so cute?" Liv asked dryly, not at all amused as she glared daggers at the lynx.

"So cute I want to throw him off a balcony," Sophia replied.

"I don't see what the problem is," Plato argued while casually licking his paw. "I'm simply helping."

"Is this like when you thought I needed a new pair of sunglasses so you scratched mine up?" Liv asked.

"You. Are. Welcome." Plato punctuated each word.

"They were perfectly good," Liv shot back.

"They made your face look tiny," he stated. "The new aviator ones you have are much better."

"You have skewed priorities." Liv went back to the plate of nachos and piled jalapeños on top.

"How exactly are you helping?" Sophia questioned.

"Well, Paul is receptive to the idea of being a librarian, I believe," Plato began. "And seeing you two at his front door, well, that has the potential to warm him to it. However...my findings state that he might need a lot of convincing, which would take time and repeated events to his place, so I decided to speed things up."

Sophia lowered her chin. "Go on."

"Well, you two show up," Plato continued. "Tell him about this great opportunity, and he'll begin to deliberate on the idea. Now if left to his own devices, Paul might weigh his options, which is the responsible thing to do since this is a 'till death do us part' contract situation."

"Meaning until he dies, right?" Liv questioned.

"Exactly," Plato chirped.

"What have you done?" Liv leaned across the table with her eyes intently focused on the lynx.

"I have made it so his home is not as comfortable as it would be, making the rush to find a new one imminent," Plato said discreetly.

"His house is on top of the volcano, isn't it?" Sophia nearly exclaimed.

"Well, it's easier to take a new job when you know your work from home one is no longer viable," Plato argued.

"But we have to trek up to the top of this active volcano to get this guy," Liv seethed.

"True," Plato stated. "Which is why you might want to leave soonish."

"How big is this small volcano you've started?" Sophia asked.

Plato shrugged. "Smaller than Mount Vesuvius, but still big enough to take out Pompeii and consequently erase Paul's mountain from your map."

Sophia stood at once, realizing that they had no time to waste. She gave her sister an urgent expression. "I think we better get a move on."

Liv moved her chin to the side and gave her familiar a pointed glare. "Something tells me that someone didn't just want to hurry Paul along to accept this mission, but also us."

He gave her a coy smile. "What can I say? If left to your own devices, my studies told me you'd be here eating and drinking all night. Chop, chop. I've got library books for someone else to reshelve."

CHAPTER ONE HUNDRED TWENTY-THREE

"That cat…" Sophia opened the Hidden Places map book as soon as she and Liv were in a private place on the beach in Santa Monica. Reviewing the book of secret places didn't seem like a good idea inside the public restaurant. Not to mention that Plato had made them exit pretty quickly after giving his orders, stating that if they didn't, then the restaurant would suddenly be shut down by the authorities for reasons that couldn't be disclosed to the public.

Now the two sisters were on the beach and listening to the Pacific Ocean lap on the shore while Liv held a light orb above the book of maps.

"Isn't he delightful?" Liv jibed. "He wonders why I threaten to take him to the pound every so often."

"I don't," Sophia stated. "Although, imagine the poor employees there when they arrive in the morning to find the black and white cat missing from a cage locked from the outside."

"Always the air of mystery, that Plato," Liv sang.

"What I don't get," Sophia began while flipping through the pages and looking for something that stuck out as Paul's mountain, which was about to erupt, "is after we locate Paul and convince him to go with us to the Great Library, how do we find it? Plato didn't give us the new location."

"No, he didn't give it to you." Liv pulled an envelope from the pocket of her cloak. She flipped it over to show that it was sealed with wax on one side. On the other side, it said, "To be opened only by Paul —the Great Librarian."

"Why do you think he did it that way?" Sophia questioned.

"Probably because for the most part, the new location for the Great Library has to remain confidential," Liv explained. "You'll have the portal from the Gullington, and there are others that will open back up when things are ready. But again, the details of the location mustn't fall into the wrong hands. If Nevin Gooseman is still out there hunting for it, Plato will have to move it again. Not to mention that there will always be busybodies that want to find the place who aren't worthy of the location."

Sophia nodded. "I'm guessing that's why once the Great Librarian is in place, the Fierce will be back on the job. If someone isn't savvy enough to find the creature who leads one to the Great Library, then they can't find it."

Liv nodded. "Exactly." She pointed at the book of maps. "So how does this work? Think, and you find the information, like in Bermuda Lauren's Magical Creatures book?"

"I wish," Sophia sighed. "No, unfortunately, it's not that intuitive. This one requires us to study and make educated guesses. I found the location I was looking for last time because I had some clues about it."

"Okay," Liv began, looking over Sophia's shoulder and studying the maps. "We know that we're looking for a mountain—"

"That's about to explode," Sophia interrupted.

"A volcano," Liv added. "And we know that it's inhabited by a Mr. Paul, no last name given."

"Oh, all the details," Sophia mock gushed. "They're simply overwhelming."

"They appear like that at first, but we're obviously missing something," Liv mused.

"Like more information?"

Liv shook her head. "I've worked with that damn lynx long enough to know he's supplied everything we need to know. We have to fit the puzzle pieces together."

Sophia thought while continuing to comb through the pages. "Well, where are most of the active volcanos in the world located? Isn't it the Ring of Fire in the Pacific?"

"Good thinking," Liv commended, but her tone contradicted her words. "However, Plato has probably just made this mountain an active volcano, remember? Because he wants to encourage this poor man who probably wants some peace and quiet to take a job."

"Right," Sophia stated. "So we can cross off all active volcanos from the list. That narrows it down to, like, several thousand mountains."

Liv slapped Sophia's arm. "Wait!"

"You want me to punch you in the face?" Sophia asked her sister and looked down at where she'd been assaulted.

"No, I already was earlier," Liv stated. "And that elf paid dearly for it."

"What is it?" Sophia watched the expression in her sister's eyes. Liv was working something out.

"What did Plato say..."

"Can you be more specific?"

"When he supplied the very little information for us," Liv stated. "He said that the mountain we were searching for on the Hidden Places map was 'smaller than Mount Vesuvius, but still big enough to take out Pompeii and consequently erase Paul's mountain from your map.'"

Sophia's eyes widened. "If it's big enough to take out poor Pompeii, already once assaulted by an active volcano, then it has to be in Italy."

"Exactly!"

The sisters flipped through the book that only had maps of places that were hidden on the globe. It took them less than a minute to find one of Italy, and specifically of a place that detailed a beautiful mountain range south of Naples.

"That has to be it!" Liv exclaimed.

Sophia narrowed her eyes at the mountain that few others would know about until it exploded and sent molten lava and ash into the air. "Mount Castiglione. That has to be it."

The location was close enough that if erupted it would again take out Pompeii. Sophia shivered while thinking about the history of the devastating eruption that killed thousands and blanketed a city in ash for centuries.

She looked up at her sister. "We've got to figure out how to get Paul to take the job, get him off the top of Mount Castiglione, and stop the eruption."

Liv nodded. "All in a day's work for the Beaufont sisters. Let's do it. Then I'm going to buy Clark's new kitten a bow."

CHAPTER ONE HUNDRED
TWENTY-FOUR

"Where is your dragon when you need him?" Liv looked at the mountain that was already smoking at the top, giving small signs of the eruption that was about to happen.

"He's always there when I need him," Sophia answered. "However, he's rarely there when you or anyone else needs him since he's not your dragon."

"Oh, but a little ride up to the top of Mount Castiglione would ensure that Tyson didn't get coal again this year for Christmas."

Sophia laughed. "Lunis had a ball batting that coal around for ages."

"Cool. What does the inconveniently not present dragon not want this year for Christmas or Kwanza or Hanukah or whatever dragons celebrate?"

Sophia didn't answer. Instead, she put away the book of Hidden Places. It had given them enough information to portal close by, then discover Mount Castiglione's location by using the maps. It was strange for the two sisters to walk through country roads alongside vineyards and open areas and glance at the map, then up again to find a smoking mountain that hadn't been there moments prior.

"That book is pure witchcraft," Liv had remarked.

Sophia agreed, having used it to find the Reflective Sea in the South Pacific along with some other strange places. Although they'd portaled close enough to Mount Castiglione to locate it using the Hidden Places book, like most magical locations, it was protected from portals, meaning that they had to climb the tall and nearing eruption mountain.

"This Paul guy must know that his home is smoking and rumbling, right?" Liv questioned as they started the trek up to the top of the mountain.

"One would think," Sophia mused. "However, I gather that he's a bit of a recluse. Otherwise, why would he fit the bill to be the Great Librarian, a position that doesn't offer much opportunity to get out? So maybe he doesn't notice that his home is rumbling and such."

"Although true, he might also fit the job description because the Great Librarian has to be able to wax eloquent on tons of different subject matters to know the largest catalogue of books in the world."

"Also true," Sophia chirped. "I still don't think this person is trekking around outside. My guess is he doesn't see what we see, and more importantly, it hasn't reached his house."

"Which is where?" Liv studied the mountain from where they stood at the base.

As a dragonrider, Sophia's vision assisted by the chi of the dragon was better than Liv's, which gave her the clues she needed to see exactly where Paul's stony mansion was. She pointed to the northern peak of Mount Castiglione, which had three. "It's there. At the very tip-top."

"Brilliant." Liv started forward and winked back at her sister. "I think I'll go first. Age before beauty."

CHAPTER ONE HUNDRED TWENTY-FIVE

"There's something I should warn you about with the Hidden Places book," Sophia began as the sisters hiked Mount Castiglione.

"It's full of deception and will lead us to danger?" Liv easily kept up with Sophia, who was hiking in full armor as usual.

"Totally," Sophia replied. "One hundred percent, but there's more."

"More, you say," Liv joked. "Like, it's also going to bring us fortunes and riches beyond our greatest dreams?"

"Truly unlikely," Sophia retorted.

"Well, I'm all out of sarcastic replies, so pony up something then."

"Fair enough. I've only used the Hidden Places book once to find something, but I've concluded since then that those places in the book aren't normal."

"What?" Liv acted surprised. "What strange world of normality do you live in, Sophia Beaufont?"

"I'm serious," Sophia urged, not trying to kid for once. "The place I had to go to remove the mark from my soul was very strange. I think it was hidden because it was extremely dangerous, and if people found it, then it would lead to really bad things."

"So you're saying that Paul didn't conceal the location of his home because he didn't want salespeople soliciting at his door, but rather he happens to live on a mountain that most shouldn't visit?"

"Bingo," Sophia affirmed.

"Okay," Liv began as the hike to the top grew steeper. "Let me get this straight. We're hiking to the top of a hidden mountain where no one can find us, that we know is about to erupt with a volcano big enough to take down Pompeii and surrounding areas, to recruit an important person who we can't allow to die—and this place is also full of unknown, hidden dangers that we'll have to cross?"

"Don't forget that we somehow have to stop the eruption after the fact," Sophia stated.

"Right," Liv chirped. "How could I forget that little milestone in our adventure?"

CHAPTER ONE HUNDRED TWENTY-SIX

"Should we play a game to pass the time?" Liv asked as they hiked, as if climbing a vertical incline wasn't enough for her and she needed an extra challenge to make things interesting.

"I'm not sure about you, but focusing on breathing is enough for me."

Liv shook her head from her place in front of Sophia. "You might want to up your cardio game."

"Well, excuse me." Sophia pretended to be offended. "Yesterday I spent half the day battling every climate change known to man in Wyoming, all so I could fix the entire water supply in Scotland."

Liv shivered violently. "Did you say Wyoming? No need to say more. I'll give you a piggyback ride if you need one. You must be exhausted, not to mention mentally beat down."

Sophia laughed. "The people were great. The weather, well, it seemed to have a mind of its own. But I guess that keeps you humble at the end of the day."

The ground under their feet rumbled, and steam issued up from below.

"The timing of your statement and that was cute." Liv faked a laugh. "Can you not say any more for the rest of the trip?"

Sophia couldn't help but laugh as they traversed the cliffs bordering what would have been an idyllic lake in other, more model circumstances. Being on yet another adventure with her sister filled her heart with joy. Yes, they were venturing up a mountain that had recently become an active volcano started by Liv's familiar. And yes, they needed to recruit for one of the world's most powerful positions and fast. On top of that, they needed to stop said volcano from erupting. Other than all those details, Sophia was happy that she was there with Liv.

She hadn't expected that Liv would come back to their family. Or that she would take the position of Warrior for the House of Fourteen, meaning that the responsibility wouldn't fall on Sophia. Or that she would become one of her best friends.

But more surprising than all that was that when it came to facing danger, there were few that Sophia wanted by her side other than Liv Beaufont. She, like Lunis and Wilder, made adventure fun. Sophia never felt scared when Liv was around, probably because she knew that she was with the very best in the world.

Sophia suddenly felt so very grateful to be a Beaufont. To be Liv's sister. To have the family and past that she did, and the upbringing that had brought her to this point.

And as it usually happened, the universe heard her thoughts and responded in kind.

Steam rose from the lake's edges as something glowing sprouted from the center of the body of water.

CHAPTER ONE HUNDRED TWENTY-SEVEN

"I'm getting tired of small bodies of water lately," Sophia supplied as the disturbance gave both sisters pause.

"Because you too had a boating incident lately?" Liv asked over her shoulder.

"You had a boating incident?" Sophia looked her sister over for injuries. "Are you okay?"

"I broke three bones, but the gnome is going to be okay, unless he doesn't deliver on his side of the bargain," Liv replied.

Sophia nodded. "Yeah, I experienced a small tsunami."

"They're never small," Liv replied. "And we'll have our fair share of tsunamis if we don't hurry up and stop this volcano." She picked up the pace, hurrying up the mountain although the glowing orange thing was growing larger in the center of the small lake.

Liv was right. Mount Castiglione wasn't far off the coast. If it erupted, there would be earthquakes and tsunamis and all sorts of aftermath that the Beaufont sisters would have to deal with. Not only did they not want to worry about evacuating innocent people from their homes and saving the lands of Italy, they had an important person they needed to get into place. Since the Great Library had been without a librarian, things had been crazy at the Gullington, and

Happily Ever After College, and who knew where else. It was time that things returned to normal. Or at least as close as they could get to it.

"So what do you make of..." Sophia's voice trailed away, not knowing how to describe the disturbance in the lake that Liv seemed keen on ignoring.

"Do you want my real answer? My fake answer? Or the funny one?"

"Well, since entertainment seems to keep me moving, let's go with all three."

"Okay, in reverse, here we go." Liv had to hunch to get up the steep hill. "It's a bad light display because Paul is one of those types who puts up Christmas decorations in early November thinking that's at all appropriate."

"Ha-ha." Sophia wished her sister had tried harder, but recognized the fear in Liv's voice. She felt it too, rebounding in her chest. "And your fake answer? What's that?"

"It's probably a lava monster who wants to make our life hell," Liv said as the lake bubbled more and steam made the air thick.

"And your real answer?" Sophia asked in a rush.

Liv shook her head erratically as something emerged from the water and threw hot droplets of water on them. "I'm sorry, that was my real answer. I think that's a lava monster, come to take us down! Run, Sophia! Run!"

CHAPTER ONE HUNDRED TWENTY-EIGHT

S omething large and round emerged from the lake that was now a bubbling cauldron of mess, and Sophia was pretty sure it was the new pits of hell. Hot water spurted up and hit them in the face and on the backs of their hands. Sophia knew they needed to keep climbing, but it was impossible to ignore the danger that had popped up from the lake and appeared to vie for their attention.

Not only that, but Liv had halted and pulled her sword Bellator. This immediately made Sophia unsheathe Inexorabilis.

"What are the chances that this is a funky Santa Claus display gone wrong?" Sophia asked her sister and blinked to see through the steam rising in the air.

"Do you want my real answer, fake one, or funny one?"

"Last time you only gave me two of the three, so what will I get this time if I ask for all of them?"

"Soph..." Liv said as the steam drifted to the side of the lake and the creature that was undoubtedly a monster rising from the center of the water became visible. "In all seriousness, run!"

CHAPTER ONE HUNDRED TWENTY-NINE

L iv shoved her sister in front of her and pushed her up the hill, encouraging her to get up there faster before the creature that was no doubt fueled by the heat of the volcano came to life.

Both put away their swords as they ran, seeing that the upcoming area was steeper and required both hands to climb.

Sophia didn't mind that Liv's hands were pressed into her behind, knowing that she was trying to propel her away from the danger faster. The monster was unlike anything that Sophia had faced, which was saying a lot.

Then, as if Liv were in her thoughts, she said through ragged breaths, "I've never seen something like that! What is it?"

Sophia shook her head as her fingers dug into the dirt to help her climb ever higher. "I don't know. I've never seen that kind of thing before either."

"Well, let's get pictures later after we're far enough away. Can't wait to post that on my Instagram," Liv stated. "I'm not sure what that monster is capable of, but I don't want to find out."

That was the thing, Sophia realized at once. The round monster that was like the top of an octopus head hadn't attacked them yet. It had simply emerged from the steaming, boiling lake with its head glowing bright orange. It had limbs much like an octopus, but as far as Sophia could tell, only two or four at the most. It was hard to be sure since she hadn't stayed by the lake's edge long enough to get a good look. And part of the body was still submerged in the glowing water. She hoped it stayed that way.

Very much unlike an octopus, the creature had three eyes side by side and a large mouth. That was the thing. Its mouth was so large. Like, almost half the size of its head. And that had been what was most strange about it, although there had been many things.

The beast was so large that it could easily take up half the lake, and the antennas on its head were strange. But it was really the mouth. For Sophia, *that* was the cause for concern. Yet, they weren't under attack. They were simply climbing a steaming, rumbling mountain the same as they'd been doing before.

Sophia suddenly halted and turned to her sister. "That thing..."

"I'm calling him Herbert," Liv supplied at once.

"Good name," Sophia replied. "What got to you most about it?"

"The mouth," Liv answered without hesitation.

"Yeah, me too, but why?"

"Maybe because it was huge, the better to eat us with," Liv stated in a rush and pushed Sophia in the bum again. "Can you hurry up? I've got places to be that don't involve an active volcano."

Sophia laughed at this, then to her devastation realized something. She halted again.

"What?" Liv asked. "Did you lose a contact? Just remember you forgot to turn in your library books? Realize you let that sub sandwich punch ticket expire before cashing it in? Left the coffee pot on in the Castle?"

Sophia wanted to laugh, but she couldn't as she squinted around. "We've lost the trail. I don't know the way up anymore."

CHAPTER ONE HUNDRED THIRTY

L iv stepped around Sophia and squinted in the waning light. The orange glow from the lake and smoke made the setting sun very eerie, but a little beautiful since it cast a strange array of colors over the sky.

"How hard can it be?" Liv questioned. "We go up."

Her eyes widened when she saw what Sophia was talking about. The trail had disappeared, and somehow they'd ended up on the side of a scree with a sharp incline that plummeted to a pit of jagged rocks far below.

"Oh, hell," Liv complained and turned to survey the way they'd come. "Well, we can double back."

"But Herbert..." Sophia indicated the direction of the lake, which was obscured from view thanks to a tree line they'd entered. However, doubling back would put them back into view.

"Honestly," Liv began, "I think I'd rather deal with Herbert at this point than take our chances moving forward. We have to cut upward on a path that will lead to the cabin at the top. That one looks like a steep slide down."

"Agreed." Sophia followed her sister as they scrambled down the dramatic decline.

"Herbert is part of that specialness you mentioned when saying the Hidden Places only has dangerous locations, isn't he?" Liv questioned as they strode back the way they'd come.

"I'm afraid so," Sophia stated. "And unfortunately, if Mount Castiglione is anything like the place I visited in the South Pacific, Herbert won't be our only surprise."

"I can't stand surprises," Liv complained, but Sophia heard the amusement in her voice.

When they came to the portion by the lake where the trees disappeared and the water was in full view, both sisters dropped to the ground at once to avoiding getting hit by the balls of lava being thrown at them.

"Seriously," Liv grumbled through a mouthful of dirt.

Both dared to look up to see what Herbert had become. He'd grown—his mouth too. He was using his tentacle-like arms to pick up wads of lava and roll them into round objects as if they were snowballs. Then he stuck them in his giant mouth and spit them around the lake, launching them far onto the shore and straight at the Beaufont sisters.

"Herbert is officially the worst lava monster I've met," Liv stated. "And I've met a few."

Sophia agreed. She knew he was also the most dangerous she'd met, and would soon take them out unless they acted fast.

CHAPTER ONE HUNDRED THIRTY-ONE

"We need a strategy." Sophia rolled behind the first set of trees, knowing that shelter from more oncoming lava balls would help.

"Playing baseball with a lava monster was my strategy," Liv retorted as the mountain rumbled under them, both still lying on their stomachs.

"Something tells me that the creature that eats lava and emerged from a pool of steaming hot magma isn't going to be harmed by a volley of balls being launched back at him."

"I don't know. I've got a mean arm," Liv argued and ducked lower as sparks flew at them from a ball of lava that burst against the dirt on the shore. It was hot. Really hot, but for some strange reason it didn't burn Sophia like she thought it would. She'd unfortunately been around lava enough to know that one feels it when it's close, even if it doesn't touch your skin.

"That's weird," Sophia mused and dared to take a moment to study the bits of lava smoldering in the dirt nearby.

"You mean that it doesn't feel as hot as you'd expect?" Liv asked.

Sophia glanced sideways at her sister. "Can you read my thoughts or something?"

"No. I know how you think because you're smart and think similarly to me," Liv answered. "And I put a protection spell on you earlier to keep you from getting burned. It's not foolproof and a solid hit from Herbert will be deadly, but it should keep us both from frying or melting, as it were."

"Thanks." Sophia offered a grateful smile. "For strategy, I think we need to consider fighting this guy with the opposite of fire and lava since that doesn't seem to be his weakness."

"Good idea." Liv pursed her lips. "The problem is that although the king of the fae thinks he's my best friend, he hasn't graced me with ice magic yet and I doubt I can manifest it willy-nilly right now."

Sophia nodded. Each magical race owned a certain element. As magicians, they had dominance over the element of wind, making producing or controlling it somewhat easy without being a huge drain on their magic. Other types of magic like fire for the gnomes and ice for the fae or water for the elves were harder for them to control. The gnomes had at one point gifted Liv with fireball magic. However, it was rare for a magical race to do that since their control over an element made them unique and gave them an advantage over others.

"Don't worry, I've got us covered," Sophia began. "The chi of the dragon gives me ice magic as well as the others."

"Being a dragonrider is the ultimate best." Liv looked impressed. "Well, besides that whole having to ride a dragon and live in the middle of nowhere."

"I like those parts of the job," Sophia argued.

"You know, at this point, I'd take a dragon over a familiar who sends us to a mountain and makes it an active volcano," Liv joked. "Los Angeles doesn't have the same charm as Scotland. The guys who wear skirts in my neighborhood in West Hollywood aren't the hearty, Viking type who refer to the garments as kilts."

Sophia dared to laugh as Herbert sent attack after attack at them. The heat was intensifying from the spray off the busted lava balls. That could only mean that Liv's spell was wearing off, which meant they needed to act fast. Plus, it appeared that Herbert's aim was getting better. Or the monster was swimming closer. Either way, they would soon be in trouble.

"I've got a plan, but I'm not sure you'll like it," Sophia said with a careful tone.

"I'm certain that I won't," Liv replied. "But I also don't much care for lying in the dirt and having lava rain down on me, so lay this strategy on me."

CHAPTER ONE HUNDRED THIRTY-TWO

"You're right, I hate the plan," Liv said darkly. "In our next life, I get to be the dragonrider with cool snowball magic and you get to be the Warrior for the House of Fourteen who serves as a diversion to distract the lava monster."

"Deal." Sophia prepared to push to her feet. "Have you figured what you're going to do?"

Liv nodded. "I'm going to be obnoxious."

Sophia laughed. "Yeah, but how are you going to distract Herbert?"

"Ha-ha!" Liv boomed. "I'll let that one pass this time. Okay, are you ready?"

Sophia held out her hand. It glowed before a snowball formed, cold in the palm of her hand but a welcome relief from all the heat.

"Awesome. After this, you're totally making me a snow cone." Liv hopped to her feet but stayed low.

"Are you ready?" Sophia tried to find a good spot behind the tree to fire from. It was important that Herbert didn't see her, or he would attack her and Liv's distractions wouldn't work.

Liv nodded. "For sure. I'm ready to sprint. Incidentally, do you know what a sprinter eats before a race?"

Sophia wasn't thinking and therefore completely seriously replied, "No, what?"

"Nothing," Liv answered with a wide grin. "We're fast."

Then she took off from behind the trees and into full view of the lava monster who was ready to hurl all his attacks at her.

CHAPTER ONE HUNDRED THIRTY-THREE

Sophia had to give it to her sister. For not being a dragonrider, she was impressively fast. She assumed that Liv had put a speed spell on herself, which was smart because Herbert was also incredibly fast.

The monster was bigger than the last time Sophia had gotten a good look at it. It was easily the size of a barge in the smallish lake, but only its dome-shaped head stuck out. The rest of its body besides its limbs remained submerged in the water, which was still mostly liquid and not entirely lava yet.

Herbert had to dig around in the lake to find some magma. When he did, his three green eyes enlarged like he was excited by his find. Then he brought it to the surface and rolled it around before sticking it in his mouth.

It was such a strange creature that it gave Sophia and Liv pause. The Warrior recovered from her momentarily fascination. "Hey, Herb! Look over here, Three-Eyes!"

The blob of a monster rotated in Liv's direction as she ran for the other side of the lake. It used its two tentacle arms to propel itself like it was a large raft. There was no coverage on the far side of the lake for Liv to hide behind if it threw an attack, which meant she had to be fast to dodge out of the way or Sophia had to serve up her distraction.

Liv put her hands to her head and stuck out her tongue like a schoolchild taunting a bully. "Didn't your mom tell you that eating lava was bad for your teeth?"

The monster roared and made the lake boil more around it, as if its anger somehow turned up the heat.

With Herbert's back to her, Sophia couldn't tell when it was about to spit a lava ball at Liv, but that didn't matter because she had a clear shot at the creature's massive back.

She pulled back her arm and launched the snowball at the monster, hoping that it didn't melt before it reached it. That was one reason Sophia had kept it in her hands a little longer, trying to freeze it into ice rather than snow, which took time and magical energy.

To her relief, the snowball was solid when it hit Herbert in the back. To Sophia's horror, the creature spun around at lightning speed and hurled a lava ball straight at the tree where she hid. It burst into flames and made her leap out from behind her hiding spot.

CHAPTER ONE HUNDRED THIRTY-FOUR

The monster spun around like a Tilt-A-Whirl ride quickly changing direction, its three green eyes suddenly larger and rimmed with red.

He was mad, Sophia realized.

Livid would have been the word I used, Lunis said in Sophia's head, spooking her.

She rolled to the side, moving fast to avoid the sparks that flew in all directions from Herbert's attack. The tree where she'd been stationed was now on fire, which sent more sparks around as the flames licked up to the branches. The whole mountain would be on fire soon unless they got this monster and volcano under control.

But it was hard to do that while on the defensive. The fire from the first tree was spreading up the mountain and taking away her shelter. Sophia tried to create another snowball but was too busy dodging the burning branches falling from the trees. She would have to go without coverage.

"Hey, Ugly Lava Blob!" Liv yelled from the other side. "Yahoo! Over here. I was hoping you'd share how you can spit so far? I'm pretty bad at it, especially with lava."

This seemed to get Herbert's attention. The monster spun to face

Liv as its tentacles dug around in the lake for more lava. With its back to her, Sophia was frustrated to see that her snowball attack hadn't made a mark. All it seemed to do was anger him, which made it so he took away her coverage and set the mountain on fire more than before.

May I make a suggestion? Lunis asked in her head.

As long as it has to do with my current situation and not some new gadget you want me to order off Instant Amazon, she answered.

Oh, well, never mind. Good luck with staying alive.

Sophia shook her head and watched as Herbert retrieved some lava bits from the bottom of the lake. It was time to act, but she didn't know if throwing another snowball was the right approach. It might deplete her, and she could use that energy to put out the fire taking over their path up the mountain.

My thoughts exactly, Lunis chimed in her head again.

I thought you were leaving me to die alone, she remarked with a laugh.

Nah, I just like to make you think I've abandoned you, he stated.

So cute, Sophia replied with no humor.

I don't think you should try the snowballs again either, he said, obviously having read her thoughts on the matter.

You don't?

No. Instead, put out the fire and also go for the bigger water source, Lunis advised. *My suggestion is that you fight lava with water.*

T*he lake,* Sophia exclaimed. *That's genius, Lunis.*

That's why I get paid the big bucks. Can I get a raise on my allowance, by the way?

You don't get an allowance, Sophia stated.

The dragon mumbled something in her head. *About that...*

Liv was doing her best to avoid getting impaled by a lava ball on the other side of the lake. She had Bellator out and was playing a batting game that Sophia had played with fireballs before. It's how they improved their baseball game. No better way not to miss the ball than wanting to avoid catching on fire if one struck out.

"Batter, batter, batter, up," Liv yelled in a taunt. She connected with one of the lava balls and fired it back at Herbert. As they expected, it didn't damage the monster. It made him angry that the attack didn't work though, and it splattered the top of the lake with its tentacles to send boiling water raining down.

"What a baby you are when you don't get your way," Liv goaded.

Sophia held out both her hands and directed them over the water. She hadn't tried freezing a body of water this big before, but when would she ever have had an opportunity? It stood to reason that it was easier to turn existing water to ice rather than create it from scratch.

And I heard that it was easier to freeze hot water because the composition had already changed once, Lunis offered in her head.

Your time watching Bill Nye the Science Guy is paying off finally, Sophia joked while directing as much of her attention as she could to the lake.

Liv caught a glance at what she was doing but to Sophia's horror, so did Herbert. The monster spun around and dug furiously for more lava.

"Hey Bulbous Head!" Liv yelled and waved her hands over her head. "Over here! Let's go back to working on your pitching skills, which are horrible. I've had Brownies throw a ball at me harder than you, Herbert."

Apparently, the beast was done with being taunted. He saw what Sophia was doing and wasn't going to have it. He might have felt his tank of boiling water getting cooler. From Sophia's perspective, it seemed to be working—the simmer subsided, along with her magical reserves.

Liv had abandoned the insults and instead had run back around the lake, picking up stones as she ran. Sophia had no idea what she was doing, but knew that she had to stay focused on the task of cooling the lake. Otherwise, they were out of options. Mount Castiglione would erupt, and Paul would be gone. There was way too much riding on this for Sophia to fail. This thought was the motivation she needed to up the ante and make progress.

To her amazement, frost began to form around the water's edge.

"You hungry, boy?" Liv asked with one arm full of large stones. She pulled back her other arm, threw a stone at Herbert, and nearly landed it in his wide mouth.

The creature was busy searching for lava in the lake. Its face contorted with anger, which increased when the rock ricocheted off his head and plopped into the water.

To Sophia's relief, it appeared that Herbert was having trouble finding any lava. She hoped that meant her freezing spell had solidified much of what was in the lake. She no longer saw orange magnum streaking through the water.

"Okay, I bought a bunch of tickets for this carnival game. Open up so I can try and get the bean bag in the clown's mouth," Liv joked while throwing another round of rocks, this time faster than before. Two landed in the monster's mouth and made its green eyes bulge.

"Oh, shoot!" Liv exclaimed.

Sophia's head jerked up. Concern nearly made her halt the spell.

"I got some in Herbert's mouth, but then I remembered something." Liv continued scavenging for stones.

"What's that?" Sophia dared to ask.

"What goes into the lava monster, most likely will come out!"

CHAPTER ONE HUNDRED
THIRTY-SIX

L iv dove through the air and rolled head over feet as the lava
monster shot stones that were now bright orange at her. She
tumbled to the side and nearly went into the lake.

"Watch out!" Sophia warned, trying to stop her sister before she
was in the water.

"No worries," Liv sang while popping back up to her feet victoriously. "Everything is going to plan...more or less."

"This is your plan?" Sophia had to ask, feeling a huge drain and
thinking she might fall down from exhaustion at any point.

"Oh, yeah." Liv ran around the opposite side of the lake. "Piss off a
lava monster while you freeze its habitat."

The ground rumbled underfoot and reminded Sophia that she was
fighting a losing battle. She was trying to freeze a lake on a volcano
that was trying to explode. *Surely Paul was aware of the commotion by
this point.* Maybe he'd come down soon and save them the effort of
having to hike up the mountain.

The trees along the path were still on fire, although freezing the
lake had slowed the progress as frost reached up them from the
ground and took over. It was a battle of the elements at this point.

"Hot potato!" Liv exclaimed and dropped a steaming rock. She wagged a finger at Herbert, narrowed her eyes, and gave him a punishing glare. "Seriously, you're not fighting fair. I give you lovely rocks to eat, and you turn them burnie hot. This isn't a hot stone massage, dude. And if it were, you'd be the worst masseuse in the world."

To Sophia's relief, Herbert didn't seem to be moving as fast, as if the absence of heat slowed him.

"Hey, Soph," Liv called. "Are you seeing what I'm seeing?" She nodded in Herbert's direction to indicate its slower speed. Freezing the monster was working to a certain extent, although Herbert hadn't given up looking for more lava somewhere in the lake.

If only Sophia could get it to freeze enough that the monster was stuck. Then they could deliver the finishing blow.

Sophia and Liv's eyes met, and they seemed to share the same thought. Sophia dropped to her knees and put her hands on the lake's surface, hoping that closer contact made the spell stronger. Sometimes that was the case.

She bowed her head, unable to focus on staying vigilant or defending herself. Sophia would have to rely on Liv for that now. All her effort had to go into freezing the lake before Herbert got another advantage and came back from near defeat.

The lake surface felt like a burn under Sophia's fingers and palms as she pressed them into the newly formed ice. Her head lolled to the side, and in the distant corners of her mind, she heard Liv laughing and taunting the lava monster. She hoped with all the strength she had left that this was enough for her sister to defeat Herbert—because Sophia didn't have much left to give.

Don't you dare give up, Soph, Lunis urged in her mind. *Don't you dare let go now.*

CHAPTER ONE HUNDRED THIRTY-SEVEN

Watching Sophia slump, nearly passed out from the effort of trying to freeze the small body of water, was almost too much for Liv. It distracted her from what she needed to do next. However, she couldn't allow that to happen.

Sophia had done her part. Now it was Liv's opportunity to rise to the challenge. She wasn't going to waste her sister's efforts.

Herbert was slowing down, but the monster was smart enough to keep its distance from Liv. She could have shot a fireball at the creature, but as they had assumed, it would probably only fuel Herbert. Her other options weren't devastating enough to firmly end the beast. She needed to get close, but the ice that had formed over the surface didn't seem thick enough to support her weight, especially after the huge dinner they'd had in Santa Monica.

Liv's eyes connected with the area around where Sophia was lying pretty much passed out. Her hands rested on the ice-covered lake, and the frost spread out around her, covering everything. Sophia wasn't conscious, then. Which was huge, because she'd passed out while expending the spell. Usually, fainting would cut off the effort to preserve her last bit of strength, but in full Sophia fashion, she'd figured out how to keep the spell going after she'd lost consciousness.

"Big Tex the dragon is probably behind this," Liv said bitterly while noticing the one good thing about Sophia passing out and still expending the energy to spread the cold and ice around the lake.

The frost crept over the trees lining the side of the lake, and had blotted out the fire completely.

But that's not what lifted Liv's spirit. Needing to distract Herbert while she got the next part of her plan into place, Liv launched the rest of the rocks she'd collected at the lava monster, along with a few more insults.

"Your momma is so ugly that she gives Freddy Krueger nightmares!" Liv spat and hit Herbert in one of his three eyes.

He roared, but was unable to pull his tentacles from where they were stuck in the ice. Liv considered grabbing Sophia at that point and hauling her up the mountain to retrieve Paul. However, her concern was that the lava monster would generate heat and come back to life if not disposed of fully.

"You're so ugly that when you were born, your momma said, what a treasure," Liv began, and threw more rocks at the lava monster as she progressed around the other side of the small lake. "And your father agreed and said, yeah, let's bury it."

With great effort, Herbert turned to follow Liv streaking around the almost frozen lake. This gave Liv enough time to take off in a full sprint. When she was almost upon the first frozen tree, she leapt into the air and kicked hard at the structure, pairing the effort with a spell. Her foot collided with the trunk, and there was a loud *crack*.

The tree split in half as if sawed down by a lumberjack, and the top portion fell into the lake, creating a bridge of sorts.

Liv didn't waste any time as she jumped onto the frozen trunk, then nearly slipped off it onto the ice where it rested. She caught her balance as Herbert turned all the way around. Its eyes widened as he realized what she was about to do. How close she was. How it was completely out of options.

Liv yanked out Bellator and shot down the length of the trunk. She didn't stop until she reached the end and plunged her sword into the bulbous creature, feeling like she was stabbing a giant pumpkin. The assault made Herbert explode, sent lava everywhere, and launched Liv into the air and straight back onto the banks of the lake where she landed hard on her back.

CHAPTER ONE HUNDRED THIRTY-EIGHT

The wind was knocked out of Liv when she landed, but she didn't let that slow her down. She rolled over while shielding her face from the lava that rained down. Thankfully, it had exploded up and out like a roman candle and fountained around the lake. So far, Sophia wasn't being hit by the spray but as the fountain of lava lessened, so did its trajectory.

Liv jumped to her feet, pulled up her cloak, and was grateful to see that the protective spell she'd put on them was still working. However, Sophia was passed out and completely exposed.

She ran through the raining lava and felt it burn through her cloak. Still, she moved fast enough that the droplets of lava didn't get to much of her.

The monster had exploded into the ice bath, which sent steam into the air, blanketed the area with smoke, and made it hard to see.

Liv darted the wrong direction at first, her bearings off after being thrown through the air.

She ran around the edge of the pond the wrong way for a good distance before spying Sophia on the opposite side. Liv kicked it into high gear and sped back to where her sister was close to being hit by the fountain of lava, which thankfully wasn't on the warrior anymore. However, she'd rather that than have it rain down on Sophia.

The concentration of lava droplets grew thicker as Herbert's innards rained down on them.

Liv would have to be fast while running through the lava shower. But coming back through it seemed like a horrible idea. She could recast the protective spell to get her through the now almost wall, but that would only work for one pass. That's when she realized that the shore wasn't being hit, and they had only one option to get out of this unburned.

Liv pulled in a deep breath, said a prayer, and sheathed her sword.

It was go time. Hopefully, she'd weighed her options well enough and wasn't about to kill her sister, but rather save her.

CHAPTER ONE HUNDRED THIRTY-NINE

L iv darted forward and kept her head low as she passed through the falling lava, which was now like sparks radiating off a welding torch. Thankfully, they rained down uniformly, making it easier to pass through.

They burned Liv's head and shoulders as she crossed, but the spell had done its job and she believed she was unharmed. She could assess her injuries later. Right now, she had to finish what she started.

Liv sped forward, not losing any momentum as she scooped up her sister's passed-out form and slapped her hard across the face as she did.

"Stop the spell!" she yelled as the strange orange magma fountain arched over their heads.

Sophia's eyes fluttered, and she opened her mouth with a gasp before falling limp again. However, to Liv's relief, the spell spilling from Sophia's hands had stopped and her heart was still beating.

With Sophia no longer trying to freeze the lake, the lava from the monster had neutralized the water and melted some of the ice.

Liv glanced back over her shoulder as she cradled Sophia in her arms. The arch of raining lava was nearing her. She couldn't chance passing through it again, especially because it wasn't a shower anymore but rather a torrential downpour.

That's why Liv didn't hesitate, but instead, lumbered forward with Sophia in her arms and jumped into the lake, hoping that it was neither too hot from the lava nor too cold from the spell, but rather their protection from the magma fountain until they could get away.

CHAPTER ONE HUNDRED FORTY

The water was like swimming in a hot tub. It made it hard for Liv to hold her breath, but she was grateful that it wasn't scorching her or Sophia.

Bubbles flew away from her mouth as she submerged, her sister in her arms. Liv found the bottom right away and kicked for the middle of the lake. She wasn't planning on crossing it, but she did need to clear the lava fountain. The hope was that she and Sophia had enough oxygen to survive that.

The biggest concern was that Sophia was passed out and breathing in the hot water. But taking her back through the cascading flow wasn't an option. Liv had to be fast.

She kicked hard, swimming with her sister in her arms. When the orange of the raining lava was overhead Liv pushed harder, knowing they were almost there. All she had to do was get to the other side of it and they could come up for air. Hopefully, the biggest of the dangers would be behind them.

Liv's strength was waning, but she didn't give up. Instead, when she was sure that she was past the lava fountain, she reached down with her feet, touched the bottom of the lake, and kicked up as hard as she could manage, shooting to the surface of the water.

Steam and hissing greeted her ears from the lava meeting the water. The air Liv pulled into her lungs was thick but a welcomed relief. However, the sight of her sister's pale face lolled to the side as she cradled her was cause for concern.

Liv swam as fast as she could to the lakeside where she'd try to revive her sister—hoping against all hope that it wasn't too late and Sophia hadn't depleted the last of her strength with the spell or drowned during Liv's attempt to get them out of the lake safely.

CHAPTER ONE HUNDRED
FORTY-ONE

With a great effort, Liv shoved Sophia's limp body onto the shore as carefully as she could manage. That was harder than it would have been in the water that was increasing in temperature by the moment. If Sophia hadn't cooled the lake so much, it would have been boiling, especially with the lava raining into it on the other side. But thankfully, it was only like a hot tub quickly getting to an unmanageable temperature.

As soon as Sophia was out of the water, Liv crawled out too and began working to expel the water from her sister's lungs. She had to have swallowed quite a bit when submerged. Liv could have used a spell to speed along the process, but she was already depleted from the effort of shielding them from the heat.

That's why Liv was grateful that she could rely on her good old mortal knowledge, thanks to John Carraway insisting that she not entirely rely on magic. The owner of the electronics repair shop had been adamant that Liv have backup options. That was one of the reasons he taught her a series of first aid techniques, just in case.

Liv went to work compressing Sophia's chest while alternating between puffing oxygen into her lungs. It was a frustratingly arduous process that didn't yield results right away.

After a few attempts, Liv worried that it was too late. That Sophia had been in the hot water too long. That she'd expended too much energy with the spell.

They were out in a hidden place where no one could find them.

No one could help them.

All for what? Liv thought erratically.

"All for a librarian!" she yelled and continued to pump Sophia's chest. Liv was ready to march up to Paul's place and kick him over the side of the volcano into a lava pit. If her sister died because of this… Well, she'd have Paul's and Plato's asses, and neither would know peace while Liv was alive.

Her anger seemed to press through Liv and into her sister. On the next pump, Sophia sat bolt upright while coughing and spitting up water. It shot out of her mouth like she was a human fountain, and she doubled over until Liv laid her on her side while patting her back and encouraging her with words.

"There you go," Liv crooned. "Take it one breath at a time. You're back with us. And damn it, you're not going anywhere…ever. Not on my watch."

CHAPTER ONE HUNDRED
FORTY-TWO

S ophia was tired of drowning lately. *Twice in close succession was quite enough.*

Her lungs burned, and her head was hot from expelling nearly boiling water from her lungs. However, it was nice to have Liv's comforting hand rubbing her back and encouraging words seeking to bring her back from the groggy places the enduring spell had sent her.

Sophia's face pressed against the lake's muddy bank as she tried to breathe without choking. She didn't care about Herbert's where-abouts. Sophia guessed that if Liv was there with her, the lava monster was gone or not a problem.

She didn't remember anything after passing out next to the lake, except that she asked Lunis to keep the ice spell going after she lost consciousness. It appeared he'd cooperated, although she'd felt his resistance in her mind.

That little stunt nearly cost us, Lunis said in a punishing voice in her head.

Sophia smiled, feeling dirt in her mouth from being so close to the earth with her face. *But it didn't, and we're probably successful because of it. Think about it. If I'd quit when I passed out, then Liv might not have been able to do whatever she did to Herbert.*

Or she would have, and you would have died, Lunis argued.

I did what I thought was right. And thanks for helping.

One day you might not be right, and it will cost us greatly. He didn't sound at all like his usual light self. *We'll pay for it with our lives.*

But not today. Sophia turned over and saw a huge look of relief on her sister's face, lying next to her.

"Hey there." Liv smiled. "Welcome back. Hope you enjoyed your time in Comatose-Ville."

Sophia managed a grin as she pushed up to a sitting position. Her chest still ached from the second near-drowning. "It was okay. The service is awful and the amenities not very memorable, but it's a trip that makes me grateful to get back to the real world, so for that I'm glad."

CHAPTER ONE HUNDRED FORTY-THREE

"I say we replenish our strength," Liv dared to say as the ground rumbled under where they laid by the lake and steam issued from newly formed cracks.

"I'm not sure if we have time for that." Sophia pushed up to a sitting position.

"Cool," Liv chirped. "You go ahead and amble off to complete this mission. Pick me up on your way out."

Sophia went to push up and found that she had zero energy. She allowed herself to settle back on her elbows and look at her sister, who held something in a wrapper.

"What's that?" Sophia asked Liv.

"A candy bar," Liv said matter-of-factly. "You wouldn't want any of this, would you?"

"Remembered to put a 'keep dry' spell on your food, did you?" Sophia extended a hand to her sister.

"I'm guessing you didn't." Liv handed over the candy bar and retrieved another from her cloak. "Amateur mistake."

Sophia nodded. "Ironically enough, I had a 'keep dry' spell on the Hidden Places book, but forgot to protect my food."

Liv held up a single finger. "Always, always protect your food.

Those are your reserves when you inevitably deplete yourself. It doesn't matter how much you carb load for a mission. The simplest snack will always replenish it."

Sophia found the strength to sit up after a few bites of the dark chocolate candy bar. "Like when you think you're going on a simple mission to recruit a librarian, and you meet the worst Herbert in the world."

Liv nodded. "I apologize for the name. A Herbert seems so unassuming, and that guy was anything but that." She waved her hand toward the still-steaming lake. "I think he was a Fredrick or a Chad."

Sophia laughed. "Yeah, but I'm glad Herbert is no longer with us. What did you do to him?"

"He and Bellator met," Liv answered. "And now Herbert is no longer with us."

"Although his lava still is." Sophia waved her hand through the air, trying to fan away the smoke and steam making her eyes burn.

"Yeah, but it's cooling thanks to your ice spell," Liv stated. "Good work there."

"Thanks." Sophia chowed down on the chocolate bar and finished it in two bites. "That was pretty exhausting. I have no idea how we're going to stop the entire volcano if stopping the lava-spitting monster was that hard."

Liv nodded. "I agree. Thankfully, we have some time to think about it because we can't stop this mountain from exploding just yet."

"But what if the top blows off in the next few moments?" Sophia asked erratically, feeling the fear from before pool in her chest again. "We'll be out of options. No way to get off this mountain. It will destroy us."

Unflustered, Liv nodded. "No doubt. But remember who started the volcano."

Sophia thought for a moment. The recent events took a moment to come back to her after all the drama. "Oh, right. Plato."

"His mission is for us to recruit Paul," Liv stated. "So I think we'll have time to do that since the volcano was created to encourage him to abandon his home for a new one. That's why we can't stop the volcano until then. However, I don't know that Plato would have considered that we'd try and plug this bad boy from exploding, so we might be on our own when we level up and attempt that mission."

Sophia nodded. "Okay, so we're mostly safe until we recruit the Great Librarian, right?"

Liv nodded. "Then all hell will surely break loose. And before then, I assume we'll probably get a few bumps and bruises."

Sophia looked over her cloak. It was burned and torn in many places. She also felt the many wounds on her body. "Well, I think it's too late for that."

CHAPTER ONE HUNDRED
FORTY-FOUR

Once Sophia and Liv had recovered enough and the mountain felt like it was fed up with their break, they pushed up and continued on the path toward Paul's house at the top.

It was night now, and the smoke and steam from the brewing volcano blotted out any stars or moon that might lead their way. Sophia used a light orb to light their path, not wanting to get off the trail this time.

The line of trees they passed before the battle with Herbert were extra strange now, halfway between being charred and eaten up with frostbite.

Sophia didn't feel completely normal, but she could move forward and create a spell if necessary. However, when she glanced up to the top of Mount Castiglione, she started to doubt her reserves for the rest of the mission. The hike in front of them seemed monumental after the battle they'd already had. With all the potential dangers that lurked around them, it was very overwhelming.

Every few steps, the ground quaked under Sophia's boots and steam shot up from somewhere on the mountain. It seemed that anyone on this hill would know that it was on fire and about to explode.

"How does this guy not know he's about to be launched into outer space?" Sophia asked after they'd hiked in silence for a long time.

"Maybe Paul is engrossed in a Netflix series," Liv reasoned. "I mean, I can't be bothered to get up for the typical earthquake in Los Angeles when I'm marathoning something good on streaming."

"Maybe." Sophia shrugged. "Just seems strange that he hasn't figured out that lava is shooting out of his backyard."

"What I don't get," Liv began, "Is why he lives on the top of a mountain. I mean, talk about having a commute to get nachos. It's unlikely that Uber Eats delivers out here."

"Maybe that's one of the many reasons he was chosen to be the Great Librarian," Sophia reasoned. "I mean, if he doesn't mind living remotely, then being locked up in the Great Library will be perfect for him."

"I think that's an accurate assumption," Liv agreed as they reached one of the last ridges. Both sisters took the opportunity to catch their breath.

Usually, a hike like this would hardly wind them, but after battling a lava monster and compromised air quality, it wasn't a surprise to either that minimal effort taxed them. However, it did make Sophia worry about how they'd fare with future battles on Mount Castiglione.

CHAPTER ONE HUNDRED
FORTY-FIVE

"You knock," Liv encouraged when they finally came to Paul's door. "I'll hold the gift basket."

Sophia glared at her sister. "You don't have a gift basket."

Liv looked around as if she'd dropped something. "I don't! Oh, shoot! I must have left it back there by the lava lake. Stupid Herbert probably ate all the apples."

"Or charred them to a crisp," Sophia stated.

"Mmmm...apple crisps." Liv licked her lips.

"We should focus," Sophia encouraged while looking over the modest house.

It might have been small, but it was definitely eccentric with multiple curvy chimneys and different shutters on all the windows. The entire house was like that of a storybook witch—totally mismatched, with varying sizes of windows, roofs, chimneys, and doors. However, that was part of the charm.

The many colors that Sophia could discern in the dark also added to the allure. Lots of flowers and strange herbs sprouted from window boxes or the beds along the house's perimeter.

There was a glow in the window closest to the door, which Sophia assumed belonged to the kitchen. Its lacy curtains swayed in the breeze and told her that the window was open.

Sophia lifted her hand to knock as a strange bird call echoed through the open window and made both sisters tense.

Sophia glanced at Liv with a tentative glare. "That was either a bird or..."

"A velociraptor." Liv winked. "Only one way to find out."

Sophia swallowed her apprehension, knocked on the door, and waited for the person known as Paul to answer.

CHAPTER ONE HUNDRED
FORTY-SIX

There was a ton of shuffling behind the door as if the resident kept a pile of odds and ends beside the front entrance.

Sophia gave Liv a sideways glance and considered backing away.

"Hold on," a voice called from the other side. "I'll be there in...well, give me a moment or two."

The guy had responded to the knock quite quickly for not having heard all the commotion related to the volcano. Or maybe it was because he felt trapped by the volcano that he was on guard. There was no portaling from Mount Castiglione. Sophia reasoned that Paul could have seen the signs and boarded himself up.

"We'll wait." Liv looked over her shoulder at a bush fire that ignited a fair way down the mountain but was still disconcerting. "No hurry. Just lava and whatnot."

Sophia didn't think Paul could hear her response over all the ruckus on the other side of the door. She reasoned that he had barricaded himself inside, trying to protect himself from the volcano, although that wasn't the smartest approach.

Finally, the many latches on the door slid back, one after another.

When the fifth had clicked, Sophia thought the door would pull back. However, Paul continued to slide more out of place.

Sophia widened her eyes at her sister and mouthed, "What is happening?"

Liv seemed to be chill with this. "Remember, Plato recruited this guy."

"So he's going to be brilliant and totally right for the job?" Sophia questioned.

Liv nodded. "And totally nuts. All the best are."

Sophia drew in a breath as the next, hopefully next, Great Librarian pulled back the door to reveal one eye as he peeked through the opening.

CHAPTER ONE HUNDRED FORTY-SEVEN

"I'm not interested in buying any magazine subscriptions," the guy that Sophia hoped was Paul said through the crack in the door. She reasoned that there couldn't be two people living in secluded homes on the top of Mount Castiglione, but stranger things had happened. How bad would it be if they showed up to the wrong house to recruit the wrong guy? She nearly laughed at how unfunny that would be.

"Do you get a lot of solicitors trying to sell you magazine subscriptions?" Liv asked quite seriously.

"Usually just Girl Scouts." The guy pulled the door a little wider after noticing that the two sisters didn't have any wares to sell him.

"Oh, Girl Scouts are the worst," Liv agreed. "You tell them a polite no and they smile, but you know those judgmental little kids are thinking that I'm being stingy by not buying their cookies."

"You are, aren't you?" Sophia elbowed her sister in the side.

"Do you know what happens if I bring Thin Mints into the house?" Liv argued. "Clark and I fight over them until he has scratch marks all over his arms."

"Sorry to bother you," Paul said in a polite voice. "I do apologize for interrupting you ladies, but you did knock on my door."

Liv straightened and came back to herself. "Right. You're totally right. Please excuse our appearances, but you might have noticed that there's a volcano happening on your mountain." She held out her arm to show the molten lava trickling out of various places on the hills below.

Paul poked his head out the door, peered down the slope of his yard, and shook his head. "I hadn't noticed. And you both look very nice."

"Thanks." Sophia blushed.

"Again, the volcano…" Liv continuing to gesture at the steam rising from the lake below where Herbert met his end.

"Thank you, but I have volcano insurance." Paul tried to close the door on them.

Liv stuck her boot in the doorway to stop him from closing it all the way. "We're not here to sell you insurance, although creating a volcano and trying to sell you insurance would be…well, the dumbest business ever. No, we're here for something else."

"And if you have insurance," Sophia began, "that's not going to keep you alive when the peak of Mount Castiglione blows."

"Oh, well, then I want my money back on this property." Paul appeared frustrated. "I wouldn't have bought this place otherwise."

"Well, then do we have a deal for you." Liv inched her way into the open door. "We've got a new place for you that's rent-free, devoid of volcanos, and probably your ideal job, according to my cat."

To Sophia's surprise, Paul opened the door wide and nearly made Liv tumble into the place since her weight had been pressing forward, trying to enter the residence. "Well, then, please do come in. I'll put on the kettle and we'll discuss."

CHAPTER ONE HUNDRED FORTY-EIGHT

"Thanks." Liv righted herself and stepped into the cozy house, which was a nice relief from the lava and monsters. "But you did hear the part about how the top is about to blow off this mountain, right?"

Paul, who wore a long white robe and a dark beard, held up a finger to pause the question. "I never make decisions without a cup of tea. Am I hearing you right that you want me to make a decision about something?"

"Mostly about whether to live or die." Liv touched a figurine and nearly knocked it off a shelf, but caught it before it fell to the floor and shattered.

Paul didn't appear flustered by the handsy houseguest he'd allowed into his place. "Now, will you two be taking milk? I gave the stuff up years ago, but keep it on hand for guests."

Liv lifted the curtains in the window and looked out. "For all the guests you get up here in the middle of no-freaking-where?"

Paul chuckled. "It's true, the milk probably isn't any good any more, but I wanted to offer it just in case. I could pop over to my neighbors and see if they have any."

"Your neighbors have evacuated, no doubt," Liv imparted.

Sophia decided to try a more diplomatic approach. "Paul, have you noticed the rumbling or that there appears to be a disturbance outside?"

He glanced up as he refilled the tea kettle as if listening for outside noises. "I thought I heard some mice in the basement. Does that count?"

Liv shook her head, still looking out the window. "So you didn't notice the storm clouds of doom building over the top of your house?"

He shook his head, put the kettle on the stove, and started the flame. "To be honest, I don't pay much attention to things, and I have a soundproof spell on the house because I was getting disturbed by a strange talking cat."

Liv turned away from the window and frowned. "Now it all makes sense why we were recruited."

"Huh?" Paul asked good-naturedly while putting some crackers and other nibbles on the table.

"You won't answer the door for a talking cat, but two girls show up, and you open it?" Liv questioned.

"Well, I figured you were lost," he reasoned and set out a full tea service, making Sophia nervous as she realized the volcano could only be getting worse. "I was told long ago never to trust anything that's not human that speaks."

"Good advice, for the most part," Liv stated. "Unless it's Plato."

"The philosopher!" Paul chirped.

Liv shook her head. "No, the cat that the philosopher was named for."

Paul scratched his head. "I don't know that history."

"Most don't." Liv casually sat at the table. "Paul, we're here because we have a job for you and it's a killer opportunity. Like, if you don't take it, you'll be in hot lava."

CHAPTER ONE HUNDRED
FORTY-NINE

"This sounds serious." Paul poured the tea after the sisters had explained the situation to him. "So I'm being offered a job I didn't apply for? Are you certain that this Plato got my correct credentials?"

"Completely." Liv took a biscuit and popped it into her mouth. "He's good about getting details right."

"But he's a cat," Paul said, a question in his voice.

"Sort of," Liv imparted. "Think of Plato as a cat, like you would Mother Nature as a woman."

"Well, I never would," Paul argued. "She's a supreme being who is holier than thou!"

"You'd be surprised." Sophia sipped her tea but found the warmth off-putting. Although it was the right temperature, if she never had anything hot for the rest of her life, she might be okay with that after her lava bath earlier.

"I'm flattered that you two came all this way to offer me this job of sorts," Paul began. "I was put off by that cat at my door. I was grateful I paid for the extra burglar insurance and security systems when he tried getting in."

"No wonder Plato sent us," Liv commented to Sophia dryly. "He couldn't get in. Modern technology has outsmarted the lynx."

"Figures." Sophia took a bite of a wafer that Paul had set out, thinking it would be good to reload her reserves in case there were more battles on the way down. They did have to extinguish the volcano after all.

"Well, and of course I had no problem opening for you two," Paul went on. "I figured you were lost hikers. I get those from time to time."

Liv looked around at the middle of nowhere that the cottage occupied. "You'll excuse me for being surprised."

"Anyway," Paul continued, apparently not paying attention to Liv, like most. "I'll need a few weeks to think about this offer. Then if I take it I'll need time to pack and think about a relocation package... there will be a relocation package right?"

"Yeah," Liv chirped. "It's a killer deal. You take it, or you'll regret it. I promise."

Sophia set down her teacup after deciding it was her time to take over. "The thing is, Paul, we're asking you to be the librarian for the greatest library in all the world."

"For which I'm very grateful and honored," he stated proudly.

"That's nice." Liv didn't sound like she meant it.

"And this type of position comes with some...." Sophia paused while thinking of the right word, "incentives."

"Incentives?" he questioned. "Like paid holidays and such?"

"More like if you don't take the job now, then the top will explode off this volcano," Liv stated in a rush. "Well, I think even if you do accept, the top will blow off. It's an incentive to get you to take the job."

Paul stood suddenly. "Are you serious? This volcano? It's real?"

"I'm afraid so," Sophia stated. "We battled it coming up here to get you. And I fear we don't have much time. You see, Plato wanted to encourage you to take the job. I'm sorry if that's wrong, but—"

"Oh no," Paul said dismissively. "I was inevitably going to take the job. It's perfect for me. But I'd probably pretend to deliberate on it for a while, then finally come around."

Liv lowered her chin and glanced at Sophia. "Clever Plato knows how to cut corners with dawdlers."

"But now you say that my place…" Paul glanced around frantically at his belongings all around the neat cottage.

"But at the Great Library, you'll have everything you'll ever want," Sophia explained in a rush. "And every book known to man, or elf, or centaur. You'll have visitors, too."

"But not too many," Liv cut in and added, "since I'm guessing that living at the top of Mount Castiglione, you're not the visitor type."

He nodded. "You guessed right. And this sounds like my perfect job. When do I start?"

Liv pulled the envelope that Plato had given her for the Great Librarian from her cloak, having also protected it with a "stay dry" spell. "As soon as you open this."

CHAPTER ONE HUNDRED FIFTY

S ophia didn't know what to expect when Paul opened the envelope from Plato. Part of her hoped that the all-powerful lynx made it so that the spell transported all three of them to the Great Library's new location, healed the volcano, and spread a huge feast out in front of them to celebrate all the victories.

Wow, was she disappointed when Paul tore into the sealed envelope.

The new Great Librarian's eyes widened. He held up his hand since it started to sparkle and disappear.

"Something is happening." Paul sounded nervous and excited.

"You're being portaled to the Great Library's new location," Liv informed him with a smile.

"Do I have time to grab anything?" He looked around his place as he faded.

Liv and Sophia shook their heads in unison.

"I'm afraid not," Sophia stated. "But we'll visit you soon. You'll be in good hands until then."

"Well, paws," Liv corrected and waved as the man faded away completely.

When he was gone, Liv looked at her sister. "So, I'm guessing we don't get to fade away to a new location then?"

Sophia showed her hand to display that she wasn't fading. "I'm afraid not."

Loud bangs rumbled the floorboards under their boots.

Both women tensed.

"What are the odds that's just the pipes in Paul's place?" Liv asked.

Sophia stood up. "Probably zero percent."

Liv stood too. "Well, looks like Paul got to take the easy way out but we've got to go down with the mountain."

"Or rather," Sophia put her back to her sister's and looked out the window that was filling with an orange molten glow, "we get to keep the mountain from going down."

Liv nodded. "Yeah, I like the way you think. Then we're buying Plato a muzzle."

CHAPTER ONE HUNDRED
FIFTY-ONE

Sophia and Liv busted out of Paul's cabin in unison, both brandishing their swords like they were going to fight the volcano.

Although after the fight with Herbert, it wasn't such an odd idea, Sophia thought. They were in a location on the Hidden Places map, so it was likely that whatever came at them next was deranged and weird.

"Any ideas about how we're going to contain this volcano?" Sophia asked her sister while looking out at the eruption that had started on one peak and spilled lava all down the mountain, and made the ground tremble.

"Do you happen to have a big plug?" Liv joked.

Sophia blinked at her sister like she was crazy, but the notion sparked something in the recesses of her mind.

Before she could focus on that, thundering noises caught their attention. Sophia would have thought it was the lava trying to surface below them. Or clouds throwing lightning at them from above. However, when she looked out at the distant hills and saw giant figures approaching, she realized it was way, way worse.

CHAPTER ONE HUNDRED FIFTY-TWO

"Are those giants made of stone and fire?" Liv asked.

"To be very specific," Sophia stated, "I think they are fiery giants made of stone."

"Oh, yay," Liv said with sarcasm. "Glad I brought you along."

The giants were shining hot with embers from the inside out, much like the molten rock. They moved like robots and seemed to have a grievance for the cabin—or the sisters peeking out of it as they thundered in that direction, heads above the tallest trees, which they knocked over like toothpicks.

"So it isn't enough that we've got to figure out how to stop that volcano?" Liv pointed at the erupting liquid magma below them on the middle peak. "Now we've got to deal with the deranged stone men who seem to have a problem with Human Resources and think we're it."

Sophia slapped her sister's arm after having a sudden idea.

"Wow." Liv glanced down in astonishment. "So you want me to take you out first, is that right?"

Sophia laughed in response. "No, but I think I know how we can stop these stone men barreling in our direction and also the volcano at the same time. You know, kill one volcano with a bunch of stones."

"That's not how that phrase goes, but we'll work on your knowledge of clichés later." Liv tilted her head. "I'm for once in my life speechless at this current situation and out of ideas. Please tell me everything."

CHAPTER ONE HUNDRED FIFTY-THREE

L iv pulled away as if the idea that Sophia had told her wasn't digestible, but then nodded. "Okay. It's worth a try."

"Are you serious?" Sophia suddenly felt like a small child. "You're going to try my idea?"

Liv shrugged. "Well, only because if you've noticed, I'm on the top of an erupting volcano with stone giants like twenty feet away and no other options and no way to escape. But I also love your idea Soph, simply because I can't think of a better one. Gold star."

Sophia lowered her chin and regarded her sister with hooded eyes. "I'm canceling the nacho-making station for your birthday this year."

"You wouldn't," Liv fired back.

"I would," Sophia replied. "But onto more important matters." She pointed at the approaching giants. "You take the ones on the left. I'll encourage the ones over to the right. Remember what to do?"

Liv nodded. "I'll use water and wind. You use ice. And remember the jokes I taught you. They'll at least buy you time."

Sophia nodded. "Okay, let's hope this works. If not, I love you, Liv."

Her sister nodded. "I love you. It will work though. Familia est sempiternum."

CHAPTER ONE HUNDRED FIFTY-FOUR

"Your momma is so ugly, Hello Kitty said goodbye to her," Liv fired at the first giant while holding her hand in the air. The thing was massive, and its stone face contorted with anger. Just the insult seemed to give the stone weirdo pause if not the tiny magician on the ground who dared to fight the monster with her hand raised as if politely asking it to stop.

It tilted its head and grunted.

"That's right, Dumb-Face," Liv continued, encouraged by the reaction. "Your momma is so ugly, she went into a haunted house and came out with a paycheck."

That's when Liv's luck ran out. The stone and fire creature opened its mouth to build up some energy, about to blow a flame at the one who had insulted it. That's when Liv gathered her wits about her and held up her hand, harnessed the magic of the elves she'd inherited, and sprayed water at the stone giant.

The blast hit the fiery creature and made steam shoot out from various places. It created awful crunching sounds, like asphalt being ripped apart by a jackhammer. The stone giant opened its mouth as if attempting to blow fire at Liv again, but nothing came out except a puff of smoke. Then its eyes closed like a robot had powered off.

The stone giant resembled blocks of boulders arranged to create a very rudimentary man. However, to Liv and Sophia's relief, it didn't take much to subdue the ordinary-looking block man and turn him to stone after extinguishing the fire within with the cold blast of water. When the smoke and steam cleared, it was evident that the monster had frozen after turning gray, all the fire within it gone. Then the giant suddenly crumbled into a pile of rocks.

"Next one is yours, Miss Beaufont." Liv bowed in her sister's direction as another giant advanced on them.

Sophia swallowed. The monster quickly approached. Its long strides carried it across Paul's yard as it closed the distance between it and the two magicians. Sophia gripped her resolve and tightened the expression on her face. She faced off with the stone giant burning from within with embers and lava and wondered if she had the same brazen nature as her sister.

No, Lunis told her in her head. *You have yours. It's different and just as good. Better in some ways. Use it to take these oversized stone men down.*

Sophia nodded and felt the victory before it came, which was the best sign of things to come.

CHAPTER ONE HUNDRED FIFTY-FIVE

"Your momma is so ugly, she makes blind children cry," Sophia fired at the stone man that she'd named Teddy. All the giants were named Teddy to keep it easy—all four of them.

Because they're so cuddly? Lunis asked in her head.

Because I can crush them like they're a teddy bear. Sophia pooled the energy in her being, preparing to shoot the ice blast at the monster.

You've never had a stuffed bear, have you? Lunis observed.

Shush. I'm fighting a monster, Sophia admonished.

Must be nice, Lunis replied. *Since you asked, I'm counting the cracks on the Cave ceiling. There are one hundred and six so far.*

Seems like a great use of your time. Sophia realized she didn't have too much longer until the beast was upon her, but she wanted to ensure she'd charged up the cold blast enough to be effective. Unlike Liv's water blast, Sophia didn't think the cold and ice would be as effective.

It is a good use of my time, Lunis replied. *I've got lots and lots of it while you're gallivanting in beautiful Italy.*

Sophia almost laughed. *I'm currently hanging out on a volcano that's threatening to erupt.*

Sounds so exotic. Lunis sighed. *Bring me a souvenir.*

How about some molten lava? Sophia offered.

I was thinking a nice bottle of wine, Lunis stated. *An expensive chianti. Only the best will do.*

At this point, I'm going to be bringing you some burn wounds.

Gross, Lunis complained. *You're horrible at picking out souvenirs. Never mind.*

As usual, Lunis' timing during a high-octane moment was perfect. It kept Sophia calm, which meant that she was able to better channel her energy. She felt Liv getting anxious beside her, but Sophia knew timing was everything. The stone monster was only a few yards away and moving faster, but Sophia didn't rush. Proximity would help with her attack.

Don't worry, she said to the dragon in her head, *soon enough there will be a battle and you can stretch your legs and test your skills.*

I hope so, Lunis stated. *I'm looking forward to meeting this mysterious villain or villains and sporting my shiny new armor.*

I'm sure you'll look quite dapper.

When Liv opened her mouth, probably to question Sophia's sanity for waiting so long, she released the ice spell and sent a blast of freezing air mixed with frost at the fiery giant.

The spell hit it straight in the chest and made the creature halt suddenly. It rocked forward and back. For a moment, Sophia didn't think it had worked. She worried that she hadn't charged up enough and the fire was too hot to extinguish, but then the spray of frostbite that had hit the monster's chest spread out like a spider's web and wrapped around the stone, taking over the fire.

It was much slower to work than Liv's water blast, as Sophia had suspected. The stone man lumbered forward, and Sophia worried it would grab for them with its massive hands as it reached out. However, she held her ground and defiantly looked up at the strange angry beast.

The crunching sound of the magma coursing through it as the lava solidified was ear-splitting. Thankfully, it didn't last for long as the monster turned into a statue reaching forward with a hostile expression covering its face like it was going to crush them, if only it hadn't been stopped first.

CHAPTER ONE HUNDRED
FIFTY-SIX

"Your momma is so ugly, she turned Medusa to stone," Liv said to the stone monster before blasting it with water. Then she turned to Sophia. "Which is impressive because I've met that witch and she doesn't bow to anyone. She nearly took out Papa Creola."

"Sounds like a great story for later," Sophia urged and pointed at the last remaining stone man striding in their direction.

"Over nachos!" Liv agreed and spun to take out the final monster.

They had made the impromptu decision that Liv would take the monsters down using the water spell since that seemed to be more effective and quicker—hopefully keeping them from getting pummeled.

That left Sophia free to work on freezing the rock that once composed the stone men. She wasn't certain that her theory would work for stopping the volcano. Although her knowledge of natural disasters was limited, Sophia knew that there was no way to stop a volcano...well, not without magic.

Her first idea was to relieve the pressure. Releasing the heat and gases inside the volcano would work in theory, she reasoned. But even with intense magic at their disposal, Sophia didn't know how they would vent the volcano. Then that idea, along with something that Liv said, gave Sophia a plan. It would either work or seriously backfire.

There was no getting down from Mount Castiglione at this point. The trek was too far and the volcano too intense. The only option was to stop it and hopefully save the surrounding cities of Naples and Pompeii.

"Your mama is so ugly, her reflection said, 'I quit.'" Liv waited until the monster cast her an offended stare. She didn't seem content unless she angered the beast before extinguishing its fire, essentially taking away its life force.

Sophia found it much faster to freeze the rocks than the water. Frost formed over the huge pile that had once been the four giants. It towered high above them when Liv "swept" them together. Having them all compiled made it easier for Sophia to freeze them and helped with the next phase.

When Sophia thought the rocks were sufficiently frozen, she turned her attention to Liv. "Are you ready? We have to do this together."

With a look of pure confidence, Liv reached out to the huge boulders as if she was going to pick them up with her fingers. "Let's get moving. My nachos are getting cold somewhere."

CHAPTER ONE HUNDRED FIFTY-SEVEN

When Liv had mentioned something about plugging up the volcano, Sophia had taken the idea literally. If they needed to stop or at the very least slow the volcano down, the best way would be to plug it up.

From studying geography, Sophia knew that volcanic plugs were an actual thing that could lead to an explosion. But she thought that if they employed magic, meaning using rocks that once belonged to giant men and were frozen, that could cool the volcano from the inside out. And if it didn't work, then it very well could make matters much worse, and not just lava and ash would rain down from the sky, but also rocks.

"Okay, ready?" Sophia let out a breath and prepared herself for the next feat. It wasn't something she could have done on her own. As powerful as Liv was, it was unlikely that she could accomplish it solo either. But together, the Beaufont sisters stood a chance. Sophia hoped with all her might that it worked because the strength it took would probably make both of them pass out.

This time, Sophia wouldn't have Lunis continue to fuel her spell when she fell into unconsciousness. They needed too much precision. Sophia had to stay awake long enough to finish things. Then she could pass out and hopefully wake to a blue sky, or least one that wasn't falling ash and rock.

"I'm ready," Liv said with conviction.

Both magicians turned their full attention to the huge mound of boulders and focused, using their collective magic to pick up several hundred tons of rock.

At first, the pile only trembled. A small boulder rolled down the stack and landed on the ground. The earth quaked under the mound, which Sophia thought was the reason for the rocks shaking. Then they all rose into the air and soared high above their heads.

Sophia didn't allow herself a moment to rejoice at their success. She needed to concentrate with everything she had. One slip-up and the rocks would fall where they'd roll and crush them—freeze them. They were in essence all big ice cubes at this point, but Sophia thought the effort to change the temperature would be worth the work.

Plugging the volcano wasn't enough. The lava had to be "calmed down" first. One of their hopes was that the rocks would fall into the volcano's mouth in such a way that they didn't plug it right away but instead created a vent. Then the smoke and steam would release, and the lava would solidify to complete the plug. That was the hope, and for someone who didn't know much about these things, Sophia had to rely on faith because that's all she had left.

CHAPTER ONE HUNDRED FIFTY-EIGHT

S weat dripped down Sophia's forehead and into her eyes, but she stayed focused. Her chest filled with heat and her breath became irregular. Her hand shook in the air and she spied that Liv's did the same. But they kept the huge pile of boulders airborne.

That wasn't enough though, and they both knew it.

"Ready," Sophia said through clenched teeth.

Liv nodded, probably the only reaction she could manage right then.

In unison, the sisters moved their hands from in front of the suspended boulders to the mouth of the volcano peak spilling lava down the side of the mountain next to them. The heat radiating off the structure was intense, but Sophia refused to allow herself to feel it. All that she gave attention to was moving the rock pile through the air to the volcano that promised to shoot bright orange magma into the air, raining down on them and the surrounding areas.

Not on my watch, Sophia thought with strict firmness.

The effort to move the mound of rocks over the top of the bubbling peak took all that Sophia had. All that Liv had. But when they finished, there was only one thing left to do, and it was thankfully the easiest thing Sophia had done all day.

"Now," she whispered to her sister, and together they dropped their hands and abandoned the spell that had the power to take them both out.

The cluster of rocks fell into the mouth of the volcano, making lava splash out and ooze over the side.

For a moment, Sophia held her breath, only allowed to watch. There was nothing left for her and Liv to do. There was nowhere to go. They could only wait and see if the plan she'd concocted with little understanding of science would work.

Steam issued from the volcano's mouth and filled the night sky. A great sizzling sound filled the air as if the loudest barbecue grill in the world stood right in front of them.

Spurts of smoke shot into the air with a few rocks.

Liv gave Sophia a sideways look that spoke of her apprehension. However, no matter the doubt that the warrior felt, she managed a smile and clapped a hand on Sophia's shoulder. "It's going to work."

Maybe faith had no power in the world after an act was done. Maybe it was simply the propeller that got things in motion and kept things moving. Or maybe it was holding onto faith when there was nothing left that created the positive results.

For whatever reason—because Liv believed in Sophia's plan, or because the rocks had cooled the lava enough, or because enough pressure had been released before the plug formed—the quaking stopped.

Sophia was startled, having gotten used to the trembling under her feet. It was like when she rode Lunis for an extended amount of time and dismounted. Her legs always felt strange as if not used to the lack of motion.

Liv's hand tightened on Sophia's shoulder. "Did it…"

Her words cut off when something like an explosion rocked the volcano. Sophia instinctively brought her hands overhead and prepared to shield herself from the lava and rocks that flew from the mouth of the volcano as if that would work.

However, nothing flew from the top of the volcano. Instead, the boulders that had previously been frozen bubbled to the surface where they rumbled and shook before becoming still once more. They glowed brightly for a moment before seeming to instantly cool and form, to Sophia's ultimate surprise, a plug of sorts.

To Sophia's relief and total astonishment, it had worked. They'd been able to plug up the volcano and potentially save millions.

CHAPTER ONE HUNDRED
FIFTY-NINE

When Sophia woke, she was lying with her head next to Liv's in the grass outside Paul's cabin on one of the peaks of Mount Castiglione. She didn't remember falling asleep or rather passing out. For a moment, she wondered if the volcanic plug had all been a dream until she looked at the nearby peak and saw the mound of rocks keeping it sealed.

Sophia sat up and blinked at her surroundings, noticing how different they looked in the early light.

She sighed and looked around as morning dawned on the hills of Italy and made the rolling lands of vineyards and orchards glisten with the fresh light.

Liv stirred next to her, and Sophia turned her attention back to her. She realized at once what had awoken her sister. It wasn't the morning sunlight or Sophia sitting up.

Standing next to Liv and pawing her face was none other than the lynx, Plato.

Liv pushed blindly in the cat's direction, but he easily moved out of her reach.

"Wakey, wakey," Plato sang.

SARAH NOFFKE & MICHAEL ANDERLE

With her eyes still closed, Liv shook her head. "Nah. I'm not going to school today." She rolled over and tugged on make-believe covers.

Plato looked up at Sophia with a sly grin. "This is a cute game we play."

She yawned and watched as the cat strode around to where Liv had turned and positioned his backend right in front of Liv's face. Sophia wondered what the sneaky feline was up to when it dawned on her a moment too late.

"What?" Plato hollered. "There's a sale on plain black T-shirts, you say?"

"Wh-Wh-What?" Liv opened her eyes groggily. Her gaze landed straight on the cat's butt right in front of her face. She grimaced and rolled the opposite direction, and sat up at once. "Oh, dude! That joke totally got old after the tenth time you did it."

"But I'm hoping that you find it funny again after the eight hundredth time," Plato sang while shaking his rear end at Liv. "Go ahead, don't you want to make a wish on the morning star?"

"After what you put us through, I'm thinking about skinning you, cat," Liv threatened.

Plato casually glanced out at the still-smoking volcanic plug. "I expected you to recruit Paul. I expected you to navigate the obstacles caused by the volcano and this being a hidden place. However, I didn't see that you'd stop the explosion. Kudos."

Liv shook her head. "You have about a ten-second head start before I run after you, animal."

Plato wiggled his whiskers, unperturbed by the threat. "Paul seems to be happy in his new role. I think he'll do nicely in the position. He asked that you two come by and visit once he's settled in at the Great Library."

"So we can open the portal in the Castle and at fairy godmother college?" Sophia got to her feet and stretched, all her muscles feeling strained from the hike and many battles.

"Oh, right," Plato chirped. "I forgot about the portals. Yeah, when I was moving the Great Library to its new location, you'd have wanted to close those. Otherwise, all sorts of weird things would have resulted."

Liv gave her sister an annoyed expression. "Do you want a mink shawl? And by mink, I mean lynx. I hear they make nice mufflers. It gets quite cold in Scotland."

Sophia laughed, grateful for the relief. "Where is the new location?" she asked Plato.

"Well, you can simply take the portal from the Castle when you reopen it," Plato stated.

"But for the rest of us who don't have magic portals and aren't allowed into the Gullington?" Liv said dryly.

"That unprivileged person would go to Timbuktu," Plato informed her.

"I see that knowing you does me few favors," Liv stated.

"I got you backstage at that Snow Patrol concert," Plato argued.

"Then you got us kicked out when you stole the drummer's drink," Liv spat.

The lynx giggled slyly. "They all like having a cat around and think it's funny when I drink until they realize the feline can drink them under the table and will empty all their expensive liquor bottles."

"And that's why I can't take him to parties," Liv said to Sophia while thumbing in the cat's direction. "Seriously, how about fur-lined boots? Or cat-lined anything? I'm buying, and by that, I mean I'm skinning the creature."

Sophia's phone buzzed in her pocket. Since they were on the top of a mountain in a hidden place, she had to guess it was someone important who knew how to get hold of her.

She pulled out her phone and read the message, then smiled. "No thanks. Looks like I'll be getting some fancy new clothes though. I've got to go."

"Okay, well, this was fun," Liv sang as Sophia quickly made her way down the path. "Next time, let's try to keep our eyebrows and not burn off our fingertips."

"Sounds good," Sophia replied. "Can't wait until next time."

"I can," Liv replied dryly and turned her attention to the lynx. "Don't go planning any adventures for me just yet. I need nachos first."

"You have two and half hours," he teased.

CHAPTER ONE HUNDRED SIXTY

"Get your paws off my slice of pizza, Angela," Evan warned as Sophia reached for the last piece. She'd been so busy telling Mahkah and Wilder about the adventures with Liv and before that with Lee that she hadn't had a bite, although her reserves were seriously depleted after Mount Castiglione.

"I haven't had any," she retorted and took the piece.

He dared to slap her hand, but it was more of a pat. "I called dibs."

"When?" she challenged.

"Just now!" He continued to slap the back of her hand, trying to make her drop the slice.

She shook her head and took a bite. "Oops, it fell into my mouth. Deal with it."

"I'll order us another one." Mahkah stood and strode for the counter in the Cosmic Pizza, a popular place on Roya Lane that served pizza with specialty toppings like French fries, macaroni and cheese, chicken nuggets, and for those who hated themselves —pineapple.

"Just don't put fruit on it," Evan called after Mahkah. "It has no place on a pizza or a dessert."

"Amen." Sophia sat back and sipped her beer.

"I can't believe you were on a volcano." Wilder looked her over. "You don't look like it."

"Thanks," Sophia replied. "The new threads help."

She tugged at the armor she wore. Jeremy Bearimy had made it and handed it off to them. That was the text message she received when on the top of Mount Castiglione. The tarantula had already sent the dragons' armor to Hiker at the Gullington and notified him to pick it up outside the Barrier. Hopefully, it all fit since the armor was custom-ordered for each dragon and there was no telling when they'd need it.

Sophia had been so consumed with fixing the water supply and the sheep and with recruiting Paul the Great Librarian that she'd almost forgotten there was something bigger looming over the Dragon Elite, waiting to try and take them down. Nevin Gooseman had to be behind it. Usually, Sophia forced herself to have confidence when it came to facing villains.

However, after the leviathan and the simurgh, she was more than worried about what Nevin Gooseman had in store for them. Besides wearing the new armor created by the best seamster in the world, her only hope was that Bermuda Laurens came through with some information on the monster Nevin planned to send the Dragon Elite's way.

"I think I look quite dashing in my new armor as well," Evan smugly interjected while looking down at his shiny and sleek new clothes.

"Be careful how much pizza you eat," Wilder warned. "If you have too much, then you might not fit into it much longer."

Evan scoffed. "I need quite a bit of food, boy. You wouldn't understand."

Wilder nodded and pushed his empty plate away. "I guess I wouldn't. After that, I was left quite satisfied."

"That's what she said." Evan dropped another of his favorite lines from the sitcom, *The Office*.

Sophia shook her head and finished her slice of fajita pizza covered in black beans, salsa, guacamole, and carne asada. "I'm glad that Mahkah is getting another pizza. I'm starving after facing those lava creatures."

"Yeah, me too," Evan stated. "I had this long contract negotiation with Nigeria that totally depleted me."

"You sound like a pretty little princess in contrast to Sophia," Wilder joked.

"She's the one who wears pink like it's going out of style," he argued and leaned over to whisper loudly to Sophia. "It totally is. Stop wearing pink."

"Stop talking to me." Sophia pressed her hand to the side of his face and pushed Evan away.

He pretended she catapulted him to the far side of the booth. When he pushed himself upright, he gawked at Sophia, then at Wilder. "You watch this one. She's abusive. I bet that if you step out of line, she'll beat you."

Wilder cocked a sideways grin at Sophia. "I can take it, and need to be disciplined now and again."

"That's what she said," Evan spouted with a laugh.

Sophia was about to reply with a sarcastic joke when she noticed a figure enter Cosmic Pizza who she didn't recognize. Still, he was strangely familiar as he looked around the restaurant as if trying to find his party waiting for him at one of the nearby booths.

The man had long black hair tied into a ponytail low on his head. Although he was an elf, he wasn't dressed like one, merely wearing jeans and a black T-shirt. It was the glint in his eyes that made Sophia think she'd met him before.

Then the man's gaze connected with hers and he strode over. "There you are, Sophia. I've been looking for you all over this place and being in public robs my soul, so follow me right away."

The man turned at once and strode back for the door while waving over his shoulder for her to follow him, a commanding essence in his every move that Sophia didn't know how to question and had a strong feeling that she shouldn't.

CHAPTER ONE HUNDRED
SIXTY-ONE

"Who is that guy?" Evan asked as Sophia slid out of the booth and started after the stranger.

"I don't know," she remarked, then followed the elf, not wanting him to get away since he didn't seem to be waiting for her.

"Good idea then, just follow him." Evan hurried after her. "Don't you know not to talk to strangers? Or to follow them when they demand it?"

Sophia nodded. "Especially since we're not short on enemies, but something tells me we need to follow him."

"Me too," Wilder agreed on her other side.

They nearly ran into Mahkah, who was hurrying in their direction. "I ordered another pizza."

"Not now, Kah," Evan stated like he was offended. "We have to get a stranger who strode in here and demanded that Sophia follow him."

Mahkah nodded. "Okay, well, we can come back for the pizza."

Evan sighed. "Do you always have to make everything about what you put in your mouth?"

"Oh, put a sock in it." Sophia sped out onto Roya Lane and looked back and forth, trying to locate the man with a black ponytail. He moved fast and was quickly making his way to the end of the street. "That way!"

They all hurried through the lane while maneuvering around passersby and gnomes who seemed to be trying to get in their way to slow them down.

Sophia nearly lost sight of the man several times, but one of the guys often helped out by spying him before he turned a corner. When the guy disappeared into the shop at the end of Roya Lane, Sophia paused, totally confused.

"Why would he go in there?" Wilder asked, standing at her side.

She smiled, finally understanding what was going on as she watched the elf disappear into the Fantastical Armory.

"There can be only one reason."

CHAPTER ONE HUNDRED
SIXTY-TWO

The man who Sophia realized was none other than the Protector of Weapons was casually waiting for the dragonriders when they entered his shop.

"Subner, that's you, isn't it?" Sophia looked the elf over. He didn't appear anything like his former appearance as a hippy, but he was still an elf—much like Ainsley and Renswick who were different from their race in that way.

"It is." Subner leaned on the counter with a long case beside him.

"This place is cooler than the last time I was in here," Evan gushed while looking around. The shop did seem to have new inventory with shiny weapons hanging all over the walls and cluttering the many cases.

"Don't touch anything," Wilder and Sophia said in unison.

"Jinx, Mom and Dad," Evan spouted at once. "Now neither of you can say anything until I say your name five times, which will never, ever happen."

Sophia rolled her eyes and strode up to the Protector of Weapons. "So Doctor Tiffanee Freud was able to help you?"

"She did. Now I've assimilated this form and won't talk in nonsensical phrases any longer. I appreciate your help."

"You're welcome," Evan cut in. "Where is my lovely wife?"

"She went back to the mortal world," Subner replied.

Evan nearly screamed like an offended schoolgirl on the playground. "How dare she? That tramp abandoned me? She spends our honeymoon with another man, then runs off—taking me for everything I'm worth."

"Which is pretty much nothing," Wilder retorted.

Evan clapped his hands to his chest. "Can't you see that I'm hurting? Are you going to kick a man when he's down?"

"Down, broken, asleep," Wilder listed. "It doesn't matter much to me. I'll kick you however and whenever it suits me."

Evan shook his head. "You know who your friends are when your wife leaves you high and dry."

"The marriage can be annulled now," Subner stated blandly, not at all entertained by Evan's antics. He was definitely back to his old self —humorless and lacking much personality.

"Fine, fine." Evan waved him off and turned to study some weapons in a case.

"I'm glad you're better," Sophia said.

"What you're probably most glad about is that my recovery means I can help you secure the weapon you'll need for your next battle." Subner patted the case sitting on the counter beside him.

"Yes, please." Evan strode over, his eyes full of curiosity. Mahkah and Wilder joined him and stood behind Sophia.

"There can only be one weapon in there," Sophia stated. "But I was under the impression that we were all going into battle together." She indicated the other dragonriders. "That's why we all had armor created and the dragons too."

"That's correct," Subner answered. "But this weapon can only be wielded by one person, and it's the only way to destroy the enemy you'll meet."

Evan held up his hands and nodded. "I'm the one. I get it. Hand over my new silver ax."

"It's not an ax," Subner corrected.

"Whatever it is, I'll take charge," Evan said confidently. "Lord knows I'm the only one with strong enough shoulders to swing whatever is in that massive case."

"You're not the one," Subner stated with authority. His pale blue eyes connected with Wilder. "It's you, Weapons Expert. You're the one who must carry this into battle. You're the only one who can deliver the final blow. If you don't, then all of you will pay the ultimate price."

Evan slapped Wilder on the back and laughed. "No pressure, son."

CHAPTER ONE HUNDRED SIXTY-THREE

S ubner unfastened the buckles on the case and lifted the lid to reveal the largest sword that Sophia had ever seen. It seemed too big for a normal magician to carry. In truth, it seemed fit for a giant or one of the fiery stone creatures she and Liv had taken down on the volcano.

The silver sword's craftmanship was simply extraordinary with the devil's face on the top portion of the hilt and his horns spiraling up toward the blade. The bottom of the hilt had a fist fashioned on it. The lower portion of the blade was serrated and the top dangerously pointy. Sophia could tell that it was incredibly sharp by looking at it.

"Dang," Evan exclaimed, drawing out the word. "That's one mega-sword."

"It's called the Destroyer," Subner imparted, his intense gaze straight on Wilder.

"Oh, man," Evan complained and threw his head back. "And it's got a cool name. Are you sure I'm not the one who needs to carry this into battle and strike the finishing blow, Sub?"

"Subner," the elf corrected. "I'm certain. It must be Wilder, although all of you have a role to play in the upcoming battle."

"Which is?" Sophia asked, a hopeful tone in her voice.

"You'll find out very soon," Subner stated. "But it would be very helpful for you if you took that call."

"What call?" Sophia looked around as if someone had entered the shop looking for her. She was still tired enough that Wilder had to indicate her cloak pocket.

"I think Subner means your phone," he stated.

Sophia growled when she realized that the Protector of Weapons knew her phone was ringing although she didn't. She retrieved the phone from her pocket and nearly gasped at the caller ID. If Bermuda Laurens called it was for one reason: She'd remembered the monster that Nevin Gooseman had asked her about.

The Dragon Elite were about to find out what they were facing— and by the looks of them and the weapon lying in front of them, they were ready right on time.

CHAPTER ONE HUNDRED
SIXTY-FOUR

Hiker thundered back and forth across the floor of his office as his hands pulled his beard.

"You're going to break the floorboards, son," Mama Jamba warned while sketching on her pad as she had been doing lately.

"Good," Hiker fired back. "How did this happen? How did Nevin Gooseman get such a monster?"

Sophia cleared her throat, knowing that question was hers to answer. "Bermuda said that he tricked her into supplying the information. Then, based on her assessment of the leviathan and the simurgh, she believes that he has someone who can do magical enhancements on the creatures."

Hiker halted, and his seething gaze landed on the old woman curled up on the couch. "Why is it that you're no help with this one?"

"Who says I'm not?" Mother Nature fired back. "These animals aren't from my wheelhouse, so I'm not sure what you expect me to do. This one in particular isn't one of mine, but rather a manmade genetic anomaly."

"One that could be anywhere and has the potential of destroying tons, as well as the Dragon Elite," Hiker nearly boomed with his hands in the air.

"The good news," Wilder began in a calm voice, "is that we have the weapon to battle this beast when we learn where it is."

He indicated the case that held the Destroyer, which sat open on Hiker's desk.

The Viking glanced in that direction and nodded. "And Subner stated that it was the only thing that could?"

"Yes, the finishing blow," Evan stated. "Which means I have to do all the work to wear the beast down first. Then Wilder puts down his turkey leg, sweeps in, and takes the glory moment by simply stabbing the monster."

"We also have the armor from Jeremy Bearimy," Mahkah added while ignoring Evan like the rest of them.

Hiker nodded. "That makes me a lot more comfortable knowing what you all are facing."

Sophia glanced at the picture on the iPad sitting on the coffee table that depicted the beast Bermuda Laurens thought Nevin Gooseman was sending after them: a tarrasque.

It was weird for a group that rode ancient dragons to look at the monster they'd face and shiver with disgust. The tarrasque looked like an ugly dragon with its large head covered in two large horns and rows of teeth in its wide mouth.

It was orange and armored in a thick-shelled back covered with more spikes. The monster's tail was the length of its body and also full of sharp horns. Worse than its appearance was Bermuda's explanation of the creature. It was quite hostile and unwilling to be tamed or reasoned with. There was only one thing a tarrasque wanted: blood.

According to the expert on magical creatures, she only knew where one tarrasque in the world was located. It was the very last of the magically created dangerous monsters.

As luck would have it—or not have it for the Dragon Elite—Bermuda had learned after some checking that it was missing.

She tried to assure Sophia that the four dragonriders shouldn't have much trouble facing off with the beast.

According to the giantess, it would be a tough battle since its hide was pretty much impenetrable by most weapons. Sophia had informed Bermuda that they had a new weapon that should help.

Bermuda seemed to think this was good news. She then explained that the teeth and horns of the monster could cut through most armor or strong dragon hide.

Sophia again felt victorious, explaining that the riders and their dragons had new armor created by the extraordinary Jeremy Bearimy.

"Then you have little to worry about," Bermuda stated matter-of-factly. "Well, unless Nevin Gooseman has enhanced the tarrasque somehow as he did with the leviathan and the simurgh."

Silence fell in the room, and Sophia felt Wilder fidgeting with nervousness beside her. Hiker went back to pacing on the far side of the study. Evan hummed. Mahkah closed his eyes and meditated.

Mama Jamba broke the silence when she pointed at the television and turned it on at once. "I hope that you're all rested up now that you know what you're facing because the beast is awake and ready for you."

CHAPTER ONE HUNDRED SIXTY-FIVE

All the dragonriders watched with wide eyes as the news coverage on the television screen showed the horrific events unfolding in Dallas, Texas.

A monster that was almost as big as the one hundred and fifty-yard-long building planned its escape from a huge, abandoned sports arena. Sophia could hardly believe it as she watched the orange horns rip through the dome's ceiling, tearing it open like it was an aluminum can.

After ripping a slit through the top, the tarrasque effortlessly shoved the rest of the dome to the side with its claws that took up most of its hand. Free from its prison of sorts, the beast stood on its hind legs in the center of the football field and roared, making the buildings in the city of Dallas vibrate all around it.

The helicopter taking the footage soared around the monster, trying to take in the creature's enormous size. Sirens wailed on nearby streets. The city was in chaos, and it was evident before the reporter came on-screen.

"What you're seeing is coverage we only learned about recently when a traffic copter caught a disturbance from an abandoned sports arena slated for imminent demolition," the reporter began in a rushed voice, her tone brimming with nervousness. "It has allegedly been acquired by the politician Nevin Gooseman, who recently went into hiding after authorities discovered he was behind the spread of distortion, a deadly disease that affected the magician and elfin populations."

"Nevin," Sophia muttered under her breath. She knew he was behind this, but getting the confirmation was good. Necessary.

Hiker nodded, seeming to agree with her silent sentiment.

"We have no idea what the massive monster is that has just escaped from the sports dome," the reporter continued. "But if this thing is loose in our streets, God help us all."

On the heels of the woman's words, the tarrasque slammed through the walls that blocked it from the city of Dallas. The move sent debris in all directions, upended cars, and toppled buildings with a casual jerk of its hand. The beast then lumbered out into the streets of Dallas and roared as its tail swished back and forth, creating destruction in its wake.

Mama Jamba pursed her lips and continued to sketch. "The only ones I'm aware of who can help are the Dragon Elite. Let's hope they're up for the biggest challenge they've yet to face."

CHAPTER ONE HUNDRED SIXTY-SIX

"No pressure at all," Evan said over the comms connecting the four dragonriders. "All of the city of Dallas is counting on us. And if we don't contain this tarrasque, then it will only create havoc as it tours North America."

Sophia shook her head at the dragonrider who was the best thing for morale as they rode into battle, after exiting the portal into the skies over Dallas, Texas. It wasn't hard to determine where the tarrasque was. All they had to do was follow the sounds of screams and sirens.

The Dragon Elite hovered in the air on their dragons while they assessed the scene in front of them. Being quick was essential to protect lives and everything else. However, rushing into battle without studying the scene would be a costly mistake, and one Sophia couldn't afford.

She glanced out at the city that stretched in front of them—flat and full of concrete. It was also easy to spot the tarrasque because it was massive, the size of a city block. It was clear that Nevin had spent his efforts to make the monster huge. Whereas the leviathan and the simurgh were massive, they were sea and air creatures. Although incredibly dangerous, they had nothing on a land-dwelling beast.

"What are your orders, boss?" Evan rode atop Coral who also wore the special armor from Jeremy Bearimy. They looked regal in the shiny gear, although Evan sported his trademark grin.

She drew in a breath and leaned low on Lunis to pull in his strength, which she'd need for what came next.

"Evan and Mahkah, you need to protect the city and mortals." Sophia pointed at the many helicopters and tanks that were speeding into place, obviously thinking they could stop the tarrasque. "They don't know any better and are going to get themselves killed faster by fighting the monster. Push them back and try to minimize damage."

Mahkah nodded at once and took off on Tala without another command.

Evan saluted and flew off after his friend.

"Wilder," Sophia began. She felt strange ordering her boyfriend into battle, but right now they were riders, and their orders were to protect. "You need to get in close, but that monster is much too hungry and energetic for that, so we're going to wear it out."

He grinned at her from his place on Simi. The white dragon flapped her wings as she stayed aloft next to Lunis. "I like this plan. Sounds like a game."

"Keep your distance until the time is right," Sophia warned. "If you get too close, that monster can swipe you two out of the sky. I don't want you going in for the punishing blow until we have the advantage, which will take a moment."

Wilder nodded, pure confidence in his gaze as he absorbed Sophia's command. "You got it."

CHAPTER ONE HUNDRED SIXTY-SEVEN

Nevin Gooseman watched the aftermath of what he'd worked on for months...years...from the top of a skyscraper in downtown Dallas.

He had wanted to help the mortal world, but maybe they needed war and destruction. There never seemed to be an end in sight to their problems. Nevin would create a piece of legislation meant to protect mortals, and they'd invent more chaos that he'd have to fix. It was never-ending. Now he saw that the solution was to take them down, so they stopped fighting. Sometimes being put out of one's misery was the only solution.

He puffed out his chest and smiled as he looked out at the evening sky full of Army helicopters outfitted with the best mortal weapons. They were nothing compared to his magitech army, and they stood little chance against his tarrasque.

In the streets of downtown Dallas, tanks also armed with weapons rolled toward the tarrasque. Those too would be stomped to bits when they got in the way of his prize.

The only ones who stood a chance against the powerful and massive tarrasque were the Dragon Elite, and not even prayers could save them now. This was most assuredly their funeral.

Nevin watched as the four dragons swooped through the air, their riders low on them and navigating in different directions. Nevin didn't know what they planned to stop the tarrasque, but he knew it wouldn't work.

The beast was too large and powerful. He had planned to be far away by the time the dinosaur-like creature was big enough to escape its confines. However, after all his efforts and losses—after everything—Nevin Gooseman needed to see this. He needed to watch the demise of the Dragon Elite and the mortals.

He pinned his hands on the side of the building and leaned forward, almost giddy about watching the battle that would ensue and mark his victory in stone.

CHAPTER ONE HUNDRED SIXTY-EIGHT

Evan was made for battles. That's what he lived for. As much as he joked, he enjoyed them most when side by side with his comrades. Few things made him as happy as sharing the victory with his fellow riders.

He and Coral swerved through the skies of smoggy Dallas, Texas, whisking through the clouds as they tore through them and made new shapes.

The helicopters and jets racing in would get themselves in trouble if he didn't intervene. They had no idea what they were up against. The tarrasque wasn't merely a beast to be reckoned with. It was one that the angrier it got, the faster it would destroy. That was the reason they had to wear it out first, then take it down. If antagonized too quickly, it could stampede across the flatlands of Dallas and take out the city with a swish of its tail.

Evan and Coral flew toward the helicopters and jets and streaked right in front of their line of sight to get their attention. The pilots undoubtedly noticed the dragon and rider, but Evan couldn't determine whether they noticed his signals to stand down.

Then a jet racing in from the opposite direction fired a missile at the tarrasque. The rocket hit the creature like a spit wad and fell to the ground below with a loud *clunk*, creating a small crater in the streets.

The beast roared, reared on its back legs, and threw its front legs in the air before it fell forward and created a sizable earthquake.

Evan nodded with a sigh. "Dumb mortals. Fire first and think second. Now we've got to clean up their mess, which will be the result of a very irritable monster."

Mahkah had the job of corralling the tanks and ground forces. That would be no easy feat since they were spread out around the tarrasque and moving in as if they thought they could block the monster in by surrounding it. Really, they were creating a wider circumference for the beast to trample.

Mahkah didn't know how he would get the ground forces to retreat. They were defending their city, and he understood that. But how could he tell them that they were better off not being present for this battle? That they were in the way?

Then something occurred to him after watching the news report earlier.

He abandoned his position alongside the ground forces. Instead, he sped for the news vehicles far in the distance, watching from the other side of the downtown area, perched on rooftops and in the streets, their news cameras trying to capture everything. Which, if things weren't soothed quickly, would be mass destruction.

Flying with the Destroyer didn't make Wilder feel extra tough. The weapon was incredibly heavy. It had strange magic about it. And his power of seeing a weapon's history told him it had killed many, and all were very powerful.

Having the weight of the final blow in this battle resting on his shoulders was a lot. But, his responsibility and allegiance were to the Dragon Elite. Wilder didn't want to let the others down. He didn't want to disappoint Hiker. More than anything, he wanted Sophia to be proud of him.

She'd done so much to get them there, as she usually did. Because of her, they had armor that would most likely save their lives in this battle against the tarrasque. Because of the youngest dragonrider, Wilder had the Destroyer, which was surely the only way they were going to take down this massive beast. And it was because of her nonstop detective efforts that they were there so quickly after the monster emerged from its "cage."

Yes, Wilder wanted to save the city of Dallas and the mortals in the midst of the tarrasque. He burned to stop Nevin Gooseman. But more than any of that, he wanted another battle for the Dragon Elite and their leaders.

"What is Mahkah doing?" Evan asked over the comm.

Sophia glanced over her shoulder and watched as Mahkah sped away from the ground forces and toward the news reporters in the distance. She shook her head, knowing exactly what Mahkah was doing. "He's being strategic. You should try it."

"I was going to take out the engines on the helicopters," Evan replied. "How's that for strategy?"

"Yeah, no," Sophia vetoed. "The mortals will think we're their enemies too. Probably assume the tarrasque is our friend and concoct the idea that we're the enemy. Make peace, not confusion."

Evan sighed. "Fine. I'll go and play nice. But you better play extra dirty to make up for it."

Sophia nodded and leaning low on Lunis, preparing for the game of cat-and-mouse they were about to play with the giant tarrasque.

Are you ready to wear this ugly guy out? she asked her dragon telepathically.

Buck, Lunis stated, like that made any sense to Sophia.

Say what?

That's the ugly dinosaur's name, Lunis answered. *Buck.*

Sophia smiled. *Okay, are you ready to exhaust Buck?*

Abso-freaking-lutely.

CHAPTER ONE HUNDRED
SIXTY-NINE

The mortals might not be the smartest of the races, but Evan wasn't going to stand by and watch them get themselves killed with their fearful reactions and lack of concern for strategy.

Sophia was right, although he'd never tell her that freely. Maybe after a bottle of whiskey. But she was still right that if the Dragon Elite didn't act correctly in this situation, the always-quick-to-jump-to-judgments mortals would misconstrue things. The dragonriders had shown up on the heels of this beast tearing out of the sports dome.

Many conspiracy theorists would believe that the Dragon Elite was behind this. Evan's job was to look like a hero by saving the dumb mortals from the tarrasque's attacks on the assaulting mortal army. They thought they were big stuff in their helicopters and jets and didn't realize the best defense was a brain, not blades and bullets.

Evan watched as the tarrasque picked up a building like it was a wad of paper and threw it through the air, its trajectory headed for a helicopter hovering close by. Although the dragonrider didn't know as much about modern technology as Sophia, he knew that the chopper wouldn't be able to escape the impact of the building colliding with it, nor would the ground troops below it.

That's why Evan sped into motion atop Coral, holding up his hand and blasting a strong wind at the collision course. It would hit the helicopter, throw it back, and cause it some trouble, but it would also save it from certain death. At the same time, Coral used her elemental water magic to make a nearby water tower explode, which sent the troops on the ground away from the building the tarrasque was about to throw.

Evan sighed dramatically. "Keeping mortals alive is a fulltime job."

"Tell me about it," Mahkah said over the comm in reply to Evan's comment.

He'd seen his friend use a diversion to help mortals get out of the line of attack and was proud of Evan's strategy. Mahkah had been too busy moving into position to reply when Evan questioned his plan, but he was grateful to hear over the comm that Sophia believed in him.

She was the queen of using strategy when fighting was an option and Mahkah had learned a lot from the youngest dragonrider. It proved to him that age meant very little when someone remained open to the ideas around them. Sophia was pure of heart, and that meant she truly wanted the best for all. Intentions were everything, Mahkah believed.

He used his magic to create an amplifying spell, something he had never tried before. As a very soft-spoken and quiet person, it had never occurred to Mahkah to be loud. He wasn't inaudible like Quiet, but he wasn't noisy like Evan. Mahkah chose to listen rather than talk. He learned a lot more that way.

However, in that moment of battle, it was most important that others learn and take note. Otherwise, they'd all suffer.

Mahkah drew in a breath and began the speech that he hoped would keep the ground forces safe.

"People of Dallas," Mahkah began, his voice booming as if on a loudspeaker. All the news cameras turned on him and zoomed in on the dragon and rider streaking through the air. "Do not go near the monster known as the tarrasque. It is dangerous and if enraged, will only become more destructive. Taking down this monster will require everything that the Dragon Elite has, so we ask that you back down. Allow us to do our job. Otherwise, you will only make this battle that much harder. Military forces, stand down. Let the Dragon Elite do what we do best and save you."

CHAPTER ONE HUNDRED SEVENTY

So the Dragon Elite thought they were going to save the day, Nevin Gooseman thought bitterly.

He ground his fist into his thigh and watched the dragonrider using the amplifier spell speed through the sky. It was all propaganda they were filling the mortal's heads with.

The Dragon Elite were no more than glorified superheroes with little to do but create problems they would later fix.

They were the reason that five hundred evil dragons would one day infiltrate the globe. They were the reason the world was out of control, and Nevin was out of power. Nevin shook his head, knowing that these were the desperate actions of a dying organization.

Soon, the Dragon Elite would be wiped out, and Nevin could come back to power.

The mortals would beg for him to help them after he took down the tarrasque. He'd figured out exactly how to do it, and that was another reason he'd stuck around instead of fleeing. He could destroy everything, and he did intend to do some of that. But he could also be the savior at the end of the day.

Nevin eyed the detonator in his hand. It would explode the device that the tarrasque had unknowingly eaten, and would be its final demise.

When the mortals finally begged for the beast to be stopped, after tearing through all of Texas, Nevin would offer them mercy and find a way to take down the monster. All by clicking a button.

CHAPTER ONE HUNDRED SEVENTY-ONE

The Destroyer's extra weight burdened Wilder and Simi, but they still sped over the head of the tarrasque and wove through its huge claws, which were the size of columns on a large building.

Wilder anticipated which direction the monster would swipe, went to the other side of it, and nearly got knocked to the side by its sharp claws. This was a beast that could rip through a diamond mine with little effort. Not only that, but it was much faster than its large size would lead one to believe.

Several times, it went for Wilder streaking between its legs and moved much quicker than he would have thought possible. The spikes on its legs grazed against Wilder and Simi and they both screamed, feeling like razors had cut them in a hundred places.

"Wild!" Sophia screamed into the comm.

He whipped around, checking his dragon first, then himself. They were unharmed. They'd felt the impact of the assault, but the magical armor had kept them protected. However, too many encounters like that and they wouldn't survive. That was certain.

"I'm okay," Wilder breathed over the comm. "Just a close call."

Sophia let out a relieved sigh and watched as the white dragon and her rider soared back up into the air, away from where the tarrasque could reach them again.

"Good," Sophia stated. "Okay, it's our opportunity to run interference and try to wear out Buck."

"Who?" Wilder asked over the comm.

"The orange nuisance who obviously doesn't play football," Sophia stated, hardly able to talk as Lunis raced toward the tarrasque like a bullet. The blue dragon streaked through the air so fast that it made Sophia's lips pull back from her teeth.

Buck caught sight of them as they were next to his face like a fly taunting a mortal. The tarrasque threw his head from side to side, trying to knock them out with its horns. To Sophia's utter astonishment and horror, Buck was successful. One of the spikes on its head impaled Lunis in the side and threw the blue dragon across downtown Dallas like he was a tennis ball.

CHAPTER ONE HUNDRED
SEVENTY-TWO

"Sophia!" Wilder screamed in the comm.

Evan had seen the tiny dragonrider get tossed through the air as if swatted like a common housefly. She and Lunis had landed on the far side of a distant city block, not far from where Evan was stationed after rescuing the mortals from getting themselves killed.

"I'm going after her," Evan stated. "Stay in position and do what you came here for, Wilder. Don't worry. Sophia will be fine."

Evan turned Coral in the direction where Sophia had landed, hoping that he was right—hoping that an assault like that hadn't taken out the dragon and rider. The Dragon Elite wouldn't recover from a loss like that.

Mahkah wanted to fly to assist Evan in helping Sophia, but he knew that his efforts had to stay with keeping the mortals safe. Despite his message, he sensed that they were on edge and ready to defend their city.

That was the thing about mortals. They didn't always think long-term because their lives were so short. He'd been on the Earth long enough to see the senseless wars they fought, usually forgetting what they were fighting for in the end.

Mahkah scanned the city from high above while flying through the clouds. That's when he spotted something on a high rooftop that caught his attention. He wouldn't have noticed it in the massive chaos surrounding the crazed tarrasque that was as confused as the residents it was set upon. However, a man standing on a rooftop and staring at the burning city was odd when most were running or defending themselves from a monster.

Mahkah always believed that he should look for the ordinary when in a rare situation and that would tell him more than looking for the bizarre in an already crazy world.

Mahkah bore down on his dragon and did something he wasn't told to do. He rarely defied orders, but this time, he would get the tarrasque to follow him. Hopefully, that would mean the monster would take out another monster—if everything went to plan.

CHAPTER ONE HUNDRED SEVENTY-THREE

Sophia could hardly breathe with Lunis lying half on her in the middle of an abandoned road. However, she could feel him breathing on top of her, and that was all that mattered.

She was pretty sure her ribs were broken. She had trouble breathing and felt like bones were poking into her lungs. But she was awake and grateful to hear the sirens in the distance.

"Lun," she whispered and coughed.

"I'm here." He picked his head up to look at her from the other side. "I think I'm crushing you."

"Are you okay?" she asked.

He tried to move but didn't seem capable of it. "I'm...I will be okay. The armor..."

"It saved us, didn't it?" she asked.

"For now," he answered, an ominous tone in his voice.

"You're okay?" she asked again.

"My leg is... Well, I need help getting it unstuck from a crack in the road," Lunis stated, but there was something else he wasn't saying.

"It's broken, isn't it?" Sophia felt her heart break.

"It will mend."

A tear slipped down her cheek.

"That's why I can't move off you," Lunis explained, his regret billowing to the surface. "I'm sorry."

She reached out and stroked her hand across her dragon's face. "It's okay. We'll be okay."

"Yeah, you will because I'm here to save the day," Evan cheered as he dove from in between buildings and landed on the road next to Sophia and Lunis.

His usually cheerful face took on a brief look of grief as he took in the sight of them.

"We're okay," Sophia said to the other rider.

Evan shook his head. "No, you're not. But you will be. Give Coral and me a few moments, and we'll have you out and back to the Gullington in no time."

"But the tarrasque," Sophia argued. "Wilder!"

Evan gave her a rare look of severity. "He can handle it. What he can't handle is knowing you're in danger. So do what you do best, and take care of your team by letting them know you'll be okay by getting some help."

Sophia drew in a breath and held back the tears. "Wild..."

"Yes," he said, a breath of relief in his voice too.

"I'm going back," she stated. "Take down the tarrasque and return home to me."

"Copy that, Soph."

Wilder didn't know what Mahkah was doing, but he didn't dare say anything with Sophia on the comm and hurt and needing to know that she was okay. Instead, he stayed silent and watched as the older dragonrider streaked through the air, nearly ramming into him, taking over his position, trying to wear out the tarrasque. Wilder trusted Mahkah enough to know that if he was jumping into battle and trying a tactical move, that he should allow it.

So Wilder hung back and watched as Mahkah streaked around the massive beast, seemingly trying to entice it into following him.

The act worked. The monster swatted at Mahkah but thankfully didn't catch him. That was the benefit of spending the last few hundred years training. Mahkah was the fastest of them on his dragon. However, he wasn't a show-off and only put his skills to the test at the moment when no one but Wilder was watching.

Mahkah kept looking over his shoulder as he zigzagged through the air, ensuring that the tarrasque was following. When he came to a skyscraper in the middle of a bunch of short, squatty buildings, he circled it three times while avoiding colliding with the tarrasque's assaults.

Then, as if he was never there at all, Mahkah and Tala dove and flew low along the deserted road until they disappeared around a corner.

The tarrasque, obviously annoyed by the pest, looked around until it spotted something standing squarely on the rooftop like a cherry on top of a sundae.

Wilder wasn't sure if he imagined it, but recognition of some sort seemed to dawn on the monster's face as if it recognized its maker. Or in this case, its captor.

"You're a freaking genius, Mahkah," Wilder remarked and smiled at his friend and fellow dragonrider's brilliance.

CHAPTER ONE HUNDRED
SEVENTY-FOUR

It had all happened so fast. One moment, Nevin Gooseman watched the battle from a few city blocks away. Then the tarrasque had thundered across the streets, crushing buildings and overturning cars as it followed the dragonrider speeding through the air.

Nevin had thought it was strange that the dragon and rider had circled the building where he stood, but then the rider had glanced at him. Their eyes connected right before he disappeared and Nevin knew…

He'd been set up. The Dragon Elite had drawn his beast to him.

They just wouldn't stop.

Now as Nevin looked up into the giant eyes of the monster he'd cared for and fostered for months, he knew one thing with certainty. The beast recognized him, and it was hungry. Nevin would be its first real meal unless he did something fast.

He turned and ran for the door on the far side that led to the stairs.

The tarrasque threw its claws into the building's side and instantly tore down a corner of it. The force sent Nevin to his hands and knees, and his face collided with the pavement.

He dared to look over his shoulder, hoping that the hot breath he felt on his back wasn't from the monster.

It was.

Nevin slid his hand down to his pocket. If he could retrieve the detonator then maybe, just maybe that would give him the chance he needed to escape the monster.

It wasn't there!

He looked around. The detonator lay some twenty feet away on the concrete ahead of him. It had fallen from his pocket.

The tarrasque's eyes connected with where Nevin was looking. He'd assumed it was a dumb beast, but something in the monster's eyes told him that it knew and wasn't going to risk it.

Nevin rolled over on his back and threw his hands over his face as the tarrasque's head came down. The monster's sharp teeth scooped him up in one single bite and crushed the politician with one crunch —ending him for good by the very beast he'd harbored for the world's demise.

CHAPTER ONE HUNDRED
SEVENTY-FIVE

Nevin Gooseman was gone, Wilder thought. He'd watched the entire thing.

It was all thanks to Mahkah who was now stationed on the far side of downtown Dallas, back to his role of keeping the mortals away from the tarrasque.

Sophia and Evan had traveled back to the Gullington where Lunis would receive the care he needed. Sophia, too.

That meant the very last of it was on Wilder. It was his job to rid the world of this monster.

Wilder didn't like killing creatures that didn't ask to be born or made evil or fed to grow large and starved to feast on the innocent. But he also knew that trying to save this creature wasn't something he or anyone else could do. Mama Jamba had made that abundantly clear.

Wilder's job was to take out this creature so that it didn't create any more destruction. Although he and Sophia had tried to tire it out, they hadn't been able to do much. Hopefully, going after Mahkah and taking down Nevin was enough.

While the monster feasted on its creator's body, Wilder sprang into action and sped through the air on Simi faster than he had in the recent past.

While his dragon closed the distance between them and the tarrasque, he pulled the Destroyer from its sheath. The weapon was incredibly heavy and bulky—hard to hold in position.

But using that weapon was less about being fast and more about the right attack. Wilder had learned something when they fought the leviathan and the simurgh. Massive beasts all have a vulnerable spot. All one has to do is find it and have the right weapon, and they can take down anything, no matter its size.

Wilder twirled the Destroyer through the air and rotated it until the blade pointed down.

The monster caught sight of Tala as she approached. It lifted one clawed hand to swipe at them, but she swerved at the right moment and feinted in the opposite direction, throwing the beast off and confusing it. That's when she made the risky decision to streak back around in a circle above its head, so close that Wilder could smell the creature's musty odor. It smelled of death and destruction. Of war. Of rot.

Without a moment more of consideration for the giant life he was about to take, Wilder thrust the Destroyer's keen blade into the soft tissue on the top of the tarrasque's head and straight into its brain. Then he pulled up on his dragon's reins and sent her straight up as the monster reeled onto its back legs and screamed so loudly that the city shook for a hundred miles.

Wilder looked down over the wings of his dragon and into the soulless eyes of the monster below. It was close enough to reach out and knock them from the air if it wanted to. But the beast wasn't able to. Wasn't going to. It had finally surrendered, and there was a spark of gratitude in its eyes as if Wilder had put it out of its misery. Then it swayed and fell, taking out more than a city block and crushing buildings, bridges, and cars—however, the tarrasque was gone and with it, Nevin Gooseman.

CHAPTER ONE HUNDRED
SEVENTY-SIX

"Are you sure he's okay?" Sophia asked for what felt like the hundred and seventy-first time.

Mahkah nodded and sat next to her. His brown eyes gave her a sensitive look. "Lunis needs to rest. That's all. The Cave will take care of the rest, like the Gullington will take care of you." His gaze fell to the thick pieces of cloth wound tightly around her midsection that bandaged her punctured lungs and broken ribs.

"I just want to be with him." Sophia looked around the dining hall for support from the others.

Wilder pushed his toast around on his plate, not eating. Evan pretended to be interested in the bagel he was spreading with cream cheese.

"There's nothing to be done, Sophia," Hiker stated from his place stoically positioned at the head of the table. "He'll recover. His leg will recover."

What no one was saying was whether Lunis would be able to walk normally again. It was the cloud over their heads. It was the worry since Evan and Coral helped Sophia and Lunis back. The blue dragon couldn't walk on the leg now. Nor would he talk to her telepathically. He probably couldn't, with all his energy going to healing.

She knew it was too soon to tell, but she needed to see that he was okay.

"Where is Quiet?" Sophia looked around the breakfast table. No one had seen the gnome since the Pond incident, and Sophia had been gone since then. But if he was still recovering, then who would help Lunis? The worries were too much for her.

"He's okay," Hiker said.

"Okay?" Sophia questioned. "As in he's still sleeping after the Pond?"

"As in he's busy," Hiker stated. "I don't know where he is lately, but he's back to normal. He'll help Lunis. We all will. Now eat your food." He indicated her untouched plate.

Sophia glanced down at it like it was fish heads. "I'm not hungry."

"You're not helping Lunis like this," Wilder stated.

She shot him a punishing look but immediately regretted it. He was trying to help. They all were in their weird ways. Even Hiker told her to eat when he usually didn't care. Evan had offered to give her his pastry. Mahkah hadn't left her side most of the morning, doting on her. But Sophia didn't want any of that. She needed to know that Lunis was okay. That he would recover. She knew that she would. A punctured lung and few broken ribs would take her out for a day, maybe two, but her dragon...

Lunis was her heart, and not knowing how he was, threatened to break the one part of her that the Gullington couldn't repair.

"You all..." Hiker began, and looked around the table, "were exceptional in battle."

Sophia pushed her plate away, feeling more defeated than before. Usually, after a successful battle there was a celebration of sorts. Maybe in a few days, when she and Lunis were better, there would be. But it felt wrong to celebrate when the dragon and rider were injured and Lunis' fate was uncertain. Also, the city of Dallas had taken many casualties and tons of damage.

Yes, they had successfully defeated Nevin Gooseman and the tarrasque, but it came at a price.

"You all were incredible," Sophia stated while looking at her full plate. "Great thinking Mahkah, leading the tarrasque to Nevin Goose-man. And you, Wilder." She looked at the man she loved and didn't think she could love him more. He had been brave and strong and delivered the final blow, as Subner knew he would. But it was Evan who stole her attention right then. Sophia swallowed. "Evan, thanks for coming to our rescue. We wouldn't have—"

"Wouldn't have to have waited so long, but I got stuck in traffic," Evan interrupted with a laugh. Then he gave Sophia a sensitive expression that pierced her from the inside out. "That's what we do, isn't it? We watch out for each other, in battle and outside of it. I believe you've saved my butt a few times. I'm just repaying a debt."

Sophia nodded and felt a fondness for her friends that she'd only felt for Liv and Clark. She took her water goblet and raised it high. "I couldn't ask for a better group. I love you guys."

No one made a joke about how she was being a girl and emotional. Instead, they all picked up their water goblets and smiled at her.

"We love you," they chorused and clinked their glasses with hers.

Sophia was afraid she would start crying, so she was grateful when Mama Jamba ambled into the dining hall a little later than her usual time. For once in a long while, she wasn't sketching on the pad of paper. However, she pressed a single piece of paper between her fingertips.

She dropped it on the dining table in front of the group. "There you are."

"There we are what?" Hiker grabbed the sheet. After a moment, he lowered it. "What is this?"

"That," Mama Jamba began while pulling close a plate of blueberry pancakes made specifically for her by Trin, "is the location of the demon dragons you asked me to track down."

"I see that." Hiker lowered the paper, which looked somewhat like a drawing of a map done by a child. "What are the stars next to them?"

"Stars?" Mama Jamba asked absentmindedly while pouring gobs of syrup onto her pancakes. She glanced up. "Oh, those. Well, those are the riders who have magnetized to them, naturally."

"Riders?" It was Mahkah who asked the question, his eyes wide.

"Well, yes," Mama Jamba chirped. "You know better than most that dragons like to have the companionship of riders if they so choose that path. And it appears that a few of your demon dragons have."

"Riders." Hiker sounded halfway between excited and on edge. "We have new riders?"

"Well, by 'we' the world does," Mama Jamba answered. "But I don't suspect those types will much want to be a part of the Dragon Elite. They never do, do they?"

She mused on her question before shrugging and taking a large bite.

"So we know where the demon dragons are." Sophia dared to take the drawing from Hiker and study it. The dragons had spread out worldwide, and there were quite a few that had magnetized to riders. Which meant things were about to intensify for the Dragon Elite.

"Speaking of riders," Mahkah began, his tone careful. "I suspect a few of the angel dragons here at the Gullington are ready to magnetize too."

"You suspect," Hiker said, a question in his tone.

"There have been talks of them leaving," Mahkah stated. "Of exploring."

The Viking sighed heavily. "More riders. Both good and bad."

"Demon and angel," Mama Jamba corrected. "Remember that good and bad is relative. The demon riders will bring advantages to the world."

Hiker rolled his eyes. "Don't think I forget my brother was one of them."

"And look at the magitech he brought," Mama Jamba argued. "It's just that he went too far. That's the thing about evil. It tends to know no bounds. But imagine if evil paired with good." Her eyes lightened with the thought. "Oh, imagine that world. The potentials would be vast."

"Yeah, maybe." Hiker didn't sound convinced.

"Hey, Soph," Wilder said, his tone careful.

She glanced at him, feeling like he was too far away on the other side of the table, but he'd been giving her space knowing that she was healing, both physically and emotionally. He pointed over her shoulder.

She turned around and looked through the window that showed the Expanse of the Gullington. Her mouth popped open, and tears jerked to the surface.

Sitting there on the grassy green lawn and rolling over like a dog that had found a treat was her blue dragon. Lunis jerked up when his eyes connected with her and she knew two things instantly. He was still hurt, his front leg bandaged. Also, he would be okay, even if he didn't make a full recovery. There was no taking away Lunis' spirit, and that was what counted at the end of the day: Spirit.

CHAPTER ONE HUNDRED
SEVENTY-SEVEN

Quiet McAfee orchestrated many things in his time at the Gullington, more than most thought or ever suspected. But there were few things as important as what he needed to do next.

Having recovered from the incident at the Pond, Quiet turned his attention to more crucial events. Those involved things outside his domain and required more of his energy than usual. Dropping hints from the past into someone's life at the Elfin Council wasn't easy. Reminding Hiker of things he was trying to forget was an arduous task.

Neither Ainsley Carter nor Hiker Wallace wanted to be the one who caved. Still, Quiet knew their truest feelings. His role as the Gullington gave him an intimate knowledge of what was in the minds of the Castle's residents. More importantly, it told him what was in their hearts.

Although Ainsley shouldn't have been able to pass through the Barrier since she had no motive to serve the Dragon Elite, Quiet allowed her to pass through that night.

She thought she'd forgotten her favorite book and had a clear memory of leaving it on the shelf in Hiker's office.

The book had never been in Hiker's office, and the memory was planted, but that didn't matter. All that mattered was what happened next and that it happened at all.

The book, a gift from Ainsley's older brother, meant a great deal to her. However, unbeknownst to her, it was still safely in her suitcase at the Elfin Council, which she'd never fully unpacked. That was because the shapeshifter didn't feel at home there, but was unwilling to admit it. What she would admit was that she needed that book once she realized it was missing. She figured that she could sneak into the Castle and up to Hiker's office where she could retrieve her good luck charm and return to her life that was full of negotiations and pretenses and nothing fun at all.

Ainsley found the door to the Castle unlocked because the one who kept it locked at night was hiding in the shadows of the entryway. Quiet wasn't seen when the shapeshifter slipped into the Castle wearing a beautiful evening gown. She'd been at a cocktail party where handsome elves with too much time on their hands and no real culture talked smugly about their adventures.

The elf paused in the entryway and looked around, like for a moment she forgot what the place looked like, or rather had missed it and was memorizing every single detail before she had to leave once more.

Ainsley was wearing a black embroidered dress that was tight on the bodice, and the lacy gown was see-through, showing her lean figure. She was beautiful, but that was true before she wore fancy gowns and had her red hair sleeked back. Ainsley was beautiful in burlap dresses with grease covering the bridge of her nose.

She hurried up the stairs and noticed that there was a small light on in Hiker's office. She remembered that he often kept it on even when he wasn't in there.

That was true, but on that night, even when Hiker tried every light in his study, none of them worked. He'd planned to stay up late and study the map Mama Jamba had made of the demon dragons and concoct a plan. Mother Nature had gone to bed hours before, saying she needed her beauty rest.

Ainsley didn't knock as she pushed the cracked-open door to Hiker Wallace's office open and strode across the space, straight for the bookshelves she knew well, having dusted them often.

She had been in such a rush that she didn't check the room before entering. But when the man stood from behind his desk, Ainsley froze, her hand reaching for a book that she knew right away wasn't what she was looking for.

"You came back..." Hiker's voice was scratchy.

CHAPTER ONE HUNDRED
SEVENTY-EIGHT

Ainsley pulled the book in front of her hands from the case and swung around, brandishing it proudly. "For this."

Hiker narrowed his eyes at the cover. "For a copy of 'Dragon Rashes and How to Treat Them.'"

Ainsley glanced at the cover and blushed. "Yeah, elves and dragons are pretty similar. I thought that maybe this would work on some of my colleagues."

"Oh." Hiker nodded curtly. "That's why you returned. For a book."

"I did," Ainsley replied while looking at the shelves longingly. "But I don't think it's here. I don't think it ever was." She scratched her head as if she was suddenly confused, her memory playing tricks on her.

"I'm not sure what you're talking about." Hiker still stood awkwardly behind the desk, not seeming to know what to do with his hands. Or his feet as they shuffled around and made noise.

"Yeah, me either," she replied. "I thought I lost something here and figured I'd pop in and find it. Guess I was wrong."

"You look..." Hiker gestured at the elegant dress Ainsley wore. "You look beautiful."

Ainsley glanced down at the dress that was of the finest quality

ADAPT OR BE CRUSHED

and hid her blush. "Thank you. I had a meeting with a bunch of aristo-crats. It was... Well, I survived."

"Sounds like you're living the life." Hiker held back, as always.

"I'm living my life," Ainsley stated. "Something I wasn't granted for a long time."

The two fell silent for a moment. Both their gazes darted in oppo-site directions. Quiet worried he'd have to shut the office door and lock them in there for the rest of their days if they didn't stop being so stubborn. He was willing to do it, even if they starved.

That's what you did when you loved others. Well, without the starving part...

Finally, to Quiet's relief, Hiker sighed, a sign he was about to start talking again.

"I never stopped you from living your life," Hiker stated. "I tried to preserve it. I'm sorry if you don't see it that way. I didn't know what to do."

Ainsley left the book on the shelf and took a step forward. "I know. I give you a hard time, but you did the only thing you could at that time. It wasn't like you had many options, and the world changed so dramatically after that."

"It was a blur," Hiker admitted. "One moment, we reigned over the world. Then there was a war, and we disappeared from the globe, unseen for centuries. And you, you couldn't remember anything without it hurting you. And that hurt so much. So I stuffed it away. I just..." He motioned to the log that he'd kept every day for the last few centuries. "I did the only thing I could and remained the pillar that the Dragon Elite needed, knowing that I couldn't help you. That you couldn't leave here or remember or be with—"

"With what?" Ainsley asked, her voice so elegant although the ache lay under it.

"With me," Hiker admitted.

She laughed at this. "You never wanted me with you. It was always the Dragon Elite first and everything else second."

He nodded. "You're correct. But things were different then. Things are different now."

"How?" she demanded at once.

"Time changes a man," Hiker began. "I thought that the only job I'd ever want was leading the dragonriders. I thought that was the only thing worthy of my attention. But in a few short months, I've seen things I never saw in all my years on this Earth before. People do things solely for love. They cross lava and sacrifice everything and think the world is over if they lose one person. I always thought my job was to steer men...dragonriders in the right direction, but the only reason we exist in the first place is because love exists. I had it all wrong, all along. My job is to preserve love in this world."

Ainsley gathered herself and looked toward the door like she might rush out at any moment. Surrendering that idea momentarily, she glanced at Hiker. "How do you do that?"

"I tell you not to leave again." He stepped around the desk, his figure in full view. He was as strong as ever, as handsome as he had been when she fell in love with him.

"But I have—"

"You have a life here, and you know it," Hiker interrupted. "I let you go before, while also keeping you here. Do you know how hard it was to look at you every day and know that you couldn't remember me? Us? I died a little having to get over our love. Then I had to let you go. I don't know what's harder—having you here and not being with you. Or have you gone and not seeing you. All I know is neither is right at this point."

"What do you want?" Ainsley kept her green eyes pointed at him.

"You."

Her mouth twitched. "Me? Me to do what?"

He swallowed. "Just you. With your memory intact. With your ability to leave here but with the hopes that you won't. You with all you are and all that we've been through and learned, not wasting time anymore. Or us afraid, although I think there will always be something of that."

"Hiker Wallace, after all this time, what are you saying?"

"I'm saying that if you aren't in the Castle, then it doesn't feel the same," he stated.

She laughed. "Because it's not clean enough."

He didn't think this was funny and shook his head, giving her eyes that spoke of his true intent.

Ainsley nodded. "I get it. My life... Well, it doesn't fit me. I was happy...I was happier here."

"Then come back," he urged and stepped forward.

She took a step back. "I don't know. It's too hard to go backward after all this time."

"But you'll be a delegate, and you can come and go as you want. I'm sure Quiet will allow it." He sighed and threw his hands through his hair. "Ains, what do you have to lose? Really? What does either of us have to lose? We've already lost so much. Why not go for love this time?"

She tilted her head to the side, surprise written on her face. "What happened to you, Hiker Wallace? You seem to have a heart all of a sudden."

He pursed his lips and smiled. "I tried teaching dragonriders a thing or two, and they ended up teaching me a lot more."

Ainsley shot him a smile back. "We think we know everything when we're young, but it's the young that teach us everything."

He stepped toward her, and this time she didn't retreat. Instead, the elf took a step toward him. They were closer than in centuries.

"I always thought you'd come back to me." She reached out and ran a finger over his sleeve, feeling it.

He glanced down at the movement and grinned.

"I never thought I'd come back to you," she continued.

Hiker reached out and wrapped his hand around her wrist, securing his grasp around her arm after centuries of missing her. It was by far better than any victory he'd ever experienced. "I'm glad you came back." He pulled her in, hoping that she always came back. For him, for the Dragon Elite, but mostly for him.

SARAH'S AUTHOR NOTES
SEPTEMBER 25, 2020

Thank you to everyone out there who has supported the books and LBMPN. We can't do this alone. And I really value you all readers, your input, your ideas, your encouragement and more! Thank you.

I will be in Scotland, yet again, when this book releases. It's sort of tradition at this point. The Scotsman can't get into the US yet because of border closures, so I go there and it helps that it always fills me with inspiration for the books. But obviously I go because of the Scotsman.

I know three things with certainty for release day of this book. The first is that I'll be in Scotland. The second is that the Scotsman always buys the books and flips to the author notes straight away. And thirdly, that he's got the best smile.

Yes, a perk of writing books is that I get to use them to communicate with my boyfriend to get reactions out of him. The notes are great for sending messages. Like for instance, Scotsman, where is my mimosa sans the orange juice? It's release day and your legs aren't broken. Strut over to the kitchen (pretty please) and grab your demanding girlfriend a cocktail. It's five o'clock somewhere...

Speaking of pestering the really patient Scotsman, some of you may be wondering about the Miranda reference in this book and the last one. I think in the 8th, Lee goes off about an ex-girlfriend she had who did all these horrible things, and her name was Miranda. Then Evan said something about how he hoped his new wife didn't look like a Miranda. Why did Miranda get this rep? First, please let me state that I don't know any Mirandas. I apologize to all readers named that. You are lovely and smart and probably much better at baking and tennis than me.

You, Miranda, were simply put in the book because I have an over-active imagination and draw on real life for my books. So the Scotsman isn't secretive per se, he just doesn't write books about his dating life or life in general for EVERYONE to read. Apparently some people aren't open books, with their life on broadcast. The Laird was a tad bit shy on details, especially at first. So I made up the idea that he had a secret life on the side, or rather that I was the side life and that he had three wives and they were all named Miranda. That's the easy way to avoid confusion, right?

Anyway, I often reference the Mirandas, asking the Scotsman how they are doing, specifically are they staying on their diets and has the acne meds started to work. I know...I don't know how he puts up with me. So now you know how the Miranda thing came about and also you realize how incredibly immature I am. And all Mirandas are lovely. Just like all the Karens of the world. Heart you all.

While in Scotland the last time, Ramy and I joined up for a little walk. If you know anything about RE Vance and his shenanigans then you know he loves to photobomb people, but he does it with his own unique flare. So we did this duel posts on the KGU Facebook page where I was like, "I wished I could have caught up with Ramy while in Scotland," and I posted these pics of the Scotsman and me, with RE lurking in the background. Then Ramy-Cans posted something that said, "It was nice hanging out with Sarah in Scotland," and he posted pics of selfies of him with the Scotsman and I in the background, oblivious to him snapping our pics. It was funny. It was clever. It took planning.

Do you know who showed zero acknowledgement of this creative effort on the part of two of his authors? If you guessed Manderle then you get a gold star. Ramy and I like to think of ourselves as siblings vying for "Dad's" attention (Oh, yeah, I did that, MA 12). But then he ignores us and we have to act out even more!

Like for instance, I recently, at Ramy's request, dressed up as Mike. Ramy-Cans messages me and says, "Will you dress up as Michael? It's because—"

I cut him off and was like, "I don't need a reason. Tell me when and where."

I then put on my LMBPN T-shirt, which I harassed Mike about getting for a year and now I'm sure he regrets letting me sport the company logo. "No, she's not associated with us. We don't know her..." To complete the Anderle look, I tucked my hair under a ball-cap, left off my make-up and then put on my old glasses. That part gave me a headache because I've had LASIK and don't wear my thick glasses anymore. But I did it for the company! And because Ramy-Cans and I think antics are funny.

Now are you wondering who said anything about this acting out, which was obviously a plea for attention? Not Dad!

On that note, I'm going to go do something really adult like talk to my accountant or look into investing in real estate to off set this childish behavior.

Funny that Mike makes me feel old and young at the same time. He alluded to this in the last author notes. We were chatting about life and stuff, as we tend to do when we're gearing up to discussing the actual books. Our conversations would be hard for most to follow. Anyway, I derail, as I tend to do, and mention going to Scotland every five minutes. He's like, "Oh, to be young and in love...or in your case, to be in love."

I was like, "Mike! I have a complex."

MA really can't bear to hurt anyone's feelings because he didn't graduate from asshole college like me. I have a graduate degree in how to offend with a minor in snark. Anyway, he's like, "No, you act really young, don't worry about it." And then I had to fire back, "So you're calling me immature now!"

Poor guy was backpedaling from there, but it ended up in the author notes, so we are cool. Or at least his teasing is now your entertainment.

In all seriousness, Manderle and I have really great discussions when we're waxing about the books. I've worked with enough authors to really appreciate our dynamic. The convos start small and then snowballs until I'm exclaiming loudly and the ideas are speeding at me faster than I can write down. I have notes from our discussions that the greatest deciphers in the world couldn't make sense of. But I absorb the gist of it usually.

During one of our last convos, I had this profound moment where I realized one of the reasons that Liv and Sophia are so much easier for me to write than other protagonists. Yes, they are based on me, but those other ones in my other dozen series were too. The thing that's changed in this stage of my life is how I view myself. If we're critical of ourselves or naïve or angst ridden, then that will be how the protagonist is portrayed to readers. It just can't be hidden.

But at this point, I'm what I call, Unapologetically Sarah. Many evolutions I went through, writing the books and launching my business and renovating my life, have gotten me here. I think I, like many of us when younger, tried to hide who I was or make excuses. But now, I don't do fake. I'm not doing things so people like me. Liv is very much that way.

So I'm grateful to be here, Unapologetically Sarah, writing characters who come to me naturally and entertaining you all. Thank you!

Much love and peace,
Tiny Ninja

MICHAEL'S AUTHOR NOTES
SEPTEMBER 25, 2020

First, THANK YOU for supporting our crazy stories here at LMBPN.

I need it, you see, because apparently, I'm acquiring more children. I hadn't expected to have adult children adopt me or anything, and Ramy (being the guy he is) hasn't mentioned any of this adoption stuff.

Only Sarah.

I have to admit, with a little reservation because it is embarrassing, I didn't clue into ANYTHING she spoke about with her and Ramy's antics.

Not a thing.

Perhaps Steve "Zen Master" Campbell can provide a bit of insight from the substantial amount of wisdom he has garnered over the years? Anything?

—> *Note from the Zen Master: Consider this a victory. Acquiring adult children gets you to grandchildren that much quicker. I'm in Texas as I write this, awaiting the birth of grandson number three. Seeing your kids raise their kids is truly a blessing. (Come on, Myles, we're all waiting....)*

I'm going to assume Steve put something that essentially means "don't look at me."

—> Nope, sorry. If you ask the Zen Master for wisdom, you'll get something. Maybe not wisdom, but something.

I know I would.

If Steve actually does put something wise (like "ignore them, they eventually grow up"), I'm going to be a little chagrined.

—> Consider yourself chagrined!

Oh @#$, she has a Laird.

Seriously? Not only does she call him her Scotsman (I hear a lady swoon every time that word is used. Kinda like take a drink when she says it. You should be pretty sauced by the end of her *Author Notes*.) She calls him her Laird as well.

I seem to remember she bought him the title for a present. That's such a Sarah thing to do.

Young puppies in love (no matter their age) are so damned cute it's annoying. It's tiring me out.

Only one of my wife and my boys has a girlfriend that we know about. He's in college, so we don't get to see too much of the cute side of it. Come to think about it, the two of them (seniors in College) seem to be more mature about the relationship than Sarah.

Figures.

RELEASE THE DRAGONS!

Stay with us through this final set of books – I ALMOST guarantee you won't figure out where Sophia goes...

Ad Aeternitatem,

Michael Anderle

ACKNOWLEDGMENTS
SARAH NOFFKE

I feel like I'm on the stage at the Oscars, accepting an award when I write my acknowledgments. I stand there, holding this award, my hands shaking and my words racing around in my mind. I'm not an actress for a reason. I'm a writer and talking to people in "real life" is hard. Not to mention a ton of people all at once.

I picture looking out at the audience and being blinded by spot-lights and forgetting every word of the speech I memorized just in case I won. The speech would go like this and it's meant for all of you, not the guild. For the fans. The supporters. The people who are the reason I would ever stand on any stage, ever.

Okay, here we go. I clear my throat and smile, looking up at the camera, holding the little golden man. And then I begin:

This was never supposed to happen. I was never meant to publish a book and then another one. And then another. I was supposed to write in private and live a life that Henry David Thoreau called a life of "quiet desperation." I would always hope to share my books, but never bring myself to do it. And you would never read my words. But then, in a crazed moment of brashness, I did share my books and you all liked them. And because of that, I've never been the same. And here I am feeling grateful all just because…

That's why I'm here. Because of you. Thank you to my first readers. The ones who picked up those books that I didn't even outline and you still liked them. You messaged me and maybe you thought it was no big deal, but when your ego is new to the publishing world, it's a big deal.

I can't thank you readers enough. I've found that reading your reviews helps me to start a chapter when I'm stuck or lazy.

I really need to thank someone who has made this all possible and that's my father. I was going to quit. I can't tell you how many times I quit. But when I wasn't making it, he was the one who told me to not throw in the towel. "Give yourself a timeline," he suggested. If I didn't get to my goal by then, I'd quit. And apparently there was magic in that advice, because I'm still doing this. Dad, you're the pragmatic one, but when you believed in me enough to tell me to not quit, I knew I had to follow your advice.

And I thank all my friends who are constantly supporting me with thoughts of love and encouragement. Most don't read my books. I'm sort of self-deprecating, although I'm working on it and will be the first to tell my friends, "My books probably aren't for you." However, every now and then a friend surprises me and says, "I was up all night reading your books." It's always a total shock. But my point is, that even if they didn't read, I still have the best friends ever. Diane, you're my rock. And I love you, even though you will probably not read this.

Thank you to everyone at LMBPN. Those people are like family to me, although I'm not sure if they'll let me sleep on their couch. Well, who am I kidding? They totally will. Big thanks to Steve, Lynne, Mihaela, Kelly, Jen and the entire team. The JIT members are the best.

Huge thank you to the LMBPN Ladies group on Facebook. Micky, you're the best. And that group keeps me sane.

And a giant thank you to the betas for this series. Juergen you are my first reader and friend. Thanks for all the help. And thanks to Martin and Crystal for being some of the best people I know. What would I do without you? A huge thanks to the ARC team. Seriously, if it weren't for you all I might pass out before release day, wondering if anyone will like the book.

And with all my books, my final thank you goes to my lovely muse, Lydia. Oh sweet darling, I write these books for you, but ironically, I couldn't write them without you. You are my inspiration. My sounding board. And the reason that I want to succeed. I love you.

Thank you all! I'm sorry if I forgot anyone. Blame Michael. For no other reason than just because.

BOOKS BY SARAH NOFFKE

Sarah Noffke writes YA and NA science fiction, fantasy, paranormal and urban fantasy. In addition to being an author, she is a mother, podcaster and professor. Noffke holds a Masters of Management and teaches college business/writing courses. Most of her students have no idea that she toils away her hours crafting fictional characters. www.sarahnoffke.com

Check out other work by Sarah author here.

Ghost Squadron:

Formation #1:
  Kill the bad guys. Save the Galaxy. All in a hard day's work.
  After ten years of wandering the outer rim of the galaxy, Eddie Teach is a man without a purpose. He was one of the toughest pilots in the Federation, but now he's just a regular guy, getting into bar fights and making a difference wherever he can. It's not the same as flying a ship and saving colonies, but it'll have to do.
  That is, until General Lance Reynolds tracks Eddie down and offers him a job. There are bad people out there, plotting terrible

things, killing innocent people, and destroying entire colonies. **Someone has to stop them.**

Eddie, along with the genetically-enhanced combat pilot Julianna Fregin and her trusty E.I. named Pip, must recruit a diverse team of specialists, both human and alien. They'll need to master their new Q-Ship, one of the most powerful strike ships ever constructed. And finally, they'll have to stop a faceless enemy so powerful, it threatens to destroy the entire Federation.

All in a day's work, right?

Experience this exciting military sci-fi saga and the latest addition to the expanded Kurtherian Gambit Universe. If you're a fan of Mass Effect, Firefly, or Star Wars, you'll love this riveting new space opera.

NOTE: If cursing is a problem, then this might not be for you.

Check out the entire series here.

The Precious Galaxy Series:

Corruption #1

A new evil lurks in the darkness.

After an explosion, the crew of a battlecruiser mysteriously disappears.

Bailey and Lewis, complete strangers, find themselves suddenly onboard the damaged ship. Lewis hasn't worked a case in years, not since the final one broke his spirit and his bank account. The last thing Bailey remembers is preparing to take down a fugitive on Onyx Station.

Mysteries are harder to solve when there's no evidence left behind.

Bailey and Lewis don't know how they got onboard *Ricky Bobby* or why. However, they quickly learn that whatever was responsible for the explosion and disappearance of the crew is still on the ship.

Monsters are real and what this one can do changes everything.

The new team bands together to discover what happened and how to fight the monster lurking in the bottom of the battlecruiser.

Will they find the missing crew? Or will the monster end them all?

The Soul Stone Mage Series:

House of Enchanted #1:

The Kingdom of Virgo has lived in peace for thousands of years...until now.

The humans from Terran have always been real assholes to the witches of Virgo. Now a silent war is brewing, and the timing couldn't be worse. Princess Azure will soon be crowned queen of the Kingdom of Virgo.

In the Dark Forest a powerful potion-maker has been murdered.

Charmsgood was the only wizard who could stop a deadly virus plaguing Virgo. He also knew about the devastation the people from Terran had done to the forest.

Azure must protect her people. Mend the Dark Forest. Create alliances with savage beasts. No biggie, right?

But on coronation day everything changes. Princess Azure isn't who she thought she was and that's a big freaking problem.

Welcome to The Revelations of Oriceran. Check out the entire series here.

The Lucidites Series:

Awoken, #1:

Around the world humans are hallucinating after sleepless nights.

In a sterile, underground institute the forecasters keep reporting the same events.

And in the backwoods of Texas, a sixteen-year-old girl is about to be caught up in a fierce, ethereal battle.

Meet Roya Stark. She drowns every night in her dreams, spends her hours reading classic literature to avoid her family's ridicule, and is prone to premonitions—which are becoming more frequent. And now her dreams are filled with strangers offering to reveal what she has always wanted to know: Who is she? That's the question that haunts her, and she's about to find out. But will Roya live to regret learning the truth?

Stunned, #2

Revived, #3

The Reverians Series:

Defects, #1:

In the happy, clean community of Austin Valley, everything appears to be perfect. Seventeen-year-old Em Fuller, however, fears something is askew. Em is one of the new generation of Dream Travelers. For some reason, the gods have not seen fit to gift all of them with their expected special abilities. Em is a Defect—one of the unfortunate Dream Travelers not gifted with a psychic power. Desperate to do whatever it takes to earn her gift, she endures painful daily injections along with commands from her overbearing, loveless father. One of the few bright spots in her life is the return of a friend she had thought dead—but with his return comes the knowledge of a shocking, unforgivable truth. The society Em thought was protecting her has actually been betraying her, but she has no idea how to break away from its authority without hurting everyone she loves.

Rebels, #2

Warriors, #3

Vagabond Circus Series:

Suspended, #1:

When a stranger joins the cast of Vagabond Circus—a circus that is run by Dream Travelers and features real magic—mysterious events start happening. The once orderly grounds of the circus become riddled with hidden threats. And the ringmaster realizes not only are his circus and its magic at risk, but also his very life.

Vagabond Circus caters to the skeptics. Without skeptics, it would close its doors. This is because Vagabond Circus runs for two reasons and only two reasons: first and foremost to provide the lost and lonely Dream Travelers a place to be illustrious. And secondly, to show the nonbelievers that there's still magic in the world. If they believe, then they care, and if they care, then they don't destroy. They stop the small abuse that day-by-day breaks down humanity's spirit. If Vagabond Circus makes one skeptic believe in magic, then they halt the cycle, just a little bit. They allow a little more love into this world. That's Dr. Dave Raydon's mission. And that's why this ringmaster recruits. That's why he directs. That's why he puts on a show that makes people question their beliefs. He wants the world to believe in magic once again.

Paralyzed, #2
Released, #3

Ren Series:

Ren: The Man Behind the Monster, #1:
Born with the power to control minds, hypnotize others, and read thoughts, Ren Lewis, is certain of one thing: God made a mistake. No one should be born with so much power. A monster awoke in him the same year he received his gifts. At ten years old. A prepubescent boy with the ability to control others might merely abuse his powers, but Ren allowed it to corrupt him. And since he can have and do anything he wants, Ren should be happy. However, his journey teaches him that harboring so much power doesn't bring happiness, it steals it. Once this realization sets in, Ren makes up his mind to do the one thing that can bring his tortured soul some peace. He must kill the monster.

Note This book is NA and has strong language, violence and sexual references.

Ren: God's Little Monster, #2
Ren: The Monster Inside the Monster, #3
Ren: The Monster's Adventure, #3.5
Ren: The Monster's Death

Olento Research Series:

Alpha Wolf, #1:
Twelve men went missing.

Six months later they awake from drug-induced stupors to find themselves locked in a lab.

And on the night of a new moon, eleven of those men, possessed by new—and inhuman—powers, break out of their prison and race through the streets of Los Angeles until they disappear one by one into the night.

Olento Research wants its experiments back. Its CEO, Mika Lenna, will tear every city apart until he has his werewolves imprisoned once again. He didn't undertake a huge risk just to lose his would-be assassins.

However, the Lucidite Institute's main mission is to save the world from injustices. Now, it's Adelaide's job to find these mutated men and protect them and society, and fast. Already around the nation, wolflike men are being spotted. Attacks on innocent women are happening. And then, Adelaide realizes what her next step must be: She has to find the alpha wolf first. Only once she's located him can she stop whoever is behind this experiment to create wild beasts out of human beings.

Lone Wolf, #2
Rabid Wolf, #3
Bad Wolf, #4

BOOKS BY MICHAEL ANDERLE

For a complete list of books by Michael Anderle, please visit:

www.lmbpn.com/ma-books/

CONNECT WITH THE AUTHORS

Connect with Sarah and sign up for her email list here:

http://www.sarahnoffke.com/connect/

You can catch her podcast, LA Chicks, here:

http://lachicks.libsyn.com/

Connect with Michael Anderle and sign up for his email list here:

Website:
http://www.lmbpn.com
Email List:
http://lmbpn.com/email/
Facebook
https://www.facebook.com/LMBPNPublishing

www.ingramcontent.com/pod-product-compliance
Lightning Source LLC
Chambersburg PA
CBHW020227110726
47898CB00004B/1178